Witchlight

Witchlight

M A R I O N

Z I M M E R

B R A D L E Y

TOR®

A TOM DOHERTY ASSOCIATES BOOK

NEW YORK

WITCHLIGHT

This book is printed on acid-free paper.

A Tor Book
Published by Tom Doherty Associates, Inc.
175 Fifth Avenue
New York, NY 10010

Tor Books on the World Wide Web:
http://www.tor.com

Tor® is a registered trademark of Tom Doherty Associates, Inc.

Library of Congress Cataloging-in-Publication Data
Bradley, Marion Zimmer.
  Witchlight / Marion Zimmer Bradley.
    p.   cm.
  ISBN 0-312-85831-0
  I. Title.
  PS3552.R228W5   1996
813'54—dc20

96-20703
CIP

First Hardcover Edition: April 1996

First Paperback Edition: September 1997

Printed in the United States of America

10 9 8 7 6 5 4 3 2

Another kind of poltergeist activity may be the expression of psychic force in tension, not around a hysterical or mal-adjusted child, but around a relatively well-adjusted adult. When this occurs, there is some unresolved psychic force in action; it could be said that the Unseen is coming in search of the individual concerned, and this does not, strictly speaking, come under the scope of this book.

In addition to the case histories in this book, consult Carrington and Fodore, cited elsewhere, as well as the monograph by Margrave and Anstey, in the Autumn, 1983, issue of The Journal of Unexpected Phenomena, *reissued by Silkie Press, San Francisco, as* The Natural History of the Poltergeist.

—The Inheritor

Witchlight

CHAPTER ONE

A WINTER'S TALE

A sad tale's best for winter.
I have one of sprites and goblins.
—WILLIAM SHAKESPEARE

THE HOUSE WAS CALLED GREYANGELS. IT HAD BEEN built in the last years of the old colony and added to in the first years of the new nation. Old orchards from its days as a farm still surrounded the house; their hundred-year-old trees long past fruiting but still able to bring forth a glory of apple blossoms each spring. But the house's days of ruling over acres of corn and squash and rows of neatly barbered apple trees were long past. Now, only the house remained. Its pegged, wide-planked floors, its lath-and-horsehair plastered walls, its low ceilings with their smoke-blackened beams, its tiny windows with their wavery, hand-rolled glass, had dwindled from luxurious to old-fangled to quaint to dowdy, before being forgotten entirely and abandoned to the mercy of time and the seasons.

Years passed. The house was nearly dead when it came to the attention of the living once more, to be gently renovated to suit the tastes of a generation raised with indoor plumbing and furnace heat, a generation which summered outside the city. But tastes and fashions continued to change, and soon New Yorkers had less desire for an old summer house on the banks of the Hudson River.

The house passed from hand to hand to hand, drifting farther even from the memory of its initial purpose, as cars got faster and roads improved and the suburbs moved north and north again, until Dutchess County was filled with New York commuters racing for their daily trains and it seemed that Amsterdam County, too, would soon fall to tract housing and the desire of the city's residents to reside in the peace of what once had been country.

But for now the house was spared, sitting on its dozen acres between the railroad and the Hudson, its nearest neighbor a private college with a lurid reputation and an artists' colony that sought anonymity above all things. For a while longer the old farmhouse still sat quietly in the quiet countryside, and nothing disturbed its peace.

That must be why I came here, Winter Musgrave told herself, although to be brutally accurate, she could not remember the precise details of her flight here, and prudence—or fear—kept her from reaching too forcefully into the ugly confusion where the memory might lie. There were things it was better not to be sure of—including the frightening knowledge that her memory had—sometime in the unrecorded past—ceased to be her willing servant and had become instead a sadistic jailer waiting to spring new and more horrible surprises on her. A day that did not bring some jarring revelation, however small, was a day Winter had learned to treasure.

The quiet helped, and the slow pace of the countryside as it ripened into spring. She had a vague understanding that she had not been here long; old snow had still lingered in shadows and hollows when she had driven her white BMW up the curving graveled driveway, and now only the palest green of half-started leaves softened the outline of the surrounding trees: birch, maple, dogwood—and the apple trees in gnarled files marching down to the river.

Winter did not like the apple trees. They worried her and made her feel vaguely ashamed, as if something had been done among the apple trees that must never be remembered, never spoken of. The orchard formed an effective barrier between Winter and the river that could be glimpsed only from the second-floor bedroom.

But she could see the apple trees from there, too, and so Winter had made her bedroom downstairs, in the tiny parlor-turned-spare-bedroom off the kitchen, which was both warmer and hidden from the sight of the flowering orchard.

So long as no one knew where she was, she was safe.

The notion was a familiar one by now; familiar enough that it might even be safe to think about.

Why should no one know where I am?

Winter picked up a heavy carnival-glass paperweight from the Shaker table and stared down at its oil-slick surface as if it were a witch's crystal and she could find answers there. Wordless reluctance and fear surged over her, making her hastily return the paperweight to the table and nervously pace the room.

The front parlor of the farmhouse was sparsely furnished; there was the Shaker table with a lamp on it, a Windsor rocker made of steam-bent ash, and a long settle angled before the fieldstone hearth. A hand-braided rag rug softened the time-worn oak-planked floor, and on one white-washed wall hung a mirror, its thick glass green with age, set in a curving cherry frame.

Winter stopped automatically in front of the mirror and forced herself to look. It could not hurt more than coming upon her reflection by surprise, when the clash between what she saw and what she remembered fashioned another of the small humiliations and terrors by which she marked out her days.

Hair: not wavy and chestnut any longer, but flat and lank and dark. The skin too pale, its texture somehow fragile, flesh drawn tight over prominent bones that said the border between slender and gaunt had been crossed long ago. Hazel eyes, sunken and shadowed and dull; a contrast to the days when more than one admirer had sworn he could see flecks of baltic amber in their sherry-colored depths. Her mouth, pinched and pale and old. She couldn't remember the last time she'd worn lipstick, or what color it had been. Did she even have a lipstick here? She couldn't remember—did it matter?

Of course it does—Jack always said I should wear as much war-paint as I wanted; it made them nervous. . . .

The scrap of the past flashed to the surface like a bright fish and was gone; pushed away; sacrificed to the need to hide.

From what? Frustration almost made Winter willing to risk the pain of trying to remember. Restlessly, she made the circuit of her world again: the front parlor, with its welcoming hearth; the kitchen, looking out on the remains of someone's garden and a windbreak of tall pines; the downstairs bedroom, bright and homelike with patchwork quilts on the white iron bed and a bright copper kettle atop the pot-bellied wood-stove; the entryway with its door to the outside world and the staircase leading to the second floor—the place that held so many frightening possibilities. From the front hall she could see the woodshed that held half a rick of oak and pine split for burning, and that held her car as well. She'd need to bring in more wood soon, for the electric heat that provided the farmhouse's heat was feeble and unreliable, and she'd learned to keep fires burning both in the bedroom stove and the fireplace in the parlor to fend off the chill of early spring.

But that would mean she'd have to leave the house; to walk outside in the open air.

How long has it been since I've gone outside? Sheer stubbornness made her demand an answer of her memory, and at last the image surfaced: Winter, carrying suitcases—

suitcases?

—slipping on patches of rotting ice in her haste to get into the house, running away from . . .

The knowledge was so close she could nearly grasp it; she shied away, knowing that the balance between fear of knowing and fear of ignorance would soon shift, and she would reclaim at least that fragment of her past. Even though it must be something terrible, to drive her to hide here, crouching behind closed shutters and drawn curtains like a wounded animal in its burrow.

I haven't been out of this house in . . . weeks, her thought finished lamely. It was no good knowing that this was April—surely it was April; the new leaves and the masses of daffodils she could see from the window told her it must be April at least—if she did not know when she'd gotten here. March? Was there still snow on the ground in March? Maybe it had been February . . .

But whenever it had been, she had spent enough time since then indoors. More than enough. Spring was the season of rebirth; it was time for her to be born.

There was a sudden copper taste in her mouth, but this time the fear seemed to spur her determination rather than hinder it. Before she could think what she was doing, Winter strode into the hall and flung open the door to the outside.

The living air of the countryside spilled in, and the sunlight and the breeze on her skin were like messengers from another world. The spaded earth alongside the flagstone path was dark and fragrant with recent rain, and tiny sharp grass blades lanced up through the soil beside the darker, more established green of daffodil and iris, tulip and lily of the valley. The flagstones curved down and to the left, to meet the graveled drive that led from the garage to the outside world.

There was no one anywhere in sight. Not even the road was visible, and no traffic noise disturbed the illusion that time had not gone forward since the farmhouse had first been built.

It's okay. It really is. There's nothing out here that can hurt me, Winter told herself bracingly. With as much determination as courage, she stepped from the house to the flagstoned path.

One step, two . . . As she left the shadow of the house a wave of giddy disorientation broke over her; she felt the same faint light-headedness that she imagined one would feel opening a tiger's cage. The rolling pastoral landscape around her seemed to rear up like an angry bear, threatening to crash down upon her and rend her to bits.

It's just your imagination! That's what they always said. . . . A sudden flash of memory swirled out of the vortex of sensation, striking sharklike without warning.

Another vista of green, but this time tamed and tended. Bright autumn sunlight warming the terrace, where patients in discordantly cheery bathrobes stared mutinously out at the sanatorium's landscaped grounds.

The sanatorium—yes! I remember Fall River. Did I escape from . . .

But no. The memory was clear of the weeks of desperate courage: first to refuse her medication, then, to leave. She was an adult, she had checked in of her own free will; they really had no reason to hold her.

And at thirty-six one ought to know one's own mind! Winter thought with a flash of gallows humor. So she had left—*why* had she left?—had they said she was cured?—surely she ought to feel better than this if she had been pronounced sane and well?

They were talking about me. . . . Another hard-won memory, and now her tottering steps brought her to the shelter of an ancient oak, and the refuge of the bench that some former tenant had built to encircle its trunk. Winter sank down on the moss-green wood and looked back toward the house.

Talking about her at the sanatorium. Saying it was just her imagination, when she knew it was not, that the tales they ascribed to the inventive fancies of a disturbed and unbalanced mind were real.

I did not make it up.

Grimly she clung to that truth, but the act took all Winter's strength, and she had none to spare for the effort of remaining outside her refuge. She forced herself to walk slowly, not to surrender to blind panic, but her mouth was dry and her chest was crushed by iron bands by the time she could shut the front door of the farmhouse behind her once again.

The staircase beckoned; the elusive second floor of the house. That, and the memory of the suitcases, and the need to draw some triumph from the jaws of this latest defeat made Winter put her hand on the newel post and her foot on the first of the risers.

This isn't so hard! she told herself rallyingly a few moments later, even risking a quick peek out the window on the landing. She could see the roof of the woodshed from here, its slates knapped and mellowed with age.

Only three more steps.

The second floor was smaller than the first. It held two bedrooms and a modernized bath, its pink and white fifties curves Rubenesquely out of tune with the house's Shaker simplicity. The largest bedroom was the back one, and Winter, peering through the door, saw two Vuitton suitcases and a Coach Lexington brief in British Tan flung haphazardly onto the bed.

She could go downstairs now. She could leave that reclamation of her identity for another day, along with that sense that to reclaim herself meant also to take up some awful burden.

But if I don't, there's no one else to do it.

She could not say where that certainty outside of time had come from—it would be so easy to dismiss this sense of special purpose as just one more of the daydreams of the delusional. When she had tried to talk about it at Fall River she'd been hushed and dismissed, until she'd prayed for the nagging sense of mission to go away, to leave her normal; to make her seem to respond to their treatment and their drugs just like all the others who came to . . .

To that privileged retreat for failed overachievers, Winter finished with a flash of mockery. But the words weren't hers. Whose?

Never mind that now. Her mind was trying to distract her with inessentials to keep her from acting, but she knew that trick by now. Squaring her shoulders, Winter stepped over the threshold into the bedroom.

These were the bags she—or someone—had packed when she went to Fall River. She emptied the contents of both Vuitton cases onto the sere candlewick bedspread; all casual clothes, resort clothes; but somehow, by accident, her pit pass from Arkham Miskatonic King was there. She stared at the photo.

I look like I've been caught in the headlights of an oncoming train. . . . Despite which, it had been her proudest possession since the day she'd qualified for the Pit. As a commodities broker. On Wall Street.

As smoothly as that, the missing past rushed in. She was Winter Musgrave, a trader at Arkham Miskatonic King on Wall Street. She'd been there for ten years, since they'd romanced her away from Bear Stearns. . . .

She remembered getting up early in the morning to walk to work when the subway was on strike; remembered her apartment. If she opened the briefbag lying on the bed now she could say just what it would contain: the *Wall Street Journal* and a bag full of throat lozenges; a pink stuffed elephant—a good-luck charm—and a spare T-shirt to change into; extra pens . . .

My life, in short.

She'd had no life, outside of the Street. And she hadn't wanted one, either. She'd ignored all well-meaning advice to ease up, slow down, find a hobby, get a life.

I had a life.

Until that break between past and present; the event that she could not yet remember. That she now knew would come in time, and explain, perhaps, this purposeless sense of purpose.

Shaking her head, Winter gathered up an armful of clothes. If she was going to stay downstairs, she might as well have her clothes with her. At least she could pretend she was normal.

But don't crazy people always think they're normal? Isn't that how it starts?

No. It had started with the breakdown that had brought her to Fall River—and now she was out of Fall River, but not because she was better. . . .

Face it—FACE IT!

Winter ran down the stairs; not running away, but running to the only thing left to frighten her; the thing that had driven her into this long fugue state.

The clothes she had gathered scattered behind her like autumn leaves. She flung herself across the serene parlor and into the cheerful kitchen. Here were the dutch doors leading out into the garden; to the orchard; to the river. She threw open the door and recoiled with a cry, even though she had seen what was there before; had seen it this morning, in fact. . . .

The creature was difficult to identify, although from the size, it had probably once been a squirrel. Only a few wisps of gray fur clung now to the ruined blob of shredded meat flecked with white spurs of shattered bone.

Like all the others. Just like all the others.

It began with pigeons. Pigeons and squirrels and mice; she'd found the tiny bloodless corpses everywhere she went until each new discovery had been almost beyond bearing. When she'd gone to Fall River there had been no more for a while, but then the bodies had begun appearing again, and when she'd sworn she had nothing to do with the deaths, Dr. Atheling said he believed her but none of the others did. They said she was doing it herself—that *she* was the one responsible: catching and hurting and killing. . . .

And so she had run away, praying that if she ran far enough, hard enough, she could outrun that vengeful shadow. And for a while she'd thought she'd succeeded.

Until today.

Winter was restless all the rest of the day, as if the appearance of the tiny shattered body had brought with it a summons that could no longer be denied. Winter spent that night sleepless before the old fieldstone fireplace, feeding the last of the woodpile to the greedy flames.

With the morning light came the certainty that she could hide here no longer. If she was sane, she could test that sanity in the outside world. If it failed, she'd . . .

What?

I can't go back there, Winter told herself, although Fall River Sanatorium was not a bad place—not like some she'd heard of, where malice was disguised as concern and sadism took the place of care.

It's just that Fall River is a place that should help people—and it can't help me.

Even without knowing where the conviction came from, Winter trusted it—even though she no longer trusted herself.

I guess the world—and I—will just have to take our chances.

The morning was spent in a thousand delaying chores. Even though each strengthened her confidence in her ability to function outside the safe refuge the farmhouse had become, they were also a form of escape from the consequences of her decision. She washed the dishes, and made a list of the things she would need to replenish her larder in town, carried the rest of her clothes downstairs and put them away in the large red cedar armoire that shared the kitchen parlor with the woodstove and the white iron bed, and even went through her purse and Coach briefbag, alternately amazed and baffled by the contents. There were a fistful of unopened monthly statements, forwarded to her at Fall River from the accountant who paid her monthly bills. Winter glanced at one of them, but the rows of numbers, of transfers and debits, were a meaningless jumble.

More real were the wads of twenties and fifties crammed at the bottom of the bag—enough to take care of any conceivable immediate expense—crumpled loose in the bottom of the purse like so much play money.

Play money. That's what it was to us. We were like kids with a Monopoly set—none of it was real to us, she thought, clutching the small pink stuffed elephant that had been at the bottom of her Lexington brief, along with a *Wall Street Journal* with last year's date and clutter of things almost unfamiliar to her now. Her years at Arkham Miskatonic King were solid but curiously distant, as if out of a particularly vivid book she'd read and enjoyed. She'd lived fast and high, bought the usual toys and paid for the usual perks, and none of it was unique to her, somehow. It was the sort of life that any of the traders could have had, as unindividuated as the life of a drone in a hive.

And we thought we were so special, and all along we were just a funny kind of moneymaking robot. Wind us up and we'd trade, and trade, and trade, until . . .

But Winter still wasn't sure what had taken her from the floor of the New York Stock Exchange, to Fall River, to here. Maybe she'd just gotten . . . tired? People did, after all. Burnout was the commonest reason for leaving the Street.

But not Winter's reason. Even if she didn't know what her reason was, she knew that much.

At last she could delay no longer without acknowledging to herself that she was running away from the outside world. She changed her scruffy jeans and worn-out sweater for something more suitable to an appearance in town. *Although Glastonbury isn't much of a town, as far as I can remember.*

The fashionable, expensive woman in the gray cashmere sweater and Harris tweed skirt who stared back at Winter from her bathroom mirror was gaunt and hollow-eyed until Winter painted the illusion of health into her skin with cosmetics labeled Chanel and Dior. Expensive accessories for a lifestyle she had once worshiped with all her heart, that now more and more seemed a silly and expensive sort of mistake. But the rouge, and the Paloma Picasso earrings, and the thin sparkle of Elsa Peretti "Diamonds By The Yard" all helped disguise the sleepless nights filled with fear.

This time Winter made it all the way to the woodshed, although the open space around her seemed vast and threatening and she felt as if the sky would fall and crush her. She ducked into the shed with a tiny cry of triumph, and rested her forehead for a moment against the BMW's white lacquered roof.

Maybe Chicken Little was right. It's a possibility. Her heart was beating far too fast, and for a moment Winter considered turning back—she'd done enough for one day; no one could ask her to do more. . . .

Except me. I can ask me to do more. . . .

And she was running out of time.

Winter wasn't certain where that conviction came from, but it was enough to galvanize her into unlocking the car and settling inside. When she put the key into the ignition, she had one wild pang of panic—suppose it didn't start? suppose something terrible happened?—but fought past it. She had to know if she could survive out here in the real world. If she could not manage as simple a task as going into town for supplies, then she had better call Fall River and tell them where to find her.

And learn to live surrounded by the baffling and terrifying deaths.

Winter turned left out of the driveway almost at random—if Glastonbury wasn't this way then she'd retrace her tracks—and drove to the bottom of a hill, where one sign identified the crossroad as Amsterdam County 4 and another said GLASTONBURY: 6.

As she followed the winding two-lane road, Winter got intermittent glimpses of the river, and more information floated to the surface of her battered memory. The grandiosely named little town of Glastonbury, New York, dated from the nineteenth century, and served the local college as well as Amsterdam County locals such as herself. There was a supermarket, a post office, even a small movie theater, though most people preferred to drive to the multiplexes in the malls south of here.

It was the sort of thing that anyone might know, particularly anyone who had rented a farmhouse and come to stay for an extended period, and the ability to remember such trivia was obscurely comforting. She was dressed, she was driving a car; if she really were . . . sick . . . she wouldn't be able to do these things, would she?

When Winter reached the town, she found it had a haunting familiarity, as if she'd been here before, but the memory was elusive. County 4 had turned into Main Street, and as Winter drove down it, she saw bright posters in the windows of the business: FREE WILL—AN EVENING OF SHAKESPEARE SCENES AND SONGS BY THE TAGHKANIC DRAMA DEPARTMENT. Students from the nearby college were everywhere at this time of day, identifiable by the universal symbols of age and backpack, trendily pierced or equally trendily grungy, but carefree in a fashion Winter could somehow not associate with herself. While stopped for a light, she watched one pair wistfully as they proceeded up the street holding hands. The boy's hair fell to shoulder length and the girl's was shaved to a spiky buzz; both were dressed identically in work boots and overalls that seemed about eleven sizes too big, and they were obliviously in love.

Winter watched them until they rounded the corner, and then forced herself to concentrate on the signal and the other drivers. This outing was as much to prove she could cope as it was for anything else. She could not afford to daydream.

The supermarket was right on Main Street; and she pulled into the lot and parked with a sense of relief and growing triumph. She climbed out of the car—remembering to lock it—and stood in the warm afternoon sunlight, looking down at the list of errands in her hands.

Groceries first. And then . . . the butcher, the baker, the candlestick maker . . . Winter thought giddily.

Her destinations were not quite that archaic, though it hardly made sense to buy grocery-store bread with an organic bakery right up the block. Half an hour later, the first part of her self-imposed assignment completed, Winter emptied her grocery cart into the BMW's trunk: crisp clean brown paper bags containing cans of soup, fresh fruit and fruit juice, and all the other household necessities she'd only realized she needed when she'd seen them on the supermarket shelves. She felt almost jaunty as she locked the trunk again and headed for the bakery; it was just around the next corner, the cashier had given her directions, speaking to her as if it were a perfectly normal thing to ask for such directions. As if everything were all right.

On impulse, Winter stopped at a liquor store as she passed it, debating between Bordeaux and Nouvelle Beaujolais as though such questions could really matter. She finally settled on a bottle of white Burgundy and a trendy California Zinfandel, and proceeded up the street with her purchases cradled in one arm. She found the bakery without trouble, and bought a dozen raisin scones and a round loaf of seven-grain bread that looked as though it contained enough vitamins to nourish the entire Mighty Morphin Power Rangers. Echoes of her old life—her *self-sufficient* life—rose up to bolster her determination as she made her purchases. She would be fine. She would *make* herself be fine.

As Winter came out of the bakery, the bright colors of a display across the street caught her eye, and she went to look. There were three clear-glass *amphorae* in iron cradles, their liquid contents dyed bright blue, red, and green: It was a drugstore, its window used to display a collection of antique patent medicines and pharmacy supplies.

Winter dawdled by the window, looking. It was truly amazing what people had been able to buy without a prescription at the turn of the century: opium and morphine and cocaine, all packaged in pretty blue and amber glass bottles, or wrapped in boxes with labels written in serious Spencerian script. Extract of cannabis. Tincture of arsenic. Asafoetida. Cyanide.

Winter raised her gaze from the quaint display of antiquated medicines to the shelves behind them filled with their modern descendants. She took a hesitant step toward the door. Was there something in here that would cure her fears and dreams—let her sleep soundly at night and return to her New York life?

No. Regretfully, Winter shook her head. Nothing she could buy here would help—if the pretty red-and-black pills that had left her disoriented and numb for days after she'd stopped taking them had not helped, how could aspirin and Sominex?

Even Seconal and Thorazine had not stopped the killing. . . .

"I don't know how she manages to do it." The memory-voice was irritated; one of the Fall River aides talking to another in the sitting room of Winter's suite. Perhaps they hadn't known she was there, in the bedroom beyond the open door. Perhaps they simply hadn't cared.

"Found another one, eh?" The second voice was knowing; resigned.

"They're all over the place; Dr. Luty gives her enough junk to tranquilize a horse and she still sneaks out at night."

"Think so?"

"Has to be. And I know she's not dodging her meds. And we're the ones who have to clean it up, dammit, not Luty or Atheling. You'd think the bitch'd show a little consideration."

"Nah. She's having too much fun."

The intrusive memory receded, leaving Winter shaking. Their remembered contempt—she hadn't even known their names—still made her stomach roil. She'd done nothing to merit such hatred.

Nothing she could remember, at least.

The trembling didn't stop; Winter clutched her purchases tighter and realized that she'd grossly overestimated her stamina and emotional endurance; she'd better get back to the car and get out of here while she still had the strength to drive home safely.

She looked back the way she'd come, judging the distance. Too far, but if she turned down that street just up ahead it ought to take her right back to the supermarket parking lot.

But the street ahead only ran half a block before it made an L-shaped turn onto another street, leaving Winter farther from her car than ever. She felt sick and light-headed, as though she'd been in the sun too long, but the spring sunlight wasn't strong enough to cause anyone distress. Winter stared around herself, hoping to see a familiar landmark or at least a place to stop and rest for a minute.

She'd managed to detour into the heart of the small riverside town, away from Main Street. Here the streets were narrow and lined with picturesque and old-fashioned shops; old storefronts intermingled with brightly renovated Victorian houses converted to commercial space. Everything was brightly inviting, but all it was to Winter was a hostile labyrinth keeping her from the safe refuge of her car and her house.

She drew a deep breath, forcing calm against the rising tide of sickness and panic. Maybe the simplest thing to do would be to just ask directions. Anyone along here ought to be able to tell her how to find Main Street again.

She turned toward the nearest shop. The sign over the storefront was carved and painted wood: a golden full moon riding a skirl of swirling purple clouds spangled with stars. The words *Inquire Within* were carved to the left of the moon in old-fashioned letters. There was also a crescent moon and a swirl of stars painted in gold on the window itself, and behind them, on the red satin drape of the display window, a "crystal" ball on an ornate stand, a long acrylic tube filled with glitter with a shiny holographic star on one end, and a spill of brightly colored paperbacks with titles like *Teach Yourself White Witchcraft* and *Mind Over Matter.* A New Age bookstore.

Winter recoiled as if she'd confronted a monster out of her darkest subconscious. The sick disassociated feeling she'd been fighting grew stronger; she felt beads of perspiration break out stingingly all over her forehead, and swallowed hard against a wave of nausea.

The signboard overhead began to rock as if a wind were blowing, though the spring day was sunny and still.

Winter jerked spasmodically, staring up at it in horror, and began to back away—from the sign, from the store—every muscle trembling uncontrollably.

A sandwich sign in front of the antique store next door flung itself to the sidewalk with the sound of a pistol-crack. Winter cried out—a sound of fear and anger and despair. The bread and the wine bottles slipped out of her arms, slamming into the pavement with impossible force.

The bottles did not break as much as disintegrate, wine and slivers of glass spraying fire-hose hard through the tatters of the ruined bag to make a glittering fan-shape on the paving. The glassware in the antique store's window began to shiver and hum in sympathy, with a sweet high keening that filled the street with sound.

Winter ran.

She did not know how she reached her car again, only that by the time she did, her body was drenched in icy sweat and she was shaking so hard the keys in her hands made a staccato rhythm as they danced across the lacquered surface of the car door. Red and black blobs floated through her sight, and waves of fever and chill wracked her. Her heart was a fast hard hammering in her chest.

"Can I help you, lady?"

Winter shrieked and spun around.

"Stay back!" she cried, brandishing her keys like a crucifix. They flew out of her hand and fell at the feet of a boy in a Taghkanic College sweatshirt and frayed jeans.

I'm going crazy. Oh, God, I'm losing control—

He started to sidle away, then hesitated, staring at the keys on the ground.

"I just wanted to—" he began.

"Go away!" Winter screamed. *Before something happens.* Waves of nausea threatened to drown her; her heart was beating hard enough to make her teeth chatter; she felt as if she were about to have a seizure. Winter clutched at the car's door handle, willing herself not to faint. She had to get out of here before any more accidents happened, because even though Winter Musgrave was accident prone, around her the accidents happened to other people. . . .

The boy backed off, giving her a frightened look, and Winter darted forward to grab her keys. The gesture unbalanced her, driving her to her knees, and as she knelt on the asphalt, she could see the signs on the buildings across Main Street begin to rock.

No— No— Not here; not again—I promised. . . .

A terror beyond fear galvanized her. Winter clutched the keys so tightly their metal edges were driven into her palm hard enough to bring blood and she staggered to her feet with the determination of the desperate.

The key left a long scratch in the car's paint before it found the lock, but then she rammed it blessedly home and turned it, and the door—safety, refuge—opened.

Winter fell across the seat and dragged the door shut, whimpering in torment. *Safe—safe—safe*—some idiot part of her mind babbled, but it was too late, she had gone too far, and as her finger touched the button for the automatic lock, the display panel of the car exploded in a violent burst of sparks.

Three hours later Winter stood beside the smoke-blackened remains of her car, glaring defiantly at the last of the gawkers as the fire truck pulled out of the parking lot and headed back up the street. Her hands still ached from battering at the sealed windows and her throat was raw from screaming.

Someone—probably the kid she'd yelled at—had called the police, and the sheriff's car had arrived to find smoke billowing from beneath the hood and from under the dashboard of the BMW, and Winter, hysterical, trapped inside. Every electrical system in the car—including the windows and the unlocking mechanism of the doors—was dead, and Winter was sealed inside a vehicle whose passenger compartment was filling with poisonous smoke. The deputy had smashed the window and pulled her out through it. Then the fire department arrived to spray foam over the hood and every interior surface of her car, replacing the stink of burning leather and insulation with the rank wet stench of chemical foam.

The only thing that had allowed Winter to hold onto any scrap of self-control was the repeated pleas of the sheriff's deputy that she go to the hospital so that they could see if she was all right. The thought that she might be sent to the hospital—and by extension, back to Fall River—was enough to crush her spiraling hysteria and drive Winter into a numb emotionless state. She knew dimly that such numbness was far more dangerous than screams and tears, but her frigid self-possession had made them leave her alone, had made them send away the EMTs with their threatening orange-and-white van, had made them all go.

The growl of a powerful engine and the clanking of winches and chains roused her. An enormous blue-and-white tow truck, with KELLY'S GARAGE AND TOWING painted on the side in rainbow letters, lumbered into the parking lot.

"You the lady that needs the tow?" the driver shouted over the noise of his engine.

Winter glared at him in disbelief, then turned back to stare at the remains of her BMW—remembering, belatedly, that its trunk was filled with melting groceries. The sheriff's deputy had not even bothered to consult her before calling for a tow truck.

Without waiting for an answer from her, the driver pulled his truck up to the front of her car and set his brake. He got out.

"What happened?" He was wearing a gray mechanic's coverall that said DAVE on it, and he looked open and friendly.

"My car exploded." She was ready to weep with sheer exhaustion, but if she could not manage to cope, she would have failed, and Winter Musgrave hated failure as theologians hated death and Hell.

Dave looked at her car. "A BMW?" he said in faint disbelief. "I don't even know if there's a dealership this side of the river. . . . Oh, I'm Dave Kelly; I own the garage." He held out his hand.

Winter stared at it blankly for a moment before reaching out and shaking it. "Winter Musgrave. I live outside of town; all my groceries are in the trunk. . . ."

"That's right; you're up at Greyangels, aren't you? Why don't you come on back to the garage—your car might not be in as bad shape as she looks, and if she is, I'll give Timmy Sullivan a ring; he and his sister run the car service."

"Yes. All right. Anything," Winter said.

Dave helped her up into the high passenger seat of the wrecker. She sank into the seat and lay back, eyes closed, while he hooked her car up to the winch and raised the front end up off the ground. She wanted to retreat to the safety of the farmhouse, to shut out the world, to return to the uncaring oblivion she'd had before.

But she couldn't. It was a seductive trap. *There is no time. . . .* It would leave her defenseless against whatever was killing the animals.

Whether it was Winter or something else. She closed her eyes.

"—never seen anything like that before," Dave said, climbing into the cab. "It's almost like the thing was struck by lightning—spark plugs are *melted* into place; don't know how I'm going to get them out. . . ."

He looked toward Winter. "Are you all right, miss?"

Winter's eyes flew open and she straightened up hastily. "Fine. I'm fine."

I'm not fine at all. . . .

Dave Kelly's garage was at the edge of town; a square white building that seemed to combine a service station and a junkyard all in one. There was a large blacktopped area beside the building filled with cars—some new, some old, some missing tires or hoods or windows. Deftly, Dave Kelly maneuvered the wrecker until the car in tow was where he wanted it, then he released the winch and shut off the ignition.

"Why don't we see about getting your stuff out of the trunk and I'll give Tim a ring? It's going to be a day or two before I have an estimate for you on fixing your Beamer. I can tell you right now you'd better call your insurance—although what you're going to tell them, I don't know."

Winter awoke in her own bed several hours later, ravenous and light-headed. The house was dark; through the open window came the high sweet song of night peepers. Groaning, Winter rolled over and flicked on the light. The warm, oak-paneled walls of the bedroom shone with a re-assuring solidity. Wincing at the stiffness of her muscles, Winter tottered to her feet and closed the window. The demanding rumble of her stomach made it plain that simply going back to sleep was not an option.

I have to have something to eat.

The thought triggered another one. *My groceries. What happened to them?* She remembered reaching the garage, and her overriding determination not to go to the hospital, but everything beyond was a jumbled blur. She must have gotten home somehow—but had her shopping?

Cautiously Winter explored the midnight house, shivering in the cold. The electric heat would take forever to warm the place; she wondered if she could summon the energy to light the stove or build a fire.

Part of the reason for the cold was explained when she got to the parlor. In the hallway beyond, she could see the front door hanging gently open, admitting moonlight and a skirl of last year's leaves. Winter pushed it shut and threw the dead bolt. She was only lucky not to have had visitors—if not burglars, then their even more destructive cousins, raccoons.

In the parlor, the bags of groceries she'd bought an eternity ago stood like battered sentinels in their tattered paper sacks. Unwarily, Winter lifted one, only to have its contents shower from its damp, torn bottom to bounce and roll in every direction. *How did they . . . ?* She didn't remember loading them into the taxi. To be honest, she didn't remember the taxi.

She pawed through the bags until she found a jar of jam. Twisting off the lid, she scooped a dollop out with her fingers and sucked it into her mouth. The fruity sweetness sent a tingle of craving through her entire body. Still carrying the jar, she hurried into the kitchen for a spoon, and had eaten half the jar's contents before she began to feel satisfied. Rinsing her sticky fingers beneath the tap, Winter returned to the parlor to see what else she could salvage.

Most of what she'd bought had been canned or boxed, and only the frozen foods were ruined. She bundled the soggy melted mass up in a plastic garbage bag for later disposal and carried the remainder into the kitchen to put it away. Once she'd done that, Winter opened a can of stew to heat on the kitchen stove.

The bread would have been good with this. And the wine. She winced inwardly at the memory of her expedition to Glastonbury. She only hoped that the consequences didn't extend beyond a few ruined sacks of groceries and a burnt-out car. Visions of people coming to her house, demanding that she leave with them and go back to Fall River or to some worse place, haunted her until she angrily banished them. She would not go—she wouldn't! She'd done nothing wrong. . . .

But what *had* she done? What had happened, exactly? It had been only a few hours ago, but she wasn't sure. She'd gotten lost, and—

I panicked, Winter told herself brutally. *That's all.*

And the car . . . ?

A coincidence, Winter told herself.

But it wasn't.

She'd refilled the rick on the mud-porch, and now she carried logs into the parlor and laid a fire in the fireplace. While it was kindling, Winter filled the stove in her bedroom and lit it, ate the canned stew she'd opened, and even found a little brandy to go in her instant coffee—a forgotten bottle pushed far to the back of the pantry. She sat in front of the fire, sipping the warming drink, and sleepily watched the flames dance over the burning wood—the way the signs had danced over the buildings, the glassware in the windows—

No! A bright jolt of fear galvanized her to wakefulness; she couldn't sleep, not when she might find anything at all here in the farmhouse when she awoke. The memory of the squirrel made her shudder. If she slept again, who knew what she'd find in the morning?

Because she was the one responsible. She had to find the strength to admit that now. There was no one else to blame. No human agency could have followed her from Manhattan, to Massachusetts, to Glastonbury, killing animals and placing their ravaged corpses outside her door. It was her. She was the one doing it.

A wave of depression mixed with relief settled over her. *Accept the blame,* a cold inner voice whispered. *It's your fault, all your fault. Don't try to find an explanation. Just accept the blame. . . .*

Winter drew a long, shuddering breath of grief. All right. She'd accept the blame—that was supposed to be the first step on the road to recovery, wasn't it? Mea fucking culpa? But if she was the cause, she could also make it stop.

Couldn't she?

In the search that had uncovered the brandy, Winter had also seen what she needed now, and although she could not imagine the necessity that had stored 250 feet of cotton clothesline in the farmhouse pantry, she blessed it now. With the clothesline in one hand and the kitchen shears in the other, Winter retired to her bedroom.

She'd built a fire in the woodstove at the same time she'd built the fire in the fireplace, and the room was pleasantly warm now. She took the time to change her slept-in clothes for heavy flannel pajamas and turn back the patchwork quilt and Hudson Bay blanket that covered the white iron bedstead.

Then she turned to the clothesline.

It's not me. It's NOT. But it was, it had to be—there was no one else here to blame. She cut a long hank of line, and knotted one end around the bedpost, tying and retying knot over knot until there was no way to undo it. She set the rest of the coil aside on the rocking chair and slipped the shears carefully beneath the mattress. Then she climbed into bed.

At least it won't happen tonight.

Winter felt her cheeks go hot with embarrassment—although there was no one to see—as she took the free end of clothesline and wrapped it around her wrist, knotting and tying it until it was as secure as the other. She tugged at it, relieved at its strength. There was no way she could break the rope, and no way to untie it. In fact, she'd set herself up for a certain amount of strenuous gymnastics in the morning, since in order to get out of bed she was going to have to get the shears out from under the mattress and cut the clothesline one-handed, something she knew she couldn't possibly manage to do in her sleep.

If she *did* walk in her sleep—and she had to believe that she did—she would not do it tonight. Satisfied, Winter turned out the light and settled herself again for sleep.

CHAPTER TWO

A ROSE IN WINTER

It was the winter wild.
— JOHN MILTON

TAGHKANIC COLLEGE WAS FOUNDED IN 1714 IN THE colony of New York to provide education to the residents of what would later become Amsterdam County. The college was first housed in a building that had once been a cider mill, and the mill was still there on the campus, though its classroom days were long past. Taghkanic College survived into the twentieth century almost unchanged from its Federalist heyday; the newest building on the campus was the "new wing" of the Margaret Beresford Bidney Memorial Psychic Science Research Laboratory, and the "new wing" was completed in 1941.

Margaret Beresford Bidney graduated Taghkanic College in the late 1860s, and upon her death, her fortune went to fund what came to be known as the Bidney Institute. From the moment of the Institute's inception, the trustees of the college were on the verge of claiming the entire Bidney Bequest on behalf of Taghkanic College, when Professor Colin MacLaren accepted an appointment as director of the Institute.

Under his guidance, the moribund Institute revived, taking the lead in the investigation both of psychic phenomena and its wicked stepsister, occult phenomena. In the waning years of the twentieth century, Tagh-kanic College, in association with the Bidney Institute, stood as one of the few schools to offer a doctoral program in parapsychology.

But the Institute's primary function began as, and remained, re-search—into parapsychology as well as "Science's dark twin," the occult sciences that Professor MacLaren so firmly believed must be studied alongside the psychic sciences in order to understand them fully.

On this particular spring morning, researcher Truth Jourdemayne, who had become expert in the glamorless field of statistical parapsychol-ogy long before she realized her allegiance was to an older stranger craft, was not thinking of science—parapsychological or occult—at all.

"An entire summer in an Appalachian ghetto—you sure know how to spoil a girl," Truth teased. Her willing victim was Dr. Dylan Palmer, both a teacher at the college and a researcher at the Institute.

Dylan simply grinned, his mild blue eyes and shaggy blond hair giv-ing him the deceptively placid air of a penitent sheepdog.

"There hasn't been an in-depth case study ever done on Morton's Fork—oh, Nicholas Taverner did a little something in the twenties, but he was more of a folklorist, gathering material about English folk-survivals."

"When what you want is ghosts," Truth said.

"Well," Dylan admitted, "you have to agree that the director of the Institute is more likely to be interested in ghosts than folk songs—and from what I can tell, Morton's Fork is the center of unexplained activity for a fifty-mile radius. I've marked this survey map—"

Dylan spread the map over the piles of paper that covered his desk. Truth bent over it to see it more clearly, and Dylan tugged at her arm so she overbalanced and fell into his lap.

There was a time not so long before when Truth would have lashed out against a gesture of this sort; fighting against it and the feelings it pro-voked. But that time had passed, and an emerald-and-pearl ring glinted on the third finger of her left hand in token of her emotional renewal.

"But maybe you're right," Dylan said wistfully as Truth put her arms around him. "It won't be much of a holiday, and I did promise. . . ."

"I think it will be the perfect vacation," Truth said, snuggling into a more comfortable position. "Just you, and me, a hundred thousand dollars' worth of temperamental recording equipment, three grad students, and some ghosts." *Or whatever* genius loci *infest the place,* she finished, with a pang of premonition.

"Sounds crowded," Dylan murmured. "But, as none of them are here right now . . ."

There was a knock at the door.

Dylan swore, and tipped Truth to her feet an instant before the door opened. Meg Winslow, the Institute's secretary, looked in.

"Sorry to bother you, Dylan, but—oh, Truth, I didn't see you there. Boy, am I glad to see both of you—we've got a real live one this time."

As a public focus for society's interest—and sometimes obsession— with the occult and paranormal and allied New Age pursuits, the Bidney Institute had become accustomed to attracting a certain amount of public inquiries, by phone, by letter, and sometimes in person. They ranged from pleas for help from those genuinely troubled by psychic phenomena, to attempts by con men and charlatans to bilk the Institute of its endowment through one fraud or another, to outcries—no less sincere and desperate for all of that—from individuals whose problems lay entirely within the scope of their confused minds and troubled emotions.

"What's his problem?" Truth asked, getting to her feet.

"Her," Meg corrected. "I tried to get rid of her, but she just keeps saying she needs to talk to one of the researchers. She's really out there, Truth; I put her in the Interview Lab—she was scaring the students."

"As if anything could," Truth muttered.

"Did she tell you what the problem was?" Dylan asked.

Meg shrugged. "All she'd tell *me* was that she was being haunted— she's got *that* right, if you ask me."

Winter Musgrave rocked restlessly back and forth, too keyed up even to pace. She wrung her hands, as if some private devil were clasped between them, until she noticed what she was doing and stopped—only to start again as soon as her attention wandered. Her jaws ached with the tension of gritted teeth, but she nearly didn't dare open her mouth for fear that the sounds that issued from it would be the keening of a madwoman.

I'm not crazy. I know I'm not. What happened—I could NOT *have done that. No matter what.*

She clung to that thought, even though she could not understand how it could be true. Perhaps it wasn't. Maybe she *was* crazy. That would be better. Because if she wasn't crazy, she didn't need a shrink.

She needed an exorcist.

Winter hadn't meant to come here at all, but when she'd called Sullivan's Taxi she hadn't been thinking clearly, and when the driver had come, he'd misunderstood her frantic demand to be taken "to the Institute" and brought her here. She hadn't really been thinking of going back to Fall River when she gave him the order; only of getting away from the house that had now twice betrayed her.

But the driver had brought her here instead—to the Bidney Institute. He'd had to tell her where she was three times before she'd get out— by then, hazy memories of the local college's pet ghostbreakers had begun to surface and Winter realized that her destination was sanctuary of a sort. She didn't remember where she'd heard about the Bidney Institute—it wasn't the sort of laboratory that was traded on Wall Street, after all— but once she'd arrived she knew it was her last hope. Her only hope.

Winter stared around the room she'd been told to wait in without really seeing it. The long window at the far end looked out over the old cider mill, with the river behind it like a bright foil ribbon. On the oak table in front of her were various things to fiddle with—blocks, a silver tuning fork, a deck of cards, and a brown paper bag, looking out of place among the executive time-wasters that Winter recognized from happier days. The back wall was lined with books and cased runs of magazines.

I am not crazy. Winter clenched her hands tighter. On the table the tuning fork began, ever so faintly, to hum.

Oh, please, I want to be crazy.

She'd been waiting for over ten minutes, and was beginning to be afraid that the receptionist—who had so clearly wished she'd go away and stop being a problem!—had simply shut Winter in here to get rid of her. She couldn't let them do that. They had to see her, had to, had to, had to—

Because I am not mad. I'm not.

When the door opened Winter had her back to it. She was so keyed up that the slight sound of its opening made her jerk and yelp. She tripped backward into the table; the deck of cards spilled onto the floor and one of the Rubik's Cubes clattered after it. Winter stared wild-eyed at the figure in the doorway, heart pounding.

She looks as if she's going to have a seizure any minute, was Truth Jourde-mayne's first thought, and the second was that the petite chestnut-haired woman ought to be in bed—maybe even a hospital bed. Her gauntness had the emaciation of hysteria rather than fashion, and even while staring at Truth and Dylan as though they were fresh out of her nightmares, she could not keep her hands still.

Another crazy, Truth thought resignedly, though some instinct kept her from being satisfied with the facile judgment.

"Hello," she said in calm encouraging tones, "my name is Truth Jour-demayne. And you are . . . ?"

"Winter." The woman's voice was a husky croak. "Winter Musgrave." She stared over Truth's shoulder at Dylan, amber eyes wide.

"I'm Dylan Palmer," Dylan said, coming into the room. Truth walked over to the table, and Dylan closed the door again, shutting out the noise of the people going back and forth in the hall outside.

"Won't you sit down, Ms. Musgrave, and tell us what we can do for you?" Truth said.

Winter Musgrave laughed; the sound came out almost as a wail.

"I need help," she said. "And not that kind! I've been—" she broke off. "No. You'll never believe me then—why should you? *I* don't believe me—don't you understand? *I* don't believe me—I don't care—all I want to do is stop it!"

She'd begun to pace, walking back and forth in front of the row of books, her voice rising as she spoke until she was almost shouting.

Dylan looked quizzically toward Truth. Both of them had been forced to baby-sit their share of cranks while waiting for the campus police to remove them—was this another? Truth frowned and shook her head a fraction, and sat down at the table.

"First you have to tell us what is troubling you," Truth said with gen-tle firmness.

Winter paused in her pacing and whirled to face Truth. As she did, two of the cased magazine sets fell off the shelf behind her; she jumped away from them, looking first at them and then back at Truth as if she ex-pected at any moment to be accused of something.

"I'm not crazy. Don't you understand? I'm not crazy—that's the whole problem—I'm not!"

"Okay," said Dylan, not moving from his watchful post beside the door, "you're not crazy. But you are going to have to tell us what you want."

Truth watched the woman gather herself together with an effort. "I want it to stop," she said, her voice nearly a whisper. "I want it to stop before someone gets hurt."

They couldn't help her, Winter realized with numb despair—and even if they could, she'd been a fool to believe that anyone would listen past the point where she told them about Fall River. "That's all I want," she repeated plaintively. "For it to stop."

"What is it that you want to stop?" the dark-haired woman seated at the table—Truth—asked her.

Winter stared at her doubtfully. She'd expected someone older—and, frankly, male—when she'd come demanding to speak with one of the Institute's researchers. This Dylan Palmer, in his work shirt, jeans, and earring, wasn't quite what she'd had in mind either, whether he said he was a doctor or not. Someone in a suit, maybe—someone with authority.

The authority to cast out demons.

"Do you—could you—I need to know . . ." The words trembled on the tip of her tongue, but she could not bring herself to say them. "Can you tell if someone's possessed?" she finally choked out.

Blessedly, neither of them laughed.

"Possessed by a devil?" Truth asked, as calmly as if she were discussing the price of a new bond issue. "Why don't you sit down, Ms. Musgrave?"

Dylan walked around the table and pulled out a chair for her. Winter sank into it, feeling drained of all strength by the effort it had taken to ask that question. She could be sane, and these things could still be happening—if she were possessed. It did not even occur to her to consider how desperate she must be to entertain this possibility.

"Now," Truth Jourdemayne said, "start from the beginning."

Winter hesitated. She'd always been a very private person—even when the catchphrase of the eighties was "Do you want to talk about it?" Winter never had. Talk frightened her; it made her feel too vulnerable. Even now she didn't want to talk. She wanted someone to wave a magic wand and make the problem go away. But they couldn't. Not until she told them what it was.

"Things . . . happen," Winter began, but even to her that sounded inadequate. She waited, but the woman across the table provided no helpful questions, and finally Winter went on. "To me—no, *around* me. These— things—happen, and I don't have any control over them; I'm not *doing* them—" she didn't think she was; how could she do things like that to helpless animals; how could anyone? "—but I can't *stop* them, either."

"What kind of things?" Truth asked, her voice still calm.

Winter flinched away from the telling. "They're . . . Look, I have to tell you: I've been in, in an institution. I had, oh, I guess they used to call it a nervous breakdown. But I'm not . . . I'm not crazy, you see? And if I am, why won't somebody just *tell* me I'm crazy, okay? I could stand that. And not just go around all the time pretending everything's great, everything's fine, like this is some sort of skinned knee that's going to get better if I just leave it alone for a while?"

She knew her voice was rising hysterically again. She couldn't help it; every time she managed to stop being afraid even the littlest bit, the rage and frustration rose to the surface until it took all the self-control she had left not to merely scream wordlessly and lash out at everything that surrounded her.

"Why don't you tell us why you came here, Ms. Musgrave?" Dylan Palmer said.

"Because you people are the ghostbusters, right? And that's what I'm dealing with—something that walks through walls and does things that nobody can do. Following me, and I thought it was my fault, so I— But I'm not going to take the blame, not if it— So you've got to exorcise me, or whatever it is you do here, so I can get back to my life!"

She could not manage to stay in her chair; she got to her feet again and began to pace, choking on her fear and rage until her heart was a thick weight in her throat.

"Ghosts usually haunt places rather than people, Ms. Musgrave," Dr. Palmer said calmly. "Why do you think you're being haunted?"

Winter waited, but the dark-haired woman—Truth—didn't say anything. But at least neither of them had laughed. A strange serenity seemed to radiate from Truth Jourdemayne, an intangible but real something that Winter could shelter beneath and draw strength from. She managed to halt her pacing and press both palms flat on the table. Finally she went on with her story.

"I'm staying in the old farmhouse a couple of miles out of Glastonbury. I went there after I got out of the sanatorium," she added, half-defiantly.

Neither of the researchers spoke. Winter forced herself to go on, to go faster, to get to the end of her tale so she could know the worst.

"Things happened at Fall River, at—the sanatorium. Nobody accused me, but they didn't have to. They never happened to anyone else. Things would disappear—little things, nothing of value—and show up later in weird places. My room had french windows that looked out onto one of the terraces; nobody could keep them locked; finally they nailed them shut. Nothing worked. The nails kept working loose."

A confused and vivid memory surfaced; a collage of images: the aides ostentatiously removing their watches before they came into her room; accusations that she'd broken—oh, she couldn't list the things; the coffeemaker in the rec room; the Coke machine; people blaming her, when she'd never *touched* the things.

"And there was something else, too—" but she still couldn't bear to name it "—but when I left there, all of that stopped."

"Completely?" Dr. Palmer asked.

"Yes. Although I'm not sure I would have noticed even if it continued, not with no one there to nag me—" She heard the whine of self-pity in her voice and stopped. "But then the one thing, the one particular thing, it's started again and it's worse, and I can't be doing it—I can't—not possibly. . . ."

She drew a shaking breath. Every nerve and muscle jangled with tension; it was an effort to keep her teeth from chattering.

"You have to tell us what it is that is troubling you, Ms. Musgrave," Truth said gently, "and even so, we may not be able to help."

"If you cannot help me I don't know where else to go," Winter said dully, "except to drive my car off the nearest cliff." Except she couldn't even do that, not after yesterday.

Winter took a deep breath and reached for the paper bag on the table. "Because of the—of the thing that happens, last night I tied myself to my bed. This morning when I got up every door and window in the house was wide open—and there was this":

She upended the bag over the table and shook it. Out fell two hundred fifty feet of white cotton clothesline, neatly dismembered into three-inch lengths.

Both of the researchers from the Institute went very still, like hunting dogs who have just sighted game. Finally Dr. Palmer stepped over to the table and picked up one of the pieces.

"The cuts are very clean," he said in a neutral voice.

"I couldn't do that—not with a knife, or a pair of scissors, or a razor blade. You tell me what did that," Winter said in a ragged whisper.

Truth picked up one of the pieces of line. The severed ends were as neat and crisp and compressed as the end of a filter-tip cigarette. Only something very sharp, wielded with great force, could make a cut like that. She pulled several more of the short pieces toward her and lined them up side by side. Each piece was the same length as all the others. Exactly.

She glanced at Dylan. His face was expressionless, but she could tell he was excited. The symptoms as Winter Musgrave described them were almost a synopsis of a classic textbook case of poltergeist possession: doors and windows mysteriously locked or open, apportation of small objects, and instances of whimsical and nearly impossible vandalism.

But the woman bringing these complaints was too old by at least two decades to be a traditional focus for a poltergeist, and the typical pranks of a "noisy spirit," while annoying, couldn't be enough on their own to bring an adult woman to such a fever-pitch of terror.

"Why did you tie yourself to the bed, Ms. Musgrave?" Truth asked again.

"Do you think I'm crazy?" the woman demanded fiercely. Her eyes blazed fever-bright with desperation, and Truth sensed the swirling currents of raw emotion which were the only things keeping her on her feet now.

"No," Truth said, glancing toward Dylan again. He was generally much more charitable in his assessments of people and their motives than she was, but he was also scrupulous in his judgments of matters touching on the psychic realm. If Dylan did not feel that the paranormal was involved he'd have no hesitation about saying so.

He nodded almost imperceptibly. He agreed, then, with Truth's preliminary assessment.

"Neither of us thinks you're crazy, Ms. Musgrave—just frightened. I will not make any promises, but it is possible that we can help."

The chestnut-haired woman across the table sagged wearily into her chair again. "I keep finding these animals," she said in a flat, exhausted voice. "Dead. Torn to shreds. Dropped on my doorstep like something the cat might drag home—only I don't have a cat. And I don't think even a cat would . . . Anyway. Pigeons. Squirrels. Mice. Some other kind of bird. And yesterday it started again. And this morning there was—oh, God, I think it was a raccoon or something. In the kitchen. *In* the kitchen." She dropped her head into her hands.

"I think," Dylan said, gently so as not to startle the woman across the table, "that you could use a hot drink. A cup of tea would be in order, I think, and then you can tell us the whole story start to finish."

Dr. Palmer left the room, leaving the door slightly ajar. Truth Jourdemayne looked at Winter.

"Have you ever read anything about the paranormal, Ms. Musgrave?" Truth asked.

"Please. Call me Winter." She said it with faint reluctance—Winter loathed false intimacy—but so far these people hadn't said she was crazy, so she at least owed them the use of her name. "And no, I haven't. Hocus-pocus bores me: Steven Spielberg and Uri Geller and all that stuff."

"That isn't quite what I was thinking of," Truth said, smiling to blunt the rebuke. "Well, to put it as simply as possible, it sounds to both Dylan—Dr. Palmer—and me as if the problem you're describing may fit into one of the rather broad categories established to describe paranormal events."

"Aren't you going to run some tests before coming up with that one?" Winter snapped. The woman across from her shook her head, not seeming offended in the least by the question.

"Unfortunately, one of the problems with these psychic abilities is that they tend to come and go as they please—and like cats, they don't respond well to being shown off for the neighbors. Anyone who says he can produce psychic phenomena on demand is probably a fraud."

"So even if you tested me, you wouldn't find anything," Winter offered grudgingly.

"Probably not," Truth admitted. "Still, we'd appreciate it if you'd let us run our standard battery of screening tests on you—"

"Screening? Why? Do you think I'm making this up?" Winter said, suspicious again.

"Screening," Truth repeated firmly, "to find out if you demonstrate any other potentials than this poltergeist you seem to have. It's rare to find a psychic only showing one ability—precogs will also exhibit clairvoyance; telepaths, telekinesis. . . ."

"I'm not a psychic," Winter protested. "You said *poltergeist*—isn't that a ghost? I told you I was haunted!"

"A poltergeist is not a ghost. The word itself is German, and means 'noisy spirit,'" Truth began. "Today we often call it RSPK phenomena, for Recurrent Spontaneous Psychokinesis. There's a whole range of activity broadly classified as 'poltergeist phenomena'—moving furniture, smashing dishes—oh, yes, and unlocking doors and windows as well—that seems to be being done by some malicious or mischievous entity; but as far as anyone seems to know, there is no ghost or spirit—Dylan would insist we call them 'discarnate consciousness'—involved. Poltergeist activity usually centers on a person, not a place, and let me emphasize that *all* cases of poltergeist activity eventually stop—usually when the *locus* matures, because most of the *loci* of poltergeist activity are girls just entering puberty."

There was a pause, while Winter digested what she'd just heard.

"But I'm not," she said flatly.

Just then Dylan returned with the tea things on a tray and passed the cups around the table. The tea was hot and already sweetened; some odd-yet-pleasant herbal blend. Winter didn't really want any, but at least holding the white stoneware mug gave her something to do with her hands. There were biscuits on a tray as well, giving the whole meeting an absurdly genteel air that somehow angered Winter.

"I agree that you're older than most victims—tell me, was there a poltergeist in the family when you were a child?" Truth asked, holding her own cup.

"Don't be ridiculous," Winter said shortly.

"RSPK is the most obvious explanation," Dylan acknowledged, sipping his tea, "because it is random, irrational, and—it can't be said too many times—not under the control of the person to which it is attached. It just seems to be a statistically random flare-up of psychism; which is why it affects ten times more girls than boys and generally occurs at puberty, when the entire body's already in an uproar. Emotional stress also seems to be a factor, and you did say you'd been under psychiatric treatment?" he added casually.

"You *do* think I'm crazy! You think I'm doing this myself!"

"Ms. Musgrave—Winter—please—" Truth began, but as Winter went to set her mug down on the table it went spinning out of her hand, hurtling across the room to shatter against the wall beside Dylan's head.

"And, of course, being the victim of a poltergeist can be very stressful itself," Dylan finished calmly.

"I— I'm sorry," Winter stammered. "I didn't mean to throw it at you—it just slipped. . . ."

She looked from one face to the other, and saw they did not believe that she had thrown it at all.

"All right," Winter said harshly. Tears stung at the corners of her eyes, and she resented her weakness with all her heart. "You've convinced me. I'm haunted by a poltergeist. Now how do I get rid of it?"

"The most important thing to do is to eliminate stress from your daily routine as much as possible, and—unrealistic as it sounds—try not to let it worry you," Truth said soothingly. "We can run a test series here, but that shouldn't affect a poltergeist one way or the other, and as I say, there's no documented cure. I *can* recommend some harmless herbal teas that may help; there's a store in Glastonbury called *Inquire Within* that keeps several mixtures made up. Don't be put off by their window display, the owner is more into herbs and crystals than black magic. I'd also suggest meditation, if you're—"

"*Meditation?*" Winter said incredulously. "I tell you there's this *thing* stalking my life across three states, killing animals and leaving them strewn around for me to find, and all you can suggest to do about it is to *think happy thoughts?*"

The tuning fork on the table began to hum faintly.

"What would you prefer—electroshock?" Truth snapped back. "Haven't you been listening? All of this—nasty as it is, frightening as it is—is coming from *you*. A poltergeist is a sort of psychic seizure, and maybe they can find the part of your brain where it's happening and burn it away, but there won't be very much of you left afterward. The only thing you can do is minimize the damage, clean up after it, and try to find out *why* it's happening."

"I don't want to know why it's happening! I want it to stop!" Winter shrieked over the sound that suddenly filled the room: the buzzing, ringing, beeping cacophony of a dozen different warning bells. Her heart hammered until it seemed that her head would burst with its next beat, and once again she was trembling so hard her teeth chattered. She flung herself out of her chair and ran for the door, her only thought to escape before worse happened. Dylan Palmer grabbed her before she could reach it; she cried out and struck at him.

"Running won't solve anything," Dylan said firmly, holding her until she stopped struggling. He released her slowly; Winter stayed where she was, panting and wild-eyed.

The sound intensified; the unholy racket of a dozen different devices, from the security system to the smoke alarm, that had all gone off at once.

"It's probably a quake," Truth said calmly. "Dr. Martello said he'd be running a series today with that new Dutch psychic, the teleport; and the machines we use to measure PK are very sensitive. But I do wish they'd shut them down." Almost as Truth spoke she got her wish, as one by one the blaring sirens stopped and there was silence again.

As if some wave had crested and ebbed, the frantic tension that had filled Winter since the discovery of the pieces of cut clothesline was gone, leaving her hungry, exhausted, and wishing only to sleep. She sat down again and took a biscuit off the tray, biting down and closing her eyes as the sweetness filled her mouth.

"Tell me, Winter, how did you come to rent Greyangels Farm? Amsterdam County isn't exactly along the beaten track," Dr. Palmer said.

"It's beautiful, isn't it?" Winter said. She heard the grogginess in her voice, and hoped he wouldn't ask a question that would make her admit that she had no idea how she'd come to be at the old farmhouse.

"You probably remembered the place from your student days," Dr. Palmer said. "Old Mr. Zacharias was always trying to rent the place—not that it ever stayed rented for very long," he added to Truth. "It isn't haunted, unfortunately."

"Student days?" Winter echoed blankly.

"When you were at Taghkanic . . ." Dr. Palmer began, and stopped when he saw the look on Winter's face.

"I went to college here," Winter said in an uninflected voice.

Both women were looking at Dylan Palmer now. "Winter Musgrave," Dylan repeated to himself, as though making certain of getting it right. "You were Class of 'eighty-two. So was I. You audited Professor Mac-Laren's Introduction To Occult Psychology course; I can't remember why—" Dylan said.

Winter stared at Dylan as if she'd never seen him in her life. "I've been here before?" she said.

Truth felt the hairs on her neck and arms rise up in a primitive animal response to the uncanny.

"You went to school here," Dylan said, taken aback by Winter's response. Whatever he'd expected when he'd brought up the subject, it hadn't been this.

"I went to school here," Winter echoed inanely. Her voice held no inflection. "I don't remember. Why don't I remember?"

But she did remember, a little. Enough to know that Dr. Palmer spoke the truth, even though she had not suspected it until this moment. She'd come back here because she'd come from here. "If this is true, why don't I remember?" Winter repeated plaintively.

"I'm not a psychologist," Truth began carefully, "but sometimes the mind, under trauma—"

"But I haven't had any trauma," Winter interrupted. "I've had a perfect life. I had a wonderful job; I liked what I did; I was good at it. I had no problems." Panicked, she cast her mind back into the past, beyond the blurred memories of the past year. There were the details of her life, sharp and clear; a comfortable, ordinary life without surprises or disappointments.

"You don't remember anything?" Dr. Palmer asked. Winter hesitated.

"What was your major in college?" Truth asked.

And now the fear began, because Winter didn't remember that either, and *everyone* remembered their college major. She couldn't even remember getting her diploma! She gazed at Truth in mute appeal.

"Winter didn't graduate," Dr. Palmer said slowly, thinking backward more than ten years. "I remember you left school a few weeks before graduation," he said to her. "No one ever knew why."

The half-echo of her own thoughts started Winter into a laugh.

"Though it's really too soon to be really sure your problem is paranormal in nature," Truth said carefully, "and I can't say this particular problem is related, I think it would help both you and us if you came to the Institute for the full battery of tests."

"But all the animals," Winter said. That was really the worst—the bodies of the dead animals left in her path like some ghoulish offering. "I have to make that stop."

"We don't know where poltergeists come from," Truth repeated, "so we don't know what affects them. I know you think it's useless, but do, please, try the tea I suggested." Truth pulled a pad of paper over to her, scribbled a name on it in pencil, and pushed the pad over to Winter. "And perhaps some meditation techniques. They can't do any harm, and they may help you to . . . stand up to it."

"I thought you said poltergeists couldn't be controlled," Winter said suspiciously, ripping the top sheet off the pad and pushing the paper into her purse without looking at it.

Truth shrugged and smiled apologetically; Winter realized that Truth Jourdemayne was much younger than she seemed.

"I said that—as far as has been reported in the professional literature—no one ever has. But that isn't to say that it can't be done—and I don't think you're the sort of woman who submits tamely to the vagaries of fate."

Winter forced herself to smile, feeling—if not hopeful, then at least that she was finally in a fight. "No," she said. "I guess I don't give up easily." *And I certainly don't believe the first quack that comes down the pike. On the other hand . . .* She hesitated. "What's the name of that store again?"

"*Inquire Within.* It's down in Glastonbury. Meg has a stock of their cards out front; tell her I told her to give you one. You can set up an appointment for a round of psi-tests with her, too, if you like."

I don't think so. Winter had always been a fighter, an instinct that had stood her in good stead in her years on the Street. Just the act of putting her darkest fears into words had strengthened her against them. She could fight this, this—hobgoblin that was trying to take over her life— yes, and reclaim her own past as well. And she didn't need anyone else's help to do it. For some reason it was better to think she was haunted than that she was crazy, and this large, official-looking building, filled with researchers and machines and civil, civilized people who took all of this so seriously, made her feel that being haunted was more than an option, it was almost respectable.

"I'll . . . think about it," Winter said hesitantly. "But thank you for your patience—both of you. I don't imagine I've been the most charming guest."

"In comparison to some," Dr. Palmer said with a twinkle of mock sobriety in his eyes, "you have been a paragon of virtue. Thank you for coming, Winter—and don't hesitate to stop by again."

"Thank you, Dr. Palmer. I'll certainly keep that in mind." *The next time the ghoulies start nipping at my toes,* Winter thought with a faint flash of mordant humor.

But the bout of febrile high spirits that had momentarily possessed her vanished when she was out of doors once more. Winter clutched the business card that Meg Winslow had given her and blinked at the bright sunlight. She hadn't taken a good look around before. All around her were apple trees white with blossom; the spring campus looked as scenic and inviting as a painting in a book. And it ought to be familiar. She had gone to school here—so Dylan Palmer said. If she could trust anything he said.

No! She brought her wandering mind up with sharp anger. Start thinking that way and she'd be mad in truth. Dr. Palmer had told her the truth—he had no reason to lie to her, as far as she knew.

But why couldn't she *remember* anything?

Despite her weariness, Winter chose a direction and started off, almost at random. Maybe more exposure to theoretically familiar sights would jog her memory back into place—and if not, the exercise would at least ensure a dreamless sleep tonight.

In spite of herself, Winter shuddered. What dreams could she have that were more horrible than her awakenings?

CHAPTER THREE

A HAZY SHADE OF WINTER

The winter I'll not think on to spite thee,
But count it a lost season, so shall she.
— JOHN DONNE

BUT AN HOUR OF WALKING AROUND THE TAGHKANIC campus failed to jog loose any hidden memories, and only served to remind Winter how recently out of a hospital sickbed she was, though once upon a time she had . . .

A ghost of a memory, of a much younger Winter, running laughing among the apple trees, being chased by . . . who?

She shook her head. The scrap of memory was gone, leaving her with nothing to do but follow the rest of Truth Jourdemayne's prescription.

Winter felt butterflies collect in her stomach as the taxi pulled up to the curb of the little storefront. She had only realized how reluctant she was to come here once she was fully committed to it. Here was where all the trouble had started.

No. Be honest. Here was where the trouble continued.

"I'd like you to wait," Winter said to the driver.

"How long?" Tim Sullivan said. He was young and fresh-faced, and looked more afraid of her than she was of him—a far cry from the New York City taxi drivers she was used to.

"I'll pay for the waiting time," Winter said. She knew that being outside the city, these cars were not equipped with a meter that could charge for waiting time. "Fifty dollars."

The driver's jaw dropped and he nearly choked. *"Fifty dollars?* But, ma'am—"

"My car's in the shop and I need a way to get around. And there isn't anyplace around here that I can rent a car, is there?"

"I—well—Dave Kelly's Garage has a loaner sometimes. . . ."

Ah, the joys of living in a small town. "Fine. Then we can go there next. If you'll wait for me here?"

"Um . . . sure." Sullivan was dubious but faintly willing. "Just let me park this thing."

He slid the car without difficulty into a space along the unoccupied curb and turned off the engine. Winter got out of the car.

There's nothing to be afraid of. . . . Winter put her hand to the door.

It was green-painted wood, and the glass panel in the top half had been replaced with stained glass; another moon on another storm-tossed celestial sea. The whole effect was clownish rather than frightening, and the silly tableau in the window of crystal ball and pointy hat completed the impression of Saturday morning cartoon magic. This was an herbs and crystals shop, nothing more.

A bell jingled as she opened and closed the door. The air inside the store was musty and sweet-smelling, and the first thing Winter focused on was a large calico cat sitting on top of a glassed-in bookcase. It blinked green eyes at her and stretched disdainfully.

"Can I help you?" came a voice from the back of the shop.

The sixties are not dead, was Winter's first derisive thought. The woman who approached her was small and slender, with long blond hair and a kittenish face. Her hair was parted ruler-straight down the middle of her head and held in place with a braided leather headband. She was even wearing the love beads and bell-bottoms of Winter's childhood. *I wonder where she finds them in this day and age?*

"Can I help you?" the woman said again, coming closer. She smiled disarmingly, and Winter saw that despite the illusion of youth, the woman was closer to forty than thirty. "I'm Tabitha Whitfield; the owner. I wondered if there was something you were specifically looking for; you look a little lost."

"I came in for some tea," Winter said. She rummaged through her Coach briefbag for the paper that Truth Jourdemayne had given her. "Something called . . . Oh, I can't remember!" And the paper was not showing up.

"Oh, don't worry; I'm sure we can reconstruct it," Tabitha Whitfield said cheerfully. "You're from the college, aren't you?"

"Why?" Winter was instantly suspicious.

Tabitha laughed. "Because when people come in with—excuse me!— your particular shell-shocked expression, they've almost always been sent down by the ghost-hunters. At the lab?" she added, in case Winter hadn't understood.

"Yes," Winter said shortly. "It was a woman named Truth Jourde- mayne."

"Oh, *Truth!*" Tabitha said. "Then I know just what she sent you for. She's quite the local celebrity—did you know her father's Thorne Black- burn?" Tabitha added, just as if she expected Winter to recognize the name.

Tabitha gestured to a stack of books on a marble-topped table in the corner. "She even wrote a book. I'll just get that tea." The proprietor dis- appeared behind the inevitable bead curtain into the back room of the shop.

Her interest piqued, Winter went toward the table. The calico cat stretched out a languid paw toward her as she passed.

The books on the table were all the same title. Winter saw a dust- jacket that was a collage of sixties images: love beads and pentagrams, and a man dressed up as Merlin the Magician. She picked up one of the books.

Venus Afflicted: The Short Life and Fast Times of Magister Ludens Thorne Blackburn and the New Aeon.

What the hell?

She opened it and read the flap copy. Along with the sight of a glossy, insincere picture of Truth Jourdemayne with fluffy hair, Winter discov- ered that the book was a biography of a sixties nutcase who'd claimed to be a warlock—and was, incidentally, Truth's father.

Winter shut the book with a snap, her lip curling in disgust. She wasn't quite sure what was so irritating about this, and she didn't feel she owed it the courtesy to find out. Anger crept back into her mind: She'd gone to the Institute for help—it was on a *college campus,* for God's sake; it ought to be at least a little bit respectable—and all they'd been able to field was a John Denver look-alike who said he'd gone to school with her and the daughter of the Archdruid of Canterbury!

Winter felt her heartbeat begin to race, and belatedly recognized the trap. Strong emotion—of any sort—seemed to bring on those spells of disastrous bad luck that were almost more tormenting than the visitations of the *thing* that opened doors and ripped animals to shreds. Even now, she felt compelled to distinguish the two, as if they were not one problem, but two. Clutching the book tightly, Winter took a deep breath, then another, groping for the iron-willed self-control that had served her so well on the Street—and felt the clutch of frightened anger fade.

"And how are you finding everything?" Tabitha Whitfield's cheery voice broke into Winter's mood of wary self-congratulation.

"Just where you left it," Winter said, trying to keep the edge out of her voice. Sarcasm had always been her first line of defense against the world; a way to lash out before she was hurt. She came over to the cash register, and realized she was still holding *Venus Afflicted* in her hands. "I'll take this, too," she said, by way of tacit apology. She placed the book and her bag on the counter beside the small parcel Tabitha had brought out of the back room—a small brown paper package with a silver-and-white label on it. *Centering Tea* was written on the label in ornate purple felt-tip.

"You should take it on up to the college and get it signed," Tabitha said, opening the book to run her scanner over the bar-code. "But I can see why you were drawn to it—you're one of the Grey Angels, just the way she is. Your aura's very strong, you know; I can feel it from here—"

"What do I do with the tea?" Winter said brusquely. Whether she was an angel—gray or otherwise—she really didn't want to hear about other people's auras. The eighties were over.

Fortunately, Tabitha seemed willing to be diverted. "All you need to do is steep it in a pot like regular loose tea, and be sure to sweeten it with honey or molasses—they're much better for you than the artificial sweet-

eners like refined white sugar. I've got a page of directions right here—"
she rummaged beneath the counter "—and a booklet of the exercises that
go with the tea. That'll be thirty-seven seventy-eight."

Exercises? Whatever the explanation for that one was, Winter wasn't in
the mood for hearing it at the moment. Recalling one of the very prosaic
stickers in the window, Winter dug through her purse again and handed
over her Visa card, incidentally turning up the piece of paper with
Truth's handwriting on it. She peered at it. *Centering Tea* it was, whatever
that was. She crumpled the paper into the bottom of her purse.

"There's a meditation group that meets here on Wednesdays after
hours," Tabitha said as she validated the card. "Some of the locals and
some of the kids from the college—you're welcome to come."

The offer, though flaky, had been well meant. "Thanks," Winter said.
Maybe in another lifetime.

Tabitha Whitfield handed Winter back her charge card. Winter
glanced briefly at the photo on the front of the Visa card. Had that vital
young predator really been her? She tucked the card back into her wallet
and took the bag Tabitha handed her. It seemed to be rather full of flyers.
Oh, well, the stove at home could always use kindling.

To Winter's relief, Tim Sullivan was in fact still waiting outside *Inquire
Within* when she emerged, blinking, into the thin spring sunlight. She
slung her Coach bag and the brown paper sack into the backseat and
climbed in.

"Do you want to go to the garage now?" Sullivan asked.

"Sure," Winter said recklessly. The more time she spent successfully
navigating the pitfalls of the world, the cockier she became. Jack had always said she was crazy and reckless with it—and that was what made a
good trader.

*"You've got the killer instinct, sweetheart, and you aren't afraid of blood.
That's what it takes to survive here."*

The killer instinct. Abruptly Winter felt as if a cold breeze had spilled
over her skin. *Was* she a killer—and using some kind of psychic power to
do it?

"I heard something funny back there." She heard her own voice,
bright and high with tension, talking to block out the voice within. "The
woman who owns the store—*Inquire Within?*—said something about

'Grey Angels.' What are they—some kind of local folklore?" The Hudson Valley was rich in folklore, Winter remembered from another lifetime, from the Headless Horseman of Sleepy Hollow to the ghostly galleon that plied the Hudson on moonlit nights, scaring hell out of the local maritime traffic.

"That's right; you live out on Greyangels Road, don't you, ma'am?" Sullivan said. "I don't know much about it myself," he went on, "it's more a local thing, and Dad just moved up here in 'eighty-seven. The old-timers say there's supposed to be angels haunting this part of the Hudson Valley. Like ghosts, you know, only good—most of the time."

How appropriate, Winter thought to herself. "Gray ones?"

"I guess so." Sullivan was dubious. "All I know is, I've never seen them—but we do get pretty heavy fogs from time to time, being so near the river and all. Maybe that's them. Here we are."

She could always call for another cab if the loaner car failed to materialize, so Winter sent Tim Sullivan on his way after assuring him she really *had* meant him to keep the fifty dollars. Walking around the building, she found Dave Kelly out in back, leaning into the engine compartment of a car that had rolled off the Detroit assembly lines five years before Winter had been born, in the company of a boy who was a younger, slenderer version of himself.

"Hi," Winter called.

Dave straightened up out of the engine. "Oh . . . hi." He didn't look particularly happy to see her. He wiped his hands on a rag. "You just keep after that, Paul; I've got to tell this lady about her car."

The body under the hood made a noise that might have been either sympathy or contempt. Winter followed Dave back around to the front of the garage, thinking that if she didn't get a chance to sit down soon she'd probably fall down.

"It's like this," Dave began, and sighed. "BMW's a damn fine car; German engineering and all. I've had it up on the lifts, and I don't know what the hell happened, if you'll pardon my French, Miz Musgrave, but there's not a thing I or anybody else this side of Bavaria can do with it. Only time I've ever seen anything like what happened to your electrical system's on a car got struck by lightning up in The Angels a few years back."

"The Angels?" Winter asked. Anything to avoid a discussion of what had destroyed her car. She was afraid she knew.

"Local mountain range—well, foothills, really, but high enough; me and my boy Paul go rock-climbing there weekends. It's called The Angels; the first guy to get this far upstate was French; the original name was *Aux Anges*."

Aux Anges—the Heights. And *The Angels* was simply a mistranslation into English. Maybe the explanation for the Grey Angels Tabitha Whitfield had mentioned was as simple.

"So that's what I'd do, if I were you," Dave finished, and Winter realized with a pang of alarm that while she'd been woolgathering she'd missed everything he'd said.

"I'm . . . sorry?" she said hesitantly.

"I said, if you want a rental you're going to have to go all the way down to Poughkeepsie to get it. It's going to be at least a month before you can get an insurance adjuster up here, and all he's going to tell you is the same thing I have. When the battery melted, it ruined just about everything else in the engine that hadn't already fried. They might not even pay up; you know how those insurance guys are."

And what do you think melted my engine, Mr. Kelly? The twee little fairies in the bottom of the garden? Winter drew a deep breath. "Okay." *So they don't pay. I can take that hit.* "I'm going to need something to get around in until I can get down to . . . Poughkeepsie?" Winter said, stumbling over the outlandish and unfamiliar name. "Tim Sullivan said you might have some kind of a loaner car?"

"Nothing I really want to offer a lady," Dave Kelly said. "Because it isn't fancy, and it isn't what I'd call dependable, either."

"I've got to have something," Winter said desperately. "Look, I'll *buy* it."

"I couldn't sell it to you," Dave Kelly said, shaking his head. "Not in good conscience. Tell you what, I'll loan it to you for a couple of weeks. Better get Timmy to run you down to Poughkeepsie, though."

"I will," Winter promised.

"Great. I'll go get you the keys." There was a brief hesitation; Dave looked at her as if she'd forgotten something. "And, uh, what do you want me to do about the BMW?"

"Keep it," Winter said. "Use it for a planter. The registration's in the glovebox. I'll sign it over." *I never want to see that car again.*

There was a delay while Dave took the plates off the BMW and wrapped them up for her, but forty-five minutes later, Winter pulled out of the garage and started up Main Street in a battered yellow Chevy Nova with one blue and one red door and no backseat at all.

And now I don't have to worry about the Beamer, she told herself in self-congratulatory mental tones. *"There's no problem so big it can't be run away from."* Who'd said that? Someone she knew? Someone she'd *known*—somewere in the lost seasons of her past?

It doesn't matter, Winter told herself, and even in her mind the words had the forlorn gallantry of someone whistling in the dark.

Though she'd left the Bidney Institute before noon, it was late afternoon as Winter stepped through her own front door again, her purse slung over her shoulder and the sack from *Inquire Within* clutched in one hand. Despite its having been the scene of so much terror, the farmhouse on Greyangels Road welcomed Winter back with an apologetic air of reassurance, like the family pet begging forgiveness for some recent transgression and offering the hopeful promise that it would not happen again.

If only that were true, Winter thought somberly. In the last day or so it seemed as if some sort of veil had been lifted from her will—*maybe those drugs took longer to wear off completely than I thought*—and she was thinking clearly at last.

Even about the unthinkable.

From ghoulies and ghaesties and long-leggedy beasties, the Good Lord deliver us. Amen.

She locked the door firmly behind her: dead bolt, chain, and the key-turn bolt that was part of the door's lock. A circuit of the remaining ground-floor rooms—front parlor, kitchen, mud room, and bedroom parlor—revealed that the windows and doors of each were firmly locked, just as she'd left them. No problems there. She looked into the bathroom and set the enormous cast-iron Victorian tub to filling, dropping in a generous dollop of Joy *de Bain* from the round black bottle on the windowsill. The luxurious scent of jasmine followed her as she headed into the kitchen.

The kitchen was tight and tidy, just as she'd left it this morning, the ancient speckled linoleum clean and dry.

Nope. No monsters here. And if it would just STAY . . . Sudden tears of weakness prickled at the corners of her eyes, and Winter felt the day's exertions catch up with her in a rush.

Some of that silly woman's tea. That's what I need. And maybe a good book. She filled the teakettle and set it on the stove, willing the tears away.

But the farmhouse's previous inhabitants weren't readers, apparently, although any place that was rented as furnished ought by rights to include a shelf of books or two. She even ventured upstairs again, tiptoeing as if she were in enemy country, and didn't find so much as a magazine.

Which left her with a choice between *Venus Afflicted* and the pamphlet Tabitha Whitfield had tucked in with the tea. Winter stood beside the bathtub, weighing them both in her hands and wondering why she'd never noticed the house's lack of reading material before. A large mug of Centering Tea, dark-steeped and liberally dosed with honey, stood waiting on the windowsill beside her bottle of bath oil.

Well, the so-called biography was longer, at least. She could look through the pamphlet later, before using it to start the bedroom stove. Winter tossed it aside and stepped into her bath, then opened *Venus Afflicted* and began to read.

The author—could it really be the same dark-haired young woman she'd met this morning?—made it clear in the preface that this book would deal in names and dates, facts and figures, which was much to Winter's taste—at least until the preface went on to refer to Thorne Blackburn as an important figure in twentieth-century Occultism, just as if all this sort of Dungeons & Dragons stuff ought to be taken seriously.

She set the book aside and picked up her tea, regarding it with equal wariness. It was a deep red, nearly the color of Burgundy, and had a woody, almost briny, scent that Winter found paradoxically appetizing. The taste of it went well with the honey she'd used to sweeten it—she realized it was the same tea Dr. Palmer had served her at the Institute, and as she sipped it, Winter finally understood Tabitha's insistence that she use honey or molasses in the tea. With plain sugar, the taste would have been unbearable.

Winter lay back in the bath, relishing the warmth within and without, letting her mind drift where it would. Hadn't there been more than a little bit of whistling past the graveyard in her scornful dismissal of

Thorne Blackburn, boy wizard? If she was going to have poltergeists, she probably ought to take books like this more seriously. She picked up *Venus Afflicted* once more, and despite herself, this time Winter found herself becoming interested in the Blackburn bio.

Fortunately there wasn't too much—at least in the early chapters of *Venus Afflicted*—that was particularly hard to swallow. She read about the history of the Western Mystery Tradition and people with names like Dion Fortune and Aleister Crowley, and about the start of Blackburn's own career as a fortune-teller in New Orleans, and by the time she came to herself again, the room was dim, the tea was gone, and the bath was cold. She felt better than she had in longer than she could remember.

Stepping out of the bath and wrapping herself in a large white towel, she addressed an invisible opponent.

You won the first rounds—but that's just because you caught me off guard. I'm ready for you now, who- and whatever you are, and if you think I'm just going to lie down and give up, you picked the wrong Winter Musgrave. I will beat this. I will survive. I will be . . . whoever I wish to be.

As if to mock her vow, calm hours became calm days—and then a week—without any disturbance at all.

The Taghkanic College library had been constructed in a time when it was considered the height of fashion to ape English models, and so Winter's notes and reference were spread out in a chamber that looked as if it would have been at home in any of Oxford's colleges. Light streamed into the main reading room through a wall of narrow, Gothic-arched windows, and a twisting iron ladder provided entrance to the library's second floor.

Opposite her chair, Winter had an unobstructed view of an enormous muddy-colored oil painting hanging on the oak linen-fold paneling depicting a dissatisfied-looking man in vaguely Puritan dress. Winter had been interested enough to inspect the engraved nameplate, and so knew that it was the portrait of Jurgen Lookerman, the original founder of the college.

Her college.

Faced with a riddle she could solve—her missing past—she had fastened on it with a stubborn determination that would not admit of failure. And she had not failed, though she had to admit that progress was maddeningly slow. Winter had walked the campus until her feet ached and the security guards all greeted her by name. She had poked into the classrooms, the student union, the dorms, trying to kindle the fires of memory.

A stop at the bursar's office had yielded proof of her attendance here, as well as a copy of her college transcript. It sat, now, atop a stack of Taghkanic College yearbooks, and a folder containing a sheaf of photo-copies from *The Angulus,* the student newspaper.

She'd written poetry once. Yes, and had it published in the paper, too. Most of it was pretty bad—the usual overdramatized self-obsession of late adolescence—but a few of the poems were actually pretty good. That girl would have been a moderately competent poet—if she'd lived.

Don't be an idiot, Winter reproached herself, quelling even the tiniest sign of fancifulness. That girl was her—she'd even checked to make sure that there hadn't been another Winter Musgrave enrolled at the college in '81—and the poems, like it or not, were hers.

And I'm not dead. At least I think I'm not.

But what had happened to that girl and her impassioned poetry?—the girl who'd taken Art and English courses with a fine disregard for the re-alities of earning a living once she graduated? The girl who had joined the Drama Club and played Juliet and accompanied strolling carolers on her guitar? Winter didn't even *own* a guitar—until she'd seen the pictures of herself in *The Angulus* she hadn't even suspected she could play one!

This is not right. This is not normal. There's something—wrong—about this.

She'd been doing a lot of research in the last several days. All the books she'd consulted said that this form of amnesia was not unknown, but they all agreed that it was symptomatic of a hysterical response to shock.

And that made no sense. She'd had a *fine* life. If she hadn't just checked herself out of Fall River, she'd have been worried about a brain tumor, but she'd been tested for every possible physical explanation of her prob-lems before she'd been admitted.

She was—more or less—young, healthy, and rich.

So, what was the problem?

Winter sighed, and turned back to her books. She'd come back to school in more ways than one. On the table before her was a stack of books; in addition to copies of the school yearbook, books on psychology, parapsychology, and any other *-ology* that could possibly help her.

She'd even found herself reading more about Thorne Blackburn, trying to understand how normal people could believe without evidence in the sort of thing that she had evidence of but refused to believe in. It was true that she continued to find the doors and windows unlocked at the farmhouse, but the weather was warming into late spring, and it was often warm enough to open the windows now—and she still did not trust her memory completely enough to know for sure if she'd closed and locked a window she'd previously opened or simply forgotten about it. A cup of the Centering Tea at bedtime seemed to ensure an untroubled sleep, and as long as there were no more dead animals, she could live with that ambiguity. Meanwhile, she continued to search for answers to her other questions.

Winter found that Taghkanic owned one of the largest collections of occult and magical paraphernalia, and *the* largest collection of Blackburniana in the world; reasonable, she supposed, since his daughter worked here, but . . .

"Well, hello, Winter," a familiar voice said.

She glanced up. Dylan Palmer stood beside her table, his arms full of books.

"The librarian told me that someone over at this table had one of the books I wanted today, and here it's you. How are you doing? Feeling better?"

"Oh, um, fine," Winter said awkwardly. "Which one is it—which book, I mean?"

"*Ha'ants, Spooks, and Fetchmen,* by Nicholas Taverner; the Appalachian poltergeist book." Without invitation, Dr. Palmer set his books down on an unoccupied corner of the table and sat down.

Winter scrabbled through her pile of books until she'd found the title Dr. Palmer had indicated. The Taverner book was one of the older ones in her stack—1924, she remembered the date was—and dealt mostly with folklore, although it did mention in passing a family of Ozark poltergeists. It didn't seem to be especially germane to Winter's current situation, but she'd been grabbing anything she could get her hands on.

"Here it is," she said, holding it out and willing Dylan Palmer to go away. Something more seemed to be called for. "I'm sorry I was so rude the other day—barging in on you and carrying on like that. I've been un-der a lot of stress lately. I'm sorry."

He took the book but made no move to go. "You didn't make an ap-pointment to come back to the lab," he said.

Winter felt her cheeks grow hot, like a child caught in a lie. "I decided not to."

"Oh." Dr. Palmer seemed to consider this. "Mind telling me why?"

"There just didn't seem to be a lot of point. Truth—Ms. Jourde-mayne—said that it would just go away on its own, and the books all agree with her, so there really doesn't seem to be a lot of point in laying out Tarot cards and gazing into crystal balls in the name of Science."

"I see." Dr. Palmer did not seem to be unduly offended by Winter's declaration, and she felt herself relax a bit. "And how's the other thing coming?"

"Beg pardon?"

"The search for your roots." Dr. Palmer tapped the stack of yearbooks.

"Oh." This subject, though loaded, was safer. "I have an appointment with Professor Rhys at two-thirty."

"You were a student of his?"

"He was my faculty advisor," Winter said. "I thought we could get to-gether and talk about old times."

"Which you still don't remember," Dr. Palmer suggested with damn-ing insight.

"I remember . . . something," Winter protested. *Like a dream that I woke up from a long time ago. But at least in the dream I was happy. . . .* "How can someone just *forget* their past?" she burst out helplessly.

"A lot of people would like to," Dr. Palmer said. "Maybe you're fortu-nate."

And maybe not. "I'm sure it will come back to me," Winter said, and this time she made the cool dismissal in her words unmistakable.

Dr. Palmer took the hint. "Well, good luck then. And if there's any-thing else you need, Winter, remember that you have friends here." He stood, adding the Taverner to his stack of books.

"Thank you," Winter said formally. "You're very kind."

She watched as Dr. Palmer walked away, and for a vulnerable moment she wished to summon him back. He had been kindness itself—maybe he *could* help.

No. She didn't need anyone's help. Whatever had to be done, she'd do herself. Needing other people only got you hurt. She glanced at her watch. It was time to go. Winter gathered her things together and stood up.

Professor Rhys's offices were in one of the older buildings on the campus, though since nothing had gone up on the Taghkanic grounds since the Second World War, none of the campus buildings could be called particularly new.

As she crossed the campus, Winter could almost imagine that it was as familiar as it ought to be; that the past year was only a bad dream and that there was some other reason that she'd come back to this place where her younger self had known so much happiness.

But if that were to be reality, Winter was slowly coming to realize, then more than the last year would have to vanish. During the past several days, she'd sought in vain for traces of the woman she'd become in the girl who'd written poetry and played madrigals, and could not imagine that child turning into the woman she knew as Winter Musgrave.

But she did. She's you, Winter reminded herself. *So what if you can't imagine it—you've never been all that fanciful.* Brusquely she forced away the insolent reminder that the writing of poetry and plays requires a certain amount of imagination, and mounted the steps of the rambling nineteenth-century building that was her goal.

Afternoon sunlight slanted whitely through the windows at the end of the long hall, and the—familiar?—scents of dust, apples, and old varnish tickled Winter's nose. She peered down the anonymous line of glass-paneled doors, wondering which it was. Professor Rhys had given her a room number, but there didn't seem to be any numbers on the doors.

"Welcome, my dear—welcome."

Winter, peering closer at the nearest door, and just realizing that actually were brass numbers on them—tarnished to black and indistinguishable from the varnished wood—jumped as she was hailed cheerily. She looked up.

From the far end of the hall a man who looked more like a professor than anyone had a right to leaned out his open doorway and waved.

"Professor Rhys?"

If he wondered, she had an excuse for asking—the glare made it difficult to see, she could say. But the reality was, she could see him perfectly well; it was her stubborn memory that refused to give up its horde, and Winter was left feeling not as though she'd never known this place and people, but rather as if she'd known them once, and forgotten.

"Yes, yes—" The voice was expansive and faintly English. "And you must be little Winter; how delightful."

Hesitantly, Winter approached. Professor Rhys beamed—a ruddy-faced, white-haired cherub of a man, he was only a few inches taller than she was.

"What a pleasure it is to have the opportunity to visit with a former student. Do come in, my dear, and tell me how you've been. Did you make a go of the theatrical life, or did you decide to stay with painting instead?"

"Neither one, actually." Swallowing dread, Winter forced her voice to match his delight and cheerful tone. "And how have you been?"

She followed Professor Rhys into his office. A corner room, it had windows on two sides, and a small fireplace on the wall it shared with the office next door.

Yes, that was right; the first-floor offices all had fireplaces; it was one of the oddities of the building's construction.

Pleased to have reclaimed even so small a scrap of her past, Winter smiled at Professor Rhys.

"How have I been? Oh, you know the academic life; moments of the most lively terror interspersed with years of boredom. But come in, do, sit down." He lifted a teetering pile of magazines and folders from the end of the cracked leather couch and gestured for her to sit.

Winter seated herself in the freshly cleared space and looked around. The office was almost a parody of what she'd expect an absentminded professor's office to be like: The built-in bookshelves were stuffed with books and papers and edged with memorabilia; the mantelpiece of the small, green-tiled fireplace was filled to overflowing with books, framed certificates, and peculiar objects less easy to identify. It was a homely place, in the oldest sense of the word—a place where one could feel at home.

"I do hope you're feeling better now," Professor Rhys went on, "although I don't know why I'm talking about it as if it were yesterday—it was fifteen years ago, wasn't it?"

"I left without graduating," Winter said, as if she were answering his tacit question. Coming here had been a mistake, she realized. Professor Rhys didn't know that she remembered neither him nor her college years—how could she expect him to give her the answers she needed unless she could bear to tell him why?

"But of course your diploma was sent later," Professor Rhys said firmly.

I wonder if it was. "Professor, I was wondering; could you tell me—"

"Ah, there you are, Johnnie!" The speaker did not bother to knock, but came sailing in as if this were his office instead of John Auben Rhys's.

Lion Welland was in many ways the physical antithesis of Professor Rhys. Tall and heron-gaunt—his blond hair worn in a flowing mane reminiscent of an old-time *impresario*—time had given him the brow of Shakespeare and sculpted the hairline into a dramatic widow's peak. He wore an open-collared shirt with french cuffs and a silk scarf tied around his throat *à la apache.*

"Winter, you remember Lionel Welland—he's head of Drama now. Lion, this is one of my former students, Winter Musgrave."

"A pleasure," Lion said briefly, his attention elsewhere. "Johnnie, love, you are not going to believe what those macho babus over in admin have done *this* time—" He leaned over Professor Rhys, his hand on the professor's shoulder, and lowered his voice to a fierce murmur.

In short, Lion was a textbook-perfect picture of a theatrical "queen," and it was obvious from the intimate way he leaned over the other man that he and Rhys were a couple.

There ought to be a place for people like that, where decent people wouldn't be exposed to them! The sudden flash of hatred was primal, irresistible—and somehow alien, as if neither the thought nor the feeling were truly Winter's. The emotion made her feel dirty, and as if she'd failed to live up to her good opinion of herself.

Had the child she'd been thought and felt these things? Winter was almost certain she had not. Confusion replaced disgust.

"It's a *pleasure* to meet you—again—Professor Welland," Winter said, with such fierceness that Rhys chuckled.

"That will serve you out for your rudeness, Lion," he said.

Lion turned to Winter and advanced upon her, both hands extended. "My dear lady—forgive my obliviousness. We of the theater tend to live in worlds of our own, you know—until someone makes it impossible for us," he added darkly.

"The administration is saying that Lion ought to charge for the Shakespeare festival, rather than ask for an increase in his budget," Professor Rhys supplied.

"The point of theater is that it should be *performed*—not paid for," Lion said peevishly. "Everyone enjoys it—and you made such a lovely Portia in your time, my dear."

The quality of mercy is not strained, Winter quoted mentally. "Thank you," she said, putting real warmth into her voice. "I don't get a chance to do much acting now." *Unless my whole life's become an act. All the world's a stage, and everyone but me's a featured player.*

"Well, not everyone can be a Hunter Greyson," Lion said comfortingly. "Tell me, how is Grey? You do keep in touch, don't you?"

Hunter Greyson. Grey. A tension headache flared behind Winter's eyes like sudden summer lightning, and the creature slumbering in her bones roused itself.

"Now, Lion, you haven't given Winter a chance to open her mouth. Not everyone keeps in touch with college friends."

"Do you?" The words came out of her mouth as a harsh croak. "See Grey?" Tantalizing hints of the past swirled through Winter's mind; kaleidoscopic impressions rather than true memories.

A vase on the end of the mantelpiece began to rock.

Grey. His hair was blond—white blond—straight, pale—worn in a tight ponytail; the harshness of the style giving his face the severe purity of an angel of judgment—until he smiled. And then Grey became a different sort of angel entirely; he—

There was a faint crackling; the noise hot glass makes when it cools too suddenly, just before it breaks.

All of them had followed Grey—laughing, mercurial Grey—into whatever fancy caught his interest. She would have followed him anywhere; she—

Winter's headache had grown to a searing lightless pressure that felt as if it would burst her head from within. But even the clamor of the blood in her ears could not block the sound that filled the room; the antic vibration of the paperweights and mementoes on the shelves.

There was a crash. Something fragile had worked its way to the edge of some shelf and fallen.

"What the *hell?*" Lion yelped.

Something very bad would happen if she stayed here.

"Winter?" Rhys asked.

"I— I'm sorry. I haven't quite been myself lately. It's just that things have been so different and I'm really not used to it yet so sometimes things happen and I really—"

She was babbling and she knew it, but it seemed that only words would keep the internal betrayal at bay. She groped to her feet, frantically clutching her purse to her, as if by holding it she retained her grip on reality as well.

"I have to go."

The atmosphere in the room was that of the oncoming storm; both men were on their feet.

"I have to go," she repeated.

"Winter, can I—" Rhys said.

"*Keep away!*" Winter cried, and the picture over the mantelpiece fell. The world burned out in a blaze of pale fire, and Winter did not stay to see more. She ran, and this time no one stopped her.

CHAPTER FOUR

ALL HEADS TURN
WHEN THE HUNT GOES BY

And every winter change to spring
So runs my dream: but what am I?
—ALFRED, LORD TENNYSON

YOU HANDLED THAT SO WELL, WINTER TOLD HERSELF
bitterly, straightening up from her retching and reaching into her bag for
a wad of tissues. She wiped her mouth, shuddering with disgust. The
flaring pain had subsided to a sick background ache, though its pressure
forced meaningless tears from her eyes. She leaned against the old cider
mill—now the Alumni House and headquarters for *The Angulus*—and
gasped for breath, every muscle trembling from the unaccustomed exertion.

And I thought I was doing better. Almost an entire week without a psychotic
break. How could I have been so stupid?

It had been the room, the closeness—the strain of pretending to remember things she didn't that had brought on the panic attack.

The *panic attack.*

That was all it had been.

A panic attack.

Old buildings settled—even New York had quakes—someone next door or upstairs had banged the wall hard enough to jar the picture loose. And the vase would have fallen anyway. The rest was just weak-willed self-indulgent hysteria.

Just another panic attack. They were what had driven her to Fall River, weren't they? There was nothing supernatural about a panic attack.

A panic attack. Nothing more. And cats killed pigeons all the time, and raccoons, probably—and weren't there coyotes around here now? She'd read something in the local paper, and if she hadn't, she *could* have . . .

The comforting rationalizations settled into place as they always had, soothing away her will to believe in the impossible. Only one bright spark of desperate self-preservation blazed through.

Who was Hunter Greyson?

Again, that frustrating tickle of half-memory; something between dream and fantasy that slithered from her grasp just as she tried to pin it down.

She'd known Hunter Greyson—rather well, she gathered, if her faculty advisor expected her still to be in touch with him all these years later. And he'd help her; he would—the conviction existed even without memory to support it. She needed to find Grey . . .

She levered herself away from the building and took a few tottering steps. She hurt in every bone and muscle as if she'd fallen down a flight of stairs, and her head still throbbed painfully, sending flashes of light through her vision. The parking lot was a long way from here—Winter wondered if she could make it that far.

Mistrustfully, she looked behind her. If she wanted to find Hunter Greyson, reason said that the alumni office was the logical place to start.

But tomorrow. Now she only wanted to crawl away and hide.

She made it home by driving with agonizing slowness, but just the sight of the old farmhouse restored some of her energy. Greyangels. Named for the road, or for the creatures that her taxi driver had said walked these hills? When Tim Sullivan had talked about the Grey Angels, she'd thought of watchful nature spirits, bound neither to good nor evil, taking their direction from the emotions in the hearts of those who sought them.

Regretfully she dismissed the notion. There was nothing in this world to reward and punish like some all-seeing Santa Claus. There were only people, and the certainty that even the best intentions turned to ashes in the end.

Her melancholy mood gave way to a spiraling absentmindedness once she entered the house; over and over as afternoon became evening Winter would come back to herself with a jolt, to discover the sink overflowing, the kettle boiled dry—though what she'd been thinking about the moment before she didn't know. When at last she found herself sitting in the rocker beside the hearth in the front parlor, staring out into the night without the slightest idea of how she'd gotten there or what time it was, Winter gave up. If this was a sample of the unconscious rebellion that Dr. Luty had been so fond of assigning her problems to, then she'd just let her unconscious win the field for once. She was going to bed. And let Dr. Luty make what he chose of that!

But tonight sleep, when it came, was an unsettled thing, filled with confusion and fear—and a sense of fleeing desperately from the truth. *But that's stupid,* Winter thought half-lucidly, *why would someone not want to know the truth?*

How bad could knowing be?

After what seemed an eternity of false awakenings and strugglings with sleep, Winter opened her eyes groggily. The room was filled with chilly morning light; and her bed was a mare's nest of knotted sheets and twisted blankets. Her head no longer hurt, but she was filled with a curious exhausted blankness, as if some fever had finally broken.

She turned over to reach for the light and felt a stabbing pain in her thigh. Grabbing for the hurt, her fingers encountered a thin hard shape— a pencil? She clutched it in her fingers, inspecting the wound. A scrape; nothing serious, but surely she had not taken a pencil to bed with her?

Winter turned on the light and looked around, shivering in the morning chill that was the inevitable result of failing to build up a fire in the bedroom stove the night before. Apparently she'd taken not only a pencil but paper as well; she recognized the notebook from the kitchen on which she'd written down her grocery list a few days before.

She picked it up—and swallowed hard as she realized that page after page was covered in writing; loopy, straggling writing; the scrawling letters nearly impossible to read.

Names, written over and over as if by some mad and desperate journalist. Janelle Baker, Cassilda Chandler, Ramsey Miller, Hunter Greyson.

She knew them. They were her friends—had been her friends. They'd all gone to Nuclear Lake together. . . .

Elusive remembrance came—for once—at her bidding. Janelle's red hair. The blond streak Cassie dyed into the front of her brunette mop; she'd looked like a demented Lhasa Apso. Ramsey had . . .

But the memory blurred into uncertainty again; its image, the distortion of shapes seen through mist, and Winter was left with the conviction that these people were real, that she'd known them, and little beyond that.

It's just a meaningless dream, she told herself uncertainly. *False memory syndrome is all over the news these days—half the time they find out that those so-called recovered memories are phantoms the mind has created under stress. You've been reading the college yearbooks; even if those turn out to really be the names of Taghkanic students you could have picked the names up from there. No matter how real this seems, it isn't. You can't trust your memory—not after what you've been through.*

But she *was* her memory! Winter cried out silently to that oh-so-reasonable inner voice. *"Who will be for me, if I am not for myself?"*

She did not think she could trust the inner insistence that she reject the evidence of her eyes and mind. That inner voice would do anything, say anything, to lull her back into unreasoning acceptance; to assure her the abnormal was normal; that flying glass and slaughtered animals had nothing to do with her; a lulling, lying voice that would prefer her to be a monster than to admit the existence of such a simple thing as a poltergeist.

She could not trust that voice.

Boy, talk about getting in touch with your inner paranoid . . . Winter gibed desperately.

But for the moment she would trust the instinct that said not to trust. She would believe that the people in her dreams were real, and that they had been her friends. The best and worst of friends—and lovers. The people who held the key to her past.

A past she had to reclaim . . . to survive.

"Have you ever heard of a place called Nuclear Lake?"

Practical to her marrow, Winter began her quest at the alumni office, to see if any of the people she remembered from the Class of '82 were on file with the office.

"Nuclear Lake? Oh, my, I haven't thought about Nuclear Lake in years."

Nina Fowler was short, plump, and pretty, with brown eyes and faintly freckled skin. She was the alumni office's one full-time employee, a combination of desktop publishing wizard and school historian, and had become familiar to Winter over the last several weeks as Winter came to her with request after request, all of which Nina had found some way to fill.

"We all used to go up there when we were kids."

Nina stopped paging through the drawer of file cards and gazed off into space. Winter had taken one look at her initially and dismissed her as "one of those women who'd let herself really go," without wondering where the knee-jerk impulse to belittle the other woman had come from. Now some life-affirming impulse to distrust her facile disdain of every human being that crossed her path made Winter reexamine her hasty judgment.

Just what was wrong with Nina Fowler? It was true that she wasn't wearing a Chanel suit and a lot of expensive makeup, but when had fancy dress or the lack of it made a difference to what a person really was? When had Winter started judging other people solely on the cost of their clothes?

"I did, too," Winter said, smiling.

"It gave us all the creeps," Nina said, laughing, "I guess that's why we went there! That—and to make out; the place is smack in the middle of nowhere, isn't it? We used to tell each other stories—how it was a research facility back in the nineteen seventies, and how some really horrible experiment got out of control and the government came in and closed it down."

"Nuclear research? Is that why it's called Nuclear Lake?" Winter asked.

Nina frowned. "I'm not sure *why* it's called Nuclear Lake; just that everyone does. I looked it up; on the maps it's Haelvemaen Lake—*that* was a surprise! I'm not even sure it's still private land; it was just a little parcel tucked into State land; somebody up in Albany probably eminent domain'd it into Huyghe State Park."

Haelvemaen. Dutch for "Half Moon," the name of the galleon that Henrik Hudson had first sailed up what would become the Hudson River almost 400 years ago.

Nina had returned to her records. "Well, I've got three of the names you asked about—Baker and Miller are current; they're getting our newsletter and say it's okay to give out their addresses. Chandler I've got marked as 'moved no forwarding,' with a last address in Berkeley. You can have that, too, if you want—but I haven't got anything on Hunter Greyson."

"Thanks, Nina—this is a real help. But don't you have *anything* on Hunter Greyson?"

Nina waved a small fan of cards tucked between her fingers. "You know how it is—people move and don't give out changes of address." She laid the three three-by-five cards out on the table in front of Winter as if she were telling her fortune.

The Fool. The Hanged Man. The High Priestess. For a moment the voice echoed in Winter's ears, then the moment of disorientation passed.

Janelle and Cassilda and Ramsey. Winter took a notepad and gold Cross pencil out of her Coach bag and bent over the counter to write.

"I was thinking of going up there today," Winter said as she wrote. "To Nuclear Lake, I mean. But after what you've said, I'm not sure I want to go alone," she added, trying hard to make it sound like a joke.

"I'll go with you," Nina said instantly. "That is, if you—"

"That'd be great," Winter said quickly, trying to cover the sense of relief she felt. "To tell the truth, I'm not sure my car would make it—I've got a loaner from Kelly's Garage, and—"

Nina hooted with laughter. "Oh, *that* old thing! I used to call it 'no *va*'—I was a Spanish major; it means 'no go.' I'm the one that turned it in to Dave! No, you're better off going with me, that's for sure. Look, my student aide comes in at twelve; you want to have lunch and then run up there afterward?"

"Sure," Winter said.

It was amazing how much nicer it was to run around a strange town when you were with someone who knew it well. In Nina Fowler's company, Winter discovered a tiny vegetarian restaurant tucked in behind Bread Alone, the bakery she'd stopped at on her first visit into town.

The dining room of Vegetable Love was in a large open courtyard, with only the kitchen and juice bar of the restaurant indoors. The courtyard was floored in loose brick and filled with small round French café tables. Arching aluminum ribs and a rolled canopy answered the question of how the restaurant accommodated its patrons on rainy days, but Winter could not imagine it could be a popular place to go in the winter. She mentioned this to Nina.

"Oh, no! It's *wonderful* in the winter—they put up these free-standing fireplaces in the corners and it's terrific! You'll have to come back and see."

"Sure." *If I'm still alive.* Winter wondered where the conviction had sprung from that she, instead of those around her, was personally at risk. Even though she honestly felt the truth of it, her emotions seemed curiously uninvolved. She followed Nina across the crowded courtyard.

Vegetable Love was an evident college hangout, filled with noisy oblivious students in flannel and denim and spandex; the sort of untidy, undignified crowd that usually made Winter irritable. But this time, when that knee-jerk reaction began, she forced herself to step back and view it dispassionately. There was no earthly sensible reason for this blast of withering contempt that roared through her, except to estrange her from a group of people who could not possibly be all that bad.

As it always did. Cutting her off, isolating her from everyone who did not match an increasingly narrow set of specifications. Until, in the end, Winter would be all alone.

Alone. *Helpless.*

Was there something that wanted that? Something stalking her?

Nina found them a table in the corner because, all tolerance and even approval aside, neither of them was interested in being stepped on by the Doc Martens that were still all the rage for the under-thirty crowd, and the tables *were* pretty close together.

"Whoa! What a crush!" Nina said, sliding into her seat. "Still, I love it. Do you remember when it opened?"

Winter felt a sudden pang of fear, which dissipated when Nina answered her own question. "But you wouldn't—sorry!—you're Class of 'eighty-two and Veg didn't open until nineteen eighty-five." With an apologetic grin, Nina devoted herself to the menu.

Saved, Winter thought with an inward sigh, and reached for her own menu. But she couldn't go on pretending forever—not when she was surrounded daily by the reminders of how easily everyone else seemed to recall their adolescent years, moving swiftly between Then and Now through the facility of their own mental time machines.

Maybe it would come back to her. Even now, she felt that if she held very still and didn't startle them, the memories of her college days were close enough to touch.

Almost.

"Are you sure this is the right way?" Winter asked nervously half an hour later. She was grateful for the impulse that had led her to invite Nina along on this expedition. If Winter had been by herself, she would almost certainly have missed the turnoff from County 4. The side-road—a few miles past the turnoff for Greyangels Road—wasn't even marked, and after about half a mile the blacktop on the one-and-a-half lane road-by-courtesy vanished altogether.

"It's the only way," Nina said cheerfully. "I'm an amateur herbalist, so I ramble all through The Angels looking for plants—there's a shop in town that sells herbal mixtures, and Tabby's always on the lookout for suppliers—I haven't been up here since my student days, but I know the area pretty well, and this is the only road that goes down to the river. Hang on!"

The gravel that had replaced the blacktop petered out, and the dirt road that remained became progressively more rutted. At last Nina tapped the brake a few times and shifted the car into neutral.

"I don't want to go any further, and the lake's less than half a mile from here anyway. Why don't you go on ahead—I've got my stuff in the back; I want to look around by the car and see if I can find anything worth harvesting."

"I don't know how long I'm going to be," Winter said reluctantly.

"Oh, don't worry about me! I go on one of my rambles and lose all sense of time. If I'm not at the car when you get back just honk the horn a couple of times, and if I get done first I'll come look for you. Just keep an eye on the sun, though—you don't want to try to find your way back here in the dark."

"I shouldn't be that long. I just want to take a look," Winter said. She got out of the car, grateful for the sensible Reeboks that made walking down the trail not only possible, but a pleasure. In a few moments she had rounded a bend in the trail, and Nina's Honda was lost to sight.

It was puzzling, Winter mused as she walked along. She remembered buildings at Nuclear Lake, and Nina had said there'd been some sort of lab here. Yet the path beneath her feet was hardly more than a trail now—how had people driven to work? Nina said there wasn't any other road leading in to the Nuclear Lake property.

She also said she hadn't been up here in years, Winter reminded herself. There must be another road in. Even if the facility had been deserted for—what? twenty years or more?—a two-laned blacktopped access road just couldn't get itself into this condition in less than a century.

Could it?

Just how much can I say I REALLY *know about the nature of Reality, considering everything?* Winter asked herself snidely.

And then she saw the lake.

It was not large. The trail she'd been following swung wide around it, and, at this time of year, the water lilies that turned the quiet backwaters of the Hudson into carpets of living green were not yet in bloom; Winter could see straight to the bottom, with its round stones, occasional Coke can, and fugitive anonymous fish. It looked both peaceful and tempting, though the water was still too chilly for wading and much too chilly to swim.

Across the lake and a little to the left of it she could see a building—the oh-so-mysterious research laboratory. Squaring her shoulders in anticipation of another hike—she was still in lousy physical shape after all that bed rest, for all that she'd used to go to the gym three times a week—Winter struck off in that direction.

The building had looked perfectly intact from across the lake; it was built in that style common to the sixties and early seventies that made no concession to the organic reality of its surroundings, as if it were poised to leap right into some hygienic future composed entirely of brushed aluminum and Formica. But once she got closer, Winter could see that the perfection was only an illusion. The loops of polychrome spray-paint graffiti covering every exposed surface and the drifts of liquor bottles and fast-food trash were evidence enough of that.

She was indignant and comforted at the same time. How dare these people trespass on grounds that were so special to her? Yet if they did come here, it certainly indicated that nothing weird or harmful had claimed the place for its own.

Winter walked closer, her memories shifting and rippling like the stones seen through lake water. Was the building a little more battered than she remembered it? Did she really remember it at all? Winter studied the sight before her carefully. The main building was two stories tall and had a long one-story wing branching off to the right. The front wall of the wing was all glass; a wall of uncurtained windows; and vines had grown across several of them. Others were broken, and Winter could see a slurry of leaves and trash on the floor inside.

For a moment a hotter sun than this shone down on her shoulders— May, almost summer, and she and the others coming here again just as they did every week, to—

What?

The memory and its certainty faded, and Winter swore under her breath. If memory was personality, then hers was fading in and out like a weak radio signal.

Enough of this. Instinct told her she'd gone inside before, so she'd go inside again now. Maybe that would trigger something more—something she could hold onto.

The cement steps at the building's front had stood the test of time, and even the front door, though glass, was reasonably intact, with only one sunburst crack marring its integrity. Winter, pulling on it, was surprised to find that it only rattled and did not move at all.

It was locked.

But that's ridiculous—the five of us were in and out of here all the time. . . .

Puzzled, she went down the stairs again and walked slowly around the building. Once there had been an apron of white quartz pebbles between the wall and the sidewalk. Now the work of many seasons had cracked and crumbled the cement paving, and storms had washed nearly all the pebbles away. Just so might all the world look, if one morning it had woken up and found that Man was gone. A brief century, a few upheavals, and no trace of humankind and its busy building would remain.

Winter shivered and hurried around the side of the building, wondering if it had been such a bright idea to come here after all. She had to have been mistaking imagination for memory—that front door was locked, and there didn't seem to be any other way in.

That was when she saw the other door.

It was in the back of the building, obviously a service entrance of some sort, and when she grasped the knob and turned, to her surprise the door opened easily.

A wave of stale, musty air rolled out. Winter wrinkled her nose, peering into the gloom. *I should have brought a flashlight.* But the day was bright and the building was filled with windows—there should be enough light to do a quick exploration.

Before going in, Winter scouted about until she found a big rock to prop the door open with. She clutched another, smaller one in her hand. Just in case.

Then she went inside.

This had once been a storage room of some sort—there were still steel shelves—rusted now—along the walls, and a number of large storage drums in one corner. The floor beneath her feet was a concrete slab. Ahead of her was a doorway—doorless now—that led into the main part of the building.

The carpet there looked almost new—apparently artificial miracle fibers were unpalatable to the microscopic life-forms that voraciously destroyed wool and wood, leather and linen. But the walls were water-stained, and in places the Sheetrock panels were buckling away from their supporting studs. Winter sneezed, and then sneezed again—there must be enough dust and mold floating around this air to send an allergist to test-positive heaven.

From the back entrance Winter was able to walk straight through the building to the front, where she inspected the glass door from the other side. She still couldn't open it; the door had a key-lock dead bolt that needed a key to release it from either side. She looked through the drawers at the built-in receptionist's desk, hoping the key was there, and was surprised to find pens and paper clips and rubber bands, and wads of paper gone to gray dust—the whole building had just been locked up and left.

But she didn't find any keys.

Why? Why leave all the stuff in the drawers as if they'd just walked out? Maybe Nina was right. Maybe there was some kind of an accident here after all. Winter peered around herself and then struck off left, down the long windowed hall. *A funny kind of a lab, though—it looks more like office space than research space.*

But what kind of offices would be out here in the middle of nowhere? This is Amsterdam County, for God's sake!

Winter tried each of the doors in the hall as she passed them. Some were locked. Some opened into small bare rooms with high narrow windows at the back.

One didn't.

The door looked like any of the others, but when she opened it she found herself looking not into an obvious office, but into a large room with a spiral staircase in the middle leading downward, disappearing through a hole in the floor.

"How curious, said Alice," Winter quoted to herself. It was dark at the foot of the stairs; the dimness of evening as opposed to the afternoon light above. But she thought her eyes would adjust once she got down there, and anyway, she wouldn't go far from the stairs.

Only an idiot would go down there in the first place, Winter told herself sardonically. She grasped the rail and shook it, testing its sturdiness. Without conscious decision, she started down.

So it was a laboratory after all. Winter stood in this unexpected basement, looking at a room illuminated by the light coming in through a line of narrow windows high on the wall. The windows were set at ground level, and weeds had done as much as dirt to diminish the amount of light that reached the room within. Down here the rank musty scent of rot, mildew, and decay was even stronger than it was on the floor above, and underneath them there was a wet mineral smell like rocks or mud or setting cement; chilly and antagonistic.

In contrast to the receptionist's station above, everything movable down here was long gone—either removed by the original owners or stolen—but the sinks along the windowed wall and the complicated sockets drilled into the cinder block above them were as much proof that this had been some kind of laboratory as Winter needed. She took a step away from the staircase, and as her eyes adjusted, the room around her became clearer and sharper. Some kind of laboratory, long abandoned. But why?

Her Reeboks grated on the grit underfoot. She looked down and saw, half-erased, some sort of design painted on the floor. Even after the passage of years, the remaining scraps of color were bright.

What . . . ?

A circle. Someone had painted a circle on the floor—no, not exactly a circle; some sort of design . . . There was a circle inside a circle and some sort of marks between them, and inside that—

Without thinking of what she was doing, Winter walked out into the center of the room. There were black dots spaced evenly around the outer perimeter of the painted circle, and she counted them: three, five, seven, nine . . . Not paint marks—*scorch*-marks, as if something had burned all the way down to the ground here.

Candles.

There was a sudden coppery taste in her mouth; without any transitional unease, Winter was terrified, as if some malign God had flipped a cosmic switch to plunge the world into horror. She swung around; her only thought to escape.

There was something painted on the wall behind the staircase. She hadn't seen it before—when she'd walked away from the stairs that wall had been behind her—but against the white cinder block the dark curls and angles of the inscribed sign were glaringly plain, and the sudden, jarring sight of it struck Winter like a blow.

"Come on, Cassie—give me that, would you?" Ramsey said, hopefully. He brandished his handful of candles and reached for the lighter. The rest of the ritual equipment was already spread out on the table behind him, and of course each of them had brought their own wand and dagger.

Cassilda clutched it to her chest, shaking her head and laughing at him. The motion made the wide sleeves of her tie-dyed dashiki flutter in the dim light of the battery-powered lantern.

"Not until Grey gets here, Ramsey—you can't light them yet!"

"So when's he getting here? He said he had a surprise for us. Oh, damn—did anybody think to bring a corkscrew?" Janelle asked in sudden alarm.

"That's what you get for buying expensive wine," Winter said, digging through the Danish Bookbag she carried as a purse. "Grey told me—oh, here it is." She placed the folding tool in her friend's hand.

"It wasn't expensive—it was on sale!" Janelle protested.

"It's got a cork, doesn't it?" Ramsey said inarguably. "That makes it expensive." The pendant he wore around his neck flashed in the lantern light. "Do you know what Grey has planned, Winter?"

"She should—she spent last night with him," Cassilda said slyly.

"In his DORM ROOM?" Janelle said, astounded.

"CASSIE—!" wailed Winter in mock protest. "Can't a girl have any secrets?"

"Only the greatest secret of all—the secret of Life Itself!" Grey's trained voice filled the room with spooky echoes, punctuated by the rhythm of his snakeskin boots as he descended the stairs. "Fellow acolytes of Nuclear Circle—"

She fell, hard, on the top step of the staircase, feeling the edge of the iron riser gouge bloodily into her skin. Winter's hands slipped on the grit of the tile floor as she scrabbled to her feet again, fleeing without knowing why she ran.

How could she have forgotten—how could she have been stupid enough to forget? And now it was almost too late—there was danger, terrible danger, she had to HURRY—

No! Winter careened into a wall and pulled herself up with an effort. Her entire body shuddered with the struggle to remain still, to stay where she was when she could see the red border of madness looming in her path.

Calm. She needed to be calm.

She breathed deep, filling her lungs until they ached, holding the air until the world around her took on an extra brightness, then letting it out slowly. It seemed to help, even if only a little.

Okay, now get out of here.

Winter forced her mind away from the flashback—the vision that had granted her another piece of her past. Of all the stupid, childish, *juvenile* things to be mixed up in—no wonder she'd felt an instinctive revulsion to Tabitha Whitfield and her store if she'd been a teenage Satanist.

Winter snorted derisively, all her fear buried now in a scalding rush of contempt and fury. If *that* was what her younger self had wanted, she deserved to be dead and buried!

Winter concentrated on her anger, letting it lull and strengthen her, erecting a barricade strong enough to seal off the awakened memories. When she'd retraced her steps to the exit again she found that the wind had picked up; the weather had shifted in mercurial Hudson Valley fashion and the day was now all scudding storm clouds against a freshening breeze. When Winter dragged the rock away from the door it had propped open, the wind slapped the heavy metal door shut with the sound of a pistol-crack. Winter looked around. There was no one in sight.

"Nina!" she shouted, before realizing Nina Fowler couldn't possibly hear her this far away. She hurried around the corner of the building and, as she did, a blast of cold rain hit her in the face. There was a black squall line running up from the south, and the surface of Nuclear Lake was being whipped into a dirty froth with the force of the wind.

"Nina!" Winter shouted again, the icy chill of awakening terror almost enough to drown her anger. It was not the wind that was causing this turbulence.

The lake was *boiling*.

"Nina!" Where was she? Was she all right? Winter took a step back from the lake. There was nothing natural about what she saw: The surface of the water was bubbling, as if some unimaginable creature were forcing itself up out of the ooze at the bottom. Coming to the surface. Coming for *her.*

Winter looked around, looking for some way to escape. But there was nowhere to go except toward the lake or back into the building, and her past was waiting inside the building. Winter began to run along the path in the direction she'd come, in the desperate hope that she could reach the car before whatever was rising out of Nuclear Lake could reach her.

The leading edge of the storm broke. Rain lashed into Winter's face, blinding her, turning the broken paving into a slick and treacherous shifting surface. Anger was gone, replaced by fear, and by some kind of tension that was building inside her, drawing every nerve achingly taut. The rain pounded down with growing force, and the roaring of the storm cut her off from her senses—blinded, numb, and deaf, Winter ran toward safety, gaining ground with the maddening slowness of a dream.

It was coming for her.

As if some part of her still stood watching the lake, she could feel that. What rose out of the lake was all blind terror and eternal appetite, and if it reached her it would leave her skinned and mutilated body as testimony to that hunger.

After a nightmare eternity Winter reached the far side of the lake, feeling as if there were a bar of hot metal transfixing her throat and her lungs. Every step was agony, but if she stopped, she would be lost. She gasped for air, knowing she had to warn Nina Fowler, knowing she lacked the strength even for that.

The storm's force pressed her to her knees in the thin icy mud, and in a flux of irresistible phantom terror Winter glanced behind her, to see the bubbling surface of the lake bowed upward like a giant lens, its surface about to split and reveal . . .

Thrusting herself to her feet once more, Winter staggered onward, feeling the pain and pressure growing behind her eyes.

Nina's Honda was right where Winter had left it, lights on and windshield wipers running. The promise of safety it represented brought tears to Winter's eyes. The driver's-side door was open and Winter could see a foot encased in a muddy running shoe; Nina was already inside, sheltering from the storm and waiting for her.

Winter felt the tautness inside her begin to uncoil and *reach;* flexing through her like electricity. An instinctive spasm brought one arm up and out in a parody of a pulp-magazine priestess's mystic gesture, and as she stared in helpless horror, she saw the spark collect on her fingers in seeming slow motion and jump from her to the car.

No!

There was a blue flash and the car's lights went dead and its wipers stopped moving—and behind her, Winter could feel the malevolence that churned up out of Nuclear Lake seeking its prey.

"Damn; it just stopped," Nina said innocently as she looked up. "Good Goddess, Winter, you—"

"No time," Winter panted, plucking at Nina's arm with trembling fingers. "Come. You've got to run."

"But it'll just—" Nina began, and Winter, using the last of her strength, hauled Nina out of the car.

"Please," Winter gasped, choking on her own need to breathe. "Hurry."

There was a sharp tang in the air now, apparent even over the smell of rain and wet earth. A sharp ozone tang, as if lightning were about to strike—again—and as Winter began to despair, it seemed that Nina caught some of her fear from her. Nina's brown eyes went wide and the freckles stood out on her face like dark raindrops. Without another word she grabbed Winter's hand and the two women began to run up the path that led to the road.

Behind them there was a crash—a flash too bright for lightning—and a howling that could be heard even over the wailing of the wind.

They ran until the exhausted Winter could run no farther, and crouched on the blacktop of the access road while Nina stood over her. Both women were soaked to the skin, bramble-torn, and covered in mud.

"Go— Go on," Winter gasped, waving in the direction of the road.

"No." Nina was nearly as winded. "No, wait. Can't you hear?"

Winter raised her head. "Hear" was not the right word, but she understood what Nina meant. It was quiet now; even though it was still raining, the raging storm and the coiling sense of dreadful passion both gone as if they'd never been.

And now that they were gone, it was hard to believe that they ever *had* been.

Winter raised her head and looked at Nina. The younger woman's round cheeks were flushed with running, her curly brown hair plastered flat against her head. Her eyes were wide and puzzled, as if she had just awakened from a deep sleep.

"Some kind of storm, eh?" she said, in cheerful tones completely divorced from her apprehensive mood of only moments before. "It's a good thing you got me out of the car—I know it's a good idea to stay in your car when there's a lightning storm, but it's not so good an idea to be in your car when a tree falls on it, is it?"

Is that what you think happened, Nina? Winter bit her lip to keep from saying the words aloud, a new and entirely mundane apprehension staggering the trip-hammer beat of her heart. Wasn't Nina's reaction just what her own had been—denial and some soothing, plausible story?

Even now, the events of the past few hours tried to smudge and blur themselves in her mind, as if some malignant hand was wiping the slate of memory clean.

No! Winter concentrated on the image of that profane fetal shape rising up out of the storm-whipped blackness of the lake, and felt her lagging heartbeat increase in response.

"Maybe the car will start now," Nina said uncertainly.

"No." Winter stood up with painful effort, forcing her legs to hold her now that the danger was past. "It won't start. The electrical system's shot." *And I did that—me—not the thing in the lake.* "We'd better see if we can flag down someone on the main road."

"Yeah." Nina straightened up and stretched, and regarded Winter with a guileless untroubled countenance. "And it isn't really too far; we can walk back to town if we have to."

Fortunately they didn't have to walk, though for Winter the worst part of what followed was that by the time they'd reached the County Road and flagged down a vehicle Nina Fowler had completely convinced herself that what had happened had amounted to nothing more than a brief but intense lightning storm.

It seems as if it would be safer to think that, Winter mused thoughtfully, sitting crowded next to Nina in the pickup truck's cabin, *just as I'd be happier thinking that all that happened was one of my panic attacks and a little overwrought imagination. But I don't think it was.*

And I don't think it's safe *to pretend it was.*

"I'll call Dave; he can take me back out there with the wrecker and pick up Old Reliable tomorrow," Nina said cheerfully. Their ride—one of the villagers—had gone out of his way to drop them back up at the Taghkanic campus.

"Why don't you take my car in the meantime," Winter said, fishing in her jeans pocket for the keys. She held them out to Nina. "I'm too whipped to drive; I'm going to take a taxi home."

"Oh, but I couldn't!" Nina protested, but Winter could see her hesitate.

"Of course you can—didn't it used to be your car? And it was my fault that you were out there in the first place, getting your car . . . struck by lightning." *And only luck that I didn't get you killed,* Winter thought somberly. *And not by lightning.*

"Well, if you're sure," Nina said, reaching for the keys. "Can I run you home, Winter? You really do look tired."

"I'll call Timmy Sullivan when I'm ready. There's something I have to do first." *And if you want to live, Nina, you'll stay far, far away from me.*

CHAPTER FIVE

THE ROYAL HUNT
OF THE SUN

When the hounds of spring are on winter's traces.
— ALGERNON CHARLES SWINBURNE

SHE'D THOUGHT SHE'D BE MORE RELUCTANT TO COME back here with another harebrained story, but it was amazing how much perspective nearly getting killed by The Creature From The Id could give you. If what Winter thought had happened at Nuclear Lake had really happened—if she wasn't crazy—then she needed help. If she *was* crazy . . .

Then she wanted drugs, electroshock—all those things that Truth Jourdemayne had said would burn to ash the part of her brain that bred these chimeras. *"The sleep of reason begets monsters. . . ."* Because she couldn't bear to go on living with them inside her.

And if, as Winter had slowly begun to believe, they *weren't* delusions, she might not have a choice.

Winter walked up the path that led to the doors of the Margaret Bidney Beresford Memorial Psychic Science Research Laboratory. The Neoclassical white marble façade looked serene as always, and the imposing oak, bronze, and glass doors gave it much the look of an ancient Greek temple.

She pushed open the door. There was no one in the reception area, and Winter glanced at her Cartier tank watch for the time, only to find that it had stopped sometime around two o'clock. But the clock on the wall said that the time was only a little after four, so where was the receptionist?

Winter walked past Meg Winslow's desk in the direction she had gone the last time she'd come here, but instead of stopping at the interview room she'd been in before, some intuition drew her on past the closed doors of the offices, until she was standing in a huge open-plan area at the back of the building, obviously of more recent vintage than the Institute's stern classical façade.

The room looked like the Hollywood version of a mad scientist's laboratory, from the banks of monitors and recording equipment to the vaguely sinister padded couches. Overhead there were swags of power lines and connecting cable, and everywhere that Winter's glance fell it rested on a dizzyingly dense array of technological objects. She looked around, confused. The lab seemed to be completely deserted.

"Can I help you?" The familiar voice came from above. Winter looked up, and saw what she had missed before: A catwalk crossed the space above, a door leading to it from somewhere on the Institute's second floor.

"Truth?" To Winter, her voice sounded very small and childlike in the vast, echoing space.

"Who— Oh, Winter. Did you— Oh, wait just a moment, I'll be right down," Truth said. She crossed the catwalk to its end, and descended to the floor via one of the starkly functional white-painted metal staircases that edged the wall. When she reached the ground floor Truth hurried over to Winter, her face concerned.

"I was going to ask if you'd decided to come for tests, but it's more than that, isn't it? Something's happened—is someone dead?"

Winter felt the same strange *flexing* inside herself that she'd felt just before she'd flung the lightning bolt at Nina Fowler's car. But this time it was weirdly perfunctory, as if some vital resource had been temporarily exhausted.

"I'm losing my mind," Winter said. Her voice shook with exhaustion and fear. "I don't know who else to come to. I know I said I was losing my

mind before—but this time I *am*—unless there's a monster living beneath Nuclear Lake!" Winter finished raggedly.

"Come and sit down and tell me what happened," Truth said calmly.
She led Winter over to a corner, where two upholstered chairs with
a small round table between them made an incongruously homey oasis
in the forbidding technology of the lab. Winter sank into one of
the chairs gratefully, all too aware that nerve and will could only carry her
so far.

And desperate enough at last to trust someone. She took a deep
breath.

"I remembered . . . that I used to go up to Nuclear Lake with my
friends when I was a student here. So I decided to go up there again and
see if I could jog anything loose—I didn't really want to go alone, so I
took Nina Fowler with me—from the alumni office?"

"I know Nina," Truth said. "Is she all right?"

"She's fine. She thinks—" Winter swallowed hard, and realized, to her
horror, that she was about to cry. "—She thinks her car was struck by
lightning. That all that happened there was a storm." Winter drew a
shaky breath.

"I'm not a psychologist," Truth said, "but even I know that denial is
the mind's first line of defense against something that just doesn't fit
with its preconceptions. Sometimes it can be pretty scary when other
people say you didn't see what you know you saw."

Winter searched the other woman's face closely, trying to see if she was
being humored. She closed her eyes tightly, willing the impending tears
away.

"I know what I saw—and sensed. It was *real*. But . . . I suppose that's
what the mad think, too. I need you to tell me if I'm crazy. I don't need
you to be kind."

Truth's eyes met hers, and in their searching blue gaze Winter felt as
if her very soul was being weighed and measured.

"You don't have to go all the way to crazy, Winter, to see what other
people don't," Truth said gently. "Any number of things, from stress-
induced hallucination to drug flashbacks to an old-fashioned psychotic
break can explain it—and they're all temporary conditions; nothing to be
ashamed of in this day and age. Are you sure you want to pursue this any
further?"

"I have to know," Winter insisted stubbornly. If this were a challenge, it was one that Winter would meet if it took her last ounce of strength.

"Even if knowing won't bring you either peace or happiness?" Truth persisted. "Even if what you discover changes your life permanently?"

She was being offered a choice, Winter realized—a choice between the truth and one last comforting lie.

"I want to know," Winter repeated. "I have to."

Truth stood. "All right. Let's go back out to Nuclear Lake."

Truth drove them in her own car; a late-model Saturn. Fortunately she knew the way; Winter was not certain she would have been able to reconstruct it. On the way back to Nuclear Lake, Winter told Truth every detail she could remember: the sudden storm, the way she had felt that it was somehow connected to her even though it resisted all her attempts to control it.

"But it wasn't as if it were something I was *creating*—there are a lot of times I've felt that—as if I were controlling events outside myself—but this was different. And Dr. Luty and Dr. Mahar both said that feelings of disassociation were a common symptom of deep depression," Winter finished bleakly.

Truth made a rude noise without taking her eyes from the road. "Psychotherapy! The so-called science of making every human peg fit the same round hole, no matter how hard you have to hammer. And like a stopped clock, it's right twice a day!"

Winter was surprised into a blurt of laughter. She'd have to stop judging people, like books, by their covers. Who would ever have expected prim and proper Truth Jourdemayne to say something like that?

"So you don't . . . ?" she faltered. *Believe them? But if they weren't right, what* IS *the truth?*

"Dylan says I should have more charity, but I don't. My sister was in an institution for years, tortured by people too stupid or too lazy to have a spark of either compassion or imagination!" Truth said fiercely.

"What happened to her?" Winter asked, after a moment.

"She's living with a man who loves her now, and who is helping her reach an accommodation with the world. And while I'd be the last person to say there's no such thing as mental illness, I'd say a good proportion of the people in institutions are just people who can't manage to survive in the world human beings have built for themselves."

"It's a pretty messed-up world sometimes," Winter admitted.

"Sometimes," Truth agreed. "But there are always ways to make it better."

When they reached the road that led toward the lake itself, Winter was faintly surprised to find Nina's car still blocking the way. Its door hung half-open and the keys were in the ignition. Truth parked her Saturn behind it and got out. She walked up to Nina's car, slid into the rain-drenched driver's seat, and turned the key that was still in the ignition.

Nothing. Not even the grinding of the starter motor.

"I think I killed it," Winter said, with a brave attempt at lightness. *I wonder what Dave Kelly's going to say—two in one week.*

Truth didn't seem particularly surprised. "Some poltergeists have an affinity for electrical systems, especially battery-driven ones. Did you do things like this a lot when you were a child?" Truth asked.

The question caught Winter off guard; automatically she tried to answer it—

—and encountered a rejection so emphatic it made her psychic teeth hurt. She tried to force words past that barrier—any words—and was as helpless as any stutterer to produce articulate speech. She shook her head helplessly, coughing.

"Well, never mind that now," Truth said in that same easy casual way. She got out of the car, shut the door, and locked it carefully. "Not that I expect much in the way of human vandals up here," she said in response to Winter's unvoiced question, "but there isn't a lot left of the inside of a car once raccoons get into it, either. Now, do you want to show me where the trouble was?"

"Where the trouble was." What an admirably neutral way of putting it, Winter thought—but, it seemed, Truth Jourdemayne really was used to this sort of thing.

"Do you have a flashlight?" Winter asked. "There's something else here that I want to show you, too."

"My," Truth said, shining her light on the sigil on the basement wall. Whether it was the company or the fact that this time it didn't come as a surprise, Winter no longer had the same sense of shocky horror she'd felt the first time she'd seen it. Of course, the fact that she was almost too tired even to stand under her own power might have contributed to her apathy.

Seen by the flashlight's bright glare, the musty basement was only that—a basement laboratory, abandoned for unknown reasons and appropriated years later by students and squirrels. Harmless.

Truth shone the light on the floor. The scuffed and faded design painted there jumped out in once-bright primary colors—yellow, red, blue. "You painted this?" she asked.

"We all worked on it," Winter said, slowly, testing her newborn memories. "Janelle laid it out—she was the Art major—but she was following a design in a book that somebody had. I don't remember."

"And when it was done?" Truth asked, a new note of sharpness in her voice.

Winter shrugged, helpless to answer.

"Were you Sealed to the Circle? How far did you get on Smoothing the Path? Who was your Gatekeeper?"

"Path? Gatekeeper?" Something out of Winter's recent reading surfaced to blend with her recovered memories. "But that's—"

"The Blackburn Work," Truth finished for her, a grim new note of worry in her voice. "So if it's true that you and your friends were responsible for putting this here, then the five of you were about my father's business. And it's nothing for amateurs to meddle in."

"You don't really *believe* in that stuff," Winter asked hesitantly, once they were outside again. The sun was setting, and the last rays through the trees gilded everything they touched.

"*A savage place, as holy and enchanted, as—*" Oh, damn, I can't remember the rest of it. But that was a normal sort of forgetting, Winter knew. The sort everyone did.

"It all depends, I suppose," Truth said, "on how you define belief. Do you believe in chairs?"

"Of course I do!" Winter said, mystified. "I see them every day."

"The semanticist would argue that you didn't 'believe' in chairs, at all then—belief, after all, implies an element of faith, and faith isn't necessary when you have the physical object available to you on a moment's notice, now, is it?"

Why are we having this conversation? Winter wondered, but dutifully asked, as she supposed she was meant to, "But what about people who believe in God?"

"For every person who says they 'believe' in God, I can show you one who says they 'know' God—or Goddess, if you prefer, and I know whose integrity I'd rather place *my* faith in. Now," Truth said, briskly changing the subject, "can you tell me about where you were when you first saw the lake boil?"

To Winter's relief, it looked as though they weren't going to discuss Thorne Blackburn or his voodoo logic anymore. She didn't know if she could handle it, especially now that she began to suspect that Truth believed that nonsense, too. *"What is Truth? said jesting Pilate."* "Here," Winter said. She stepped into the place on the walkway where she'd stood to look back at the lake, but even to her strained nerves there remained no sense of menace.

She watched as Truth opened her shoulder bag—a Coach bag even more enormous than Winter's—and took out what Winter first thought was a necklace.

It was a length of bright silver chain almost three feet long. There was a large ring at one end and at the other, a cone-shaped pendulum of quartz or glass, big and heavy enough to pull the chain straight without jouncing. Winter remembered seeing much smaller versions of this in the glass case at Tabitha Whitfield's store. "What are you—?"

"Quiet now," Truth said gently. "It's a pendulum, and I just need a moment or two without distraction."

Winter watched as Truth stretched out her arm until the pendulum hung straight down from the end of it. The chain swayed slowly back and forth, the quartz weight at the end gathering sunlight and distilling it into small flashes of gold. As Winter stared at it, fascinated, the pendulum settled and became perfectly still.

She glanced at Truth. Truth was standing with her eyes closed, breathing slowly and deeply, her face relaxed.

The pendulum began to move—slowly at first, and then faster, until it was describing an agitated elliptical orbit. It seemed as if Truth must be swinging it, or at least moving her wrist, but as far as Winter could tell, Truth hadn't moved at all.

Pendulum power. Is this what I'm reduced to believing in?

But dowsing—which could use a pendulum such as this as well as the more familiar copper-sheathed rod—was something, Winter knew from her reading, that even multimillion-dollar oil companies relied on to save themselves the expense of fruitless drilling. It was a legitimate—though inexplicable—method of gaining information.

Slowly the pendulum settled to a stop again. Truth opened her eyes.

"What was here—and after seeing that basement I'm inclined to think that *something* was—isn't here now, Winter."

"But you believe that it was here before?" Winter asked. *You said I wasn't crazy—do you still think so?* It was true that she didn't feel crazy— or even afraid. What she did feel was a faint but nagging sense of urgency—a sense of some unrealized omission, and that the time in which it would be possible to make amends was drawing to an end.

Truth hesitated, watching her. "You know that you fit many of the protocols for the identification of the adult poltergeist, so I'm inclined to believe that the phenomena you're reporting center on you rather than upon a specific location."

"What do you mean? Are you saying that *thing* wasn't here? I *saw* it, Truth," Winter said, trying to keep the pleading out of her voice.

"But you might have brought it with you," Truth said compassionately, "even though it doesn't seem to be anything like what you've described as happening before. But if in fact it isn't, as you say, something which comes from you, that leaves—if you'll allow me to theorize in advance of my data—the possibility that your—for lack of a better term— psychic *locus* is 'charging up' any potential manifestation it comes near. So you both could and could not be responsible for the phenomenon at the same time."

"Like plugging the battery into the Energizer Bunny," Winter said slowly. "You mean that something like that monster in the lake couldn't happen until I came along?"

"Something like that." Truth chewed upon her lower lip, brooding. "But—" she broke off, as if she'd been about to say more. "First let's try to find out *definitely* what's plaguing you before we decide what to do about it—although I think we can rule out insanity for the time being. And now, let's go home. There isn't much more we can do here."

Much to Winter's surprise, she found that "home" was literally what Truth meant. Over Winter's admittedly feeble protests, she was borne off to Truth's tidy two-bedroom bungalow just outside of Glastonbury, where she was put to work washing and slicing greens for a salad while Dylan Palmer tended both the pot of what he claimed was "killer spaghetti sauce" and the loaves of homemade bread baking in the oven.

The moment she'd crossed Truth's threshold Winter had felt an overwhelming sense of sanctuary, and now, sitting in the cheerful red-and-white kitchen with the mound of scrubbed vegetables before her, it was all she could do to keep her eyes open.

"Is it the hour or the company, Winter?" Dr. Palmer's voice was gently amused.

Rousing with a start, Winter realized she had been all but dozing, her chin upon her chest. Reflexively, she opened her eyes wide.

"Oh, don't tease, Dyl, she's had an awful day. Winter, why don't you go lie down for a half hour or so before dinner—otherwise, I think you're going to end up facedown in the main dish."

The chance to lie down, to sleep, was sweetly tempting—Winter could not imagine having nightmares in this house. "The salad—" she protested automatically.

"Has been duly scrubbed, and you've done most of the chopping. I can finish up—it will let me contribute more to making dinner in my own house than boiling the water for the vermicelli," Truth said.

"Well if you think—"

"I do. Come on." Truth took Winter by the elbow and led her, unprotesting, off to the bedroom.

The bedroom was spartan and simple, with a single bed covered by a white candlewick spread flanked by Shaker reproduction night tables. The room's severity was softened by the braided rug on the floor and the wealth of framed photographs on the wall.

"Just make yourself comfortable," Truth told her generously. "There's a bathroom through there that should have anything you need."

But after Truth had left, it was the photographs, and not the bed, that drew Winter.

Some of the pictures she recognized from reading that book *Venus Afflicted*. Here was Thorne Blackburn, dressed for some New Age Shriners' convention. There, a photo of the same man in the casual dress of thirty years before, swinging a small child up over his head. There were other pictures—a dark-haired woman with long, wild tresses; an older woman with short-clipped graying hair. There was one of Dylan, standing in front of a *Ghostbusters* poster and waving a vacuum-cleaner hose, with a manic expression on his face.

Friends. Family. And the love and caring in those frozen images made Winter curiously uneasy, as though they presented a threat—or a vital clue to a riddle she must solve.

She turned away from them and stretched out on the bed.

"She reminds me of Light," Truth said, coming back into the kitchen a few moments later.

"She's nothing like her, you know," Dylan pointed out reasonably.

"She's a psychic in danger," Truth said inarguably, "and, if this is poltergeist activity, all I can say is that atypical doesn't begin to describe it. I'd almost be happier to see her setting fires—and you know how troublesome pyrokinesis can be to channel and control. But that's not the worst of it—did you know that she was part of a working Circle when she was at college here?"

Dylan turned to stare, giving Truth the full benefit of his attention, his lips pursed in a soundless whistle. "A Blackburn Circle? Are you sure?"

"They'd been working in the basement of the abandoned building out there—an uncontrolled, unsecured site—I saw the North Gate sigil on the wall and somebody'd done a pretty good job of painting the marks for Laying the Floor of the Temple. They probably just walked off and left it when they were through playing; I'd better go out there as soon as I can and close it down completely.

"Stupid kids!" Truth burst out. "How *could* they? Playing about with forces they have no comprehension of—and then surprised when the Unseen gives them a good swift kick in the—"

"Now, now—is this the same woman who only about a year ago was telling me that my ghosthunting was only an excuse to cater to my obviously delusional megalomania?"

Truth's cheeks turned pink. "It's a good thing I've got you around to yank me down off my high horse," she said meekly. "But at *Taghkanic,* of all places."

"Of all places," Dylan agreed. "And Hunter Greyson was on the parapsych track—he should definitely have known better than to go fooling around like that. Remember the 'Philip' experiments in Toronto back in the seventies? The group generation of psi phenomena, including RSPK? Colin would have pinned his ears back if he'd known—Grey was in his Occult Psychology seminar in his senior year. Come to that, so was Winter. I've been doing some checking," he added in explanation.

"Hunter Greyson? Winter didn't mention him," Truth said, frowning.

"She's very cagey about letting on what she actually remembers and what she doesn't, have you noticed? It isn't normal to have memory gaps like that—not without organic trauma or at least a history of drug abuse," Dylan said.

"Or physical abuse," Truth suggested. "Repressed memory—"

"—will mask single isolated incidents for which there is no corroborative reinforcement, not the kind of ongoing abuse that someone would need to just drop four years of their life. Besides, she was living on campus, and you know how closely the faculty, proctors, and student services watch those kids. If she'd exhibited anything like an abuse pattern then, they'd have spotted it," Dylan said firmly.

Truth reached for the uncorked bottle, and Dylan moved to intercept her and pour the wine himself. Truth smiled at him over her glass.

"It sounds like you've done your homework on Winter Musgrave," she acknowledged. "Should I be jealous? And you never did tell me who Hunter Greyson is."

"Hunter Greyson's file is missing from the admissions office, but most of the faculty still remember him—Professor Rhys even suggested that Grey'd stolen his own file; apparently he was known for pranks like that. Winter Musgrave and Hunter Greyson were quite the item their senior year, and with three other students had quite a close-knit little clique. They ran twenty percent over baseline in group telepathy experiments—those records are still in the file over at the Institute."

"I'd like to see them," Truth said soberly. "I bet Winter would, too."

"I'd think twice about showing them to her—at least until I found out what she remembers—and why she can't remember the rest," Dylan said.

"Maybe you're right," Truth said, unconvinced. "I just get the feeling . . ." She paused for a moment, then went on. "That there's something she needs to do, and not much time left for her to do it in."

Winter had been sure she wouldn't sleep, but to her surprise, Truth actually had to shake her to awaken her, and when she did, Winter found she'd slept for almost two hours.

"Don't look so tragic!" Truth teased. "Dylan says the sauce could use the extra time, and since I'm usually up at the lab half the night, I'm more used to late dinners than early ones, and so is Dylan."

Winter regarded her dubiously, her mind awash with suspicion and reflexive guilt.

But why? She frowned. It was almost as if she were split into two people inside herself—one with a rational response to events, the other determined to assign blame for everything, usually to herself.

"All right," Winter said with an effort. *If there's any blame to assign here, it's Truth's, not mine. She's the one who knows when she wants to eat dinner.* "Just let me wash my face and I'll be right with you." *I'm not responsible for the entire world, after all.*

That defiant vow actually seemed to have some effect; the beclouding guilt receded, and Winter found that without its choking presence her grasp of those newly won memories that she'd tested today was stronger—vague and wavery still, like something seen through heat-haze, but persisting even in the face of that inner voice's disapproval.

Those people were real. Her past was real—and if the past, as everyone always said, was a foreign country, then she'd just gotten her passport back.

It only remained to make use of it.

Winter found herself eating with real appetite—and dinner, she told her inner censor fiercely, certainly didn't seem to have been ruined by any delay. The pasta was tender, the sauce was savory and filled with meat, and the bread was still warm, with a chewy golden crust and soft white interior.

They did not talk about Nuclear Lake or its monster through most of the meal, but toward the end, when the pasta had been removed and the salad bowl set out, Winter broached the subject to Truth again.

"You said—at the lake—that there was a way to find out what's really causing all this," she said to Truth.

Truth hesitated. "There are some things I can try that I didn't mention before," she said, sounding faintly reluctant. "Knowing that you've been involved with the Blackburn Work . . . That changes things."

The Blackburn Work. All Winter really knew about it was what she'd read in the book about Truth's father—that and a confused memory of shadows in candlelight, music and incense. . . .

And Hunter Greyson.

"Is— Was— Was Grey a Satanist, then?" Winter asked hesitantly. "Those drawings . . ."

"The Blackburn Work isn't Satanism," Truth corrected her firmly, "any more than astrophysics is. Thorne—my father—created it—drawing on older sources—to be a way of knowing; a way of gathering information from the universe. Of course, it has its risks, but everything does—from climbing Mount Everest to crossing the street."

"It isn't that far from gathering knowledge to gathering power," Dylan said, glancing meaningfully at Truth. "As you well know."

"And I think I would have noticed if that were so, even after all this time," Truth shot back. "Anywhere there is faith, there is a danger of its perversion."

"You're saying you're a psychic," Winter said, her voice quivery as she attempted to keep disapproval out of it.

"It's just as foolish to say you're not when you are, as to say you are when you're not," Truth said pragmatically. "And haven't you had enough proof that psychism is real?"

Winter flinched inwardly. "I'm just . . . crazy," she said defiantly. "All this—it's coincidence, nothing more. Really."

"You're not crazy," Truth contradicted determinedly. "And you don't really want to be, do you? You're not making things up just to get attention, as so many so-called psychic sensitives do. But that is what you are—a psychic sensitive. You're having your life invaded by a change you aren't ready for—a psychic change; and just as a physical growth spurt will cause aches and pains and make a person clumsy for a while until she adjusts, you're having problems."

"Problems!" Winter exploded, thinking of the pathetic corpses of birds and squirrels she'd found on her doorstep and in her house. Was it better to think they were her fault—or that they were not?

"Problems," Truth repeated firmly. "Some of them are frightening for you—and I admit they worry me, too, insofar as they don't follow the standard pattern for poltergeists. There is no conventional treatment for poltergeist phenomena, as I said—but in your case, considering that you may have been Sealed to the Circle, there are some other things I would be willing to try, with your consent."

Winter poked at the soggy remains of her salad. The thought of madness would have been almost comforting—madmen were not responsible for their actions, after all. Truth Jourdemayne's insistence on her sanity was nearly as frightening as her own willingness to surrender to insanity rather than face reality.

And was that what the inner voice—the censor, the spoiler—wanted? Unthinking surrender?

"I'll try anything," Winter said aloud. "Do what you like." Her voice was as hard and steady as ice.

But Truth refused to take the matter farther that night, saying that it would be too dangerous for her to proceed with Winter so close to exhaustion. She and Dr. Palmer drove Winter home in Dr. Palmer's car.

"This is a lovely place," Truth said, standing in the front hall of Greyangels. "But it's wide open."

"I can't seem to keep the doors and windows locked," Winter said, with the odd feeling she was misunderstanding Truth's meaning. "I just keep closing windows and hoping for the best."

"That isn't—" Truth began, and stopped. "Forgive me—you came to me for help and here I am proselytizing, which is utterly foolish. At least let me take a look around and see that everything's all right before we leave." Without waiting for a reply, Truth started up the stairs, and Winter was left staring at Dr. Palmer.

Excuse me, but do you know that your girlfriend's delusional? a sarcastic inner voice prompted her. Aloud, she said only, "I feel as if I'm missing half the conversation."

"The absent referent," Dr. Palmer said, smiling. "I was here a few times when Professor MacLaren owned this place; I think you'll probably want a fire tonight."

"You knew the owners?" Winter said, following Dr. Palmer into the parlor. A fire was laid in the fireplace, and she tried to remember if she'd done that this morning, but somehow the memory wouldn't come.

"Colin MacLaren lived here while he was the director of the Institute," Dr. Palmer said, kneeling by the hearth. "I know he sold it afterward, but I'm not sure who to. It's a great old place, isn't it?"

"Sometimes," Winter said cautiously. She could hear—or thought she could—Truth moving about on the second floor, and wondered what Truth was looking for so intently.

There was a scrape and hiss as Dr. Palmer stroked one of the fireplace matches alight, and then poked its flaming head in among the kindling and paper scraps beneath the logs. After a few moments, pale orange flames licked up over the wood.

"That should do it," Dr. Palmer said with satisfaction.

"Can I offer you some coffee? Tea?" Winter said dutifully, though her bones felt as if they were filled with lead and the need to sleep again was a passionate ache in her entire body.

"You look like you need bed more than either," Dr. Palmer said bluntly, "and while ghosts are my specialty, I've also worked with enough mediums to know that what they do takes a tremendous toll on the nerves. Psychics need to take better care of their health than most people, or they suffer for it later."

"Isn't Truth a psychic?" Winter asked. There was a swift patter of footsteps descending the stairs.

Dr. Palmer hesitated, much as Truth had earlier. "Not exactly," he said, "but I'll leave that for her to tell you, tomorrow."

Truth came into the parlor and regarded the fire approvingly. The crystal-and-silver pendulum was looped in her left hand.

"Nothing here," she said. "No manifestation centering on the house. There's probably a residue down in the old orchard, but nothing that can reach the house, and it isn't malignant anyway."

"What's in the orchard?" Winter asked. She avoided the upstairs because you could see the orchard and the river from most of its windows—she wondered what dire associations the place had for her unconscious mind.

"Oh, Colin used to let some student groups meet down there," Truth said. "Wiccans and so on. Nothing to worry about."

"Wiccans?" Winter said, then: *"Witches?"*

"Harmless," Truth said firmly. "And nothing you'd notice unless you were down there and knew what you were looking for." She dropped her pendulum back into her purse. "And how to look for it," she added, almost as an afterthought. "Have a good night, Winter. I'll call you tomorrow." She picked up her coat, and she and Dr. Palmer turned to go.

Tell me, Ms. Jourdemayne, how do I learn to see things that aren't there—and ignore things that are? Winter's inner voice asked bleakly. But once again she said nothing, following the researchers from the Institute out into the hall, and closing the door behind them as they left.

She was starting to realize there were a lot of answers she didn't really want.

Once she closed the door, Winter dropped the antique bolt that should—in theory—keep the door barred to all intruders. In practice, by the time morning came the door would probably be standing wide open and the bolt would be somewhere else in the house.

Two weeks ago the thought would have maddened her; now, she only felt a weary acceptance of the truth. It was the work of a poltergeist, and Truth Jourdemayne said it would go away.

Of course, Truth had also said it wasn't a *normal* poltergeist. . . .

The fire that Dr. Palmer had lit was burning invitingly now, reminding Winter that if she did not light the stove in her bedroom she was in for an uncomfortably chilly night. Moving slowly she put the kettle on to heat and then stoked the stove, adding a couple of pieces of coal among the kindling to ensure that the warmth would last. Her expedition to Nuclear Lake that afternoon seemed to belong in another universe.

By the time Winter was done with her bedroom stove the kettle was whistling, and she poured boiling water over the last of Tabitha Whitfield's herb tea mixture. She'd better go and replenish her stock tomorrow; while it might not do everything the proprietor claimed, it did seem to help her sleep, and Winter had gotten used to the taste.

Thinking about *Inquire Within* made her remember the pamphlet of "grounding and centering" exercises that Tabitha Whitfield had included with the tea. Feeling oddly guilty, Winter hunted around until she found it wedged behind the clothes hamper in the bathroom.

She wandered back into the kitchen, holding the pamphlet in one hand. It was crudely—or perhaps simply would be a kinder word—done, just half a dozen sheets of photocopied typing paper saddle-stapled with a beige card-stock cover. *Fundamentals of Grounding and Centering* was printed on the cover in hand-drawn letters above an intricately woven pentacle.

It seemed harmless enough.

The tea was ready; Winter poured it out into one of the heavy stoneware mugs that seemed to have come with the house, and added a liberal dollop of honey. She made a note to pick up more honey, too, while she was in town. Hadn't Dr. Palmer said that psychics needed to keep up their strength?

She wasn't, Winter told herself firmly, psychic.

Pamphlet in one hand and cup in the other, Winter went back into the parlor. The undersides of the logs were bright poppy-red now, edged with brilliant gold lace, and the massed bank of coals was radiating a welcome heat into the room. Winter settled herself into the rocker and drew the cream-colored wool afghan over her legs. She'd just sit here a minute. . . .

It was dark, and she was running, being driven farther and farther from the place she needed to be. Months had grown to years—how COULD *she have shirked her responsibilities for so long? It was not as if she was free to do so; she had chosen the Path; had dedicated all of her lives to it. Such a promise was not something she could set aside when the burden grew too heavy! She was* NEEDED; *he had asked her for help—*

Asked her for help?

WHO *had asked her for help?*

What—?

The confusion drove her up out of the dream; floundering about, Winter capsized the rocker and went sprawling onto the cold, hard floor.

Serves me right, Winter thought groggily, getting painfully to her hands and knees. Folded paper slid beneath her palm—the pamphlet.

The fire had died back to embers. The room was ice cold. Winter crawled over to the hearth and pulled a log from the pile in the scuttle, tossing it clumsily onto the embers and ash. She hoped it would have the good grace to light; she was too fuzzy-witted at the moment to build a proper fire.

Winter groped around the floor until she found the afghan and pulled it around her shoulders, getting painfully to her feet. There was the faintest suggestion of light visible through the parlor windows, but it couldn't be later than 5:00 A.M. at the latest. She might as well finish the night in her bed—at least it was harder to fall out of.

What had she been dreaming? Winter groped after the tattered rags of her dream and could only recollect a sense of mission, of tasks left undone—the same sort of feeling that would awaken her in her early days at Arkham Miskatonic King; bringing her up out of a sound sleep to the conviction of trades left undone and deals unmade.

But this was something more. A summons she must answer.

No, Winter told herself firmly. *Your nerves are shot and your emotions are running wild. You can't trust them. Poltergeists I'll believe in, but not these . . . delusions of adequacy.*

Go to bed.

When Winter passed the kitchen on the way to her bedroom, she found that both halves of the dutch door were open—no wonder the house was so cold. Sighing, she pulled the door closed and bolted it again, then did the same for the kitchen window. Her bedroom was freezing as well; the windows, which opened outward, shutter-style, were wide open, filling the room with the faintly marshy scent of the river, and the more insistent smell of wet grass and spring leaves. The stove—and she was almost *sure* she'd lit it—was stone cold.

Grumbling to herself, Winter pulled the windows shut and locked them, and by then she was awake enough to think she might as well go around and shut everything, as all the doors and windows were sure to be open. Just because she'd been lucky so far didn't mean that she couldn't find city crime in Amsterdam County—and she didn't think Tim's Grey Angels would be of any particular help if a housebreaker decided to come calling.

The sky was already appreciably lighter than when she'd first awakened. Winter pulled the afghan tighter around her shoulders and went to check the front door.

It was open, of course, and the crossbar was nowhere in sight. Winter sighed, looking around herself helplessly. Maybe the crossbar was outside this time; by rights she ought to just consign it to whatever limbo poltergeist-stolen objects respired in, but her irritating sense of responsibility demanded she make at least a cursory search. She shoved the door open wider, intending to take a quick look around the yard and then shut the door and go in to bed.

That was when she saw the body.

The first thing she registered was the slick red mass and the fact that there was no blood. The object was dull-finished with the time it had spent drying in the open air; it was somehow more frightening that there was no blood, because there was no way that something that large could have been killed so hideously and leave no blood behind, as if it were a drained carcass from some demented butcher's icebox.

It was as large as a child.

The fear that came on the heels of that thought was what drove Winter forward, because even if it was not her fault, even if it were some energy working through her, using her as a focus, she could not bear to be responsible for murder.

But the outflung limbs ended in hooves, not toes and fingers. A deer, flayed and shredded and left on her front doorstep.

I seem to be moving up in the world, thought Winter with desperate gallows-humor, because if she could not turn mockery against this thing she thought she would begin to cry and never stop.

Moving up in the world.

From birds, to rabbits, to deer.

And what comes after deer, Winter dear?

She would not think of that.

She wouldn't.

CHAPTER SIX

THE HEART IS
A LONELY HUNTER

The red blood reigns in the winter's pale.
—WILLIAM SHAKESPEARE

IT WAS QUITE LATE THAT EVENING WHEN WINTER ARRIVED at the Bidney Institute. Truth had phoned that morning, and then Winter had spent the day doing determinedly normal things, such as taking Sullivan's Taxi down to Poughkeepsie to arrange the lease of a more reliable car. Now that the danger was so clear and so close, she almost wasn't afraid of it. She had been more frightened, she realized, of the half-real phantoms of her own mind—and they had possessed far less power to hurt her.

But this thing—creature, poltergeist, whatever the official ghosthunters wanted to name it—this was not under her control. This thing that hungered for the pain and blood of living flesh and grew stronger as it fed, was so clearly, so obviously a real and present danger that there was little room for fear and none for hysteria.

Winter parked her new car—a Saturn like the one Truth had driven, and very reliable, so the dealer had said—in the college's guest parking and walked up the steps. Truth had told her to come directly in through the lab wing, so she detoured around the back of the Institute's building, to where the Federalist brick and marble façade gave way to the pragmatic stressed concrete of the only new construction on the Taghkanic campus in the last seventy-five years.

Just as she'd been told, the door marked PRIVATE—NOT OPEN TO STUDENTS was unlocked. As Winter stepped through it and into the vast warehouselike building she had visited briefly the day before, she could hear voices.

Truth and Dr. Palmer.

Unwilling to eavesdrop—but equally unwilling to give up any advantage she might gain by it—Winter stood where she was and listened.

"Do you really think Winter's causing the phenomena herself?" Dr. Palmer asked.

"Not consciously, Dyl—and not all of it. The part that can be blamed on an adult-onset poltergeist worries me almost as much as the part that can't, though," Truth answered.

"'Another kind of poltergeist activity may be the expression of psychic force in tension, not around a hysterical or maladjusted child, but around a relatively well-adjusted adult. When this occurs, there is some unresolved psychic force in action; it could be said that the Unseen is coming in search of the individual concerned. . . .'"

"I know my Margrave and Anstey, thank you, my love. And since our girl seems to have a fairly high psionic index—go ahead and laugh, but I'm not *quite* taking that on faith, what with the series she ran here as a student—she's probably summoned up some Elemental and bound it to her without being aware of it."

Winter felt she'd overheard quite enough—if eavesdroppers never heard any good of themselves, neither did it follow that they heard anything good of others. "Hello?" she said, stepping out into the room.

The central space of the laboratory had been cleared, the machines and couches moved back out of the way and a nine-foot circle chalked out on the floor. Four large candles—as yet unlit—were spaced evenly around the border of the circle, and a completely prosaic wooden chair stood in the circle's center. A black-handled knife lay on its seat.

Winter recoiled inwardly. This looked more like witchcraft than like science. What was she letting herself in for?

The oddest thing, however, was not a part of the circle at all. Suspended above it, almost like a deep lid about to be lowered onto a saucepan, was an enormous square cage of copper wire—and looking down, Winter could see a gleaming metal square set into the floor, with sockets into which the pegs of the hanging cage could fit.

"It's a Faraday Cage," Truth said reassuringly, noting the direction of Winter's gaze. "It's perfectly harmless—once it's switched on, it generates a magnetic field that insulates you from all outside influences—the ones that make up the electromagnetic spectrum, at least."

"What does that do?" Winter asked with grudging interest.

"Some of the psychics we work with feel that the Faraday Cage enhances their abilities," Truth said, and Winter could tell she was choosing her words with care. "But what it seems to do best is insulate whoever is inside from influences outside the cage—PK doesn't work through the field, for example—and that's what we're going to use it for tonight."

Winter glanced at Dr. Palmer. He was standing next to a formidable collection of machines that seemed to have enough toggles and dials and LED displays to equip all three seasons of the original *Star Trek*.

"Tonight I'm just an observer," Dr. Palmer said. "The polybarometer will record and measure gross physical changes in the environment, from temperature and pressure fluctuation to any earth tremors that might occur. I'll also be running a wide-band tape recorder and two cameras—assuming, of course, that I have your permission. If you agree, I've got a release for you to sign." Dr. Palmer grinned at her engagingly, holding up a clipboard.

Winter walked over to him and reached for the pen. "Sure." She couldn't see that it made much difference, at this point. "Do you get your ghosts to sign these things, too?"

"We try," Dr. Palmer said, grinning. Winter scribbled her name to the bottom of a sheet saying that she'd been notified of all risks attendant upon these experimental procedures and consented to having the case history and any photographs taken compiled as part of the experimental findings of the Institute; her name would not be used, etcetera, etcetera.

"What do I do?" Winter said when she was done. When Truth had told her yesterday that she was going to try to get rid of at least some of the phenomena plaguing Winter—including the part that killed animals so horribly—Winter had assumed it would involve some kind of injection or treatment, not hex signs and candles.

"The first thing you should do is take off anything you have on that's made of metal," Truth said briskly. "Do you have any fillings in your teeth?"

Winter looked at Truth. Truth was wearing a set of green surgical scrubs and a pair of terry-cloth slippers on her feet. Her shoulder-length dark hair floated free about her shoulders, and she was wearing no jewelry that Winter could see.

"No fillings." Winter set her purse on a nearby table and took off her earrings, ring, and bracelet. She hadn't replaced her last watch yet—the damned things were always stopping and she wasn't really sure why she'd taken up wearing one again in the first place—so she didn't have that to remove.

"Shoes," Truth said, and Winter slipped off her shoes. The utilitarian gray rubber tile of the laboratory floor was chilly beneath her stockinged feet. She blessed the impulse that had made her wear a sport bra with no snaps or hooks, because she could tell that Truth wasn't wearing a brassiere and that Truth would probably have asked her to remove hers without so much as a by-your-leave.

"That's your lot—I'll take on any airport metal detector in the land," Winter said, trying for a light tone.

"Okay." Truth smiled; it made her look very young. "I'll try to keep this nonthreatening. Just come inside the circle—don't step on the chalk marks—and sit down in this comfy chair, and I'll try to answer your questions." Truth picked up the knife on the chair seat and set it on the floor beside one of the candles.

Winter stepped carefully over the chalk mark and walked to the chair, looking dubiously at the line on the floor as she stepped over it. It didn't seem to her that a chalk mark was going to be much protection against anything. Winter sat down in the hard wooden chair and arranged her limbs self-consciously. She placed a little more faith in the cage hanging overhead, though it, too, looked too flimsy to be much of a defense.

"What are you going to do?" she asked.

Truth gestured to Dr. Palmer. He went over to the wall and began lowering the copper cage over both women.

"Like any fan of the scientific method," Truth began, "I have a theory and I'm going to test it. The poltergeist—doors and windows and missing objects—isn't bothering you as much as the slain animals—am I right?"

Winter agreed. "The open doors and missing objects are just a nuisance, really, but . . . it killed a deer this morning," she finished, her voice flat and ugly. "It looked like something had run it through a grinder."

Truth nodded, her expression remote. "What I'm betting is that, since its appearances are so linked to blood and death, you're dealing with something more than simple RSPK; very likely it's an Elemental which you've somehow attracted to yourself. Strong emotion, especially anger or depression, often draws them; I'm not sure why. If the disturbance has its source in Nuclear Lake as you believe, we may be dealing with a water Elemental; they're highly destructive, and often too lazy to return to their own Plane of Manifestation. . . ."

The copper cage rattled as it brushed the floor, and Dr. Palmer cut power to the winch. He checked his watch and made a note on a clipboard.

"And so?" Winter prompted. Truth was so briskly matter-of-fact about everything that it made it easy for Winter to ignore the fact that what she was saying came straight out of an episode of *Mystery Science Theater 3000.*

"You're a cool one," Truth said approvingly. "First of all, I'm going to call upon your Elemental to present itself here so I can identify it, and once that's done, I'm going to use the proper formula to banish it back to its own Elemental Plane. If I can't manage that—some of these things are remarkably tenacious—I can at least dislodge it from you and attach it to myself, and then really give it a run for its money."

Winter glanced through the wires of the cage at Dr. Palmer, but he didn't seem particularly disturbed by anything Truth had said. She wasn't quite sure what an "Elemental" was, but *Venus Afflicted* had mentioned them also, and she could always ask later.

"All connected?" Dr. Palmer said.

Truth checked the perimeter, and fitted the last pegs into the sockets on the floor. "Ready," she said.

"Charging," Dr. Palmer answered back. He threw the switch.

The lights flickered, then slowly dimmed. Winter felt a faint, not unpleasant vibration that seemed to enter through the soles of her feet and leave through the top of her head, and the room was suddenly quieter.

Truth turned to her and smiled, and Winter saw that she was now wearing a magnificent amber necklace with a hanging gold pendant; a sumptuous piece of jewelry that clashed oddly with the prosaic green surgical scrubs. *I wonder where that came from,* Winter thought.

"Sometimes when it's really crazy at the Institute I just wish I could come in here and switch this thing on. Quiet, isn't it?" Truth said.

"Yes," Winter said, surprised.

"And if we could only figure out whether a strong magnetic field enhances psi—or damps it—and why, we'd know something," Truth complained good-naturedly.

She walked over to the nearest of the candles and retrieved an object from the floor beside it. When she straightened, Winter saw that she was holding the small dagger in her hand.

"I told you I was going to call up the Elemental that's bound to you. To do that, I'm going to have to use a symbol set it's familiar with. Don't worry," Truth soothed. "While the Elemental has what you'd call an objective reality, these things *are* only symbols—the candles, the chalk marks, everything here is only a symbol of what I'm going to do with my will. These things have no power except what I give them, really. The unconscious mind communicates by symbol—just think of it as a very powerful computer with very stupid software. Now, I'm going to want you to sit here and be very still for a while, no matter how peculiar things start to seem. I know Tabby gave you a set of centering exercises along with the tea—have you been doing them?"

"Sort of," Winter said. After yesterday she'd meant to, anyway.

"Well, just concentrate on breathing slowly and deeply—and stay in the chair, please, until I tell you to stand up. No matter what you see and hear, you are in no danger—that's what the circle's for. To protect you."

"Okay," Winter said, taking a deep breath.

With that, Truth seemed to forget her completely. Barefoot now, she walked toward one of the candles, holding the black-handled knife high, like a madwoman in grand opera.

I must be tireder than I thought, Winter told herself. Her head didn't hurt, but everything had developed colored haloes: The copper web of the Faraday Cage was outlined in violet fire and she could locate Dr. Palmer in the dimness beyond by the faint corona of blue about him. Within the cage itself, Truth Jourdemayne left trails of blue fire as she walked, and the knife she held flared and wavered brightly in Winter's sight.

Winter tried to push the illusions from her vision and see the world the way it was, but try as she might, the web of colored light superimposed on the real world wouldn't go away.

Maybe I'm starting a migraine, she told herself hopefully, willing momentarily to welcome the thought of the pain rather than to surrender to this new flood of unreason. But it was false reason that was the villain here, Winter told herself fiercely. There was too much at stake for her to afford the luxury of self-delusion. Conscientiously, she took the deep slow breaths that Truth had counseled her to, and forced herself not to care what she saw, no matter how weird it was.

Truth had Laid the Floor of the Temple and saluted the first Guardian, Winter saw, and did not question where the knowledge came from. The first candle was a pillar of scarlet fire that somehow held the wavering form of a stag; as Truth approached the second, it erupted into a bolt of pure silver light.

Red spirits and white; black spirits and gray
Come horse, come hound, come stag and wolf to bear my soul away. . . .

South, then, and a pillar of blazing ebony brighter than any color became the Black Dog. West, and a white blaze; the White Mare. Then back again toward the North, and it seemed to Winter now that Truth carried a star in her hand instead of the knife she had seen before—a star that pulsed and waned in time with her heartbeat. Truth held the star out to the North pillar and the Grey Wolf, and Winter felt a sense of completion, as if some great machine had wakened to throbbing life.

Truth walked around the chair where Winter sat again, and this time stopped facing her. She sketched a shape in the air between them: white fire that dimmed to silver, to a shape as real and tangible as the dinner plates in Winter's kitchen cupboard. She almost reached for it, but Truth anticipated her, taking it and tossing it in the direction of the scarlet pillar. Winter saw the white spark submerge in the red, and then Truth was facing her again, drawing another symbol into the aethyr and flinging it away to the white pillar of the South.

I've fallen asleep, Winter said to herself. *How embarrassing.* But she watched as Truth repeated the action twice more, all in a silence that was somehow more unreal than the polychrome light, and realized that what she was watching now was the summoning of the creature that Truth had promised to bind.

This isn't going to work. The voice was outside her, but part of her; the voice Winter had learned to trust even as it urged her to doubt. For the first time since she had come here tonight Winter was afraid—not of Truth's magic, or even of the idea of magic itself, but of the too-real unimaginable danger that Truth was so casually calling up.

I've got to stop this, Winter thought in tardy alarm, half-rising from her chair.

But it was already too late.

A wave of cold rolled over her, as if someone had just opened the door of a gigantic freezer. The violet fire of the copper mesh flashed into darkness as the Faraday Cage was sucked empty of current. The lights in the laboratory beyond flared into full illumination for a moment, blenching the flaming pillars into pallid might-be illusions, and then everything went dark.

There was a crackling noise and a cascade of purely mundane sparks. Winter heard Dr. Palmer curse and say something about the circuit breaker and emergency overrides. She heard him stumble away in the darkness, and over the sound of his shuffling footsteps she heard the first mutter of thunder.

"It's coming," she whispered, and heard the fright in her own voice.

"I know. Hush," Truth said.

At the lake it had come in the full force of its power, willing to terrify by its mere display of strength. This time it slipped in, at first only the faintest of presences as it challenged Truth's wards, then—as if it were some astral cat bored with its terrestrial mice—came more fully real; strengthening as the storm did, as the thunder crescendoed and the candles of the Guardians flickered and died.

"Oh, damn," Truth said in a quiet voice.

Winter had not realized how much she had trusted in the circle until its protection deserted them. Lightning lit the laboratory's high windows to a strobed blue-whiteness, making the following dark seem even more impenetrable. She felt suddenly naked and, as every exposed piece of glass in the darkened laboratory shattered, she screamed at the sound of breaking. The tumult served only to underscore their vulnerability, and raw impersonal terror made Winter's throat tight and her mouth metallic.

Winter would have run if she could have seen somewhere to go, except for the fact that the cage, which had looked so flimsy before, was still locked in place, and despite its seeming fragility the inert web of copper wire formed a completely mundane trap. It marked out a killing floor, on which Winter Musgrave would die.

"I charge you—" Truth's voice rang out diamond hard, defiant despite the loss of all her protection. She placed herself between Winter and that which had been summoned—Winter could sense this, even in the choking blackness—and seemed to gather darkness in her hands, weaving a net to tangle the summoning in.

But what had come would not be bound. It swatted Truth aside, and then instead of going on to attack Winter, it coiled around Truth, distracted by pure elemental fury from its lawful, rightful prey.

Winter sensed Truth's struggle, and for a moment the too-real surroundings of the Institute's lab blurred; her past reared up like a cresting wave and drowned her in the sights and urgency of the trading floor, where deals that defined the economic nature of reality rested on the heart and mind and will of one frail human vessel.

And she was there, amid the puts and calls, her blood hammering hot with the sheer predatory joy—of the victory that meant others were forced to lose. Hers would be the victor's crown—the triumph and the spoils—there was no room for second-best on the Street and she was the best; she would defeat them all—

In this uprush of passion the tiny voice that dared her to question her assumptions was all but lost—

How did it reach you so easily? How did it get here?

—but Winter's third self, her *real* self, the self that was battered and hauled between these two opposing forces, listened, and saw:

Just who the hell does this bimbo with her mumbo jumbo think she is? If she thinks she's going to take me for a ride here she's got another thought coming—

The Elemental had not needed to breach the barriers Truth had made, because its ally was already within them: the serpent of Winter's hate; the rejection of everything that might defy it—blind intolerance and knee-jerk prejudice, a hatred that fenced Winter in to a safe and ever-shrinking circle of things that would not challenge her preconceptions. Winter could almost see the darkly luminous umbilicus projecting from her body, reaching out to and twining with the serpentine elemental form, rising ice-pale and malevolent to devour anything that opposed it.

It. Opposed *it.* Not her.

She clung to that one thought as to a promise of salvation. *It.* The serpent-hatred was not her. She was not her hate—it was something that sheltered within her, pursing its own goals—*using* her.

She would not be used!

Hot human anger—a blind determination to be free at any cost— drove Winter toward the place where Truth lay, and sought something to lash out against.

"No!" Truth shouted. "Don't! You'll make it worse! Don't give it power!"

Truth's cry was like a dousing of cold water, washing away anger and disbelief, leaving behind only the fear. With clumsy, untutored instinct Winter tried to draw her anger back into herself, to defeat the serpent that way, by making a still center of quietude in which she could shelter.

But all the effort she could muster wasn't enough. The creature fed on her, was bound to her, but was not *of* her. She could not control it.

From the storm outside the lightning flashed, giving Winter a snapshot image of Truth crouched upon the floor by the melted puddle of what once had been one of the candles and its silver holder. She heard Truth cry out, a hoarse, furious sound of pain and rejection.

"Truth!" Dr. Palmer's voice. There was a high mechanical hum; the laboratory lights flashed as the emergency generators came on-line, and Winter heard a firecracker popping as half the bulbs and fuses in the lab's equipment blew. But raw electricity sizzled into the copper wire, completing the circuit, and the magnetic field surrounding Truth and Winter snapped into place with the violence of a gunshot.

Now! Winter heard Truth's voice plead silently within her mind. It was nearly too late. With one last effort Winter struggled with the phantasm, dragging it back from its alliance with the Elemental Truth had summoned.

Refusing to hate.

I see you. I know you for what you are, she told it silently. *I won't dance to your piping.*

Without her cooperation, it had no power. Without her consent, it could not act.

Tears oozed slowly down Winter's cheeks as she stood rigid, eyes closed and hands clenched into fists, exerting all her will neither to act, nor to permit action. Behind her closed lids, she could see Truth win free for long enough to sketch a white fire image in the air.

Winter felt the moment when the Elemental chose not to press the battle further. With all its power, Truth had vexed it; it withdrew, and when the glyph Truth had drawn burned to blackness and vanished, its going closed off the vortex of fear, rage, and pain as absolutely as a slamming door.

It was gone. The Elemental was gone. Winter fell to her knees. Above her, she sensed Dr. Palmer cutting power to the cage, and the weird magnetic tickle over the surface of Winter's skin ceased.

And there was silence.

Slowly Winter opened her eyes. The storm had passed, and the laboratory lights were on, albeit dimly. She heard a mechanical whine as the winch raised the Faraday Cage, freeing them. . . .

She turned toward Truth.

Just as in her nightmarish vision, the candle—wax and metal base both—was a pool of commingled slag, and Truth was huddled in a heap beside it. As Winter stared, Dr. Palmer ran to Truth, clearing the smudged chalk-mark boundary of the circle with a leap, and cradled her in his arms.

"Truth! Are you—?"

"I'm all right," Truth croaked unconvincingly. She tried to push herself upright against him, and her hands left bloody prints on Dylan Palmer's shirt. Truth shook her head as if to clear it, and Winter watched in horror as a shower of fine blood drops sprayed from her mouth. "Fine," she said again, as Dr. Palmer drew her gently to her feet.

"You are *not* fine!" he scolded fiercely. "For God's sake—"

"Not that god," Truth corrected him thickly. "Winter?"

"I'm all right," Winter said, though she was chilled and drained of all energy. "Better than you are," she added bluntly. Truth's face was green-pale; her hands and mouth were as bloody as if she'd crawled across a field of broken glass and then tried to eat some.

Truth shook her head again, coughing. "I don't—" she began, then, "Dylan, get me—"

"All right," Dr. Palmer said soothingly. "It's okay, honey. Everything's under control."

He led Truth over to the chair that Winter had sat in only yesterday, and picked up a Thermos from a nearby table. Winter followed him, worried about Truth, and saw Dr. Palmer pour a cup full of a thick dark-purple liquid that smelled honey-sweet even at this distance.

"You should probably have some, too," Dr. Palmer told Winter, while wrapping Truth's fingers around the cup. Truth slugged the drink straight back and coughed again, but she had a little more color in her cheeks. She reached for the towel that Dr. Palmer had laid by and wiped her hands and face, leaving bloody smears on the white terry cloth.

"Welcome to the glamour world of statistical parapsychology," Truth said dryly. Dr. Palmer handed a second cup of the mixture to Winter.

"What is it?" Winter said.

"First aid for psychics: It's sweet wine mixed half and half with raw honey," Dr. Palmer said. "The alcohol shuts down the psychic centers and the sugar replaces energy."

"It's horrible," Truth added dolefully, and Winter, dutifully drinking her cupful down, had to agree: The mixture was gaggingly sweet, and the wine probably came out of a screw-top bottle. But she felt better after drinking it and she could see that Truth, drinking a second cup more slowly, did, too. Slowly the jangled, exposed-nerve sensation that seemed to hang in the very air faded.

"Okay," Truth said a few minutes later. "What happened here tonight, Dylan?" She seemed to have stopped bleeding, and, looking closely, Winter could not see where the blood could have come from, though there were still dried smears of it on Truth's hands and mouth. Though the sight should have terrified, or at least revolted, her, Winter remained curiously unaffected, as dispassionate as if she were merely a surgeon watching a new procedure being demonstrated.

Was this what she had been once, in her college days? Someone like Truth?

"I lowered the cage and powered it up," Dr. Palmer said, in answer to Truth's prompting. "Winter was sitting in the chair, you were walking clockwise around the inside perimeter of your circle." He stopped, frowning, and thought hard. "You walked around a second time—oh, the usual gestures and so on," he added, and Truth snorted affectionately, "and then the circuit breakers all blew and you told me to go get the power back up."

Winter started to protest, but Truth shushed her with a raised hand. "And then?" Truth said.

"I think I was downstairs about five minutes—I flipped the circuit breakers but nothing came back up, and it took me a couple of tries to get the backup generator started. When I got back up here, you were on the floor and Winter was standing; the chair had been knocked over."

Winter, surprised, looked back toward the circle. The chair was indeed lying on its back, though she didn't remember it falling over. She shivered; the laboratory suddenly seemed very cold.

"What about the equipment?" Truth asked, wiping her mouth again before taking another drink.

Dylan shrugged and laughed shortly. "Let's see what we get. The poly-barometer didn't even know there was a storm going on outside, so it's probably a wash."

"And you didn't see anything?" Truth went on. Winter envied the other woman her composure.

"Other than the basement?" Dr. Palmer asked jokingly. "I'm not really sure. Phenomena consistent with a Class Two haunting—the railway-train sound, coldness, vertigo, disorientation. Other than that? I don't even know what I *think* I saw." He shrugged.

"What about you, Winter?" Truth asked.

Winter steeled herself. There was more than one time and place and way to oppose all that the serpent stood for, now that she had seen her enemy clearly at last. "I'm not sure about the right words to use for this sort of thing. I remember Dr. Palmer turning on the cage—I don't remember hearing you tell him to turn the lights back on, though. You did whatever you did with the four candles and the animals—" Only belatedly did Winter realize that she couldn't have seen all that she thought she had.

The red pillar was directly behind her—and how did she know it was red? The candles in all four of the holders had been white.

"And then?" Truth prompted. "Don't worry if what you think you saw happen sounds impossible—"

"It *did* happen," Winter said stubbornly. "But it sounds so stupid—I watched you draw pictures in the air and throw them into the pillars— there *were* pillars—and I— And something— I knew you shouldn't call it, but it was too late, and everything went out."

"It sure did," Dylan said. He walked back to the circle, stooped, and held up a dinner plate–sized splodge of wax and silver. "I think you're going to have to get these recast, darling."

"Later, Dylan," Truth said briefly. "Do you remember anything after that, Winter?"

"You told me not to help it," Winter said, slowly, "and I realized that part of its power came from me—that you couldn't keep it out while I was inside the circle."

"Something I should have thought of myself," Truth said ruefully. "And after I'd gone and said that you'd be safe, too."

Winter shook her head; the danger hadn't been Truth's fault, but hers—and Truth had paid in full measure for any rash promises she might have made.

"It hated . . . it *was* hate." Unconsciously Winter put her hand over her heart, as if denying expression to something still inside her. "But I don't think it wanted to kill me." Not kill, no, but something far worse, for when the mind, the *self* is gone, what can it matter that the body still lives?

"No," Truth said. "It wasn't here to kill. There was something else it wanted from you." She took a deep breath. "I can't do what I said I could, Winter; I'm sorry. I could try to call it again—"

"No," Winter and Dylan said in unison.

"—but I think I'd have even worse luck than I did this time, even ready for it. I was expecting a *doppelgänger* or one of the Lesser Elementals. . . ." Truth's voice trailed off; she seemed to be looking inward. "What I can't understand is *how;* that Circle was broken fifteen years ago—"

"Sweetheart, you aren't making a lot of sense," Dylan said.

Truth ran a hand through her short dark hair and winced as if her hands still hurt, unmarked though they were.

"All magical systems have a signature—like an artist's style: Wiccan, Christian, Rosicrucian, Golden Dawn; each leaves its own distinctive mark on the magic it makes. For someone very familiar with a particular school of magic, even the lodge—or coven—using the system can be told; sort of like telling Picasso's blue period from his late period, and so on.

"Well, it's no secret to anyone that I know a good bit about the Blackburn Work, and the damnedest thing . . ." Truth's voice trailed off again, and Winter saw her rouse herself, making an effort to say something that would make sense to them.

"What came to me tonight wasn't a true Elemental at all. It was an artificial Elemental—what some schools call a *magickal child*—something created out of a magician's life force, and sent to perform a task somewhere its creator can't or won't go. They're easy enough to create; this one was created by someone trained in the Blackburn Work and sent to Winter, and since she'd worked in a Blackburn Circle I thought she might know who . . ."

"A magician!" Winter burst out in disbelief. "I don't know any magicians—and I don't want to, either!"

"Well a magician knows you," Truth said shortly, "and if I were you I'd find out who it is, and what he wants."

"Can't you just—well—make it go away?" Winter begged, hating herself for asking, when the first attempt to help had nearly killed Truth.

Truth shook her head, and Dylan put a comforting arm around her shoulder. "It's always going to come back. Throwing up a barrier powerful enough to keep it away from you would probably kill you, and would certainly kill me—Blackburn magic is tied to the living world and needs life to power it. Living energy. Sometimes even blood."

"Which is why it keeps killing things," Winter guessed despairingly. And why Truth's hands and mouth had bled.

"It's using the power generated by those deaths to stay in the realm of manifestation—the earth-plane—the world," Truth said. "The fact that it's taking larger and larger lives at increasingly frequent intervals worries me; it must need the power for something—but what is it doing with it? So far it's only attacked wild animals, but if it tries for humans, for children—or pets, domestic animals linked to humankind . . ." Truth was almost mumbling now, keeping her eyes open by an effort of will that Winter could recognize.

"You've got to get some rest," Dr. Palmer urged. "I'll take both of you back to my place and then come back and clean up here."

Only now did Winter take a good look around the laboratory. Every flat surface glittered with broken glass from the shattered windows, giving the entire lab a grotesque Christmas-card sparkle. If the chairs she and Truth sat in had been anywhere near a window, they too would have been covered with broken glass.

"Winter, will you stay with her?" Truth made an annoyed sound but Dylan continued. "I've got a guest bedroom, and I don't really want to think of either of you alone tonight."

Dylan Palmer owned an old white-painted wood frame house on a quiet residential street in Glastonbury. It was a part of town that Winter could tell had been open fields not so many years ago, and the old farmhouse looked faintly out of place among the modern tract housing. Winter had gone along with Dr. Palmer's insistence that she accompany Truth— more for Truth's sake than her own—but after Truth was settled and sleeping and he had driven back to the Institute, Winter went out onto the porch and sat on the railing, staring out into the night.

What did it all mean? The unanswerable vagueness of the question made her smile ruefully. Where to begin? Was the beginning the place where her life had stopped with a crash—or after that? When she'd decided to seek out her own truths—or when she realized what they were?

It's in me. Not the power that had nearly killed both her and Truth tonight—and which *would* kill her if she could not manage to accept its unbelievable reality—but the other. The force that stopped watches and drained car batteries and knocked pictures off of the mantelpiece. *That* was part of her—the part that called to the—what was it Truth had called it?—that called to the *magickal child.*

Winter held her hand out, palm up, and regarded it dubiously. She tried not to care that she might be on her way to becoming a deluded spoon-bending crank—no, that wasn't right. She wasn't deluded, and what she had to try not to care about was suddenly being forced to live in a world where this sort of unreasonable fairy tale was real. Where telepathy coexisted with magic, where invisible entities could walk through walls, where the faint electrical pulses of the human nervous system could become lightning powerful enough to . . .

To blow out a car's electrical system, at the very least. Poor Nina—that was MY *fault. I hope I can find some way to make her let me pay for it. . . .*

Thinking this way was stupid, a reptilian inner voice assured her. It was magical thinking—megalomania—disassociative delusional conditions characteristic of the borderline schizophrenic state. Believing in these intangible things was not normal. It was not healthy. It was not *sane.*

Then I won't be sane, Winter decided with despairing clarity. *I can't afford to be. The price is too high.*

Clinging to the safety of what she had always believed would only free the hatred that lived beneath her skin to do as it pleased. In order to make a conscious choice to stop it, she had to believe in the serpent, and if she believed in it, she had to believe in everything its existence implied: that an unseen world existed side-by-side with their own, where Grey Angels walked the Taconic hills and ghost ships sailed the Hudson. That in that world, things like telepathy and poltergeists were real.

"Choose," Winter told herself. *And don't snivel about it afterward. And don't look back.*

Believe.

Believe as she had once, when she was a girl on the threshold of life, and anything had seemed possible. Before she had known that all the possibilities dangled before her eyes led only to grief and disappointment.

Winter sighed and stretched, rising to her feet. She walked back inside the house and went into the bedroom where Truth lay sleeping in Dylan's bed, dark smudges of exhaustion like moth-wings under her eyes.

I cannot disbelieve, Winter told herself. *If this is madness—delusion—hypocritical self-indulgence—then so be it. I think I've come about as far as rationality can take me.*

And I think I know where I have to go next.

Satisfied that Truth would sleep on uninterrupted, Winter called for a cab to take her back to her car and took the time to scribble a note to Dr. Palmer. She knew he hadn't wanted her to be alone tonight, but she wondered if he'd really understood what Truth had said: that this *magickal child* was coming for *her.*

Why?

That was the question everyone ought to be asking, Winter thought as she waited on the steps for the cab. Assume magic, assume magicians—if that was what they were called—why would a magician be sending monsters after *her?*

"If he wanted to send a message, why didn't he just use Western Union?" she asked herself crossly, just as the cab pulled up.

Winter paid the cab off in the college parking lot—her new Saturn was in guest parking, and Dr. Palmer would be using the faculty section, so there was little danger of running into him. Winter didn't know how long it would take him to clean up the lab—considering the mess it had been in, she wondered how he thought he could possibly do it alone—but she was fairly sure that clean-up efforts would keep him busy for a few hours, and she could be home at Greyangels before he knew she was gone. But Winter stood in the empty parking lot after the cab had driven away, making no move to unlock her car and go.

It was close to midnight; the spring night was chilly and she was glad for the warmth of her wool-lined Burberry trench coat. Only the hiss of the wind through the pines and the reproachful wail of a northbound freight train on the other side of the river broke the silence. How long had it been since she had stood anywhere like this, relaxed and open to the world around her? For as long as Winter could remember she'd been running—running to get somewhere, running to stay in the same place. Even her fun had been frenetic—weekend jaunts to London, to L.A., to wherever there had been people and noise and parties that had in themselves been another form of war.

How long since she had questioned why she ran—in the rat race, where the rats were winning?

It always kept coming back to *"Why?"*

Why was the *magickal child* after her?

—no, go farther back—

Why had she left Fall River?

—farther back—

What had put her in Fall River in the first place?

—farther still—

Why had she chosen the work she had?

Close, now, but not there yet . . .

What had made her do it? What had turned that girl into the woman Winter Musgrave was now? It was more than just time and growing up; there was something . . . not *right* here.

She wanted answers. She wanted reasons. She wanted her friends, her past, her *life* back. Her *real* life.

And she was going to get them.

A sense of relief, of triumph—of guessing the answer that could not be revealed to the riddle that must be solved—sent a surge of pleasure through Winter's weary body. She pulled her coat more firmly around her and fitted her key to the car door's lock. She got in, and tensed for a moment as she turned the key in the ignition, but whatever vengeful power she possessed was quiescent now, and the Saturn started smoothly. Winter turned out of the college parking lot, heading down Leyden Road to Glastonbury, and from there to home.

The farmhouse felt more welcoming than it ever had before—if this was a delusion it was a benign one—and despite the amazing horrors of the night Winter opened her front door without fear. For the first time in longer than she liked to remember, Winter did not feel thwarted at every step in her attempts to accomplish even the simplest tasks. She put water on for tea—she hadn't been back to *Inquire Within* yet, so it would have to be chamomile—stoked the woodstove in the bedroom, and laid a new fire in the parlor, all the time thinking of what she must do now.

Truth had seemed to think that the Blackburn Work had something to do with the *magickal child*'s existence, and the fact that Winter had— so evidence if not memory told her—dabbled in the Work in college seemed to mean something important to Truth as well. She had said that the creature stalking Winter was the creation of a magician, and one trained in the Blackburn Work at that. But Hunter Greyson—if Winter stretched a point nearly to breaking—was the only magician she knew. Why would Grey do something like that?

For that matter, *where* was Grey, and what was he doing? Nina had been able to find everyone from Winter's college days but him—and how could Winter have lost touch with him so thoroughly if they were as close as her memories hinted and Professor Rhys had implied?

What happened?

She kept coming back to that question, Winter realized. What happened, and when had it happened? And, as she'd realized earlier this night, the stakes were too high now to worry about looking foolish when she asked it. She must find Grey, find the others, find herself, find the answer to the monstrous riddle of the dark and bloody creature that stalked her.

Before it was too late.

I'm running out of time, Winter thought desperately. *Won't someone tell me what's going on before it's too late?*

CHAPTER SEVEN

THE WINTER CARNIVAL

In spite of all their friends could say,
On a winter's morn, on a stormy day,
In a Sieve they went to sea!
—EDWARD LEAR

IT WAS LATE AFTERNOON WHEN WINTER TURNED HER new Saturn down the dead-end street in the working-class New Jersey suburb where Janelle Baker lived. *Why every single house in this development has to look the same I'm sure I don't know—and if they* DO *have to, why don't they make the house numbers bigger?* It would also help if there weren't both a Medmenham Drive and a Medmenham Lane in the development. Winter checked her jotted notes for the twentieth time since turning off the main road.

She'd left Glastonbury this morning just as the sun was coming up, and just managing to get this far had given her a purely physical sense of accomplishment that had done much to bolster both her spirits and her determination. Though it would be foolish to pretend that she was not still physically weak and out of condition, and certainly she lacked the stamina she remembered having, just knowing her limits and being able to push them was a source of ongoing pleasure for her.

It's like being reborn.

She'd wanted to leave Glastonbury without telling anyone, but a sense of guilty responsibility—for Truth's injuries as well as for Nina's car—had made her phone Dylan Palmer at the Institute yesterday, as soon as she was back from her errands. It was the morning after the disastrous Elemental summoning, and weariness still dragged at her. The interview had not been pleasant, but she hadn't expected it to be.

"You can't just go running off like this!" Dr. Palmer's voice crackled over the telephone line.

"Perhaps you'd like to tell me, then, just how it is I ought to run off," Winter shot back coolly, in a tone her former colleagues at Arkham Miskatonic King would have recognized and backed down from. "And I don't believe I need your permission. I'm notifying you as a courtesy, nothing more. How is Truth?" Winter added, ruthlessly changing the subject.

"She's . . . okay," Dr. Palmer admitted grudgingly. "But I hope you'll reconsider this, Winter. It's not as if you're alone in this . . . thing. You have friends, allies. . . ."

"I appreciate your concern," Winter said, a shade more warmly. "But I think I need to do a little more research before accepting your offer." The sentence was a ghost out of her past and its resonance made her smile briefly. "I think I may know how to find out who this 'magician' is that you and Truth say is after me."

"You think it's Hunter Greyson?" Dr. Palmer asked shrewdly.

NO! *Some powerful instinct within her could not accept that Grey could be responsible for something that carried so much of hating and hurting with it. Aloud she said, "Grey's the only magician I ever knew, Dr. Palmer. Maybe he'll know where to start looking for yours."* IF I CAN FIND HIM. . . .

But if Hunter Greyson remained maddeningly elusive, at least the rest of her school friends were not so hard to find. Winter had reached Rappahoag around noon, checked into the first large hotel she saw, and called the number Nina Fowler had found for Janelle Baker.

Only I have to remember she's Janelle Raymond now, Winter reminded herself as she pulled the car to a stop outside 167 Grammercy Park Road. Janelle was married, and, like the others, had gotten on with her life, but she'd been delighted to hear from Winter when Winter phoned her from the nearby Marriott.

Should she tell Janelle that she didn't really remember her? Winter fretted. She was hoping she wouldn't have to—she was counting on the sight and presence of the woman who had once been one of her closest friends to shake loose her repressed memories.

Repressed? What an odd idea. What on earth could there be to repress about four years of college?

"Winter!"

But the thought vanished at the sight of the plump redhead standing on the porch of the small tract house. Janelle stood on tiptoes, waving and wearing a kelly-green sweatsuit with a row of plaid heart appliqués across the bosom, and a matching plaid bow holding back her wavy flame-red hair.

She looks like a Cabbage Patch doll with no fashion sense, Winter thought with automatic unkindness, before guiltily curbing the thought. But there was something about her friend's appearance that generated a faint impulse of alarm, though Janelle looked clean and healthy—and certainly well fed.

Oh, stop it! Winter told herself sternly as she got out of the car. She waved back at Janelle and started up the walk.

The inside of 167 Grammercy Park Road was as relentlessly ordinary as the outside; Janelle led her into a living room that looked to Winter as if it had been furnished with one of those "decorator room groupings" from a national chain department store. There was a gray velveteen La-Z-Boy with the Scotchgard label still on it in the corner and French Provincial end tables in white pickled polyurethane waterproof finish flanking the overstuffed couch upholstered in peach floral Herculon. The floor lamp coordinated with the two peach-colored ginger-jar lamps on the end tables. Wall-to-wall acrylic pile in a harmonizing shade of gray swept across the floor to vanish beneath the edge of the companion entertainment and media center. The open spaces on the shelves of the entertainment center were filled with untidy piles of the current popular videos and the sort of soulless decorative "accents" that came from the same place that everything else in the room had—creating a room that was both cluttered and impersonal.

Winter felt a faint sense of recoil, and didn't think the cause was anything as simple and unflattering as snobbery. It was true that the room

125

looked like a page from a less-expensive catalog, but that wasn't what gave the room the ambiguously chilling sense of emptiness. Winter pushed the thought away, unwilling to follow it to its logical conclusion.

The only thing that didn't fit in with the rest of the room was the picture over the couch.

It was a landscape, painted with all the hot bright colors of a New England summer—a forest surrounding a mixed field of poppies and lupines, leading the eye inevitably to the flash of gleaming silver at the center; the pool in which the rising moon was reflected even at midday, and the unicorn that waited beside it.

"Do you still paint?" Winter burst out impulsively, cheered by remembering. Janelle had been an artist. She was sure the memory was a true one.

But . . .

"Who has time?" Janelle said, shrugging. "If you only knew. . . . But here I am babbling on and you're hardly in the door. Give me your coat— um, Burberry, very nice—and you're going to stay for dinner, right? Of course you are—then you can meet Denny; I've told him so much about you that he's just dying to meet you. But let me hang up your coat; come on back to the guest room, it's in through here. Where are you staying?"

Following Janelle down the hall, Winter felt a traitorous pang of relief that she was already checked into the Marriott. The small suburban tract house was the very antithesis of Greyangels Farm, and Winter did not think she could have borne to accept Janelle's hospitality overnight.

"Oh, that's too bad," Janelle said when she answered. "We've got the cutest little guest room—you'll see—it used to be my studio—but no one ever uses it now except Denny's mother. I wish you'd called earlier— you could have stayed with us."

Oh no I couldn't have.

The guest room Janelle conducted her to was very much like the living room. All the furniture seemed to have been purchased by someone less concerned with their own taste than with satisfying some arbitrary external standard. There was a prim single bed and a chest of drawers, and a couple of tired-looking prints of flowers on the wall.

"I used to have my own stuff up, but Mama Raymond said it made her head hurt to look at it, and then she gave us these," Janelle said, talking over her shoulder as she opened the closet and hung Winter's coat inside.

"Just toss your bag anywhere—how do you ever manage that thing; it looks big enough to smuggle babies in!"

Winter smothered a laugh and felt a pang of wistful tenderness for her friend. Janelle had always been a clown, hiding her shyness behind a flurry of one-liners. Winter threw her briefbag on the bed.

"So how have you been, really?" Winter said awkwardly. "It's been a long time."

"You never call, you never write. . . ." Janelle teased impishly, "but then, I didn't ever get around to thanking you for the wedding present, and it's been—what?—eight years now?"

Winter wondered what she'd sent.

"And it's so great to see you again—you look really terrific." Janelle stood in front of the closet door, regarding Winter with frank envy.

"Thanks," Winter said, "so do you."

"Hah!" Janelle laughed dismissively. "We can't all keep our girlish figures. But come on; let me get you some coffee, and try to spoil yours."

The eat-in kitchen was decorated country style, in French blue and beige with pictures of geese everywhere. Janelle had always had a penchant for things the other members of the group considered unbearably corny, Winter thought, with a surmise that owed more to intuition than memory.

"Do you still collect teddy bears?" she asked.

Janelle beamed, her gray eyes disappearing into smile-crinkles. "Yeah. Sometimes. Remember the Lost Bears?"

"And you were Wendy," Winter said, only half-guessing now.

"And Tiger-Lily Bear, and Cub-tain Hook. I sure do miss them," Janelle sighed. "But sit down," she urged, changing the subject quickly. "I'll put up the coffee."

Janelle chattered on as she bustled around the kitchen, putting out cookies, pouring coffee, and filling in the story of the last several years without any need for Winter to ask any questions.

"Would you believe it? I met Denny working at a computer store— we'd get two or three deliveries a day from shippers and he was the UPS guy. We ended up seeing a lot of each other, and, well . . ." Janelle shrugged again, and popped a cookie into her mouth.

Somehow this was not the sort of future Winter would have predicted for Janelle all those years ago. "Computer store?" she asked, sipping at her coffee. Janelle had put in the sugar and it was far too sweet for Winter's taste.

"Yeah, well," her friend said evasively. Despite Janelle's insistence that she wanted to have a conversation, she wouldn't sit down, fussing and hovering about the kitchen as if she both wanted to talk to Winter and wanted to avoid it.

"But what about your art career?" Sudden recollection made Winter blurt the question out tactlessly, but the image was crystal-clear: Janelle with her sketches, Janelle with her portfolio . . . "You sold some paintings to that gaming company, and—"

"It didn't really work out," Janelle interrupted hastily. "Besides, there isn't a living in book covers unless you're Michael Whelan or somebody. So what are you doing these days?"

Well, I just got out of a mental institution and I'm being followed around by some kind of invisible monster. . . .

"I guess I'm taking a much-needed vacation," Winter said diplomatically. "I almost feel guilty about just calling you up out of nowhere like this—"

"Oh, pooh—what are old friends for? Emphasis on the old," Janelle said, finally lowering herself into a chair with a sigh. "Don't mind me— I was up at five this morning, cleaning up the yard—again."

"What happened?" Winter asked idly. She glanced past Janelle to the window above the sink. The goose-printed café curtains shifted in the breeze, and Winter suddenly noticed that there was a long jagged crack across the glass beneath.

"Damned kids. Denny says its a Satanic cult, and I *think* he's joking. They go through the whole development dragging the trash cans out into the road and emptying them, mixing up the recyclables, that kind of thing. But what's really sick is the way they keep scooping up roadkill off Route Seventeen and leaving it around. It's gotten to where you have to look twice before you step out your front door in the morning." She made a face.

"Anything else?" Winter asked, mouth suddenly dry.

"Anything else what?" Janelle asked, frowning puzzledly.

"Anything else weird—like doors that won't stay shut, and unexplained storms. Trouble with your car. Things that break." She was too paranoid to believe in coincidence any more—and Janelle's description sounded all too much like Winter's own litany of complaints . . . of her poltergeist, and of something darker.

Janelle laughed. "You don't need any other explanation for why things break when I'm around! Denny says we ought to buy our dishes by the carload! Honestly, Winter, do you think New Jersey's gone over to the dark side of the Force or something?"

"No." *Yes, but how could I even begin to explain?* "Of course I don't, Jannie. But do sit down. Have some coffee. Do you ever hear from any of the others?"

It was a clumsy way to change the subject, but Winter had the growing sense that their conversation was built around awkward silences, as if there were some great secret that they both shared but couldn't speak of. *Only I don't know what it is . . . do I?*

No matter the cause, Janelle was grateful to follow Winter's lead.

"Oh, you know how it is—there isn't a lot of point in keeping up with everyone else, is there? Ramsey's the only one, really, and just Christmas cards, that sort of thing. I thought about going to our ten-year reunion, but Denny didn't want to stand around all day talking to people he didn't know, and it *is* a long way. . . ."

But I drove it in a day! Winter protested silently, and Janelle, as if she could read her mind, answered, "Some places are different distances depending on who's going there."

By the time Dennis Raymond arrived home from work, Winter was already half-prepared to dislike him, and nothing she saw in the first five minutes after his arrival changed her mind.

Dennis Raymond was somewhere around forty, although his overall air of dissatisfaction made him look older. When he came in, he was wearing a cheap, unbecoming suit and carrying a large, overstuffed briefcase. Winter instantly pegged him as some sort of salesman, in the male equivalent of a woman's dead-end secretarial job. His hair was thinning and greasy; not so much slovenly as given up on. In fact, everything about Dennis Raymond said that he was a man who had given up; who was simply serving out his time and waiting until he could move on.

But this is your life; not a dress rehearsal, Winter thought against the sudden clutch of tension in her chest.

Dennis came into the kitchen, slinging his jacket and briefcase onto one of the kitchen chairs, and fixed Winter with a challenging stare from his small cold eyes that made her feel he was assessing the dollar value of everything she wore, from the casual Aigner pumps to the wheat-colored cashmere sweater and the diamond studs in her ears. Assessing . . . and resenting.

"So this is your old girlfriend, huh, Neenie?" he said. His voice was like the rest of him; aggressive and uncared-for; and Winter, whose entire working day had been spent shouting at the top of her lungs and then trying to repair the damage afterward, winced faintly in sympathy at the rough rawness of Dennis Raymond's voice.

"This is Winter; you remember I—"

"What's for dinner?" Denny said, cutting her off. He looked around the kitchen, sniffing exaggeratedly.

For the last few hours the fragrant scent of pot roast with red wine and onions had been slowly filling the kitchen. Janelle was a good cook but an anxious one, fussing and worrying over every ingredient.

"Pot roast; I thought—" Janelle began again.

"Well hurry up with it, would you? I'm starved. A man who has to work for a living—" he said, with a baleful glare at Winter "—has a right to expect a few things when he gets home, you know what I'm saying?"

Yes; but he hasn't got the right to make other people slave for him without a word of thanks. Winter had worked longer and harder days than Dennis Raymond ever had, she suspected, rising while it was still dark in order to get the news from Tokyo and the gold-fix from London; sipping her first coffee of the day staring at the big display over the Pit and waiting for Chicago to wake up so that the most frantic part of her working day could begin. She'd had people to shop for her, cook for her, clean for her—but she'd never assumed these things were hers by right. She'd paid for them, and been grateful she was in a position to be able to pay.

"Sure, honey." Janelle's tone was apprehensive, and she kept darting worried glances at Winter. Without being told, Janelle got a glass from the cupboard and filled it with ice, then retrieved a bottle from under the kitchen sink and poured a generous splash of bourbon into it.

"Would you like a drink, Winter?" Janelle said, trying to turn the moment into a social one.

"Women shouldn't drink," Denny said, taking the glass.

Winter repressed the urge to ask Janelle for a double bourbon and see if she could drink Denny under the table.

"And what is it, Mr. Raymond, that you think women *should* do?" Winter asked silkily. She crossed one leg over the other and leaned back in her chair, feeling a small sense of triumph as the gray flannel skirt slid up over the gleaming Evan Picone stockings and Denny's eyes followed the movement. Sex was a weapon, Jack had always told her, and she should use every weapon the good Lord had given her to get what she wanted.

God, she missed Jack. He'd been her mentor; she'd clerked for him when she'd first arrived on the Street, and been a good friend to him and Lorna both. When he'd died last year—

"I think they shouldn't try to be men," Denny said, knocking back the second half of his drink. His face was flushed now from the alcohol, and his mouth was set in a thin line.

Heart attack within the year, Winter prophesied automatically. She readied herself for another retort—she'd been annihilating assholes like this since she was twenty-five—but then she glanced sideways at Janelle. Her friend's gray eyes were wells of pain, and she looked pleadingly at Winter.

Winter took a deep breath, only now realizing how disastrous the consequences of losing her hold on her temper could be. If the poltergeist should strike here . . . She took a deep breath, and visualized the muscles of her chest and stomach—where, according to the pamphlet from *Inquire Within,* anger energy accumulated—relaxing.

"I'm sure you're right," Winter said. "Jannie, shall I help you set the table?"

Although the bungalow had an eat-in kitchen, there was also a small dining room, dutifully furnished with an eight-piece early American dining suite from Sears. Denny Raymond—on his third bourbon by this time—bulldozed his way through pot roast and carrots in a silence broken only by monosyllabic demands for more food. Winter found herself sneaking surreptitious glances at her watch, counting the moments until dinner would be over and she could gracefully leave.

But I have to ask Jannie about Grey.

It was true that Janelle hadn't mentioned him by name earlier when she'd been discussing how out of touch she was with the others, but even if she weren't in touch, she might at least have some idea of where Winter could begin looking for Hunter Greyson. Only Winter wasn't entirely sure of how to broach the subject, not with Dennis Raymond sitting across the table from her glaring at her as though she were his worst enemy.

Which of course I am: a woman he can neither bully nor defeat. In the fashion that Dennis measures success—money—I'm better than he'll ever be, and he just can't stand it.

She glanced out of the corner of her eye at Janelle, who, for all her chatter earlier, had been silent since she'd sat down, looking at neither of them. Considering Denny's manners—or lack of them—Winter wondered why Janelle had asked her to stay for dinner. Surely it would have been easier all around if Winter had merely left before Denny got home?

Or would it? The sudden doubt chilled her. What were evenings like here at 167 Grammercy Park Road, shut up in this little house in the middle of suburbia with a man who obviously resented any spark of competence shown by a woman?

No wonder Janelle doesn't paint any more, Winter thought, and felt a little like crying.

"So. What do *you* do?" His first hunger satisfied, Dennis Raymond was now prepared to make what was his version of small talk. But, with senses abraded raw by tension and stress, Winter knew that what the world would see as small talk was only Dennis's method of setting up another attack.

And unfortunately, any retaliation on Winter's part would have a price that was paid by Janelle, and not by her. A *high* price.

"I have a seat on the New York Stock Exchange," Winter said, although that wasn't quite true. Arkham Miskatonic King paid the five-figure rental fee each year, not her, and she was sure that by now her pit pass had gone to someone else.

Still, it sounded impressive.

"Well la-di-dah," Dennis said archly, waggling his hand. He was not entirely sober. "I guess you're one of those women who thinks she can do just fine without a man."

For some reason the statement made Winter think of Grey again; if she concentrated, she could almost imagine him here, now, one slanting golden eyebrow raised and a mocking smile of deliberation playing about his mobile mouth.

"Denny—" Janelle said.

"Shut *up,* Neenie; I'm talking to our guest. Isn't that right, *Miz* Musgrave, that you're one of those women who thinks she's as good as a man?"

I'm as good as some and better than some. And you aren't even a man, Dennis Raymond—you're a willful, spoiled brat and someone should spank you. Hard.

There was the sound of shattering glass from the kitchen and Winter started guiltily. Had she caused that breakage?

Dennis swore and shoved his chair back. "Gaw-dam *kids,*" he said, his words more slurred than they had been a moment ago. He lurched to his feet and shambled off in the direction of the kitchen.

Winter looked at Janelle.

"The local kids," Janelle said. "They throw rocks at the house. They broke the kitchen window last week—cracked right across."

Oh no they didn't, Winter thought with despairing certainty. She heard another crash from the kitchen, and the ugly sound of Denny's cursing. She heard the kitchen door open and slam.

"He's gone outside. But he never finds them," Janelle said dejectedly.

This might be my only chance.

A clear cold sense of purpose cut across the tangled emotions of the evening, sharpening Winter's will and senses as if she'd inhaled pure oxygen. If she did not ask about Hunter Greyson now there might not be another chance.

"Jannie, do you remember Hunter Greyson? Do you remember Nuclear Circle—the things we used to do?"

Janelle's face lit up; she looked eager and wistful. "Oh, golly—Grey! I haven't thought about him in years! I guess the two of you broke up?" she asked Winter.

Or . . . something.

"So you don't hear from him?" Winter asked, just to be sure. It was only later that she realized that Janelle had sidestepped her question about Nuclear Circle completely.

"No." Janelle's face was losing its animation, regaining its defensive

mask of vagueness. "Maybe Ramsey does; I don't know. He's never mentioned him."

Denny Raymond stomped back into the dining room. His face was an
alarming shade of crimson, and he'd taken the opportunity in the kitchen
to refresh his drink. This time the short glass was half full of straight
bourbon—no ice.

"Well, your little friends got away again," he said to Janelle. "She en-
courages them," he added to Winter. "They're always sucking up to her,
hanging around—she feeds them, that's what it is, when honest to God,
they've got their own homes to go to, don't they?"

"Most of the women around here work," Janelle murmured apologetically. "All I do is—"

"All you do is get taken advantage of, Neenie, and don't forget I told
you. You don't work—I told you when I married you I was going to take
care of you, didn't I? And these guys that say it's okay for their wives to
work—well, you aren't going to be the one taking care of their kids—or
anything else of theirs for that matter—and when I catch those little bas-
tards . . ." His voice trailed off ominously, and he glared at both women
as if they'd contradicted him.

Was this what Denny thought of as taking care of his wife? Winter
wondered. For that matter, was this what Janelle had wanted out of their
marriage? Someone who would make all the decisions, take all her freedom, so she would not have to face the pressure of her own success or
failure?

Surely not. She'd been eight years younger when she'd married him,
and in the flush of romantic love. Surely she hadn't known what Dennis
Raymond was—or would turn into.

But she knew now. And she was still here.

There were several other unexplained noises during the rest of dinner,
but Denny didn't get up to investigate them. Instead he complained
about the quality of the meal, the housekeeping of the immaculate house,
and even about the way Janelle looked until it was all Winter could do to
hold her tongue. She could not keep the treacherous, dangerous thought
out of her mind that if the creature that stalked her—and which apparently, in defiance of the laws of space and time, was here in Rappahoag,

New Jersey, at the same time it stalked Glastonbury—wished to hurt and kill, here was one candidate who would not be missed. She prayed very hard that she had no influence over it, since if Denny turned up dead Winter would find it difficult to forgive herself, no matter how pleasurable the thought of his death was to contemplate now.

Finally dinner and dessert—a gooey bakery cake—were over, and Winter, hastily rising to her feet, thanked Janelle for a lovely evening while saying she had to go.

"I've got to hit the road bright and early tomorrow morning, you know. It's been terrific seeing you again, Jannie—and a pleasure to meet you as well, Mr. Raymond."

Winter had learned, on Wall Street, to lie passionately and convincingly on short notice, and she drew on those skills now.

"Yeah, stop by anytime." The inflection Denny put on his words turned them into their opposite. He did not get up; he merely stared into his empty glass.

Janelle went back to the guest room with Winter to retrieve her coat and purse. Winter just happened to be looking toward her as Janelle reached for the hanger, and that was how she saw the mottled green and yellow bruises that circled Janelle's wrist like a bracelet. She took no pleasure from having her suspicions confirmed.

"You could leave him, you know," she said to Janelle.

"Yeah." Janelle turned toward her, holding out the coat. "But where would I go? And what does it matter, anyway? I'm not anybody."

"Yes you *are*," Winter told her fiercely.

But she knew that no words of hers would pierce the impenetrable hedge of psychic thorns that Janelle had woven around herself. Denny, monster though he was, was only the tool by which Janelle Baker—clever, talented Janelle—had made it impossible for herself to succeed and unnecessary even to try. And for that form of freedom Janelle would pay any price.

Even this.

Janelle saw where Winter was looking and pushed the sleeve of her sweatshirt back down so it covered the bruises.

"It . . . it's only sometimes. But he doesn't mean it," Janelle said dully. "It was an accident, really."

Winter wondered with a flash of despair just how many other marks the baggy, all-encompassing green sweatsuit hid. And she knew that with no one to stop him, Denny Raymond would go from sometimes to always—if he hadn't already—and that at his fists someday Janelle would find in truth the oblivion she sought.

"How could it happen?" Winter asked, and it wasn't the beatings that she meant. Janelle shrugged, and now there were tears glittering in her eyes.

"I don't know, Winter. You make choices, and by the time you figure the first one wasn't that good and ought to be unmade, you've already made five more on top of it, then ten—and you can't go back. It's just easier, I guess, to let it ride. Because you're all tangled up, and even if you could get loose and shove everything back to square one, the chances you thought you had when you were twenty are all gone—and there's no way you could have known how they were going to work out anyhow. I'm just not that brave."

Winter nodded, biting her lip to keep from crying. "If I could—"

Janelle put a hand on her arm.

"It's too late, Winter. It's too late for all of us. Even for Grey, wherever he is. It's too late."

CHAPTER EIGHT

WINTER AND ROUGH WEATHER

Blow, blow, thou winter wind,
Thou art not so unkind
As man's ingratitude.
—WILLIAM SHAKESPEARE

BACK IN HER NEAT, ANTISEPTIC HOTEL ROOM—AS SOUL-less and bland as Janelle's house but with more justification—Winter paced and fretted. She was not completely well even yet, and should have been exhausted from the long drive and everything that had happened that day, but somehow the frustration energized her until her body and mind were racing like an engine with no cut-off switch. How could she leave Janelle in that horrible situation, married to a man who beat her and despised her?

And who would someday kill her. Someday soon. Truth Jourdemayne might have called it a psychic flash; Winter Musgrave only knew that it was an unwelcome and unprovable intuition that she had no trouble at all believing. And the guilty, angry suspicion that Janelle would welcome that release did nothing to make Winter feel better.

All her life Winter had been a realist—accepting with good grace or at least good manners the things she could not change, however much she hated them. *And I did hate them—a lot of them, anyway.* But the daily realities of Janelle's life filled her with a monstrous sense of *unfairness;* even if Janelle were afraid of her artistic talent, surely she did not have to be punished so much for choosing not to use her gifts.

That horrible, pompous, arrogant, mean-spirited little hypocritical coward of a man! Winter dug her nails into her palms until the flesh bled. Dennis Raymond's face filled her mind's eye. He was not evil—she had a hazy acquaintance with evil, at least enough to know what it was not—but he was the sort that let evil in, and then whined afterward, desperate to escape the consequences of the actions they'd relished at the time.

Warmth and strength filled her, a tingling rush of power that was curiously numbing, though Winter felt achingly alert. The inoffensive neutral tones of carpet, walls, and bedspread that made up the Marriott bedroom seemed to take on vividness, as though they were painted with light, and the plain yellow illumination of the lamp on the dresser seemed to be filled with patterns of coruscating color. She felt a hot congested warmth beneath her heart; a predatory certainty. . . .

The row of cosmetics lined up on the dresser began to dance upon its surface, trembling as if perturbed by a small earthquake. With horrified intuition, Winter saw the hate-serpent that lived inside her wake, its aura pressing out through the surface of her skin until she could look down and see a shimmering mist of sequin-bright scales overlaying her skin, as the monstrous intolerant guardian within her spread its patterned hood and sought for prey.

No!

Winter sank slowly to her knees, the faint trembling of the objects on her dresser sounding as loud as the rumblings of an avalanche in her ears. She would not let this happen here—the creature that stalked her, the *magickal child,* that creature she could not control—but the poltergeist, born of her very marrow, should be hers to command. She could master this shameful shadow-twin; she'd found that out that night at the Institute. But the tension in her body was nearly sexual in its intensity, unambiguously demanding release. Winter nearly panicked and surrendered to its craving—but to panic would be to lose all.

To panic would be to *fail.*

Winter drew the refusal to fail about her like an icy cloak, like the season for which she was named. She tried to concentrate, but could not remember what would stop the thing that drew its life from her, and it had seduced her on until she was far too keyed-up to release the energy and the tension within her.

She took a deep breath, forcing her lungs to expand against the iron weight crushing her chest. And having nothing else left to fight with, she set her mind and her bare will against the power in which she still only half believed.

No. I will not let you. They aren't yours to play with. They aren't mine to make over in my own image. They're people—they belong to themselves, and what they choose to do is their own business, even if what they do makes me unhappy. Leave them alone. I do NOT *give you permission to act in my name!*

The power raged through her; she was flame, within and without, surrendering even her name. The only thing she clung to was that she would have her own way—what *she* wanted was what would happen, and anything that lived in her, or worked through her, would learn to understand that.

But it was a long hard fight.

Winter awoke as dawn was coming in through the open curtains. She was lying on the floor of her hotel room. Her gray flannel skirt was rumpled and her pantyhose were run; every muscle was stiff and she felt sick and light-boned as if she'd been on the mother of all benders. When she sat up, a bolt of pain behind her eyes made her cry out in protest.

What was I drinking—furniture polish?

She managed to make it all the way to the bathroom before she threw up what was left of last night's dinner, retching until her entire torso ached with the spasms and her throat felt raw and scoured. There were bruises on her forearms as if she'd been grappling with something—or, more likely, had banged into the hotel furniture while she was on the floor. The marks were black with angry red centers; severe and painful. Bruises that would take a long time to heal.

Bruises like the ones on Janelle's arms.

Winter repressed a reflexive pang of hatred for Denny, letting it sweep away in the dawning realization of what she'd done. She'd gotten her own way. She'd won, even if it'd almost killed her. The serpent had not struck—all her instincts said so.

Before—in Glastonbury and at the Bidney Institute—she'd panicked and been too weak. Her unconscious mind had been able to seize control and throw its angry tantrum, acting out a rage that Winter could not fathom the source of. But now she was stronger. And she'd stay stronger— and be ready for it the next time it decided to coil up out of its lair.

A poltergeist, eh? Well, we'll see who's going to haunt whom!

She tried to stand then and found she couldn't, no matter how great a victory she'd won the night before. On hands and knees Winter crawled out of the bathroom—ruining her clothes further—and dragged her purse down off the bed where she'd carelessly slung it. She dug through its considerable contents with dogged desperation until she found Tabitha Whitefield's battered little pamphlet, tucked in between two fresh packets of Centering Tea. Slumped on the floor, holding her eyes open with an effort of will, Winter began at last to read.

Half an hour later, the raging hunger that hammered her body was so great that Winter realized it would be impossible to concentrate until she'd done something about it. Cudgeling her brains to remember what Truth and Dylan had said about first aid for psychics, she scrambled awkwardly over to the built-in bar. With a reckless disregard for the charges that would appear on her room bill later, she opened the small refrigerator and crammed her mouth full of chocolate, then slugged down a can of Coke Classic. The quick sugar fix cleared her brain; sipping a second Coke more slowly, she placed a call to Room Service—

"I'd like some waffles or pancakes or something—whatever's fastest. Hot water for tea. And lots and lots and lots of maple syrup."

—and then retreated to the bathroom to finish cleaning up.

Two more cans of Coke and a couple of candy bars later—the sugar seemed to vaporize as it hit her bloodstream—her breakfast arrived. Winter dumped Centering Tea into a carafe of hot water to steep, and tucked into scrambled eggs and French toast with a morning appetite she hadn't felt in longer than she could remember.

As she ate, Winter read through the pamphlet a second time. The "centering" (centering *what?* Winter wondered) exercises started out very simply—timing and counting breaths—and then went on to what Tabitha called directed visualization. First Winter was to imagine a white square, and when she could do that, she was to go on to a blue circle. Finally, when she had also mastered holding the image of a red triangle in her mind's eye without distraction, she was to attempt to see all three at once, superimposed one on the other, while she breathed slowly and regularly and sensed her body's energy flowing in a regular circuit from the top of her head through the soles of her feet and back to the top of her head again.

Sounds loony, Winter declared, *but at this point what have I got to lose?*

She almost wished she could call the Institute and ask Truth's opinion of the practice—she'd formed a stronger bond with the young researcher than she yet wanted to admit—but realized that to do that would simply be to entangle herself further with Truth Jourdemayne and Dylan Palmer. And this particular quest was something she had to accomplish alone.

Only, if the point is to outrun the thing that tried to kill Truth and seems to be fixated on me, I'm not doing a very good job of it. It seems to be here ahead of me, at Janelle's house.

Everything Janelle had mentioned—the vandalism, the dead animals—pointed to the artificial Elemental rather than to Winter's poltergeist, but Winter somehow felt she was being offered a stalking horse. As if, even if the creature were here before her, its true motive in tormenting Janelle was to force *Winter* to surrender to it.

Well, I won't, Winter vowed simply. *Now, who's next on the list?*

The next name that Nina Fowler had given her was Ramsey Miller, and Janelle had also mentioned being recently in touch with him. Winter took out the copy of the 1982 Taghkanic yearbook that she'd bought in Glastonbury and stared at the picture of a youthful Ramsey Miller wearing long sideburns and a soup-strainer mustache. His hair curled over the edge of his dark turtleneck in an oddly antique fashion. She wondered what he looked like now.

So Ramsey's next, but do I really want to go on with this? Ramsey might be— oh, anything. I can call—I really ought to call today—but that won't tell me what he's going to be like. Janelle sounded all right on the phone yesterday, but then look what happened. What if he and Cassie—and even Grey, if I find him—are the same way? All . . . changed?

It would be a two- or three-day drive to Ramsey's home in Dayton, Ohio—closer to four, Winter told herself with brutal frankness, if she considered how tired she was likely to get and how many stops she'd have to make along the way. She could drive to Newark Airport, though, and be in Ohio within a couple of hours by plane.

And if the plane's electrical system blows on the way? Not that it was really likely—the serpent fed on her emotions, and, at least so far, it had never managed an appearance when she was completely calm. But while the need to reach Ramsey was imperative, now that she'd seen Janelle, Winter felt strangely reluctant to see what cruel tricks Time had played on her other college friends. A few days by car wouldn't make a lot of difference, she told herself, and that way she'd still have her car with her when she arrived in Dayton and wouldn't need to rent one.

As Janelle had said, places were different distances depending on who was going there. Winter thought that for her, the distance between Rappahoag, New Jersey, and Dayton, Ohio, would be short enough to drive.

But going anywhere at all today would be foolish. Winter spent the morning in a hot bath—much to the annoyance of the maids, who wanted to turn out the room—and in the afternoon she called Janelle again. She had to be completely sure that something terrible hadn't happened to her—or to Denny—last night.

"Hello?" Janelle's voice was slurred and slow as she answered the phone, although it was well after one in the afternoon.

"Janelle?" A sudden pang of terror made everything go faint and cold. "Is Denny all right?"

"He's at work," Janelle said dully. "He's fine." There was a ghost of resentment in Janelle's voice, and it was all too easy for Winter to imagine the reason her friend sounded that way. A sudden fierce prayer filled her heart.

Grey Angels, whatever you are, come down from the Hudson and look into Denny's heart. And Janelle's, too. But make something right happen in her life. . . .

"It's Winter, Jannie. How are you?"

"Oh . . . hi, Winter. I didn't . . . I thought you had to get an early start?" Janelle's voice was leaden, her interest forced.

"My plans changed. Look. We didn't get a lot of chance to talk yesterday, why don't I come out, and—"

"I'm busy." There was life in Janelle's voice now—life, and fear. "I've got a lot of things to do today, and—"

"Jannie!" Winter cried.

"Go away," Janelle whispered. "Just—go away." The line went dead.

*   *   *

Winter stared at the phone in her hand until the strident warble of the off-hook sound dragged her attention back to the present. Slowly she hung up the line.

There were people she could call about what was happening to Janelle, agencies she could notify. She could even call the police. But if Janelle refused to acknowledge what was going on, refused to admit what was happening, there was so little anyone could do for her. The transformation had to come from within. Winter couldn't accomplish it for her.

Winter stared at the Taghkanic yearbook on the bed. It was open now to Janelle's picture. She could still see the ghost of that girl in the woman she'd visited yesterday, but that girl had been fearless.

Or had seemed to be . . .

Winter turned the page in the yearbook, and looked at the smiling, dark-haired young man in the turtleneck and dark jacket. Time had not yet written its book on the pages of his face; it was an innocent face, lacking, in 1981 when the yearbook picture had been taken, the ingrained stamp of personality. Her flickering memories of Ramsey were all sunny, with never a cloud.

But how much had changed for him in fourteen years?

"Don't give up now."

The words and the tone were Grey's, dredged up out of some sinkhole of traitorous memory. If she turned the page of the yearbook Winter could see his frozen image—but if she closed her eyes, she could see him leaning against the wall of the hotel room, wearing cowboy boots and blue jeans tighter than sin, arms crossed over a snugly fitting Taghkanic College T-shirt, regarding her mockingly through lowered lashes.

"Don't give up now. Work yourself up to the verge of success and quit then. Be a BIG *failure."*

She opened her eyes, but of course there was no one there. There never had been. The wisp of memory remained, however: Hunter Greyson, perverse overachiever. She turned to his page in the yearbook and stared at his portrait. The face that looked back at her was unfinished. So . . . young. Innocent in a way, although of course they'd all thought themselves the height of sophistication at the time.

Winter felt a faint smile tug at the corners of her mouth. She could feel the pull on the muscles with the unaccustomed use; she hadn't had any reason to smile in a long time. But Grey had always had the knack for turning disaster inside out like a paper bag; things still were just as important, but somehow they managed not to hurt as much.

She could use a little of that knack now.

Where was Grey, and could she find him? With money and private detectives almost anyone could be unearthed from anywhere, from Elvis to your birth-mother, but private detectives took time—sometimes years—to find a person, and even though Winter had a lot of money and an investment portfolio that brought in a tidy sum each year, if she went on spending like Ivana Trump, there'd be a piper to be paid sometime. She closed the yearbook and slipped it into her suitcase again. Going on as she had been still seemed to be the best choice—at least until something changed.

Or until the creature stalking her lost its patience.

It took Winter the rest of the afternoon to work up the nerve to call Ramsey. She'd dialed the number several times and hung up before the fourth ring, and in between she'd even called Cassie in Berkeley, although Cassie's number just rang and rang until Winter had hung up in disgust. How *could* Cassie not be there when Winter was actually feeling brave enough to talk to her?

At 8:00—7:00 Ohio time—Ramsey finally picked up the phone.

"Hello?"

For a moment Winter sat paralyzed on the edge of the hotel bed, listening to the half-remembered voice across the miles.

"Hello?" Ramsey said again.

"Ramsey Miller?" Her voice was a dry croak.

"Who is this?" There was a thread of suspicion in the pleasant masculine tenor now, as if he might be about to hang up—and if he did, Winter wasn't sure she had the courage to call him back.

"I don't think you remember me; my name is Winter Musgrave; we went to school together? College?"

"Winter!" The warmth that filled his voice made her giddy with relief. "Of course I remember you—where are you? Are you in town?"

"I'm in New Jersey, Ramsey, but I was thinking of coming out to Dayton and seeing you, if that would be okay?"

She suddenly realized that she and Janelle had done almost no talking yesterday about their shared past and their college days—the one thing you'd expect old friends meeting after a long separation to do. Yesterday had challenged none of the blanks in Winter's memory. She had to make sure things would be different with Ramsey.

"Okay? It'd be great! You're calling at a good time; things are pretty quiet here—"

With a sinking heart she heard the change in Ramsey's voice; the tension that meant there was something he didn't want to say—something bad. Winter resolved to go anyway. *At least I won't find him being beaten by his husband. I hope.*

"—so I can meet your plane. When is it coming in?" Ramsey finished, and Winter realized she'd lost a few sentences out of the conversation.

"I'm going to be driving, Ramsey; I've got a new car and I'm dying to break it in," Winter said with spurious cheer. "Is there a good hotel in the area?"

In OHIO? a part of her mind asked in mocking disbelief.

"Hotel, nothing. You're staying out at my place, and I don't want to hear any arguments. Look, I'll give you directions—"

There was nothing to do but accept gracefully, though Winter privately assured herself that she was more than capable of finding a hotel and checking into it before she met with Ramsey. For some reason it seemed important to have a secure line of retreat available, just as if Ramsey Miller had ever been capable of hurting anyone in his entire life.

But did she really remember what Ramsey had been like, or was this just another layer of smoke and mirrors?

They chatted for a few minutes more, with Ramsey giving her directions to his place from I-80, the interstate that had replaced old Route 66 as the preferred means of automobile travel from coast to coast. Winter promised to give him a call the day after tomorrow to let him know how far away she was, and after a few more half-empty pleasantries, Winter hung up.

She stared at the telephone pensively. Would meeting Ramsey again be of any more use to her than seeing Janelle had? There was no reason to do it, otherwise.

Then don't do it, the inner serpent-voice suggested. *Janelle's a loser, Ramsey's a loser—you're the only one who played it smart, who got into the game. And you won big, too—don't forget that. One look at you and good old Ramsey's prob-*

ably going to hit you up for a loan. He probably just wants to see you to ask you for money, anyway. Who needs the aggravation? Don't go.

Winter rose to her feet and crossed the carpet. She'd drawn the curtains earlier, but now she pulled back both the printed room-darkening shade and the sheer liner to look out.

There wasn't much to see; just New Jersey and a scrap of the New York skyline in the distance beckoning like the towers of Camelot. Winter spread her fingers against the glass, pushing gently at the cold slickness with her palms. The bridges connecting the two states, lit for night, looked like expensive diamond necklaces, so tiny that Winter could imagine lifting one up and clasping it about her throat, there to burn like captive stars.

She could be home in her apartment in an hour. Chuck it all, get back to her life—maybe two weeks in Saint Barts to round things off, and then see if Arkham Miskatonic King was interested in hiring her back. Not this . . . shadowboxing.

The serpent-coils shifted beneath her skin, the serpent wondering if it had won.

No. Even if she surrendered to the serpent and let it take over her life once more, there would still be the other thing—the creature that Truth had summoned into her magic circle at the Bidney Institute, the thing that killed squirrels and rabbits and deer and left their bloodless corpses for Winter to find. The thing that Truth said was a magician's servant, an artificial Elemental sent to seek Winter out.

Why?

It always came back to "why," and the answer was hidden in the place Winter could not reach—her past. She could not stop now. She had to go on. If Ramsey kept in touch with Janelle, he might be in touch with Cassie—and Grey.

When it was that Winter had developed the notion that Grey could help her—never mind "would"—she wasn't sure. Dr. Luty would have pegged it as wishful thinking, one more defense against personal responsibility. Make someone else a talisman, and you absolved yourself of all need to do anything yourself. In Dr. Luty's cosmology, everyone was completely and personally responsible for everything that happened to them.

A comforting idea, but what if it's wrong? Winter watched the cars crawl by like glowing insects on the streets below. *What about all the times that it IS wrong?*

Still, the notion that she was only searching until she found somebody who could fix her life grated on Winter's sense of fitness. She wasn't doing that—was she? The poltergeist was her problem, and she was handling it herself, as was right.

But the other . . . to think she could handle the other alone was true madness.

Either the door and windows of the Marriott were exceptionally poltergeist-proof, or whichever of the entities tormenting her was responsible for unlocking doors and opening windows had taken the night off. Winter awoke to a hotel room that was no messier than it had been when she'd gone to sleep the night before, packed her bags and settled her bill, and was on her way by 9:00.

By noon she had reached the Delaware Water Gap, once the gateway to the West, and now the gateway to Pennsylvania. Despite the sprawling urban blight—and it really was a blight, Winter decided, studying the eight lanes of highway flanked by expanding shopping malls critically—the region was genuinely pretty, and there were some places along the road that looked just as they must have thirty or even fifty years before, when America was a slumbering giant, just awakened from sleep by two world wars. Winter stopped for lunch at a diner that looked as if it had been dropped down on the roadside fresh from a time machine, and decided that no matter how early it was she ought to find someplace to spend the night. Pennsylvania was something like 700 miles of signs saying BRIDGE FREEZES BEFORE ROAD SURFACE, and she was going to have to drive past every single one to reach Dayton, Ohio.

"Do you know of any place around here I can spend the night?" Winter asked the fresh-faced waitress in jeans and a polo shirt who brought her pie and coffee. Winter had never had a sweet tooth before, but now it seemed as if her metabolism ran on sugar—the quick burst of energy and the equally quick slide into insulin-induced weariness. Either state was preferable to the jittery overstimulated panic that presaged one of her poltergeist attacks, though Winter didn't worry about them so much now that she knew there was some hope of controlling them.

"Some place to stay? Well, there's the Hilton back up the road," the waitress said.

Winter had passed it on her way here, and felt a pang of distaste at the thought of its hundreds of sterile identical rooms. "I was hoping for something a little friendlier," she said hopefully.

"You mean like a Bed-and-Breakfast? Well, there's Lily Douglas's place. There's one of her cards over there on the wall; you could call her and see if she's got a bed free tonight," the waitress said dubiously. It was clear that she could not imagine anyone passing up the chance to stay in a Hilton's luxurious accommodations.

Oh, but there are better things than perfection. . . .

"Perfection is so deadly dull. No wonder Eve kicked the serpent out of Paradise," Grey said.

The voice was so real that Winter, rising off the counter stool to go in search of Lily Douglas's number, actually looked around to see who was speaking. But it was only Grey, popping up out of memory and imagination once more to offer up his opinions.

This time her mind presented him to her as he'd been his sophomore year at Taghkanic. They'd done *Camelot,* and he'd been Mordred. She saw him now, in dusty Danskin tights and black ballet flats, wearing a shabby moth-nibbled green doublet that would look glorious from across the footlights, gilded by theatrical magic. In her mind, Grey swung back his cloak and rested his black-gloved fingers on the hilt of his dagger.

"As Mordred says, virtue can be deadly. And as Blackburn teaches, every virtue, carried to its extreme, becomes a vice—usually when it starts dictating the behavior of someone else."

The memory dissolved. Was this something Grey had said to her, or was it her wistful mind manipulating his image like a puppet to give her good advice? It didn't matter; whether the words came from Grey or from her own mind, they were worth heeding.

They just don't seem particularly applicable right now, Winter thought, staring at the bulletin board. *Why should I be worrying about virtue—or perfection?*

The Water Gap Diner was the sort of place that had a cork board where the locals could pin up business cards and notices. Most of them were for snowplowing, game butchering, or taxidermy, but eventually

Winter found the one she was looking for. It was on pearlized pink stock printed with raised lavender ink and said *Justamere Bed-and-Breakfast,* with the name—Lily Douglas—a phone number, and a street address that was meaningless to Winter. She carried it over to the pay phone.

Two weeks ago you'd have cut your throat rather than telephone a stranger and go to a strange house. True, but those hadn't been the actions of her real self, but the actions of a Winter Musgrave who was sick, frightened, and all but beaten. *And two years ago you'd have cut your throat rather than be seen in such a tacky, unfashionable place as this,* her malicious other self added.

But that woman—that sleek Wall Street shark—wasn't the real Winter either, was she? Winter could not go back to living that stranger's rapacious, self-centered life—but if she didn't step back into that life, where was she going to go?

The phone was answered on the third ring.

"Hello?" A kindly voice, far from young but without the fragile breathiness of true old age. "Justamere Bed-and-Breakfast. Lily Douglas."

It was only then that Winter understood the play on words in the name—*Just a Mere Bed-and-Breakfast*—and amusement colored her voice as she replied.

"I need a room for tonight; I know it's short notice, but the lady at the Water Gap Diner said you were local and might have something."

"Well bless her heart! You tell Amy that good angels must be watching over her—I just had a cancellation—well, a postponement—this morning. Only it's a double," Lily Douglas went on conscientiously, "and you might not want to take it because it's so large; it's my best room with a bath and all. . . ."

"Why don't I come out and see it," Winter said. And if it wasn't to her taste, there was always the Hilton back up the road.

Justamere Bed-and-Breakfast was only five miles from the diner. This part of the Delaware–New Jersey border was farm country; on both sides of the road the trees were rich with new leaf and in the fields tiny spears of green were poking up through last winter's dead stubble. Winter was almost certain she had gone too far when she rounded a curve in the road and saw it.

How in the world did something like that get all the way out here? she wondered.

The old Victorian house had been built in the style known as Queen Anne Gothic, with garlanded turrets, bay windows, and gingerbread lace and jigsaw ornamentation everywhere. It was painted a pale custard yellow with the detailing picked out in white, and looked pretty enough to eat. The gravel driveway was wide enough to accommodate half a dozen cars at once, and Winter felt no qualms about pulling her Saturn in beside what looked like a battered old farm truck.

The door was answered by a pleasant woman in her fifties, figure long gone to matronly plumpness. She was wearing a cardigan sweater over a flowered cotton housedress and perfunctory makeup. Winter waited for the reflexive condemnation from within, but for once it didn't come, although Society would certainly have judged Winter to be the "better" of the two women.

Okay, so she'd probably be a failure on Wall Street. But for that matter, I don't know how to run a Bed-and-Breakfast, do I? Winter told herself.

"Ms. Douglas," Winter said aloud, "I'm Winter Musgrave—we spoke on the phone? I'm here about the room."

"Of course you are!" Lily Douglas said. "Come in and take a look—do you have any luggage? I'll just get Gary to bring it in. Gary! *Gareth!*" she raised her voice. "You come down here right now!"

Almost instantly Winter heard the clatter of footsteps on the stairs, and a moment later Gary-or-Gareth appeared.

"This is Gary—Gareth Crowther. He takes care of what needs doing—and in a place this big and this old, that's everything."

Gareth was a big bluff hearty puppy-dog of a man, with untidy blond hair and soft blue eyes and muscles worthy of a lumberjack bulging the fabric of his red-and-black flannel shirt.

"Hello," he said, holding out a painfully clean and callused hand for Winter to shake. "I got the storms off in the tower, Mrs. Douglas, so I can open up the windows now to paint the third-floor back."

"Good boy," Mrs. Douglas said, as if Gareth were the slow and patient draft animal he so much resembled. "But you just wait around—this is Ms. Musgrave that I told you might be coming and taking the Lilac Room, so you just hold on and see if she needs anything moved."

Gareth nodded seriously.

"I'm sure I'll love it," Winter said, gazing around the parlor. Her fears of shabby untidiness had been groundless. The immaculately clean front room of Justamere Bed-and-Breakfast was decorated in the Victorian high style of the era in which the house had been built. The fireplace was of white marble, carved with elongated sphinxes on each upright, and the face of the fireplace carried out the Egyptian motif, with lotuses and scarab beetles embossed into its sky-blue tiles. There was a high Victorian settee in carved rosewood flanked by matching chairs with crocheted doilies on their backs and arms and surrounded by half a dozen little tables. The whole room had a jumbled, lived-in feel to it, as if uncounted generations had lived and played here and loved each other and the house.

"Four generations in the same house," Mrs. Douglas said. "That's what putting down roots means, but with things the way they are these days, who'll want this place when I'm gone? I don't have anyone to leave it to unless one of my daughters comes to her senses, but I suppose nobody wants to live in the middle of nowhere any more."

As she spoke, Mrs. Douglas conducted Winter up the stairs and down a brightly lit hall. Each of the closed white doors had an oval brass plaque screwed into the wood.

"You're in Lilac; I have to keep track of the rentals for the tax-man somehow, so I thought I'd name all the rooms after the flowers I did them up in. There's Rose and Violet down the hall, and Daisy across the way, that's the other double." She unlocked the door—the interior lock was the first indication Winter had been given that she was not in a private home—and ushered Winter inside.

Winter looked around at a large spacious room with an Oriental carpet on the floor and wallpaper covered with sprigs of lilacs. A vase of lilacs—silk at this time of year, but pretty nonetheless—stood on the dressing-table, and through the half-open door at the other end of the room, Winter could see the promised bathroom. Dominating the room was a massive four-poster canopy bed, with a crisp white bedspread and masses of lilac-printed pillows mounded on it.

"I'll take it," Winter said instantly.

Mrs. Douglas explained that the room came with a Continental breakfast, and that she could only have it for two nights at most, as the couple who had reserved it would be arriving after that. The price she quoted was, of course, higher than Winter would have paid to stay in a Hilton, but it was worth it, Winter felt, to stay in a place that did not have the cold institutional feel of a chain hotel.

"Probably arriving, I should say, but I did promise to have it for them," Mrs. Douglas said. "And I like to keep my word to folks—or why give it?"

"I won't be any trouble, Mrs. Douglas. I'm planning to leave tomorrow morning, anyway," Winter said.

"Virtue in the defense of extremism is no vice," Grey said, punningly, out of the depths of Winter's memory.

More riddles.

Winter unlocked the trunk of her car and let Gary carry the bags into the house before he returned to what must presumably be the ongoing renovation of Justamere. Gary hefted the two large suitcases and the carry-on bag as if they weighed nothing at all, and Winter thought he could probably have carried her as well without any particular problem. He brought the bags up the stairs and into the room—two on the floor, one on the pretty embroidered suitcase stand—before leaving to resume the painting of the third-floor back.

"If you need anything, Ms. Musgrave, you just ask Mrs. Douglas. She's usually downstairs in the parlor."

"Thank you, Gary. I will." You didn't tip-as-you-went in a Bed-and-Breakfast, but Winter made a mental note that Gary Crowther deserved a generous remembrance when she left. Those bags weren't light—and besides, he hadn't leered at her legs once.

He closed the door behind him as he left and Winter was alone in the room. It was only midafternoon, and a guilty part of Winter's mind reminded her that she could have gotten in four or five more hours of driving before dark.

But I don't want to get so tired that I can't keep the poltergeist under control— and what if the magickal child *finds out where I've gone?* Winter told herself. She opened her suitcase but didn't feel any impulse to unpack—and she'd be leaving tomorrow morning, anyway.

If nothing more went wrong.

Winter sat down on the edge of the bed and pulled Tabitha Whitfield's pamphlet out of her purse. *Besides, I can get in a couple of hours of psychic aerobics before it's time for bed.*

With Mrs. Douglas's guidance, Winter located a local restaurant where, if the food wasn't quite up to Manhattan standards, she was able to make a tolerable meal. Driving into the driveway at Justamere afterward, she looked up at the floodlit exterior and the warm light coming from the expansive windows. *I'd like to have a house like that,* was her automatic thought. But not to live in alone, nor to run as an inn. A house like that was for children, a family; a place to share with the right man.

The direction her thoughts were taking pulled her up short, even as the car coasted to a halt. Husband? Family? Winter had always dismissed marriage out of hand before, and now, in her thirties, she suspected she was getting too set in her ways to compromise enough, even for love, to be able to make a home with someone else. And certainly no "right man" had ever presented himself.

Maybe you're looking in the wrong place. The image of Hunter Greyson flitted across her mind again and Winter sighed. If—when—she found Grey, he'd probably introduce her to his wife and their two adorable children. He was her age, after all; they'd been in college together. By the time they reached their thirties, most people knew the direction they wanted their lives to go in and were settled somewhere. They'd become what they wanted to be.

The way that Janelle did?

Automatically Winter rejected the thought. Janelle hadn't become what she'd wanted to be; she'd opted for safety instead, and even if it was a poisonous sort of refuge, at least Janelle had known what she was running away from.

It was only Winter who still didn't know what to run from . . . or to. Or scratch that—who'd known once but discovered she was wrong.

She got out of the car slowly and locked it, then turned toward the steps. There was one thing this wild Grey-chase was doing for her, and that was postponing the moment when she would have to try to reenter the current of her normal life and make a success of it once more.

Whatever it turned out to be.

And assuming she lived to do it.

That night, lying in her canopied bed in the Lilac Room, Winter dreamed of Grey.

She stood in a dream-landscape, knowing she wouldn't remember the dream once she awoke. It was a place she'd been many times before, though she knew she wouldn't remember that either. The light was ghostly; Winter stood in the middle of a plain so vast it seemed to have no end, a horizonless place where the sky met the ground without any demarkation line. In the distance stood the remains of a ruined watchtower, alone in the emptiness, and, having no other goal, Winter headed for it.

A spectral wind plucked at her clothing, making a low irritating keening in her ears. Where was Grey? He was supposed to be here already, waiting for her.

As if her thoughts had invoked him, the scene changed: a dream within a dream. She sat at her desk in the Taghkanic dorm, working on a paper for her music class while Grey lay on the bed, her guitar across his stomach, plunking idly at the strings.

She looked over toward him, to where his blond hair spilled over her pillow, gleaming in the lamplight. His eyes were half shut, and lashes like dark honey nearly brushed his cheeks.

"What are you going to do after you graduate?" she asked him, and realized that this was a memory, not a dream. This had happened, once upon a time.

"Get rich, get famous, do whatever I want." Grey's answer was flip. "Be a singer in a rock 'n' roll band. What about you?"

I want to stay with you, Winter thought to herself, and Grey, as if reading her mind, set the guitar aside and held out his arms to her, his smile mocking and welcoming at the same time.

"Too much study makes you go blind," he said huskily.

She reached for him, but instead of flesh her hands touched jagged rock. She was back in the gray place again, and she cried out at the unfairness of it, at being snatched out of that lovely dream, away from Grey.

"Help me, Winter. Help me, my love."

Beneath her hands was the ruined stone of the watchtower, and half erupting from it was Grey's body, face and hands yearning toward the light, as if he had been trapped in the stone like an insect in amber, trapped forever—

"Leave me alone!"

And suddenly it was spring; the apple trees were in bloom, and petals were showering everywhere. . . .

* * *

Winter sat up in bed with a gasp, heart pounding. It was nearly two in the morning, the wolf hour, the hour when suicides and premeditated murders happen. The room was dark, with only a faint glow from the security lights outside the house penetrating the translucent curtains.

The images in her dream scattered, until all that was left was the memory of Grey and the feeling of panic—and the cloying scent of apple blossoms out of season. Winter took a deep breath. She couldn't remember having nightmares before, even at Fall River; only meaningless jumbled dreams that left her more tired than before when she finally awakened from them. Dr. Luty had tried to get her to tell him her dreams, as if knowing the trash her unconscious mind threw onto the beach of sleep would let him know *her.*

But this dream was different—both a true nightmare, and something worse. Winter got herself under control enough to switch on the bedside light, and the bright glow through the hobnail milk glass made the pretty Victorian room bright and defined. Any shadows left would be merely a trick of the light, and not messengers from the unseen world.

She rubbed her forehead. What had the dream been about? Something about Grey, and trouble. But not trouble that could still be averted. Trouble that had already happened. *But if it's already too late then why do I have to hurry . . . ?*

What utter nonsense. The thought was sharp and bracing, lending her strength. *I suppose that poltergeists have to be real, and maybe even the thing that chased you out of Glastonbury,* the brisk internal censor went on. *But just because those two things happened you don't have to embrace every half-baked idea from Spiritualism to UFOs! Prophetic dreams and poltergeists don't exactly go together. There's got to be a limit somewhere. You're upset, you're worried, you want to find Hunter Greyson—it doesn't take a rocket scientist to realize that this means you're probably going to dream about him. Like Freud said, sometimes a bad dream is just a bad dream.*

Winter drew a deep breath, uncertain of whether the thoughts were good common sense or hysterical denial. *A dream is just a dream,* she repeated, feeling her body relax. Every bad dream didn't have to be a message—if she started thinking that way, she'd be wearing crystals and looking for omens in tea-leaves next.

That's right. Just a dream. Not an omen.

The dream had left her too keyed-up to sleep, however, and she didn't want to run a bath at this hour for fear of disturbing Mrs. Douglas's other guests. With a sigh, Winter swung her legs over the edge of the bed and went looking for the pamphlet from *Inquire Within.* The way things stood, she wasn't going to get any sleep for a couple of more hours at least. Thank heavens she'd managed to be sensible about the whole thing, or she'd probably be in the middle of hysterics right now. And over a bad dream, no less!

It was not until many days later that she recognized those words of rationality for the trap they were.

CHAPTER NINE

EVERY MILE IS TWO
IN WINTER

It was not in winter
Our loving lot was cast!
—THOMAS HOOD

TO EYES ACCUSTOMED TO THE MANHATTAN SKYLINE, Dayton was a small clean city with a scattering of skyscrapers and no smog to speak of. It had taken Winter three days, taking the trip by easy stages, to cross Pennsylvania, and by the time she was done, she was heartily sick of the rolling landscape, the endless fields being planted with nameless springtime crops, and the signs for Stuckey's. Pulling into the traffic tangle that was Dayton's outer loop was almost a relief after the endless hours of high-speed highway driving.

There had been no more dreams or peculiar incidents of any sort, and though Winter continued to do the psychic exercises from the pamphlet and drink her Centering Tea, it was more for the help they gave her in falling asleep than for any arcane benefits. Her physical stamina was rapidly returning, her mirror told her she was putting back on the lost weight and softening the sharp edges of her gauntness, and she was beginning to wonder if the "artificial Elemental" that Truth had told her about might be nothing more than an elaborate network of coincidences. The smaller animals she'd found could easily have been a cat's prey, dragged so far from the place where they were killed to seem like bloodless deaths. The deer could be chalked up to poachers. Even the night at the Institute's lab probably hadn't happened the way she remembered it now—and the rest? Coincidence, hysteria, bad luck—it didn't even really matter if everything had happened as she thought it had, so long as it went away now. Hadn't Truth said that the poltergeist would just give up and go away at some point? Well, maybe it had. She should be glad the thing wasn't around to get up to its old tricks with her new car.

Winter felt more optimistic than she had in weeks. The problem hadn't been nearly as bad as she'd thought it was after all. And besides, it was over now.

Winter took the exit that Ramsey had indicated in his directions, and immediately found herself in the middle of the downtown area, lost in a bewildering tangle of secondary streets. Where was—? Oh, here it was. With a little more verve than prudence, Winter cut a sharp left and found herself on a main street: four lanes plus turn lanes divided by a grassy median, the edges dotted with fast-food restaurants and chain hotels.

This doesn't look much like a residential district. Or a business one.

She followed Ramsey's directions until large buildings gave way to small ones and to outlet warehouses, an area where real estate prices were lower. She'd nearly given up hope of finding the address when—

Oh, for heaven's sake.

Why couldn't he just have SAID *so?* she asked herself, even though she knew how much Ramsey Miller liked practical jokes—assuming they were harmless ones.

Winter hit her turn-signal and made a left just under the sign that said MILLER'S USED CARS.

She'd barely brought the car to a stop before Ramsey was walking out of the prefab office in her direction. She was pleased that she recognized him, even with the new mustache. He was of average height, with brown hair and eyes, and the years had been kind to him; he still had the same hairline he'd had in college, and had also escaped the swinging, pendulous beer-gut that so many men his age didn't seem to be able to avoid.

Winter got out of her car and stood beside it, waiting for him to reach her.

"What can I do for you today?" he asked, his tone professionally polite. He was wearing the loudest sport coat Winter had ever seen—a polyester horror of green and yellow and orange plaid, with a few red and blue stripes thrown in for good measure.

"You can throw away that jacket for starters; it's the most horrible thing I've ever seen," Winter said, smiling.

Ramsey's face lost its expression of formal politeness and broke into a genuine grin of recognition.

"Winter! I told you to call me the day before you got here!" he said, enveloping her in a hug.

"I forgot," she said meekly, hugging him back, "and Dayton was closer than I thought it was. But just *look* at you."

"I'd rather look at you," Ramsey leered, in the style of a borscht-belt comic. "You look ter*ri*fic! What have you been doing? What brings you to my humble city?"

"I'm looking up old college friends—you know, the group?" The Blackburn group, Winter meant, but Ramsey didn't take her up on that.

"Well, when you find Grey, give him my best—and tell him I haven't forgotten about the twenty bucks he owes me. But come on inside—oh, don't worry about moving the car; Mike can keep an eye on it. Lends a touch of class to the place. And if I sell it, I'll make sure you get top price."

"Gee, thanks," Winter said mockingly. "And it isn't even mine."

"You're stealing cars these days?" Ramsey shot back, never missing a beat.

Ramsey's office bore a faint kinship with the place in Poughkeepsie that Winter had leased her car from: automotive calendars on the walls and clusters of tagged keys everywhere. Ramsey gestured, indicating she should sit where she liked, and Winter passed up the couch beneath the window in favor of one of the verging-on-antique chairs opposite the battered metal desk.

"Soda?" Ramsey said. Winter nodded, and he went over to a small refrigerator. "Coke all right?"

"Great." She'd never been one for sweets before—let alone soft drinks—but ever since these *things* had started happening, she couldn't keep away from the stuff. She'd developed a particular fondness for Classic Coke.

Carbonated glucose in a can. I don't even want to know what's in it, but knowing that plumbers soak fittings in it to get the rust off is enough for me. Despite her flip and mordant thoughts, Winter popped the top on the deposit can and poured the paper cup full. She drank, and let the sugar rush flush the weariness from her body for a while.

While Ramsey was getting his own drink, Winter took a surreptitious look around. The bright spring sunlight beat down on the cars outside in the lot, making the place look about as good as it ever would. Turning across four lanes of traffic she hadn't had much of a chance to look over Ramsey's place of business as she came in, but now Winter could see that none of the cars parked out there—with the exception of her leased Saturn—was less than five or six years old; almost obsolete by the standards of the market, and certainly not prime-quality preowned automotive goods.

It was true that the lot was clean and well kept—as were the cars—and the fluttering pennants and the gaudy sign lent a certain liveliness to the place, but with her finely honed predator's instincts, Winter was willing to bet that business at Miller's Used Cars was not so hot.

A used-car lot. Who would have thought it?

"So," Ramsey said, sitting down on the side of the desk, club soda in hand. "How've you been? As for me, I am as you see me."

"Pretty good, all things considered," Winter said, fencing cautiously. She might be willing to tell him about her inconvenient lapses of memory later, but at the moment, she wanted to feel her way into the conversation—and find out what had made Ramsey so cagey when she spoke to him on the phone.

"I went into Wall Street," Winter admitted, expanding on her story. "I did a whole *Bonfire of the Vanities* thing. I survived the eighties. Now I'm . . . taking some time out," she finished lamely.

"Don't worry about it; you'll get another job," Ramsey said with dismaying instinct. "Especially with your looks. You don't look a day older, you know."

"Neither do you." If it was stretching the truth, the truth wasn't being stretched too far. And she liked Ramsey. She always had. Even if he did automatically assume she'd been fired. "So, what are you doing these days?" she asked. It was a pallid conversational gambit, but at the moment Winter was more interested in normalcy than drama.

Ramsey nattered on about trivia, and Winter let the sound of his voice, his look, his gestures, carry her back to their shared days at Taghkanic. The tissue of evoked memory was too fragile to bear much weight, but even without being able to recall specific details, Winter could *sense* the time they'd spent together; the emotions they'd all felt for each other—all five of them.

But if that's true, why didn't the others stay together, even if I left? What happened to all of them?

More mysteries.

"—so after Ellie left, I got this place, and, I don't know, I think it's worked out pretty well," Ramsey was saying. "Who can ever be sure how their life is going to turn out at eighteen or twenty?"

"Ellie?" Truth was roused to a sense of her social responsibilities. "I never even asked—is there a Mrs. Miller? I don't want to come barging into your life like an old girlfriend." Which she'd never been—she and Ramsey had been that rarest of all male/female pairings: friends and nothing more.

Ramsey laughed ruefully. "Mrs. Millers? Several, but none of them wants to know me any more. I'm divorced, Winter—I just took it for granted that you knew, but of course there's no way you could. Number Three just left about a month ago—that was Laura. Ellie was Number Two, and Marina was the first one, back in 'eighty-three."

"Just out of college," Winter said. They'd all been Class of '82; Ramsey had graduated even if she hadn't. What had he gone on to do? She could almost remember. . . .

"I was working at the *Chicago Daily Sentinel* then, back in the good old days when I was going to have matched Pulitzers for my mantelpiece. But you don't want to hear about that." His tone was definite, and now Winter remembered clearly. Ramsey had been a journalism major; he'd been the one who was going to find the truth and change the world. "How long are you staying?" he added.

"What?" The question startled Winter out of her reverie; for a moment the world around her became hyperreal; from the slanting bars of sunlight across the dusty goldenrod rug to the dents and scratches in the old metal desk. Ramsey's office. The office of a used-car salesman, a stage-set in some horrible alternate reality to the future he should have had.

"Staying," Ramsey repeated patiently, "in Dayton. I admit it's not the garden spot of the universe, but its a nice little town; a person could do worse. Look, it's pretty dead here on the lot; I usually stick around until nine or so, but people don't buy used cars in the spring, and if anyone decides to buck the statistics, Mike can have the commission. Why don't you come on back to the house? You can have your pick of the bedrooms, although I admit they don't all still have beds in them."

When Winter reached Ramsey's house, carefully tailing his blue Subaru out into the Dayton suburbs, she found out he'd said nothing more than the truth.

Ramsey Miller lived in a development of the sort that realtors liked to call "better homes." The houses were good-sized, and some care had been taken by the architect and the landscaper to give each one a little individuality. Ramsey signaled and turned into the driveway, the automatic garage-door opener in his car raising the door of his attached two-car garage as he did. He pulled in on the left side with the ease of long practice. Winter pulled her car up beside his.

"All the comforts of darkest suburbia," Ramsey said with slightly forced cheer. There had been a blue-and-white realtor's For Sale sign stuck into the lawn, and the sense of failure, of abandonment, was strong.

"Ramsey, if this isn't a good time . . ." Winter said doubtfully.

He met her gaze directly, with the honesty that had always made him a good friend. "It's just as good a time as any other, Winter. Believe me. It wasn't a noisy divorce, and it's over. Laura has the kids and the bank accounts and she's moved back in with her family in Cleveland for a while. I've got the house—at least until it sells—and it's probably not going to sell in the next week, alas. You're welcome to stay here."

He pointed the control wand at the garage door and the door descended, shutting them into darkness once more. Moving through the dark with the ease of long habit, Ramsey made his way over to the wall and flipped a switch. The overhead light went on, throwing the walls and accumulated domestic debris into sharp relief. Winter could see the pale shadows on the walls where bicycles had hung.

Ramsey opened the kitchen door. "Come on. I'll give you the fifty-cent tour of *Chez* Miller."

The garage entrance led into a spacious yellow-and-white kitchen several steps up the social scale from Janelle's. It seemed oddly empty, and after a moment Winter realized why: The normal kitchen-counter clutter, from canisters on the counter to microwave, was absent.

"This," said Ramsey unnecessarily, "is the kitchen. I'll show you over the rest of the house and then we can decide what to do about dinner."

When Laura Miller had taken the kids and gone to Cleveland, Winter discovered a few minutes later, she'd also taken practically everything that wasn't nailed down. The four-bedroom ranch house was nearly empty—the dining room was bare, the living room held only a few pieces of furniture, and what—judging from the wallpaper—had been the kids' bedrooms were empty to the walls. Winter was only surprised that the woman hadn't taken the wallpaper, too.

"She seems to have been very thorough," Winter commented in what she hoped were neutral tones.

"Laura always was efficient," Ramsey said with a trace of pride. "I came home and the place was like this; she got the movers in while I was at work. Called me from Cleveland and let me know she was leaving me."

"Didn't you *mind?*" Winter asked disbelievingly. If anyone had done something equivalent to her, she would have hunted them down with a scalping knife, not recounted their exploits with this sort of fond proprietary delight.

"I guess I wasn't surprised; she put up with a lot before she called it quits. And it wasn't the first time I've been left. She played fair, though—left me the bedroom set and some of the living room furniture, and there's a fold-out couch in the guest room you can use. It was her office—Laura was a CPA; she kept up her business after we got married."

The former office was a small room about ten by twelve with a window that overlooked the house next door. It contained no furniture except the couch, and Winter wondered why that item had been spared. There was a couch in the living room, too. Perhaps the former Mrs. Miller didn't like couches?

But it would be a place to stay, at least for the night. And she wanted the chance to spend more time with Ramsey than she could over a piece of pie in some very public diner.

"It looks fine. If you're sure I'm not putting you out . . ." Winter said in a last token protest.

"How could you ever do that?" Ramsey said fondly. "One for all and all for one, remember?"

"Whoever is my brother or sister in the Art, let them be my brother or sister in all things." Winter shook her head, trying to dislodge the intrusive voice. *"Were you Sealed to the Circle?"* she remembered Truth saying. She and Ramsey had shared stronger bonds than blood or love once, so she was told.

"Okay," Winter said, capitulating gracefully. "You've sold me. Now, what about dinner?"

Either Laura Miller had taken all of the food with her, too—an idea Winter was not prepared to rule out—or Ramsey was no different than any other bachelor. Both the cupboards and the refrigerator were nearly bare. Ramsey volunteered that there was a supermarket not far from the house, and Winter proposed an expedition to it. Like most busy professionals— male or female, single or married—she wasn't much of a cook, but she could make an omelette and a salad providing she had the ingredients.

The grocery store seemed immense by East Coast standards—vast and gleaming and containing every item known to modern man, from potted plants to motor oil. In Ohio something called a "package store"—a liquor store—was attached to the supermarket, and Winter picked out several bottles of wine. White for tonight, red for some future meal. Maybe spaghetti; that was supposed to be easy, and maybe Ramsey was a better cook than she was. Winter filled the cart with whatever caught her fancy as she and Ramsey chatted, but some part of her knew the real talking would come later.

The Blackburn Work. *Venus Afflicted* was still in her suitcase, that biography of the magician whose "work" Truth said the five of them had repeated up at Nuclear Lake. What connection did their adolescent dabblings in whatever it had been have with what was happening to the members of the group today? She needed to talk to Ramsey . . . about that and so many other things.

* * *

By the time they got back to the house and had put their purchases away, the sky was growing dark and there were cars in the other driveways along the street. Winter opened one of the bottles of wine while Ramsey washed and diced ingredients for the omelette.

"But what about you?" Ramsey said, after a while. "It looks like I've been doing all the talking—you know about my wives, my kids, my gambling debts. . . ."

"Gambling debts!" Winter tried and failed to keep the shock out of her voice. *What can there possibly be to bet on in Ohio?*

"Oh, yes." Ramsey's voice was without regret. "I was quite the lad. In fact, when the house finally sells the money's going to be split between Household Finance and Laura; after I settle my debts there isn't going to be a lot left. No thanks," he said, as Winter offered him a glass of white wine. "I'm on the wagon these days." He sighed. "After Marina left and I lost my job—in no particular order, those two—I just felt numb. Placing a bet was a way of feeling something, and I told myself that at least I wasn't sniffing coke. Only they had to be *big* bets, and you could write the rest of this story in your sleep. So there's my dark secret; what's yours?"

"I had a nervous breakdown," Winter said quickly before she could censor herself. "Only I'm not really sure that's what it was. And . . . I'm trying to find out. That's all." She sipped her wine.

"That's the short version, anyway," Ramsey said. "But—other than that—are you okay? How are you fixed for cash? I don't have much, but a few thousand won't make any difference one way or the other."

"No, I'm fine," Winter said quickly. *And to think I expected him to hit* ME *up for money.* "At least I'm fine that way." *For now.*

Ramsey laughed sympathetically. " 'Partially fine, says former Wall street broker,' " he quipped. "Well, it'll do. But let's move on to the big questions of life—do you still like onions?"

Now that her biggest secret was out in the open Winter felt more at ease. Ramsey was happy to talk about old times—he'd been Grey's roommate at Taghkanic, something she'd forgotten.

"Everybody's an eccentric in college, but I've never met anyone like Grey—then or since," Ramsey said, waving a fluffy forkful of omelette. The built-in breakfast nook in the corner of the kitchen was one of the few parts of the house that had escaped unscathed, and when the food was ready, Winter and Ramsey had taken their plates and the bottle of wine there to eat.

"He really didn't care what other people thought of him, so long as he had a good opinion of himself. Oh, not arrogant, not exactly . . ." Ramsey said musingly.

But he had a tongue like a whip and less tolerance for human stupidity than anyone I ever knew, Winter finished silently. The one thing Grey had never understood was that people weren't being stupid on purpose—he'd really thought they could change if they were motivated enough. And Lord knew he'd done his best to motivate them. "There never was anyone like Grey," she agreed aloud.

"Which is probably a good thing when you come to think about it," Ramsey said solemnly, "because Grey didn't exactly lend himself to the quiet life. But you'd know that best."

I wish I did. "Do you keep in touch with him?" Winter asked with sudden hope.

"Don't you?" Ramsey sounded surprised.

She shook her head, surprised at the strength of her disappointment. "I was hoping you did."

Ramsey shook his head. "For a couple of years, yes, but you know how Grey was—detail-oriented wasn't his style. I'm surprised you two didn't . . ."

"Well, things never work out the way we expect," Winter said hastily. Why did everyone who remembered Hunter Greyson seem so surprised that the two of them weren't still together? "Who would have expected me to wind up on Wall Street?"

"Considering your family and all, I'll admit I'm amazed," Ramsey said. He emptied the seltzer from his glass and filled it with wine from the half-empty bottle. Winter said nothing. "But by the time you figure out what you want in life, you've usually pretty well arranged things so you can't get it."

It was so close to what Janelle had said that Winter was startled at the echo. She regarded Ramsey narrowly. "Are you saying we're all doomed to be failures?" Winter asked evenly.

Ramsey glanced up at her and grinned engagingly. "Comforting if true, don't you think? But as a matter of fact, I'm not." He lifted his wineglass toward the light, studying it intently while the planes of his young-old face fell into somber lines.

"The way I see it," Ramsey said, "—and this is the fruit of many hours of philosophical deliberation as the Steelers and the Buckeyes ran off with my money—is that sooner or later we all turn into our parents. Well, I ask you: Who else did we spend all our time watching when we were kids? We live our parents' lives—I am, anyway."

"But doesn't everyone become their parents? You make it sound awfully grim. As if it's some kind of trap." Something stirred beneath the surface of her memories. Winter pushed it away.

"It is," Ramsey said seriously. "Because we don't become the best of our parents. We become them at their worst, and there's only a small window of opportunity for escape—to become someone else, someone unique. Anything you do in that golden time sets the patterns you'll live out for the rest of your life. Everyone gets a chance at it—back when we're all too young to understand what we're getting—but of all of us, Jannie and Cassilda and me, I always thought that only you and Grey really made it out. Well, you know what Morrison used to say: 'No one here gets out alive.'"

But I didn't get away, Ramsey, and Jim Morrison's dead. And I'm still trapped, and I don't know how to get free.

There were more questions to ask, but Winter didn't quite have the heart for them tonight. She helped Ramsey wash up after dinner, but after that she pleaded tiredness caused by the long drive.

A short time later Winter was sitting alone in the guest room, a last glass of wine in her hand, staring down at the gaudy cover of *Venus Afflicted.* She could hear the sound of the living room television faintly through the door.

Everybody grows up, Winter told herself sternly. *There's no tragedy in becoming an adult.*

But there was tragedy in a wasted life—and Ramsey's life *was* a waste, Winter told herself with clinical detachment. It was on a—what was that buzzword?—on a downward economic spiral. That used-car lot could never have paid for this house; gambling debts aside, Ramsey must have been making more money once—money enough to afford everything that Laura Miller had taken with her, and this house as well.

. . . And all who sail in her, Winter thought, raising her glass in a

faintly tiddly salute. Laura-the-wife, and the children now in Cleveland. It didn't sound as if Ramsey was going to even try to sue for visitation or joint custody. What had he said at dinner? Something about a golden time, a window of opportunity when you had the chance to set the pattern of your life, where to fail was like a bad hand of solitaire that you would play out forever.

Could it be true?

Winter shook her head, refusing to think about it. She ought to do some work: make a list of questions to ask Ramsey, try to find out what he remembered about Nuclear Circle's work. See if he had ghosts, for that matter—if the thing had visited Janelle it would probably be after him as well.

If the Elemental even existed. If the Elemental was visiting all the former members of Nuclear Circle. And if it was—why?

But she didn't have the energy to be so organized tonight, not after seeing what had happened to her old friend. If the trap that Ramsey had fallen into was not as obvious a one as Janelle's, it was no less destructive.

"I fling open the gates of Dayton, Ohio, and shower its cultural riches upon you," Ramsey said, tossing a ring of keys onto the blanket as Winter started groggily awake. "I figured you wouldn't want to be cooped up in the house all day. There's a mall up the road if you want to do any shopping; there's a street map on the kitchen table and I've marked it for you. See you later."

Winter sat up, stiff from sleeping in the unfamiliar bed. "G'bye, Ramsey. Have fun," she said sleepily. *Don't sell any Corvettes to Arnold Schwarzenegger.*

Later, when he was gone, Winter got up and prowled around the deserted house. Paradoxically, it did not seem as empty when Ramsey was gone. Without his presence to remind it of what it had been, the house could be just any empty house.

Underfurnished, of course, and downright weird in spots, but . . .

Ramsey's bedroom was more or less intact—at least Winter didn't see any pressure marks in the rug to show where heavy furniture had been taken away. The suite was that heavy dark mock-Mediterranean style that had been popular a few years back, and looked as if the only way you'd get rid of it was to burn the house down around it. Winter closed the door behind her and tiptoed off, in search of the kitchen and coffee or tea. She vaguely remembered buying both last night at the store; she and Ramsey, two old friends—acquaintances now—playing house.

It gave Winter an odd detached thrill to pretend for a few moments that this could be her house and her life—a woman just moved into town, most of the furniture still on a moving van in another state, but all poised to settle into domesticity and family life. A kind of life she had— bypassed? Run away from? Tried and found wanting?

Was it really too late to go back and pick up the pieces of her life that she'd jettisoned?

In the kitchen Winter found the kettle and put water on to boil, deciding on tea. She wanted toast, but couldn't find a toaster—more of Laura's efficiency, Winter supposed—and decided to settle for dry cereal instead. She found the box in the cupboard and carried it over to the table.

What should she do today? She picked up the street map and tossed it aside. If she wanted to go shopping, there were better stores in New York. In fact, there was better *everything* in New York—what in Heaven's name was she doing out here in the middle of nowhere?

Ramsey's here, she reminded herself. And she needed to find out what Ramsey remembered about the Class of '82, and Nuclear Circle. Assuming that their teenaged occult dabblings didn't just constitute a silly coincidence, and really had anything to do with the things that were happening to her now.

It had been nearly two weeks now since the night at the lab at the Bidney Institute, and already the events were becoming hazy in Winter's mind—a memory-of-a-memory, soon to dissolve completely into unthinking acceptance of things as they were. The thought that something so vivid could just vanish was disturbing on a primal level; how many other thoughts, experiences, feelings, memories was she losing every day?

No more than anyone else, Winter told herself brutally. *Now is all we have. Now is all that matters.*

But the danger that followed her—and the growing suspicion that there was something she must do—mattered, too.

"Ramsey, you remember that Thorne Blackburn stuff we were mixed up with in college?"

Cartons of Chinese take-out food were strewn over every countertop surface of the kitchen. Ramsey was no better a cook than Winter was, and tonight he'd taken this easy way out.

"Thorne who?" He paused with chopsticks full of noodles halfway to his mouth.

"Thorne Blackburn. You know, the . . . occultist?" The unfamiliar term came clumsily to Winter's tongue. "You and I and Grey and Jannie and Cassie—back in school."

Ramsey regarded her with responsive interest, but without comprehension.

"We used to go up to Nuclear Lake." *And do something I can't quite remember, and this book of Truth's isn't much help, either.* "Just the five of us. You remember," Winter said coaxingly. *I do. Don't I?*

"I guess I don't." Ramsey's tone was regretful but uninterested. "I must not have gone with you."

But you did! You were there—I saw you! "We used to go up there quite a lot," Winter began cautiously. "For years. It was Grey's idea at first, I guess, but we all fell in with it. He was doing something called the Blackburn Work, and we were all involved in it with him."

"Not me," Ramsey said, a little more decisively than could really be expected from someone searching through memories more than a decade lost.

As if he doesn't want to remember—and Janelle didn't talk about it either. And I WANT *to remember, but I can't,* Winter thought in frustration.

"I went back to visit the campus, you know," Winter began, trying another tack.

But while Ramsey was willing to discuss the campus, and professors they'd had in common, and even the Bidney Institute itself, Winter could not find any way whatever to bring Nuclear Lake back into the conversation.

But Nuclear Lake *did* exist. Nina Fowler'd had no trouble remembering it—and driving there. And neither had Truth Jourdemayne—in fact, Truth had seen the basement room where they'd all done what Truth had called the Blackburn Work.

Another memory, swiftly flickering like a butterfly's wing: the laboratory basement at Nuclear Lake, bleached white by hissing propane lanterns; Janelle on her knees, carefully painting a line on the floor as Ramsey held the jar of paint ready for her . . .

"Ramsey, don't you remember anything about Nuclear Lake?" Winter asked in frustration.

"It doesn't look like *I'm* the one having memory problems," Ramsey said with unusual asperity.

"'Touché, you little yellow devil,'" Winter said, quoting *Doonesbury* with a smile. "You're right: I'm not sure about what happened there either. There are a lot of places where my memory's just . . . jumbled."

Ramsey put a hand over hers in sympathy. "Sometimes, you know, it's better not to remember," he said gently.

And normally I'd agree with that, old friend, but unfortunately, this time the stakes are too high, Winter thought sorrowfully.

"Do you remember why I left Taghkanic, Ramsey? I know I left before graduation and I don't remember keeping in touch with any of you—Janelle says I sent her a wedding present, but—"

"Janelle may be mistaken," Ramsey said, very gently. "I suspect things aren't going all that well for her, you know."

"I know. I saw her before I came here. She doesn't paint any more. Ramsey, we were all—" The grief came with an overpowering rush; Winter set down her chopsticks.

We were all going to be famous: Janelle was going to be an artist, and you were going to be a famous journalist. And what was I going to be? I don't even know any more, but it wasn't what I became.

"—we were all going to be kings and queens in Narnia; I know. But everybody has to grow up sometime, Winter, and in the real world it just isn't possible for everyone to be beautiful, famous, and rich. We were kids, with kids' dreams. And we learned that dreams don't come true." Ramsey refilled both their glasses.

She was probably drinking too much, Winter warned herself, but just for tonight it wouldn't matter. And Ramsey, for all his talk of being on the wagon, drank heavily as well. But this was no time to lecture him on his habits or apologize for hers. And even Dutch courage was a help in asking the questions she needed to ask.

"So why did I leave school, Ramsey? I've always wondered."

He grinned at her, and a trace of the boy he'd been lingered on in the lines of the man's face. "I'm afraid it's one of the great unexplained mysteries, along with where missing socks go and the egg in the egg cream.

All of us but Grey went away for spring break in April, and you never came back."

Winter had taken a large bite of dumpling a moment before, and now she waved her hands, semaphoring agitatedly: *I just* LEFT? *Didn't you look for me? You just let it drop? What if I'd been eaten by Bigfoot?* "Murph!" she said aloud.

Ramsey laughed at her agitation, then shrugged. "The Registrar's office said you'd withdrawn. I think Cassie called you a couple of times, but I'm not sure. It was a long time ago. It sort of hurt that you just dumped us," he added after a pause.

Winter felt an instant rush of guilt. It had never occurred to her how the matter must look to the others, and Janelle had given no hint that she'd felt rejected by what Winter had done all those years before.

"Ramsey, I swear to you I don't remember doing that; either leaving or . . . why. I'm . . . I'm sorry. I don't know why . . ." Her voice trailed off momentarily. "I *still* don't know why I did it. I don't remember." *And what must Grey have thought, when I just went off and didn't come back?* She blinked back sudden tears.

"Life goes on," Ramsey said, although Winter could still detect a shadow of hurt in his voice. "And anyway, six weeks later we'd all graduated, a gaggle of fledgling BA's unleashed upon the world."

"Do the rest of you keep in touch?" Winter asked, trying once more to lead the conversation back to Nuclear Lake.

"Oh, I send Jannie a card from time to time," Ramsey said evasively. "I tell her about my divorces, and she tells me which room she's redecorated now. Speaking of which, have you seen—"

The conversation slid away from personal matters into current events, and Winter was finally willing to let it go. What Ramsey had told her disturbed her profoundly, as well as making her feel strangely ashamed.

She'd just walked out on them. She, Winter Musgrave, who prided herself on honoring every pact, meeting every commitment, had just turned her back on four of her dearest friends and left them without a single word of explanation.

But *she* would not have done it—and neither would that girl from the yearbooks and newspapers, the Winter Musgrave-as-was.

What had happened? Oh, God, what had happened to her fourteen years before?

* * *

If Winter had entertained fantasies of suburban domesticity earlier in the day, she got to play them out that night: Ramsey set up a card table in the living room and beat her soundly at Scrabble three games out of four. She enjoyed it far more than she thought she would—or ought. It was such a placid pastime; harmless and conventional.

And don't forget inexpensive, Winter chided herself. It had not been so very long since she'd measured her enjoyment of things by the amount they cost. Now she was playing board games in a suburban living room with an old college buddy, and thinking of how nice it could be if there could be more times like this in her life; if they could just go on forever.

But not with Ramsey. The automatic amendment was swift. Ramsey Miller was a failure at the game of matrimony in too many times and ways for Winter to believe him capable of being a success now.

What had happened? Winter asked herself again, counting out tiles and trying to figure out if she could spell any words with what she had. The methods Janelle had used to run away from the chance to succeed was plain—but what had happened to Ramsey? He'd even had a job on a newspaper once, heading in the right direction for the career he hoped to have—and now he was here. And while it might be hard for some people to see this as a failure, she'd known Ramsey before, and Winter could not believe that he had freely chosen the life of a used-car salesman over his bright college dreams.

What were the choices that had brought Ramsey to this place in his life? Wrong ones, obviously, but had he known that at the time? Or had they been detours he thought he could get away with, unaware that he, too, had been living out the golden time that set the patterns that would dictate the rest of his life?

As she brooded, Ramsey's theory about the golden time became muddled in Winter's thoughts with the Grey Angels of the Hudson Valley, until for a brief bewildered moment she believed that the Grey Angels controlled the golden time; that its light shone from beneath their wings, and what it illuminated had the power to be different, really different, to throw off the chains of karma and—

"'Qwozle' is not a word, Winter—though I admit you'd get a lot of points for it," Ramsey said dryly.

Winter looked down at the board and felt herself flush.

"I guess my mind was wandering," she said.

"If you see my mind out wandering, be sure to send it back," Hunter Greyson said, suddenly vivid in her mind. Winter wondered, with adult insight, whether he'd kept up that barrage of Noël Coward bon mots to be clever—or to mask a compassion that he knew could have no outlet. If he were here now, seeing what had become of Ramsey, he'd be just that prickly—because there was no way he could help. There was nothing anyone could do for Ramsey, any more than anyone could help Janelle. In their separate ways, each had given up.

"I'm sorry, Ramsey. I guess I'm tireder than I thought," Winter said neutrally. *Are all of my old friends emotional basket cases? They're* ME *friends—what does that make* ME*?*

"Well, you know what they always say—quit while you're behind, right? Go to bed, Winter, have a good night's sleep. I'll see you in the morning."

But when she was sitting on the end of the fold-out couch, gazing down at her meager library—*Venus Afflicted* and Tabitha Whitfield's manual of psychic hygiene—Winter was far from ready for sleep. She spread her hands out before her and stared at her fingertips. She felt a need to *do* something, and right now her options were limited. Of course, if she got upset enough about that, she could probably arrange to have a poltergeist fit; now *that* would really liven up the place. . . .

Winter's gaze unfocused as inspiration struck. She was almost certain that she could call up a psychic storm—all it really took was intense emotion and loss of control, and God knew she'd experienced enough of both lately. And after that night in New Jersey, she was also fairly certain she could also stop one from happening, provided she had warning in time.

Was there some middle ground, then? If she could start them and stop them, didn't that imply that more was possible?

Like what? Winter wondered. She wasn't all that sure what a poltergeist *did:* opened doors and windows, threw things. . . .

So why not see if you can move something through the power of mind alone, as the comic books say? And bring your personal demons under conscious control. Winter wasn't sure she wanted to believe in controlled psychism any more than in magic, but she knew that she no longer had the right to automatically reject the strange and uncanny. She looked around.

The room contained the fold-out couch she was sitting on, a floor lamp, and a folding tray-table that currently held her half-full wineglass and a litter of oddments. Her car keys. A lipstick. She rummaged through her bags until she had five objects lined up on the tray: her stuffed elephant good-luck charm, her hairbrush, a roll of Life Savers, the car keys, and a lipstick. She tossed off the last of her wine and tucked the glass out of harm's way on the floor. She wanted nothing breakable in sight.

Now what? Winter felt unbearably silly, staring at her makeshift test subjects. *Wonderful. I've discovered the psychic equivalent of cutting out paper dolls.*

She refused to simply abandon the idea, however. Her sense of fairness demanded that it at least be given an objective test. She arranged herself cross-legged on the foot of the bed and looked fixedly at her collection.

Nothing happened.

How long do I have to wait? Winter wondered, and for that matter, what exactly was she waiting for? If she were a character in a book, she'd feel an absolute certainty, a conviction of rightness, an instant uprushing of power, and . . .

But she *had* felt an uprushing of power—just before the ball of lightning had hit Nina Fowler's car. She'd been half out of her mind with fear, but even then the sensation had been distinct and memorable. Could she re-create it less disastrously now?

Almost out of habit Winter had fallen into the slow measured breathing of the exercise she used every night; the one out of Tabitha Whitfield's pamphlet. With each breath she pushed envisioned power through her body until she felt both energized and supremely relaxed. Because she was sitting up, this time she didn't fall asleep; instead, as she gazed at the tray full of objects she felt the illogical clarity of dreams—in which there are no limits, and everything seems possible.

The hand is the extension of the mind; now make the mind become the extension of the hand. . . .

It was almost as if some familiar presence stood beside her, guiding her. Winter became aware of a subtle tingling sensation in her chest, almost a heaviness, as though she had suddenly discovered the existence of a new internal organ whose presence she had never before suspected. This was the source of the strange painless flexing that was the somatic cue for one of her psychic storms.

There. That's it. That's your center.

The discovery pleased her—everyone always talked about how important it was to find your center and now she'd found hers. Holding her awareness of this feeling firmly in her mind in the way she had held the practice images, Winter concentrated on the objects on the tray. She would move the key ring. . . .

Now!

The ring of keys on its silver Tiffany tag jumped as if falling upward, and slewed sideways off the end of the table. The bang it made as it hit the bare wood floor made Winter jump, shattering her state of dreamlike alertness.

But unlike a dream, the sensation did not end with waking. Winter's sense of triumphant success was submerged in the dawning realization that it was much easier to uncork the genie than it was to put it back into the bottle. Her skin tingled and the hairs on the back of her neck stood up; she could feel the intensifying *potential* pressing outward through her skin, seeking release in violence.

I've got to get rid of it somehow—ground the charge—

But it was too late. She felt the power gather itself; slip free of her control. She felt something deep inside her *flex*—

The bulb in the lamp did not so much shatter as dissolve, imploding with a clap and a fat blue spark that left the darkened room reeking of ozone.

Winter felt the residue of power drain from her body, carrying her energy with it—as though the effort she had just made was not merely psychic, but physical as well. Every muscle in her body ached, a familiar—if unwelcome—sensation. It was just like all those times at Fall River—and before.

"Happy now?" Grey said to her inside her mind. *"Or just scared? Once you take responsibility for things, they belong to you—and you belong to them."*

But the exhaustion was swirling through Winter's veins like a drug, and it was so much easier to let it carry her into sleep than to answer.

CHAPTER TEN

THE HUNTING OF THE WREN

*Summers pleasures they are gone like to visions every one
And the cloudy days of autumn and of winter cometh on.*
—JOHN CLARE

THE COLD AIR ON HER SKIN ROUSED HER. WINTER AWOKE early that morning with the virtuous sense of well-being she usually associated with an intense workout at her health club, and for a moment after she opened her eyes that sense of satisfaction was so compelling that she could not imagine what she was doing in this stark unfamiliar room. Then the memory of recent events returned, and with them, the sense of guilt and uncertainty—and the nagging sense of blame.

But for what? Winter could not think of anything she had done—other than end up in Fall River—for which she had to apologize. She shivered in the chill, pulling the blanket haphazardly around her. To be fair, there might be a number of sins in her past that she just couldn't remember right now, but this feeling of *omission* seemed much more immediate than something like that could account for.

But she was feeling too restless to chase this particular puzzle for long. Winter swung her legs over the edge of the bed, wincing at the chill, and barely missed stepping on her keys. They were lying in the middle of the floor.

So I did do it! That discovery made her check the lamp as well, huddling the blanket around her as she stood. It confirmed her recollection; while the shade was untouched, the remains of the bulb were fused into the socket. There was no sign of broken glass anywhere.

Still a little room for improvement, Winter thought ruefully. She ran her finger gingerly around the welt of melted glass. *I guess I owe Ramsey a new lamp.*

The flutter of the curtain caught her eye. No wonder it was so cold in here—the window was open. She went over to it and pulled it slowly shut.

But did I open it last night before I went to bed?

Suddenly it was important to know. With a haste that left no time for shoes, Winter pulled on slacks and a sweater and hurried out of the room.

"Ramsey?"

Her voice was so low he could not possibly have heard it. Winter swallowed hard, and pushed the front door shut, locking the spring lock and dead bolt and security chain.

All the living room windows were open. The heavy drapes were drawn back and the thin white curtains underneath billowed in the morning breeze. She closed the windows and pulled the drapes and then went back through the house. Every window in every room was open, as well as closet doors, cabinet doors, everything that could be opened. The dull resentful anger was a physical ache. And escape was only an illusion.

It's here.

She'd saved the kitchen for last, out of an unconscious expectation that the worst demonstration of the *wrongness* that stalked her would be there. But when she arrived, all she found was Ramsey, incongruous in T-shirt and jeans, scrubbing his hands in the sink.

Scrubbing them to the elbows.

Scrubbing them *hard.*

"Is everything all right?" Winter asked. She'd hoped for bright neutrality, but what came out was fear.

"You're up early." Ramsey's voice rang as hollowly false as her own.

Winter glanced up at the clock. 6:30.

"Careful where you step, it's—" Ramsey stopped.

It's wet. Winter mentally completed the sentence. She looked down at her bare feet, at the gleaming, freshly scrubbed, *recently* scrubbed kitchen floor.

Who mopped a floor at 6 in the morning?

"Ramsey, what happened here?" Winter asked him, voice low.

"Nothing," he said with gallant dishonesty. But he could not meet her gaze.

Scrubbing and scrubbing . . . was it only in her imagination that Winter could smell that faint sweet stench; stale and organic like swamp water on a hot morning, or spoiled meat. . . .

"I have to go," Winter Musgrave said.

He did not argue. Ramsey's curse was that he could not tell comforting lies to himself or to others, no matter how unwilling he might be to face the truth. Huddled together forlornly in the kitchen's breakfast nook, they shared one last meal, and Winter wondered if she would ever see him again. On the counter in front of her a cup of tea stewed and cooled, and scrambled eggs neither of them had the appetite for turned rubbery and dry.

"You'll be okay, won't you? I guess you're going back to New York now?" Ramsey said hopefully. There was an undercurrent in his voice Winter didn't quite understand.

"I need to find Grey," Winter said stubbornly. Lately it seemed as if everything she tried to hold onto slipped through her fingers like grains of sand, until she existed alone, without anyone to reach out for or to touch. There was no time left to be patient with Ramsey's evasions. "Do you know where he is? Have you kept in touch with him?"

Ramsey shook his head, but it wasn't an answer. "It wasn't the same at Taghkanic after you left, Winter." But that was not an answer either.

"Where is he?" she said urgently.

"I . . . don't know. Cassie would," Ramsey said, relief obvious in his voice at having even this much answer for her. "Cassie kept in touch with him. I'm sure she did."

"I've got an address for her in Berkeley. . . ." Winter began doubtfully.

"No. That's old. She moved to SF about four years ago, when she got the job managing that bookshop." Ramsey spoke with decision, just as if Winter should know what bookshop and why Cassie should be managing it. "I'll get it for you." He left the kitchen quickly.

Winter pushed her nearly untouched breakfast away from her. Ramsey was as helpful as if he were anxious for her to be gone, and after what she suspected had happened this morning she did not blame him. *But he didn't act outraged or puzzled about it, or try to blame someone. As if he expected it . . . or as if it had happened before.*

"Ramsey?" Winter called, suddenly apprehensive.

"Here it is," Ramsey said, coming back into the kitchen. He set a three-by-five card on the table in front of her, an address copied out on it in Ramsey's neat penmanship.

Ancient Mysteries Bookstore, Winter read, and an address on Haight Street in San Francisco. She felt a faint surge of discomfort; with a name like that it almost had to be a place like *Inquire Within;* one of those whole-hearted surges into the irrational. How could Cassie *do* this to her? Of the lot of them, Cassie had always been the sensible one, the one with both feet firmly planted in reality. . . .

A reality, anyway.

"Are you going to go see Cassie?" Ramsey asked.

"If I can." Winter wasn't sure what impulse made her qualify her promise. "Ramsey, about this morning . . . it wasn't you; it was—"

"If you do, will you do something for me?" Ramsey interrupted her as if he hadn't heard. "I'm—oh, God, I'm no good at this."

He sat down across from her. The harsh illumination of the alcove light made him look suddenly old, harsh downward lines pulling his face into a frozen mask of age. "If you're going, you have to understand, I . . . When you were asking about Nuclear Lake . . ." His voice drifted to a stop.

"All my life I never took anything seriously I couldn't see or touch. Used cars; there isn't much more rock-bottom real than that, is there? I didn't want to be blindsided by things I didn't have any chance of beating—you know me, Winter; I always liked a fight, but only if it was a fair one. Up at Nuclear Lake . . ." His voice trailed off in a sigh.

So he DOES *remember!* Winter felt a primal flash of triumph.

"I didn't like it, but what we did, what happened there, if it didn't come from outside—from objective reality—then it came from *me,* do you see? I had two choices and I didn't like either one. Jannie was just the opposite; she loved it and I think when she couldn't find that magic any more something in her just . . . broke. A long time before Denny." He picked up his mug and fiddled with it, not meeting her eyes. "Anyway, I didn't forgive reality for being different than I expected. And lately . . ."

Winter could feel him gathering the determination to go on, to say what was obviously so hard for him to say.

"There was something Cassie wanted to tell me, Winter. Something that worried her. She wrote to me—pages of stuff. I wouldn't even read it. She even called, and you know, we didn't stay close, at least not that way. But she called me, and I wouldn't even let her talk to me about it. She was looking for help, I think—and I wouldn't let her ask for it. Because I knew that she hadn't run away; she'd stuck with, you know, this *stuff*—"

And then she was in trouble—or you thought she was—and you couldn't bear to think about it, because of what it might be. "Oh, Ramsey," Winter said with soft compassion. She put her hand over his.

"So when you see Cassie, help her, would you? Find out what she needs?" Ramsey said.

"I will," Winter promised.

A half an hour later she was on her way.

As she backed out of the garage Winter could see Ramsey watching her through the living room window, as isolated as a castaway on a desert island. Although she was only yards away, Winter already felt as though she couldn't go back, as if there were some force pushing the two of them apart. She willed herself not to care, to look to what came next. There was no way to go back, after all—there was no "back" to go to.

She turned onto the street and drove away, and by the time Winter had reached the cross street the house was no longer in sight.

Surrounded by the sights and sounds of weekday-morning Dayton traffic, Winter brooded. Ramsey had been completely honest with her at the end. Motivated by fear . . . or because he had given up trying to protect her? Winter's fingers briefly touched the bag on the seat beside her. It held Cassie's address. Or what Ramsey said was Cassie's address, anyway.

Now that she was on the road and heading for the interchange that would put her in I-80, Winter realized that her hasty departure from Ramsey's house had been motivated as much by panic and guilt as anything else. She'd taken off without a clear plan in mind, and California was a long way to go by car. There were major air-travel hubs in Chicago and St. Louis; surely it would be more sensible to drive to either place and fly out from there?

But a part of Winter disliked the thought of being without a car once she arrived—unless she rented one—and, searching her emotions further, she realized she was reluctant to face Cassilda Chandler at all. Had Cassie changed? *She was the only one of us who kept faith,* Winter thought with an odd pang. From Ramsey's hints, Cassie was still deeply involved in . . . whatever the five of them had been deeply involved in. Magic. Occultism. "The dark twin of Science," according to the Thorne Blackburn biography. Taken up during their college days, as far as Winter could reconstruct, and never quite abandoned.

Not completely.

Not by all of them.

She turned onto one of the six-lane roads that led to the interstate, her body moving the car smoothly and automatically through the rush-hour traffic. Could it be *Cassie* who had sent the *magickal child?* The idea had a certain repugnant logic.

"After all, if you can't suspect your friends, who can you suspect?" Grey said out of memory.

"I wish you were here to tell me what's going on," Winter muttered to the absent Hunter Greyson.

Somehow she thought that he knew; Grey had always known, or seemed to know, the answer to everything—at least as much as a college student could be expected to know. It was hard now to remember how young they'd all been then. They'd felt like adults, and thought that was all that mattered, but they'd been kids. And now, all these years later, how well could she say she still knew any of them? Janelle, entombed in her sad marriage, Ramsey, complacently accepting his myriad failures—maybe Cassie had undergone the same sort of dark alchemical transformation, into . . .

The interchange for I-80 West loomed ahead in a blaze of red-white-and-blue shield-shaped signs. Accustomed to making instant decisions, Winter pulled onto the on ramp and merged smoothly with the heavier traffic, buying herself more time to think. She had to go west anyway—to reach Chicago, if she decided to fly; to reach I-90 and California if she didn't. Once she'd settled into the light autohypnosis of long-distance driving, her mind returned unerringly to her original problem. The artificial Elemental—the *magickal child.*

A power created and sent by a magician was stalking her. Beyond reason or sense, here, in the declining years of the twentieth century, her problem was a magickal assault by a person or persons unknown. Its danger increased with every day, and she had no idea what to do about it.

She'd been searching for Grey because he was the only magician she knew. She could not believe he would have returned from nowhere to harm her; but how could she be certain she'd had no contact with Grey since college? Could he be carrying out some agenda she'd forgotten?

Winter frowned. She remembered the farmhouse outside Glastonbury, and before that, the sanatorium at Fall River. She remembered Arkham Miskatonic King, the day she'd started work there still as bright in her mind as a new-minted penny. . . .

And before that came the garbled half-memories of college, like bright fish in murky waters. She hardly remembered Grey at all, but she could not believe she could ever have done something to kindle that degree of hatred in a sane person. And Grey, whatever else she might have forgotten about him, had been radiantly sane.

But not, now that Winter came to think about it, the only magician she knew. If she could believe what Ramsey had said, Cassilda had "kept up with" the Blackburn Work as well, so Cassie could be as much help to Winter as Grey could.

Or as much harm. Face it, Winter, while sorcerous assault strains the credibility, being a victim chosen at random snaps it right in half. It has to be someone who knows you—and who you know.

Not Cassie. Not Grey. With the obstinacy of a child lying alone in the dark, Winter clung to that belief. They had been her friends. They would never hurt her. Even Ramsey and Janelle, strange as they were, *changed* as they were, had meant her no harm.

I need time.

Time to reason things out, in a situation where no reason was possible. Time to think. Time to plan.

Time to *learn.* About herself, at least, if nothing else.

* * *

But Ramsey had said Cassie's problem might be urgent, and so, a couple of hours later, when Winter stopped for gas and to stretch her legs, she sought out a pay phone to call Cassie.

She was at one of those mass-produced rest stops on the interstate that seemed to have evolved in defiance of every tenet of Lady Bird Johnson's "Keep America Beautiful" campaign thirty years before. The pay phones were located in a not-very-quiet corner where the noise of tired children, cash registers, and Muzak made a deadening background mush of sound. Winter cradled the phone to her ear and thanked her lucky stars that her PhoneCard still worked—she hated to think how many quarters she would have had to feed the phone if it didn't. Fortunately the escrow account that had taken care of her bills during the time she'd been at Fall River had seen to it that her checks didn't bounce, her charge cards were paid, and there was money in her drawing account.

Now that she knew what city's directory assistance to consult, she got Cassie's home number easily. Winter carefully crossed out the old Berkeley number in her Filofax and wrote in the new. There was only one Cassilda Chandler in the San Francisco phone book, but there was no answer at that number. After a moment's hesitation, she dialed again and asked directory assistance for the number of the Ancient Mysteries Bookstore on Haight Street, and once the synthetic robot voice had provided it, dialed it before she had the chance to regret doing so.

The phone rang mindlessly on; after a dozen rings, Winter lost count and simply watched the second hand sweep around the dial of the clock that was hung over the entrance to the rest-stop cafeteria. As the clock measured off the seconds, Winter felt herself losing patience. Surely any bookstore, no matter how New Age-y and laid-back, would answer a phone that had rung for over a minute?

Finally she hung up and moved slowly away from the bank of phones, worry and relief combining into a disoriented, unsettled feeling. How could she ask Cassie what was wrong if the woman wouldn't even answer her phone?

She'd have to try again later.

There was no answer when Winter stopped for lunch, either. Pretty soon she'd cross the Indiana border, and then she was going to have to make up her mind whether to head north for Chicago and fly the rest of the way, or drive straight through, which would take two or three days minimum—at least if she took it easy and didn't push it.

Driving did have a certain perverse appeal. Behind the wheel Winter could always tell herself that she was on the verge of turning back; that this was a pleasure trip; that her destination was not as fixed and irrevocable as the stars in their courses. Behind the wheel, Winter felt *safe*.

And safety—real or illusory—was a commodity in short supply in her life just now.

That's it then. I drive—unless and until I get through to Cassie and get some real information. And anyway, almost every major city has at least a small airport—even Indianapolis. No matter where I am, I'm only hours away from the West Coast if there's a real emergency.

By evening Winter had crossed the border from Indiana into Illinois. She'd taken to trying Cassie every time she stopped, and had gotten no answer at either of the numbers. While Cassie might be out of town, surely the bookstore would still be open?

Maybe they've gone out of business. Places like that do. Ramsey didn't tell me how long it had been since she called him—and I didn't think to ask, dammit.

But that, at least, was easily remedied.

A few hours after dark, Winter stopped for the night in a shabby little motel that offered a night's lodging for the price of a Wall Street lunch. The room she got was run-down and depressing—surprising partly in the fact that, unsatisfactory as it was, people would still pay to rent it—but it had a phone.

The nearest restaurant was in the town beyond. Winter, reluctant to face food that might match her lodgings, settled for a Coke out of the machine. She shouldn't put off the call anyway. Picking up the phone, she dialed in the fourteen-digit access number, then Ramsey's number. A moment later she heard him answer.

"Ramsey?"

The sense of relief she felt when she heard his voice made her giddy; she realized that in some part of her mind she'd just expected him to be gone. Vanished without a trace, like her past.

"Winter!" His voice was politely cheerful . . . and faintly slurred.

He's drunk, Winter thought in surprise. "Hi, I'm in Illinois. I thought I'd call and see how you were."

"It was good to see you. We'll have to do this again."

Winter recognized the tone in his voice. Someone skating on the thin edge of memory, not quite sure of the context.

"Maybe the five of us could have our own private reunion," she said. "And actually, that's sort of why I'm calling. I've been trying to reach Cassie all day and I haven't been able to get through to her either at home or at that bookstore you said she has. I'm hoping she hasn't moved on; when did you say you'd talked to her last?"

The sudden strained silence at the other end of the line made Winter think she'd just said something wrong—but what?

"Ramsey, you said you'd talked to her," Winter prompted, almost pleading. "When?"

"A couple of weeks. Maybe a month. Or two. I didn't exactly write it down in my DayTimer." There was a sullenness in his voice she had not heard before.

And I bet you forgot all about it—until this morning. And something about dead animals in the middle of your kitchen brought it right to mind, Winter thought grimly. The creature that stalked her—that seemed to stalk all of them—somehow played upon the memory, withholding recollection at will.

But hadn't she read somewhere that the brain generated its own electric current? Winter remembered the ball of lightning that had destroyed Nina's car; the spark that had melted the lamp in Ramsey's guest room. Maybe *she* was what had made Ramsey remember. And if so, could she do it now—at this distance?

"Well, of course not. Why would you do that?" Winter answered soothingly. "But I can't reach her at her home, and the bookstore doesn't answer, so I'm starting to worry. Was it after Christmas that she called you?" He'd said he exchanged Christmas cards with the others. It would be a logical time for a letter. But not if the situation were urgent.

There was no answer from the other end of the line.

"You said it was important, Ramsey—that Cassie had a problem. You asked me to look her up."

"You told me you were going to go see her." Ramsey's tone was as near to hostile as she'd ever heard it. If she *was* the force that had made him remember, apparently she couldn't manage the trick from where she was now.

"Of course I did. I'm just wondering, now that I can't reach her . . ." Winter tried to think of some question that would pierce the veil of forgetfulness that her disembodied opponent had woven around Ramsey Miller.

"Look, Winter, I'm glad you called, but I'm pretty busy right now. Catch you later, okay?" The phone went dead.

She called back immediately but the line was busy, and after half an hour she admitted to herself that Ramsey had probably taken the phone off the hook.

That left Janelle.

Winter stared at the phone doubtfully. Ramsey said that Janelle's memory was unreliable, but Winter had only *Ramsey's* word for that. On the other hand, Janelle hadn't seemed to be in touch with Cassie when Winter had asked before. There was probably no point in calling her at all.

Since when did you become a coward? Winter demanded scornfully of herself. Balancing her Filofax on her knee, she quickly punched in the combined digits of her PhoneCard and Janelle's number.

This time she'd work into things gradually. She could tell Jannie about visiting Ramsey; it was a reasonable call for old friends getting back in touch to make—

"Hello? I'd like to speak to—"

"She isn't here," Denny said, and slammed down the phone.

At nine o'clock at night? Winter slowly replaced the receiver in its cradle. Whether Janelle was there, or out—*Or dead,* a chill inner voice added— Winter was not going to be able to talk to her. Not tonight, anyway.

She tried both of Cassie's numbers again—it would only be 6:00 on the West Coast—and got, as she had learned to expect, no answer.

No answers anywhere.

They were in the apple orchard below Greyangels—somehow she knew that, although she had no conscious memory of the place. The close-planted rows of trees were covered with masses of pink-white blossoms, so new that the tightly clustered petals had not yet begun to fall to the ground.

In his fringed white leather jacket and acid-washed jeans, Grey blended into them; a snow-leopard against a field of ice. His eyes were as pale as the rest of him—quicksilver mirrors of crystal and light.

"Stay with me," Hunter Greyson said. "Stay with me, Winter." He reached for her.

There was no reason for the words, the gesture, to frighten her so, but terror was a sudden cold weight beneath her heart. She began to back away, out of reach, but she was too slow. Grey grabbed her arm, and she could feel his fingers sinking into her flesh like hot iron into snow.

"Stay with me. Stay with me, Winter. Stay with me stay with me stay with me—"

She felt his fingers break the skin and knew that in a moment the blood would come—and that when it did, Grey would tear her to ribbons. She had to get away. If she did not, he would destroy her.

She struggled against him one final frantic time, but it was too late. The sluggish blood flowed over her skin like cold acid, and as it did, Hunter Greyson began to change.

His face elongated, the cool patrician features sliding sickeningly out of alignment, until instead of a mouth there was a muzzle, and his teeth were long and sharp. Helplessly she began to cry, and her tears burned, too, melting the flesh from her face.

"Stay with me. . . ." He leaned toward her, raising his other hand to begin the flensing of her, and she could not bear it, not again—

She screamed, and tore free of him, the blood was everywhere and would not stop. Grey snarled, and the scent of apple blossoms was gaggingly strong, like the smell of rot and decay. She ran, but the apple blossoms were falling now, and she slipped on their slick white softness and fell, helpless. . . .

The sound of her own scream woke Winter moments before she crashed to the floor. For a moment she fought frantically against the cocooning sheets until the very ordinariness of her fruitless struggles brought her fully awake.

A dream. It was only a dream.

For a moment Winter lay there panting, almost whimpering with relief. She was soaked in clammy sweat and her heart hammered as if she had, indeed, been running.

He'd wanted her. To stay with him always. He'd wanted her to stay, and the flowers had been everywhere. She hadn't been able to get the scent out of her hair afterward. . . .

With hands that shook uncontrollably, she untangled herself from the sheet.

Grey had wanted her.

The memory of that nightmare hunger made her shudder. It was as vivid as if she still dreamed, and even now it seemed as if she could smell the apple blossoms. No wonder she hadn't even wanted to *see* the orchard behind the house, if that was what had happened there. . . .

But how could it have?

Winter frowned, confused, feeling the borders of sanity and unreason slide over each other in her mind. What she had dreamed could not have had any counterpart in reality. People's bodies did not shift like quicksilver; and when they killed, it was not with fangs and claws. She was not dead. She had dreamed. That was all.

Only a dream . . .

She kicked her feet free of the blankets and sat up to turn on the lamp. The warm illumination banished the last of the night shadows and cleared her head. She stood, stretching, and winced at the stiffness in her muscles. She must have been lying there rigid as a board until she'd knocked herself out of bed. But the nightmare was only a manifestation of her anxiety—a projection of her fears about the others. She could have dreamed of Cassie just as easily. Grey had not turned into a monster and tried to devour her alive.

She thought.

Wearily she ran a hand through her hair. Who could tell where reality ended any more? At Nuclear Lake and in the Bidney Institute Lab she'd already seen and experienced things that were starkly unbelievable by modern standards—and Winter was wise and honest enough to admit that if they happened to her, similar things probably happened to others as well. The world was a stranger and more frightening place than anyone was willing to admit; a place without limits, where wonders and horrors occurred every day and miracles were commonplace.

Wonderful. A whole culture in denial. Is there a twelve-step program for the refusal to see ghosts?

Winter stretched again. If she could not work the stiffness out of her muscles she might have to think about staying here an extra day—without rest, she'd be a danger to herself and anyone she encountered on the road.

The nightmare was still too vivid to let her even consider sleep, but maybe a shower . . . ? And she supposed she should remake the bed, even if she didn't think she'd be getting back into it anytime soon. She reached down for the bedclothes, and stopped.

The mattress and the floor around the bed were covered in apple blossoms.

Winter left the hotel fifteen minutes later, driving west in the dark.

By the time the sun had risen that morning, Winter—inspired by the same instinct that causes the prey to lead the hunter astray—had left the bland artificiality of the interstate for the blue highways, the thin twisting map-lines that led through real lives and real towns. By evening she had come to accept that there would never be an answer at the phone numbers she had for Cassie Chandler—and to realize, too, that this slow westward journey was necessary in itself.

For the next week she worked her way slowly west, through Fayetteville, Fuller's Point, Antigua, Grimsby, Lemuria, Broken Choke . . . a journey not through the Madison Avenue version of America, but through the real one, until Winter finally understood how far out of true her own life had been.

Fayetteville. The waitress in the town's one restaurant had directed her to the justice of the peace, and Winter had spent the night in a spacious second-floor bedroom that looked out over a quiet street and the lazy river below.

It was not even so much that the life she had was not what she could have expected to happen to the young college girl whose past she had so painstakingly researched. It was that, in the final analysis, even the life she'd had—that of Winter Musgrave, Wall Street broker and analyst— had been unfinished, incomplete. Just as Ramsey's life was, and Janelle's. She'd never built anything that could grow.

Fuller's Point. An ancient rooming house on the edge of town, the sheets cool with long storage and smelling faintly of lavender and pine, where Winter continued to practice the gifts that came to seem more and more ordinary. She could summon the lightning with a touch, and slam a door from across the room, and knew it was nothing but meaningless theatrics.

Because just like the others, she had staggered down some spiritual blind alley somewhere in the past she could not remember.

Because of Grey? Somehow that felt right. The largest part of her unfinished business had to do with him. Ramsey had said how surprised they'd all been when she left college without a word to any of them.

Antigua, and a brightly impersonal motel meant to serve the nearby Air Force base. Each night as she slept, Winter felt Grey waiting for her beneath the surface of sleep, and could no longer say which she dreaded more—the bad dreams or the good ones.

Had she just walked off and left them—left *him?* What had he thought—how long had Grey waited before realizing she was never coming back? If that was what she'd done, then no wonder the dreams began with him begging her to stay, and ended in blood and terror.

Lemuria. No town at all, simply a cluster of battered, time-bleached wooden buildings, and Winter too tired to go onward or back. She'd driven into the sagging barn and slept in cramped discomfort on the back seat of her car as coyote howls crossed and blended in the night. In the morning she had driven four hours down the ruler-straight desert highway before she saw a roadside café.

She had wronged him. She owed both of them some closure to that part of their past, an ending in place of a thoughtless adolescent cruelty. And perhaps that closure could help her end the inhumanity that stalked all of them. Truth Jourdemayne had told Winter that she must take the *magickal child* back into herself to destroy it, but at the time she hadn't even known where to begin. She felt stronger now. Perhaps it *was* possible, Winter thought with dawning hope.

She would ask Cassie.

Cassie would know.

There are two U.S. cities into which the Automobile Association of America earnestly advises its members *not,* under any circumstances, to bring their automobiles.

Boston is the other one.

Yesterday morning Winter had crossed the border near Needles, circled wide around the L.A. Metroplex, and headed north along California 1, the Pacific Coast Highway. Coastal California's amazing and dramatic beauty captivated her just as it did on every visit: the hillsides still green at the end of the rainy season, the mist-hung redwoods marching all the way to the ocean's stark edge.

She'd stopped that night at a Bed-and-Breakfast just south of San Jose, and had a reservation for tonight in San Francisco at a B-and-B somewhere near a neighborhood called Russian Hill.

The rest ought to have been easy. And it was, until she crossed the Oakland Bay Bridge.

San Francisco, like Rome, is a city built on seven hills—and like the Eternal City, Winter discovered that the City by the Bay was a magic labyrinth of dead ends and one-way streets: of streets that vanished while she drove down them and streets that appeared on her map and nowhere else. She ended up down at Fisherman's Wharf almost immediately— learning in the process that cable cars always have right-of-way— and at the end of three frustrating hours she was back there again; no closer to Haight Street and Cassie's bookshop than she'd been to begin with.

Winter pulled into a parking lot and rolled down her window. The ocean smell was strong and fresh—Winter, who lived in the country's other great seaport, could not remember ever having smelled the sea so clearly.

Tourists seemed to be everywhere, carrying shopping bags full of sour-dough bread or pennants advertising *Ripley's Believe It or Not Museum.* The balloons carried by children and offered by vendors gave the Wharf the look of an open-air carnival, and seemed to underscore Winter's angry ungracious mood. She wondered if she ought to give up, if only for the day. Or stop for lunch, at least—the box of granola bars she'd consumed instead of breakfast was not an adequate substitute for two missed meals, or so her body told her.

"Can I help you?"

Winter glanced up. The voice belonged to a young man with long brown hair, wearing overalls and a tie-dyed T-shirt and looking as if he was as much a part of this place as the fishing boats that clustered in the water beyond.

"You look lost," he went on, smiling.

Winter regarded him with habitual suspicion, resisting the impulse to roll up the driver's-side window in his face. On second glance, he wasn't as young as all that, but something about his friendly, open, features held the ageless grace of the High Elves—as if some woodland sprite had chosen to mingle with the tourists on a spring day in SF.

"I'm actually trying to find the, um, Haight-Ashbury," she said. *Make what you care to of that!*

"You *are* lost," he said ruefully. "And that isn't really such a good area for . . ."

For a tourist, Winter mentally completed the sentence. "A friend of mine lives there," she added, unbending slightly. "Can you help me? The map I have says you can get there from here, but—"

"There are a couple of streets closed because of the construction. Can I see your map?"

Winter passed it over, and, looking to her for permission, the stranger pulled a felt-tip out of his pocket and marked a route. "This is the best way to get there. What address are you looking for?"

Winter couldn't see any harm in giving him that information—the bookstore was a public business, after all—and rattled off the number of the Ancient Mysteries Bookstore.

The man seemed to recoil for a moment, as if what she said had more than ordinary meaning to him.

"Oh." The liveliness that she had heard a moment before in his voice was gone. "Oh," he said again. "I'm sorry."

"Is something wrong?" Winter said, an edge to her voice.

There was a silence, long enough that Winter wondered if she'd run into one of the loonies San Francisco was supposed to abound in.

"Let me give you my card," the man said finally. "I have a shop in that area, right down the street. There's a map on the back that should help you get . . . where you're going. And you might stop by sometime. We'd like to see you. Really."

When Hell freezes over, Winter thought grimly, but she took the card. As he'd said, there was a map on the back, and the directions looked fairly clear. She turned it over.

Handmade Music, Luthiers. And then, below, in smaller type: *Antiques restored. Tuning—Harpsichord and Piano. Paul Frederick.*

Winter relaxed a little. As a small-business owner he was a bit more respectable than the traveling street person and lunatic he acted like.

"Well, Mr. Frederick, thank you for your help," Winter said decisively. "I'm sure I'll find it now."

"Good luck," Paul Frederick said somberly, stepping back from her car.

He knew. He knew while he was talking to me!

But the anger at being mocked was a pale, reflexive thing in the face of what confronted her.

Winter pulled her car to a halt in the open space at the curb in front of the Ancient Mysteries Bookstore. She was blocking the fire hydrant, but that hardly mattered now. She got out of the car and walked slowly over to stand in front of the shop.

Large sheets of plywood were tacked up over the doors and windows, but streaks of soot against the pale storefront still showed where the flames had shot upward, scorching everything in their path. The sheets of plywood gave the ground floor a smooth anonymity, blotting out the evidence of destruction.

There were wreaths and bouquets nailed to the plywood front door, some draggled and withered as if they had been there for weeks, some bright and new. Their meaning was unmistakable.

Someone has died here.

Winter felt a wave of angry panic that blotted out every other sensation. There was no need to ask who had died—it seemed to her that she had always known. The one hope she'd had was gone. It had been too late to keep this appointment even before she had left Glastonbury, and now there would never be time.

Oh, Cassie. I didn't even get a chance to say good-bye.

A bitter heaviness descended upon her aching heart, as if all hope of reclaiming her past had been ripped irrevocably away. She came closer, her fingers brushing the laurel leaves of one of the wreaths. Laurel, that crowned triumphant athletes and victorious generals. Laurel, for victory and death.

The card beneath the wreath was enclosed in plastic to protect it from the rain. Water had leaked in, blurring the dates, but Winter could read the rest: *Mary Cassilda Chandler—Born Again to the Goddess.*

Cassie had loved her, understood her, cared about her. Cassie would have helped her now—giving herself freely without judgment to solve the misfortunes besetting Winter's life. And with her death, the mirror that Winter had hoped to see herself in was smashed forever.

The scene before her wavered, and Winter blinked back hot tears. The pain of her loss was so raw, so intense, so shocking in its force that even to acknowledge it was to court her own destruction. Desperately Winter sought refuge in glib flippancy. So this was it. The trail ended here. Cassie was dead.

Murdered.

CHAPTER ELEVEN

LORD OF THE WILD HUNT

See, Winter comes to rule the varied year,
Sullen and sad.

—JAMES THOMSON

WINTER HAD NO IDEA HOW LONG SHE STOOD THERE, grieving in her own bleak autumn. Cassie was dead, and Winter mourned for her as if they had been closer than sisters until the moment of Cassie's death.

Abruptly, without any saving sense of transition, Winter became aware of someone watching her.

She started up, as wild as if she were being stalked, but the only thing in sight was a rather ordinary woman in denim jeans, T-shirt, and a green down vest. The only thing unusual about her was the cloud of frizzy bright red hair that framed her face like some Pre-Raphaelite madonna's. It made Winter think momentarily of Janelle. How could she tell Jannie that Cassie was dead?

"Hello . . ." the young woman said. "Are you Winter? Winter Musgrave?"

No! Winter's mind shouted in reflexive denial. She took a step backward.

"Don't run away!" the other woman said. "I'm Rhiannon—I was a friend of Cassie's! She told me to wait for you—that you'd come."

"When?" Even to Winter, her voice sounded hostile and grudging. Cassie was dead, and she didn't want to share her memories of her with anyone.

"Please," Rhiannon said. "Please don't run away. I just want to talk to you. Just for a moment."

Winter took another hesitant step backward, although if this woman was going to cause a really unpleasant scene, Winter doubted if she could make it to the safety of her car in time.

"There's a restaurant around the corner," Rhiannon said. "We could go there. We have to talk."

It was, Winter realized belatedly, long past lunchtime. Her body still wanted food, even if her heart was sick at the thought. And this woman seemed determined to talk to her. Nothing much could happen to her in such a public place—and if she didn't like what this woman had to say she could always get up and leave. Wondering if she was listening to her instincts or defying them, Winter made a grudging gesture of acceptance and followed Rhiannon around the corner.

The Green Man was a bright and rather archaic oasis in the middle of modern urban decay. The Haight-Ashbury district, though faddish thirty years before, had always been a shabby and neglected part of San Francisco. It had been precisely because no one else wanted it that the flower children had flocked to it in such numbers; despite their avowed desire to create a new world, most of them had found their homes in the cracks of the old one. But The Green Man was shining and defiantly welcoming, with polished wooden tables made out of discarded cable spools, cane-bottomed Bentwood chairs, and salvaged panels of stained glass hanging in the windows. There were plants everywhere, giving the café even more the look of a green oasis in the midst of the city's steel and stone.

The waitress greeted Rhiannon by name and showed her and Winter to a booth in the back.

"So," Winter said coolly, when the woman had taken an order for tea and departed. "What can I do for you?" *Probably not much,* her tone implied.

Rhiannon flinched away from her coldness and Winter regarded her scornfully, anger displacing grief. She knew Rhiannon's kind—meddlers, and incompetent ones at that, wandering through life like some self-proclaimed New Age secret agents, dispensing occult wisdom and psychic Band-Aids to anyone they could manage to catch.

Ice numbed her heart, but ice was better than the unbearable pain and guilt. *Cassilda, oh, sister—*

"Well, I thought—" Rhiannon stumbled over her words in the face of Winter's obvious disapproval. "You see, Cassie and I were friends. . . ."

Not as I was her friend!

Rhiannon's eyes reddened and began to fill. She groped in the pocket of her down vest for a wad of tissues as Winter watched implacably.

You've had a lot longer to get used to her death than I have, and you don't see ME *sniveling! Is sympathy what you're after? You won't get it here; I've suffered more than you can possibly imagine. . . .*

"Yes," Winter drawled mockingly, "I can see that."

Rhiannon flushed and glared at her. She opened her mouth to speak and reined herself in with an effort. "The point is," Rhiannon said, taking a deep breath, "we'd been friends for a long time. We met through Circle of Fire—that's a Blackburn Work group that meets in the East Bay—but Cassie felt it was more important to take responsibility for your own life than to expect another set of gods to come to people's rescue—which is what the New Aeon *ought* to be about, really. So she started a Wiccan coven *based* on the Blackburn Work, but more Goddess-oriented, really. . . ."

Fortunately the tea arrived—if it hadn't Winter would probably have walked out right then. Cassie was dead, and in the face of that disaster Winter had no taste for listening to New Age drivel.

"We sort of worked as astral police, you know, like the Grey Angels," Rhiannon said, and with that phrase got Winter's entire attention. What did Rhiannon know about the Grey Angels? "So we knew it was coming."

"You'll forgive me," Winter said tightly, "if I ask what this has to do with anything?" She pushed the raw anguish of Cassie's murder from her mind, courting the blessed numbness that hovered on her mental horizon. This was how it could be, if she only surrendered to it: no more fear, no more pain, no more weariness and tears. There was no need to wander in the wilderness looking for some better answer that she would never find: She could become winter in fact as well as name, and if she could not heal, at least she would never be hurt again.

Only surrender, surrender, sang the seductive serpent voice. . . .

"Cassie knew the Elemental was coming," Rhiannon said, and now her eyes glittered with anger as well as tears. "She knew she was going to die. We tried to stop it, to bind it, but Cassie said it drew power from the fact that the task it had been created for was undone. We put up the strongest wards we could. . . . Cassie thought you might be able to control it—she tried to find you but you never answered your phone; she called all your old friends and none of them could help. . . ."

The fury in Winter blazed up until she felt clothed in invisible lightning, like a character in a book she'd read once, whose anger alone could kill. The power of the poltergeist struggled to break free, but she had chained it, chained it forever to her service and it would never be free.

"I've heard about enough," Winter said. How dare this . . . *person* drag her in here simply to whine that Winter had not been there when Cassie died? "Thank you for the tea." She got to her feet.

"No! Don't go—I'm sorry! But she knew it was coming for her for weeks and there was nothing she could do—she tried and she tried, she knew it would kill her, and I loved her—" Rhiannon was crying openly now, her pale freckled skin turned blotchy and unattractive by her tears. "She never blamed you—she knew you'd come, only you'd be too late— she knew what you needed; she told me to give you a message—"

"*You?*" Winter said in blazing contempt. Everyone in the café was staring at both of them, which angered her further. She dug in her purse for some money, and threw a handful of ones on the table. "I wouldn't trust you to deliver a pizza. Now leave me alone." *Leave Cassie's memory alone!*

Winter turned and strode from the restaurant. She heard Rhiannon scramble out of the booth behind her and walked faster, her heels beating a quick tattoo on the wooden floor.

Rhiannon followed her up the street. "She knew you'd be coming!" she shouted at Winter's back. "She wrote you a letter—to explain—it's in my apartment—it isn't far from here. I can get it if you'll wait. *Will you at least give me some place I can mail it to?*"

Winter managed to keep ahead of Rhiannon, but when she reached the car she had to stop in order to unlock the door. It took her three tries to get her key into the lock, and by that time the other woman had caught up to her.

"Won't you even *read* it?" Rhiannon said from behind her. "Please—" She put her hand on Winter's arm.

Winter shrugged her off with a gesture that was barely less than a blow. Rhiannon staggered back, staring at her in incredulity.

"Get your hands off me, you filthy little—*coward!*" Winter spat. Cowards, all of them, running away from Reality's hard truths with their fairy tales of specialness and purpose!

Rhiannon retreated another step in the face of Winter's white-faced fury, but stubbornly held her ground. "I'm not the one who's running away," she said shakily, as Winter climbed into the driver's seat and slammed the door in Rhiannon's face.

Winter tucked the ticket for Long-Term Parking into her purse and started in the direction of the distant airport terminal. As much as she strove for calm, every time she thought about Rhiannon, ghoulishly haunting the sidewalk in front of the burned-out bookstore, waiting for her, her hands began to tremble and invisible lightnings danced behind her eyes. . . .

Winter took a deep and steadying breath. It was over. Everything was over, and there was no point to dwelling upon it. What mattered was that now any hope she had of finding Hunter Greyson was gone, unless she wanted to hire a private detective.

And the MAGICKAL CHILD—*the Elemental? What about it? It killed Cassie.*

No. The denial was automatic. There had been a fire; the bookstore had burned with Cassie trapped inside. The rest was lies. There was no vengeful ghost stalking the five—the four—of them.

A wave of vertigo washed over her, forcing Winter to clutch at a nearby car for support. She closed her eyes, willing herself to stay upright. After a moment the dizziness waned, but every time she tried to think things over it got worse.

There was a reasonable explanation, a logical one. Fires did not start of themselves, nor objects move—nor intangible monsters stalk the living. . . .

She could feel her heart beginning to race as—trapped and frightened by her own mind—Winter sought for a way out.

Breathe. Grey's voice in her mind was a calm demand. *In—out—you've been doing it for years, remember? Breathe.*

Winter filled her lungs, fighting not to gasp with sheer terror. The sense of threat receded, but not the feeling that there was something left undone, and little time to do it in.

Oh, Grey—help me! But this time there was no answer, and even the certainty of Grey's presence that Winter had come to expect—self-delusion or not—was missing.

This one she had to do on her own.

"I . . . believe," Winter said. Her voice was a croaking whisper. She held a hand out in front of her, fingers spread, and was pleased to see how little it trembled.

I believe in the Unseen World. I believe in the power of the mind to obliterate time and distance, to know what it cannot possibly know and do what it cannot possibly do. There was a creature at Nuclear Lake, and in the Bidney Institute laboratory. I saw it, and I saw what it could do. It was there, and then it was here.

And it's won. It killed Cassie.

Strength and anger drained out of her together, leaving only weariness and grief. She tried not to think of Cassie, dead and mutilated like the animal corpses that haunted all the survivors of Nuclear Lake. If the fire had killed Cassie before the creature reached her, that death would have been more merciful. Had Cassie set the fire herself to achieve the only escape she could?

Had it been Cassie's death that had been the creature's goal all along?

If that's true then I'm free, Winter thought. The thought was barely formed before it was drowned in a torrent of guilt. How could she bear to buy her safety at the price of Cassie's death?

It wasn't my choice to make, Winter told herself desperately. Oh, but once she'd held Life in her hands and been asked to choose, and then . . .

Winter gagged and swallowed hard against the sickness in her throat. She closed her eyes tightly; she did not understand where the certain knowledge of her personal guilt had come from, but its crushing weight was enough to drive her mad. . . .

*Mad. How simple. How convenient. Oh, stop it—Stop It—*STOP IT! HOW CAN I MAKE AMENDS WHEN I DON'T KNOW WHAT I'VE DONE—

"Lady, are you okay?"

Winter opened her eyes and stared at the man with the suit coat flung

over one arm and his keys in an outstretched hand, obviously a business-
man returned from his trip and on his way to claim his car.

"Lady? You okay?" he repeated dubiously.

Why do people keep asking me that when I'm not? Winter shook her head
and began to laugh helplessly, the sound rising and falling in the evening
air like jagged arpeggios.

"I must say, you look perfectly dreadful. When you called from the plane
we didn't know what to think. Of course Father and I knew that you
weren't at the spa any longer, but *San Francisco*—"

"It isn't exactly Ultima Thule, Mother."

"Don't be rude, dear. Now, where's your luggage?"

I think I left it in Long-Term Parking. "I'm traveling light, Mother."

"Well, I can loan you some things, especially now that you've lost a
few pounds. I didn't like to say anything, dear, you know I don't meddle
in my children's lives, but you were getting just a touch portly there for
a while."

I weighed a hundred and ten pounds, Mother.

The Mercedes was waiting, parking lights flashing, in the drop-off zone
at the entrance to La Guardia Airport. A ticket already fluttered under
the windshield wipers. Mrs. Musgrave snatched it and stuffed it into the
pocket of her mink baseball jacket.

"Mother—" Winter said in exasperation.

"Oh, they don't mean it," her mother said, fishing for her keys. "And
I suppose I was supposed to park in *Ultima Thule?* It's not as if the chauf-
feur could just circle the block, now, is it?"

"Let me drive," Winter said.

Her mother's brows rose in well-manicured surprise. "Oh, do you still
have your license? I'd thought, after your accident . . ." Mrs. Musgrave
delicately let the sentence drop, and got behind the wheel.

Winter's jaw tightened, but after all these years it was reflexive habit
rather than a feeling of true anger. When her mother unlocked the
passenger-side door, Winter slid in across the leather seat, reaching for
her seat belt. Mrs. Musgrave took off before Winter was belted in, sliding the car into traffic with the serene assurance of one who knows all
traffic will stop for her.

Winter leaned back against the seat and glanced at her mother. Cole-Haan shoes and Pendleton slacks, the silly-lavish jacket over a taupe cashmere turtleneck and Mikamoto pearls; her mother had not changed a bit. There might be more gray in the perfect blond hair, but with weekly visits to the salon in Manhattan—an excuse for lunch with "the girls" and shopping, or maybe a show—no one including Mrs. Musgrave would ever know.

"You ought to take better care of yourself, darling. You really have let yourself go." Mrs. Musgrave tapped manicured fingernails on the steering wheel and watched the traffic as if she suspected it of cheating her.

In that case, I wonder where I went. And if I had fun there. "How have you been, Mother?" Winter said aloud.

"Oh, life goes on. Kenneth is very pleased about, oh, something-or-other at work—you know I haven't any head for business—we had to cancel the trip to Bermuda last winter because he wanted to stay on top of things, and of course it was impossible to get a refund at the last minute, so what could we do? We sent Kenny Junior and Patricia down, and then of course I had to hear your brother Wycherly hinting around about 'special' treatment—"

Winter smiled a little bitterly at the mention of her brothers. Their names brought them to mind with almost painful clarity. Kenny was Kenneth Junior, the oldest, whose wife Patricia sold real estate for a Long Island broker. Wycherly was her younger brother, named, as Winter was, for the well-researched ancestors of the formidable Musgrave lineage.

"You spoil Kenny, Mother." And Wycherly resented the obvious favoritism shown to his golden and glorified elder sibling. "And you know that Wych—"

"I suppose you think I ought to have sent *Wycherly* and Patricia?" her mother said with a silvery laugh. "Well, never mind. I know you're tired and aren't feeling well; we'll be home soon, and then you can rest. I hope you'll be planning to stay for a while; you've been quite the stranger these past few years, and though Father would never dream of mentioning it I know you've hurt him terribly. You really ought to think more of others, Winter, dear; but then you never did think of anyone but yourself." Satisfied with the placement of her last barb, Mrs. Musgrave changed to another subject.

Why did I come here? Winter wondered, half-despairing. Her mother's voice purled on, like a quiet stream deep enough to drown in, but Winter tuned it out, watching the cars slide past them on the Brooklyn-Queens Expressway.

She'd gone home because she had no place else to go, because she'd owed this visit ever since she'd left Fall River, because they were her parents and deserved to know how things were with her.

But nothing here had changed. Kenneth still got all the attention and the lavish marks of parental favor—and drank too much, as far as Winter remembered, though certainly that wasn't something the family ever spoke of. Wycherly still drifted from this to that, looking for some position that would engage his talents and ending up living back at home more often than not—and at thirty it was becoming obvious that the youngest Musgrave sibling was what previous generations had not hesitated to label a wastrel.

Mother tended her house, her wardrobe, and her friendships, serving on this committee or that, all indistinguishable from one another except for the names of the benefiting charity and the committee members she was fighting with.

Father worked, eighty-hour weeks at the brokerage on Wall Street, barely home enough to interfere in the lives of his family.

Nothing had changed.

"Are you listening?"

"Yes, Mother," Winter answered dutifully.

"I said, you ought to see my doctor while you're here. He's very good, you know; keeps up with all the latest literature on depression and nerves. I don't know if you really ought to even consider going back to work for a year or so at least. Your health has never been terribly good, you know, and work isn't all there is in the world."

What alternative are you offering me? Winter wondered, knowing there was none. She reached for the comforting illusion of Grey's presence, but it wasn't there. All she had was the sick heavy outliers of a headache that owed nothing to poltergeists or the paranormal, and everything to coming home again.

When it had been built in 1916, Wychwood had been considered a tiny jewel-box of a house—only twenty-six rooms, built as a wedding present by Great-Grandfather Wycherly for his daughter and her husband.

With the Great Depression, the family fortunes had declined to such an extent that when a fire had destroyed the stables and one wing of the house they had not been rebuilt, and time had taken the tennis courts, the boxwood maze, and the formal gardens that Winter knew only from her study of old photo albums. But what remained of Wychwood was, by today's standards, a stately home indeed, and as the Mercedes pulled in through the high iron gates—now rusted permanently half-open—and slid up the long graveled drive, Winter could feel privilege and expectation wrap her in bonds as unyielding as the grave.

Who's the coward now?

Winter stood at the top of the stairs, looking down at the archway that led into the dining room. Her encounter with Rhiannon in San Francisco was only a jumbled collection of impressions now, but the irony of that taunt remained: Winter couldn't remember the last time she'd been this scared. The headache she had expected had never quite fulfilled its promise: The worst of the pain remained in the future, and its potential made everything in the house seem to be taking place under water. With damp palms Winter smoothed the thin silk *voile* of the borrowed Hannae Mori dress against her thighs and reminded herself that what waited at the foot of the stairs could not be so very bad. It was only her family, after all. What harm could they wish her?

Coward. Coward, coward, coward. If you were going to run, you should have run AWAY.

Memories just beyond her grasp roiled the sluggish surface of Winter's consciousness, troubling but not enlightening her. But if there were something here in the house where she'd grown up that she no longer remembered, it could hardly be important—to her or to Grey.

With that thought, a dull spike of pain began to throb monotonously behind her right eye. She really ought to go down. Waiting would not improve matters, and would only give Mother more ammunition in her campaign to render Winter a homebound invalid.

And why not? Isn't she right? All I proved by leaving Fall River was that I'm not capable of coping with the real world. I set out to remember the past, and all I did was confuse myself further. I don't even know what's real any more. I've lost Grey forever, and now I feel guilty about that, too. And as for whatever it is that's chasing me . . .

It wouldn't follow her here to Wychwood. It couldn't.

There was something so disturbing about that certainty that it made dinner seem innocuous by comparison. Winter smoothed her dress one last time and hurried down the stairs.

Despite her penchant for continual redecorating, Mother had left the dining room alone. It was just as Winter remembered it: cream and Wedgwood blue, the colors echoed in the Aubusson carpet and the stiff damask curtains that stayed closed no matter the hour or the season. The first course was already on the table and five places were laid. Winter wondered who the holdout was, Father or Patricia; her mother and her two brothers were already there, waiting for her.

"Winter! How good to see you." Kenny came around the table, looking formidably stuffy in his three-piece Brooks Brothers suit in banker's gray. He hugged her in a distant formal fashion, and Winter could smell the mingled scents of bay rum and expensive bourbon. Kenny was the eldest; in his early forties now. More whiskey, less hair, but otherwise unchanged from her last memory of him—how many years ago?

"Kenny," she said. "You're looking well. Is Patsy joining us?" Those were the things people said, weren't they? Normal people—and people passing for normal?

An elaborate Waterford chandelier showered light on the silver and crystal on the table and the mirrors on the walls; a setting as pristine and inhuman as the surface of the moon.

"Patricia had to stay late to show a house farther out on the Island. Father will be along when he can," Mrs. Musgrave said from the foot of the table. She'd also changed for dinner, into something floaty and formal the color of ashes of roses. Heirloom diamonds glittered in her ears. "If only you'd let us know you were coming—"

"He'd have had time to beat it out for Frankfurt instead of just a late meeting—but I forget, Winty, you were always his favorite," the last of the dinner party guests said.

The childish diminutive brought back an instant snapshot memory of her sixth birthday party—and of the toddler, crowing with delight as he buried his face and both hands in her birthday cake, ignoring Winter's hysterical screams of rage.

"Hello, Wych," Winter said. "And it was Kenny who was his favorite, not me."

A ripple of surprise spread among the others at this plain speaking; Kenny coughed and Wych grinned maliciously and Miranda Musgrave sat up straighter in her chair. Disapproval etched stark lines into her face.

"Do sit down, Winter. Father will want us to start without him. And you do need to keep up your strength."

"Yes, Mother," Winter said meekly, her flash of defiance over. She sat down at the table across from her brothers. The ghosts of dinners past crowded around her as she picked up her soupspoon and tried to will herself invisible.

"And how are things at the bank today, Kenneth dear?" Mrs. Musgrave asked, smoothly taking command of the conversation.

Kenny began his reply—which would be exhaustive yet diplomatic, as always—and under cover of her mother's ostensible absorption in the discussion with her elder brother, Winter studied her youngest brother. Everything else was the same—was he?

Wych was dressed much too casually for a dinner at Wychwood, wearing a rumpled sport coat over an open shirt. His hair was several weeks late for a haircut. Like Winter, he possessed the pale chestnut hair and hazel-brown eyes of their Wycherly grandmother, but instead of the stubbornness that dominated Winter's face and the set of her mouth, Wycherly's features seemed forged by some streak of cowardly cruelty.

Why am I thinking these thoughts?

She glanced toward Kenny. Though he was only a few years older than she, Kenny's hair had already faded to the color of tarnished brass, and in place of cruelty, his face showed nothing so much as a bovine indifference to the world around her.

"But you're not eating, dear," her mother said. "Shall I have Martha fix you something else?"

So that one moment you can say I'm putting on too much weight and the next try to force-feed me? "No thanks, Mother," Winter said briefly.

"Wycherly, do try to sit up straight. I'm sure Winter would like to hear what you've been doing."

Wycherly regarded Winter with sullen resentment. "Oh, I don't think so," he began nastily, but stopped at his mother's expression of doe-eyed injury. Surrendering, he'd only gotten a few sentences into a hopelessly muddled explanation of some venture partnership when Kenny interrupted with the tale of a boat that he and Patricia were thinking of buying.

"—I'd heard that Stevenson down in Term Mortgages had been looking at something like it but couldn't quite swing the financing, so naturally I took the opportunity to ask his opinion—"

And make sure he knew you were buying a boat he couldn't afford, Winter finished for him silently. The atmosphere in the room shifted like water; water to put out fire. . . .

Something was wrong here—more wrong than the clash of weak and spiteful personalities—but she could not be quite sure what. Of course everyone's family were perfect horrors; Mother wanted her own way no matter who was hurt, Kenny was a snob and a tyrant, and Wych was as much of a bully as he could get away with being, but somehow she didn't remember them being quite so *blatant* about it.

And if they were all of these things, what was she?

Dinner seemed to last for an eternity.

Kenneth Musgrave, Senior, arrived as predicted, about the time dinner was over and the dessert service had been laid out by the ever-faithful Martha. They had always had servants, and if Winter had thought about it at all, she'd considered it an automatic sign of privilege—but how much of a privilege was it, really, to have to wait for and depend on other people to do things you were perfectly capable of doing yourself?

She welcomed her father's arrival with relief. It had taken all her ingenuity to skate around the gaps in her memory; the only reason she was able to manage was the unwillingness of the others to mention anything that might open the subject of Winter's stay at Fall River. She wondered what they'd say if she told them her problem had been diagnosed as poltergeists, not nervous collapse!

"Daddy!" Winter cried, flinging herself into his arms with the first unmixed emotions she'd felt all day.

"How's my baby girl?" Kenneth Musgrave greeted her.

Now in his late sixties, Winter's father was tanned, silver-haired, and vigorous; so perfect a depiction of a prosperous Wall Street financier that he might almost be a symbol and not the thing itself. He hugged his daughter hard and then released her, studying her with acute steel-gray eyes.

"And what brings you to our humble hacienda?" he said, smiling. "I thought you were settled in to that place you bought upstate. Randa, get me a drink, would you?"

Winter let the baffling reference pass as her mother hurried to get her father his drink. This was what life at home had been like as long as Winter could remember: Kenneth Musgrave would enter like a conquering lion, and the Musgrave women would scurry to do his bidding.

And the Musgrave men . . . ?

She stepped away from her father, glancing at her brothers, the princes in waiting, to see them both regarding her father with identical expressions of resentful envy.

"I hope you'll be getting back to work, soon," Mr. Musgrave said. "You can't let one failure define your entire life."

With her father's arrival, Winter realized, the last player in the family tragedy had appeared, and events settled into their accustomed paths as if they had been repeated every night for a thousand years.

"Oh, Kenneth," her mother fluttered, "don't you think it's too soon? After all, Winter is so fragile. . . ."

"Fragile is another word for failure," her father said flatly. "Ken Junior might not be as bright as his sister, but he's risen right to the top. Persistence is what matters. You aren't going to fail me twice, are you Winter?"

His pale eyes transfixed her, allowing no room for evasion. All Winter could think of was every time she'd failed, every occasion on which she'd disappointed this man.

"I won't fail," she said in a low voice.

Her father smiled, and it seemed to Winter as if there were something of gloating in it, as if some victory had been achieved that stretched far beyond her obedience.

She looked around the table, and it was suddenly as if each of them stood in the shadow of someone she knew: Kenny was Janelle, who'd surrendered everything she was good at for peace and security and found neither; Wycherly was Ramsey, afraid to try and knowing that the failure was killing him. . . .

Both of her brothers had lost the golden time that Ramsey had talked about, and were doomed now to repeat their parents' failures until the end of time.

And her parents? Her father and mother? Whose failures were Kenneth and Miranda Musgrave doomed to re-create? Ramsey had said she'd escaped—she and Grey—but had he known how easy it was to fall back into failure? No matter what she did now—fail or win—Winter would disappoint one of her parents, and the realization was an unbearable, inescapable pressure.

"I— Excuse me; I don't think I feel very well." Winter flung down her napkin and all but fled the dining room.

Her mother had given Winter her old room, but no trace remained now of Winter's childhood occupancy. The room had long since been converted to the perfect guest room, from the Laura Ashley Ribbons & Roses wallpaper to the trendy country look of the hand-painted furniture and patchwork quilt on the bed. The room was light-years from Janelle's Sears, Roebuck kitchen, but even at its stifling worst there had been something more . . . human . . . about Janelle's house.

The illness she had feigned appeared for real; Winter bolted for the bathroom as her stomach tried to eject what she'd managed to swallow of the evening's meal.

Afterward, trembling and sore, Winter opened the medicine cabinet in search of toothpaste and found instead several miniature bottles of liquor.

So Wycherly's following at least one family tradition.

The only thing that surprised her was how much sadness the knowledge gave her. But she knew it had to be his; Kenny didn't live here and neither of her parents would have felt the need to hide their liquor.

Winter twisted the cap off one of the little bottles, rinsed her mouth with vodka and spat, then opened another and drank it straight down. Cold eighty-proof fire spread through her aching stomach, soothing the pain. Every instinct urged her to leave right now, to flee, but that was madness. This was her house; her family.

"What family doesn't have its ups and downs?" Winter tipsily quoted James Goldman as she reached for another of the little glittering bottles. *I'm having a relapse. Another breakdown. Whatever.*

And whatever it was, she couldn't bear it. Why had she come back here, if coming was going to cause her so much pain? What kind of coward was she?

A pretty stupid one.

She'd been smarter before she'd gone to Fall River. The last time she'd been here was the summer she'd left school. She hadn't been back since then. Not for Christmas, not for Thanksgiving. Not in fourteen years.

And you'd think, wouldn't you, that someone in the family would have mentioned that on the evening when Winter Musgrave came home again at last?

Suddenly she was crawlingly cold to the tips of her fingers. All the secrets she'd cavalierly tried to unearth weren't tidily deposited elsewhere. Some of the puzzles were here.

And I said I wanted to know the truth. How stupid can you get? Oh, Grey, darling, help me!

Winter retreated back to the bedroom, taking a third little bottle with her. Her headache was coming now in waves of chill and nausea, and in the world outside it had started to rain. The storm that had been threatening all afternoon and evening was breaking at last, and when Winter looked out the window she could see white lines of rain illuminated by the security floodlights.

It had been raining that night.

No! She could feel the effect it took to shove the memory beneath the surface, but she managed to make it. Her heart beat faster with fear, and the exertion left her dazzled and weak. She fell into the chair and stared morosely out the window.

There were memories in the rain:

—*Winter Musgrave! That plate was Limoges!*

—*But I didn't touch it, Mommy! I didn't!*

But her mother didn't believe her. She never did. *Just wait till your father gets home, young lady*— And Winter had no way to rationalize the things she'd never done—or couldn't remember doing.

—*If you're going to go around trying to be different, don't come crying to me that you're not popular.*

—But, Daddy, all I wanted to do was . . .

—If you'd spend less time trying to make yourself interesting and more on your schoolwork, young lady, you wouldn't have time to complain that no one wants to take you to the prom.

It wasn't like that, Daddy! Winter protested, years too late. *All I wanted was someone who would like* ME, *not Kenneth Musgrave's daughter. . . .*

The rain gusted against the window. It had been raining that night, too.

No. Oh, please, not that. Not here. The pain behind her eyes shook her, making her surroundings glow and waver.

By the time she'd reached her teens Winter no longer remembered the imaginary playmate of her childhood who had yanked pictures off the walls and broken plates with a gesture; nor that the blinding headaches she'd once gotten had coincided with electrical shorts in any machinery close by. She'd only known that there must be more to life than the garden club and the boardroom—something beautiful, meant for her alone. She'd wanted to go to UCLA or Berkeley, but her parents had insisted on an East Coast college. She'd chosen Taghkanic over Albany, even though Taghkanic was closer, because of the liberal arts program at the college and because the fact that it hosted the Bidney Institute horrified her mother.

Don't think I'm going to let you fill this house with a pack of scruffy college students after all my hard work, young lady. If you think you're bringing any of them to this house, think again—

—I wouldn't bring anyone here that I LIKED, *Mother!*

And then she'd met Grey. And he'd been all of her dreams come true.

No—no—no—! Winter pounded her fist on the windowsill, knowing that in some sense she had planned her own agony. Why else come back, when she'd sworn she'd never return here, after—

She'd never return here—

It was raining, and—

Never come back here. Never—

It was raining that night fourteen years ago. She hadn't told them she was coming; she'd taken the train downstate to New York, then the LIRR to the closest station, then a taxi to the foot of the drive. . . .

Winter groaned aloud. In a moment more she would remember; she could feel the psychic scars opening, leaving the wounds as raw and bleeding as if it were yesterday.

She'd walked up from the foot of the drive—to give herself time, to prepare for having to tell them—and the rain had soaked her to the skin, first chilling, then numbing her. She'd wished she could be as numb inside; she would rather feel nothing than the pain. . . .

She would rather feel nothing than the pain.

She could still refuse to remember. To sit here looking inward took more courage than she would need to face a loaded gun; Winter had always thought she had courage, but she knew now those beliefs were a lie. All her life was a lie, carefully constructed.

And now she knew it.

The girl raised her hand to the door-knocker, trying not to think. About what was to come, and what had already happened.

CHAPTER TWELVE

PAST REASON HUNTED

Age makes a winter in the heart,
An autumn in the mind.
— JOHN SPARROW

IN THE ORCHARD BEHIND GREYANGELS, THE APPLE TREES
were in full bloom. When she'd gotten back from the doctor earlier today all she
could think of was finding some way to tell him privately—but on a small cam-
pus where both of them were so well known, privacy was hard to come by. Profes-
sor MacLaren didn't mind Taghkanic students trespassing in his orchard, so she'd
asked Grey to bring her here.

But now that she had him alone, Winter Musgrave, age twenty-two and in
her senior year at Taghkanic College, didn't know where to begin. "I have some-
thing I need to tell you," she'd said, and then had chattered on about meaningless
things: spring break, the graduation ceremonies only a few months away, plans for
the coming summer that she now knew were meaningless.

"Come on," Grey said. He'd leaned toward her, the fringe on his white buck-
skin jacket swinging. A stray sunbeam glinted off the glass-bead embroidery
across the jacket's shoulders; a blue more brilliant than the sky. "You've been danc-

ing all around SOMETHING. *What?" he'd demanded. "Did you hear something about the internship? 'Dandy' Lion was supposed to hear this week—"*

They'd both applied for summer intern positions with the American Shakespeare Company, and Professor Welland had thought there was a good chance that Grey, at least, would get his. Winter brushed the thought aside. Like all her other plans for the future, it no longer mattered.

"I'm going to have a baby," she'd blurted out.

Grey had gone instantly still, staring at her with wide gray eyes. Even in this moment, knowing he was going to reject her, Winter could not help loving him the way she loved the wild beauty of the hawks or the Taconic hills. The spring breeze from the river had fluttered through his pale hair and the beaded fringe on his jacket, and it seemed as if the world held its breath.

"A baby." Grey had taken a deep breath and smiled. "A baby! Our baby! Why didn't you tell me? How long have you— How do you know?" He'd reached for her and Winter gestured irritably, stopping him.

"I went to the doctor," Winter told him in a small cross voice. "Dammit, those pills are supposed to WORK.*"*

Grey had laughed. "Everything always works out for the best." He'd tried to put his arms around her, but Winter whirled away, glaring at the inoffensive apple tree directly before her and willing the tears not to come. Flower petals were everywhere, covering the spring grass in mock snow. She'd brushed them forlornly off the shoulders of her fake-fur jacket, hating the mess.

"For the best! Grey, what am I going to DO*?" she'd wailed, leaning suddenly against the tree. It was somehow worse that he'd accepted it. When she wasn't facing active resistance, Winter had never known quite what to do.*

"Don't you want a baby?" Grey said then, and the sober note in his voice had made her turn back and look at him. "Do you want to, uh . . ." His voice trailed off awkwardly.

I DON'T KNOW, I DON'T KNOW—

"I don't KNOW*!" Winter wailed. "You aren't— We aren't—" She gestured helplessly, unable to put her thoughts into words, conscious only of feeling trapped. "What am I going to do?—Mother said they'd send me to Europe for the summer after graduation—mostly to get me away from you—and Daddy wants me to go to work for a friend of his on Wall Street—or get married—and I don't even know what I'm going to tell them, and—"*

"Marry me," Grey had said. "We'll have the baby, and if that internship

thing doesn't work out I can do the Renfaire circuit out in California full time. We have the Blackburn Work, and I know some people out in the Bay Area who'll help us. Everything's going to work out. You'll see."

Winter had gone on the circuit with him last summer, doing the pseudo-Elizabethan Renaissance Pleasure Faires up and down the West Coast. She'd played the guitar; Grey had done stage magic. They'd spent the summer sleeping on friends' couches or in the back of Grey's van; fine for a few weeks, but for a life? With a baby coming?

"I don't know," Winter began, hesitantly. She could see the beginnings of confusion on Grey's face; the question he was too proud to ask: "Don't you love me, Winter?"

I DO, GREY—I DO! BUT I'M SO AFRAID—

"Stay with me, Winter," he said, holding out his hand one last time. "Stay with me."

She put her hands behind her back, afraid that if she took his hand she'd lose all common sense and blindly follow her heart.

"I . . . I have to think, Grey. Take me back." It wasn't true—she hadn't been able to think, not with so much uncertainty swirling around her.

"It's my baby, too; don't you think it's my decision, too?" Grey sounded hurt then and she couldn't bear it.

"NO!" Winter exploded. "No I don't! It's my body and my life, and I can't just—"

He'd closed the distance between them and put his arms around her. She'd clung to him as if she were drowning and cried as if everything she loved were already gone. He held her until her tears were exhausted, teased her until she smiled, and promised her the sun, the moon, and the stars.

And he'd thought everything was settled then, with the easy confidence of one who had never known defeat. But she'd had no faith in the future he painted for her.

And that night, without telling anyone, not even Cassilda, she'd taken the train south.

Home.

Winter opened her eyes. The storm had softened to a steady drumming rhythm that could go on for hours, and through the open window the room was filled with the smell of rain and wet earth. Laboriously Winter picked herself up off the floor of her room. When she moved, she found that her entire body ached with chill and tension, but the headache had passed, leaving a light-headed lethargy in its wake. Unwillingly she looked around. For a moment she expected to see the rows of carefully preserved stuffed animals, but that belonged to the past; she'd given them all away years ago.

Winter's eyes brimmed with the unshed tears of a grief too long deferred. She had built her self-image on her risk-taking and courage, and all of it was a lie. She wasn't brave. She'd betrayed everything and everyone she really loved. Unforgivably. Irrevocably.

Winter climbed shakily to her feet, wondering how long she'd been lying on the floor. She no longer wondered why no one had come to look in on her and see if she was all right—she knew all of Wychwood's secrets now. Automatically she looked out the window, but could tell nothing of the time. It was late, that much she knew. The rain spilling from the gutters was a silvery waterfall in the house's security lighting, and the rest of the house's inhabitants must long since be in bed. Low blood sugar made Winter's hands shake, and her skin felt cold and clammy. That much, at least, she could fix.

All trace of use had been cleared away; the cloth changed, Grandmother Winter's sterling centerpiece returned to its accustomed place. Winter walked into the dining room. Everything was where it should be. Nothing was out of place—not the furniture, not the children. Any exceptions were swiftly dealt with.

And they kept at me and at me—they were my parents—they were supposed to know what was best—not just what was convenient!

But that wasn't true. She hadn't been a child any longer by the time she'd come home to Wychwood that spring. She should not have given them the kind of control an adult took of a child's life over hers.

But she had. She'd given them that power through fear or cowardice or even stupidity. She'd known she wanted something different than her mother's life and her father's, but in the end she hadn't trusted herself enough to take charge of her own future.

She'd paid for that.

But she wasn't the only one.

She—and Grey—and the child who had never been born—all of them had paid. And the girl she'd been, like some spell-cursed princess, had been doomed to dream away her life inside the arctic armor Winter had forged about herself to numb the pain of that disastrous choice.

Until . . .

Winter felt the flickering feeble attempt of the destroying angel to rouse beneath her skin. She pushed it away, back into the world of dream. She had made her power into a dream—a bad dream—and had dreamed on, insensible, until something had come looking for her.

Something that was tithed in blood. Something Winter had retreated into madness to escape, not knowing that to do so would free that long-denied, long-betrayed, part of herself—or that, freed, it would fight to reach her across the borderland of her unconscious mind.

With one last clutch, Winter felt the coils of her hate-born shadow-self relax forever. All that was left was Winter Musgrave.

Who's a fool.

For a moment she allowed the self-hatred to well up, then let go of that, too. Even after her mother had gotten her way about the baby, Winter could still have taken back her life—but grief and self-hatred had paralyzed her and she had let others choose her future for her—choices that had not been made out of love, but out of anger. Wychwood held little love within its walls.

Winter laughed a little shakily, and flipped on the dining room lights. *By all means, let's have all the demons out of the box in one go.* She walked through and into the kitchen and began opening cupboards, her body's demands uppermost in her mind. She found a box of raisins and began stuffing the fruit into her mouth, swallowing almost without chewing.

But even while her body concentrated on the food, her mind refused to stop spinning. Something inside her wanted her to understand everything she'd refused to face for all those wasted years.

Parents were supposed to love their children. But love didn't necessarily make someone wise. *God knows I'm living proof of that. . . .* And anger at their own missed choices had become anger for its own sake, anger that, like the serpent, was willing to strike at any target.

Even at their own children.

So no one could be allowed to escape. Because if someone did manage to break free, it proved there was another way, another life possible, and all the sacrifice and pain would have been for nothing. . . .

There was a sound behind her. Winter turned around just in time to see Wycherly walk through the dining room into the kitchen.

He was rumpled and disheveled, his hair as wet as if he'd been walking outside in the storm. His jacket was gone and his feet were bare; with a small disinterested part of her mind Winter wondered what he'd been doing. He glared at her balefully before seeming to recollect that she was his sister and there was no particular cause for enmity between them.

"What are you doing here?" he asked ungraciously. Without waiting for an answer he crossed to the enormous built-in refrigerator and pulled open one of the doors.

"Leaving," said Winter, and as she said it, it was true. The mistake that had led to everything that followed had been lack of faith. She would not make it twice. It wasn't too late; she could still change, take back the life she'd relinquished.

And even if she couldn't, at least she could keep from hurting anyone else. She could stop the rage, the hunger. . . .

"I doubt it." Malice gleamed in Wycherly's eyes—the only honest expression of his feelings she'd seen since she'd come back. But without the poltergeist-gift, the expression of Wych's anger would be controlled by his conscious mind. He made a mocking salute with the bottle of orange juice in his hand, and drank.

"Believe it. I have what I came back for," Winter said. *Even if I didn't want it very much.* "I have nothing more to say to any of . . . them." She hesitated on the last word, mentally absolving Wycherly of any part in the events of that horrible summer. He'd been eighteen, then, on the verge of his own life.

And was still, fourteen years later, on the verge of his life.

"Wych, get away from here," Winter said impulsively. "I know it seems like staying is the only way, but it isn't. If you—"

"That's rich coming from you, sister dear. Isn't it supposed to be the cuckoo that throws the other chicks out of the nest? But you're a true-born Musgrave, right enough: our motto, 'Expediency *über Alles.*'" He closed the refrigerator with a careless slap and strode over to her. This close, she could see the faint red-golden stubble along his jaw.

"You haven't had much use for us while you were feathering your Wall Street nest, but now I suppose you think it's time to make amends in order to be on hand for a favorable redrawing of the will. Well, go ahead!

Let Mother pick you out a trophy husband—something chic, a thirty-eight-long in legal sharkskin—and Pats can sell you a crackerbox palace nice and close, so Mommy Dearest can manage your life, too—"

Wycherly stopped, but more from lack of breath than because he'd run out of things to say.

Winter shook her head, holding up her hand as if she were calling a time-out. Somehow the venom in Wych's words only strengthened her faith in her choice. They carried no pain with them—it was as if they were addressed to someone else.

"No." *I had a lover, once, and I threw him away.* "Wych, I think you should leave, but I'm not going to run your life for you. But I'm leaving. Things happened here—" *And I can't forgive my parents for them, even though they're partly my own fault.* She shrugged. "I'm leaving first thing tomorrow morning and I'm never coming back here again. That's all."

"I don't believe you," Wycherly said uncertainly.

Winter laughed, and felt the crushing weight on her heart ease slightly at last. "Oh, Wych! As the man said about life after death, sooner or later you'll *know,* so why fret about it? Believe me or don't—I don't care."

She watched doubt and sullen anger chase each other across Wycherly's face until he settled on a guarded blankness.

"Mother will have a fit," he pronounced with faint satisfaction.

"Let her," Winter said. *It'd be a shame to waste all that practice.*

When Winter finally returned to her room, her sleep was too deep for dreams; the felled coma that followed an emotional purging. The alarm clock she'd set jangled her awake at 5 A.M.; moving with machinelike precision Winter dressed quickly in the clothes she had worn on the airplane yesterday, made one quick phone call, and then hurried downstairs.

As she had believed, her parents still had morning coffee together before the car came to bring Kenneth Musgrave into the city. As Winter stepped into the breakfast nook, she saw that this morning they were not alone; Wycherly was with them.

Well, what did you expect? she scolded herself, sighing. Theirs was not a family for loyalty; Wych had been right: "Expediency *über Alles*" would be an appropriate family motto.

"Winter! Come in, dear," Miranda Musgrave cooed.

A less suspicious person than Winter would have heard the tension in Mrs. Musgrave's voice. Her mother's rings flashed as she twisted her hands nervously.

Winter took a deep breath.

"Mother, Father. I have something to say to both of you. It won't take long, but I'd rather it was private. Wych, you really ought to pick a side and stick to it; it's much less confusing. Now go away."

"I think he should stay," her mother said tightly.

Winter looked at her father. Kenneth Musgrave glowered back, his baleful eyes piercing.

"I don't think you have anything to say you can't say in front of your brother," he rumbled. Only last night his displeasure would have terrified her, but not now. Never again.

"All right." Now that she was committed, a curious peace settled over Winter, akin to that which she'd once felt on the Street, on the trading floor. It was almost as if she was being reminded that some good things could be salvaged from even the worst mistakes. She took another steadying breath.

"Fourteen years ago I came to you for advice. I was pregnant, as you'll remember. I will not speculate about your reasons for the choices you made then; I will only say now, as I did then, that Grey was willing to marry me and help me raise the baby. I loved him then, and I still love him. If I find him, I will ask his forgiveness for what I did.

"I am to blame for giving in to you; I'll take responsibility for that. But I trusted you, and you betrayed me. I have no intention of giving any of you that kind of power over me or my life ever again. So, good-bye."

Wycherly was staring at her, stunned. Looking at him, it was impossible to believe he'd known. She glanced at her parents. Her father's face was bland, but her mother's was a mask of fury startling in its intensity.

"How *dare* you come into my house and speak to me like that?" she hissed.

"Now, Randa." Her father's voice was unhurried; in control. "Winter. Sit down, sweetheart. Nobody's going to hurt you. I'll call a friend of mine and you can be back at Fall River by this evening. You'd like that, wouldn't you?"

His voice was steely and soothing, with an undercurrent of threat: *Whether you'd like it or not, you're going back there until you learn to behave.*

"No," Winter said simply. "I'm not crazy and I'm not having a nervous breakdown. I'm just angry. And if institutionalization is your idea of how to deal with family problems—"

She stopped, looking at Wycherly, and with sudden intuition knew more than she'd ever wanted to know about her family's way of dealing with family problems.

"I'm leaving now. Good luck, Wych. Good-bye Father. Mother."

She turned and walked out.

"Winter!" her father shouted after her, showing anger at last. But neither of her parents followed her—all the anger and the veiled threats were only bluster: They lacked the will to act.

The monsters only have the power you give them. Dylan and Truth had both said that, and they'd been right. Now she'd taken back her power.

She was free.

Winter picked up her purse from the table in the front hall and walked down the drive to the waiting taxi. Just as she'd walked up the drive, fourteen years before.

It was a good twenty minutes before the three locks on her Upper East Side apartment door yielded to Winter's keys. The set she'd remembered keeping in her purse had been gone when she'd looked for them, which had necessitated a quick stop at her lawyer's to pick up her spare set. She made a mental note to stop by her accountant's as well—after a year and a half her emergency financial arrangements were in desperate need of an overhaul, but even at her most overwrought she had not wanted her parents to have control of her money, and now Winter blessed that stubborn paranoia. She suspected it was the only thing that had made her able to leave Fall River.

Winter pushed open the apartment door—it seemed to be stuck—and walked in, locking the door behind her. After so long an absence she saw her expensive apartment as a stranger might: a sterile place of gray carpet, white walls, white leather sofa. White vertical blinds masking the view of West Seventy-first Street. Chilly modern art for the walls.

Only now the art wasn't on the walls anymore, nor was the sofa on its legs. Winter stepped cautiously into the living room. Her shoes grated on broken shards of glass. She flipped the switch that should turn on the track-lighting. Nothing happened.

The sofa—what was left of it—was lying on its back in the middle of the room. The arms had been yanked from the frame, the springs pulled out, and the leather shredded. Cotton batting was everywhere. She didn't see the cushions at all.

Why had no one called to complain when this had happened—about the noise, if nothing else? Not that she would have been around to take the message if they had, Winter noted scrupulously. And somehow she didn't think her answering machine had survived to record any messages, either.

There was glass everywhere—from the broken dishes, from the splintered television, from the posters under now-shattered glass. Her dining room table had been a sheet of industrial glass on a granite pedestal. Only the pedestal remained, surrounded by what looked at first like uncut diamonds.

So much anger . . . Winter thought wonderingly. Her own, or that of the creature who stalked her? It hardly mattered now, did it? Whoever had done it, there was nothing left intact in the entire living room.

The bedroom was no better. The mattress and box spring were broken and gutted. The lamps and tables were smashed. The sheets and blankets were shredded. There were papers everywhere, blasted into confetti-sized snow, and Winter breathed a sigh of relief that all the really important papers that defined her life were split between a box at the bank and a file at her lawyer's.

If even they were safe.

With a forbidding sense of dread Winter opened her closet, and quickly wished she hadn't. Her cedarwood hangers were a splintered, tangled mess, and her suits lay on the floor beneath them in tatters.

Twelve hundred plus a pop and you could stuff pillows with them now. I wonder if my insurance covers "poltergeist rage"?

Even her shoes—expensive leather pumps in an entire spectrum of neutral shades—were all somehow mangled: bent and folded, heels torn off, leather gouged.

Nothing salvageable was left.

It's just as well that they aren't really "me" anymore, Winter told herself bravely. In truth, if her work wardrobe—those rigid, colorless suits—had still been intact she probably would have just donated it to some charity boutique. Ungaro and Calvin Klein didn't really fit her new look.

Whatever it was going to be.

Maybe even colors, Winter thought sarcastically. *"When I am an old woman, I shall wear purple. . . ."*

Grimly, she finished her catalog of havoc. The destruction was the same in the kitchen—though messier—and none of the lights worked. Knives and forks were warped and bent and even tied into knots. Her microwave seemed to have . . . melted.

The Geller Effect. What a pity I can't repeat it on demand and earn a million dollars. . . .

The only fortunate thing about the whole disaster was that she or someone had cleaned out her refrigerator and kitchen cabinets before she'd gone to Fall River, but in the bathroom she wasn't as lucky. The bathroom was spattered with a dried rainbow of shower gel and grooming products. The glass bottles were—predictably—shattered, but the plastic bottles were turned mysteriously inside out, something that Winter was not entirely sure was even possible.

She tossed a shampoo bottle, the outside caked with the dried slime of its former contents, into the tub. There was nothing here to salvage, and no point in searching the wreckage. Whatever had destroyed the apartment had been thorough. It saved her the time and labor of packing, really—all Winter had to do was call someone to empty the place to the walls and then repaint.

And then live here?

No. Whatever else she knew, Winter knew also that she could never take up her old life again. Nothing in it seemed to matter now. What mattered was to make what reparations she could for the damaged lives she was responsible for. Winter sighed, making one last survey of her demolished apartment. If she had needed any final proof of the danger stalking her, it was here, in this smorgasbord of destruction. The thing that Truth Jourdemayne had named "Elemental" had killed Cassie. It had invaded the lives of everyone Winter had known—and, it seemed, Winter was the only one who could stop it.

But to do that she had to confront it—as Truth had, as Cassie had.

She didn't think she'd survive the encounter.

Grey could help her, but Winter was no longer sure he would. He might even already be dead—perhaps that had been Cassie's message to her, that the creature had killed and would kill again?

There was no point in guessing—not when she could know.

Winter thought of Rhiannon, blushing with shame as she remembered the meeting. *"Won't you even tell me where to send it?"* the girl had cried—but now that Winter was willing at last to accept the message, she didn't know how to get in touch with Rhiannon.

The business card Paul Frederick gave me. If he was a friend of Cassie's he'd know Rhiannon, too.

Winter shook her head ruefully. She had a long way to go to become even half as brilliant as she'd always thought she was. Finding Rhiannon would not be that hard, and her message was Winter's only possible link to Grey.

And unless Grey was dead, she had to see him one last time.

He isn't dead. I'd know if he were dead. The inner certainty was slight-though-real comfort. She and Grey had been bound together by love and magic, once.

Then why didn't he come for me? her younger self wailed inside her, while an older Winter found the bleak and simple answer: Perhaps he had. That hideous summer she'd gone to Switzerland with her mother to "take care of things"; any New York clinic would have done as well, but that wouldn't have gotten Winter out of the country. If Grey had come for her while she was gone, who knew what her father had told him—and what Grey had believed?

And that September she'd started at the brokerage, using work as a drug to blot out all uncertainty and pain, until the work had taken on a life of its own and become her world.

For as long as it could.

She had to find Grey.

Before the elemental found *her.*

As if the thought had summoned it, Winter felt a sudden chill breeze skirl through the apartment. The vertical linen-weave blinds fluttered, exposing tightly closed windows.

Something was here.

Winter felt her hair stand up in a purely primal response to its presence. Her skin tingled, drawn tight by the lightning in the air.

Just like Nuclear Lake.

But this time she did not react with blind terror. Her panic had come from denial, and now at last Winter consciously knew the things she had been trying so hard to hide from herself. Now the fear she felt was the purely prosaic one of facing an elemental storm in a room full of broken glass. It would cut her to pieces. . . .

Time to leave. Perhaps the creature would not follow her out of the apartment. A few steps took Winter to the front door; she unlatched the dead bolt and turned the knob.

Nothing.

She twisted and pulled—the knob turned freely, but the door wouldn't open. She slammed her fist against it in frustration—a sturdy, expensive, New York door, sheathed in steel, with three-inch dead bolts, and totally immovable.

She was trapped. There was no phone to use to call for help, and help would arrive too late if she did. Winter heard the faint clicking of the blinds as they wavered in the ghostwind.

I have to stop it. I have to make it go away.

But how? Could she control it as she did her own psychokinetic abilities? The Elemental was *not* her, but Truth Jourdemayne had said it was linked to her somehow. Could the link run two ways?

It better, Winter thought grimly, or she was dead and so was her chance of stopping it. The atmosphere in the room felt now as though she were standing directly in front of an air-conditioning vent—a stream of cold air playing directly over her skin. It did not matter that outside her windows it was high noon on a sunny spring day—inside the apartment there was no time left.

The force of the ghostwind increased: Now papers and scraps of cloth on the floor began to shift sluggishly. Soon heavier objects would move. The pressure of what was coming for her made Winter's skin ache. She thought of the pressure building in the room, the windows bulging outward, to burst and shatter piercing fragments on the noon-hour pedestrians jamming the sidewalks below.

No! Take me if you must, but not here! Not where there are other people to be hurt!

The pressure strained to crush her, and Winter pushed back. It was a thousand times harder than shifting a book or a ring of keys—it was as if she struggled to lift the earth itself. The confrontation made her lose control of her own body; Winter sank to her hands and knees in the wreck-age of her apartment and barely felt the shards that cut her hands and knees.

She could not afford to lose. Sweat beaded up on her forehead and splashed down over her hands. She curled her fingers into the carpet, and resisted the elemental pressure with all the furious will she had once brought to denying the truth. She heard the crackle of glass as it was forced into the carpet around her, heard the splintering of glass and plas-tic, heard the walls groan with the pressure. . . .

And became, as Hunter Greyson had once taught her, pure will.

The apartment was gone. She chose what was real. She chose the parts of reality that were used. Winter seemed to hear the roar of the trading floor around her: sheer information, flowing faster than thought, faster than reason, shaped and controlled by human desire. She could make and unmake the world with a thought, with a choice, with her wish to make it so—

She curled her hands in the carpet, driving glass into her skin and never feeling the pain, and with the will that had triumphed over every circumstance in her life, Winter fought back.

There was a yielding, a tearing; Winter was jerked back into the here-and-now, holding to consciousness in a world that seemed to pulse redly and swarm with dizzying black spots. Her lungs ached with breath too long held; she gasped for air, and as oxygen filled her lungs she finally be-came aware of the pain in her hands.

Winter sat back and raised her palms from the carpet. Glass splinters showered from them like a dusting of sugar. Her right hand was cut across the palm, and bled freely; the other hand had several small splin-ters jammed into it. Winter swore, getting awkwardly to her feet, and only then noticed that one leg of her khakis was sliced open along the calf. Blood covered the surface of her skin and wicked into the ragged edges of the cloth. She was only lucky that she wasn't cut more seriously.

I'm just lucky I wasn't killed. Reaction set in, the rush of nausea and adrenaline almost sending her to the floor again. The Elemental was gone. She'd won.

Winter leaned against the wall and began to pick the glass out of her left hand, only then realizing that the bleeding in her other hand had not stopped. Blood ran down her wrist, staining her cotton sweater.

I must look like all six Nightmares on Elm Street.

Winter tottered toward the bathroom and stopped, her attention arrested abruptly by the sight before her. The front door was open—now, when it wouldn't do any good. She shook her head and continued toward the bathroom. The Elemental wasn't coming back today, and unless she cleaned up a little before she went out, she'd probably be arrested.

Fortunately the water still worked, even though none of the bathroom lights did. Winter ran her gashed hands under the cold water until the bleeding slowed, then picked the splinters out of her palm, wincing queasily at the pain. With a salvaged bit of towel she cautiously wiped the gash on her leg. It was clean and free of glass, but there was nothing she could do about the blood and the torn cloth. The bloody towel in her hand would be little use as a bandage.

Oh, well. This is New York. Probably nobody's going to notice, Winter told herself hopefully.

Everything hurt. It was hard to believe that this was the same day that she'd stood in her mother's kitchen and told her parents the truth. What she wanted most right now was a hot bath, a first-aid kit, and a lot of Room Service.

Walking with stiff care, Winter went into the bedroom to see if there was anything else she could salvage for makeshift bandages.

The smell was the first thing that hit her when she crossed the threshold. Winter flinched away from it before she understood what she was reacting to. Sharp, unmistakable . . .

The bed, the floor, every surface was covered with drifts of apple blossoms. It looked like the ruins of a bombed city in winter.

The shock was like a slap in the face, and only exhaustion kept her from crying out. Tears burned in her eyes. She walked slowly over to the ruined bed and scooped up a handful of the petals. They stuck to the blood on her hands, turning stickily pink. *Apple blossoms. I can never see them without remembering telling Grey. And what came after.* She closed her hand painfully over the flowers.

There was something else on the bed.

Winter touched it gingerly, fearing it was something horrible. She recognized the knotted handkerchief as hers; she'd used to buy them by the dozen; you could use them for so many more things than you could a Kleenex.

But she didn't remember it being on the bed the last time she'd been in here.

She untied the handkerchief and shook its contents out onto the spilled blossoms. Just before she got a good look at it she realized what it had to be.

The porcelain had been smashed, as though struck with something heavy, but the pieces were large, and she could tell that it once had been a Limoges box, playful and delicate, painted blue and pink with swirling clouds. And on the top, the comical figure of a white-bearded wizard, pointed hat and star-tipped wand and long blue robe.

Grey had sent this to her.

She cradled it in her bleeding hands, trying to fit the pieces back together years too late, until the tears filled her eyes and spilled over. Too late. He'd sent it to her to wish her well—touching it, she could feel the faint echo of the icy fury that had broken it, that had sealed her pain off behind a wall of ice, hurting in order to avoid being hurt.

Because she had been afraid. Because she had run away.

Winter looked around the ruined bedroom. She'd been so certain she could go to Grey for help. She'd been sure Grey could have no reason to hate her this much.

She'd been wrong.

In New York, money can buy nearly everything. Over the next forty-eight hours, it got Winter Musgrave a hotel room, some new clothes and a suitcase to carry them in, an industrial cleaning service to empty and repaint her apartment, and a realtor to sell it once it was ready to show. Money also hired a private detective to trace Hunter Greyson; Winter sat with reasonable patience through the long explanation of how they could not guarantee to find him, and how it would be weeks, perhaps months, before she could expect any information at all.

I don't have weeks-perhaps-months! I don't even know if I have days!

She didn't say anything to the bored man behind the battered desk. The detective agency wasn't her only hope; it was just that she couldn't afford to overlook any means, however unlikely, that could lead her to Grey. While they worked, she was going to go back to San Francisco and see if she could find Rhiannon again. Maybe that strange musician who'd helped her find the bookstore and seemed to have known Cassie could help her. She couldn't afford pride any more. She had to find Grey.

And there was one more thing she could try.

The last thing that money got for Winter Musgrave in New York City was another rental car. On a weekday afternoon toward the end of May she headed north along the Hudson River, to the only place left that she could call home.

CHAPTER THIRTEEN

WINTER SOLDIERS AND SUNSHINE PATRIOTS

A little rule, a little sway,
A sunbeam in a winter's day,
Is all the proud and mighty have
Between the cradle and the grave.
—JOHN DYER

TRUTH JOURDEMAYNE WAS NOT, AS ANY OF HER COL-
leagues could have confirmed, the sort of person who let sleeping dogs
lie or well enough alone. Dylan Palmer, who knew her best, had said on
a number of occasions that for a woman with advanced degrees, she had
an amazingly poor grasp of English—particularly the phrases "for your
own good" and "mind your own business."

Since he knew that much, Truth had told him the last time he mentioned it, he ought to realize it was a lost cause to ask her to just drop the
Winter Musgrave investigation, even if—or perhaps because—it had
nearly gotten her killed.

"And she's gone, anyway!" Dylan said, adding what they both knew
already. "I tried to talk her out of it, but she's gone off looking for—"

"What?" Truth had asked.

"I don't know," Dylan admitted. "The truth?"

"What the truth is," Truth had said, "depends on where you're stand-ing. But don't ask me to give up on this one, Dylan."

"Why not?" her partner and colleague had asked suspiciously.

"Because I won't," Truth had said simply. "And I'd hate to squabble with you."

"If you backed off from a fight, it'd be the first time," Dylan had grumbled, but mercifully dropped the subject.

And so, as Winter was driving toward New Jersey, Truth began an in-vestigation of her own into Winter's past.

The place to start was obviously the Blackburn Circle at Nuclear Lake, where Hunter Greyson and his coven had conducted their slapdash ritu-als. *Without,* as Truth commented to herself, *anything much of an idea of what they were doing.*

Normally it would not have annoyed her so much. After all, the Blackburn rituals that had seen print were harmless enough—it was only the last one, The Opening of the Way, that presented any danger in the wrong hands, and there was currently no printed copy of it available.

No, the trouble was not so much in the experimenting—it was that Nuclear Circle had accidentally gotten its hands on a psychic to give their undisciplined playacting the psychic force that would otherwise have come only after years of dedicated study and practice.

Truth wished Winter had remembered more about what she and her friends had done here—or that Truth herself had been luckier in trying to contact the others. Without knowing how closely they'd been follow-ing the dictates of the Blackburn Work, it was difficult to know just what sort of psychic residue she'd be dealing with here—but no matter what it was, a simple Banishing and Unbinding should take care of it.

Unless, as Winter insisted, Nuclear Lake itself was the problem. In that case, Truth might be biting off more than she could chew.

Truth frowned, navigating her Saturn slowly over the rocks and ruts of the dirt road leading into Nuclear Lake. Her working tools were in the plumber's bag on the seat beside her. She did not really need them—the power was in her, not in these reminders—but they helped in focusing her will, just as using the pendulum focused the perceptions of her un-conscious mind.

Someone—not me!—really should sweep this whole area with some sort of psy-

chic Geiger counter to locate the hot spots and shut them down. Most people would be much better off without a psychic locus *running wild in their backyard. . . .*

But most people would never know if there was one. The Unseen World truly did not exist for those without the senses to perceive it—and some lucky few had the power to choose whether they would see its manifestations or not.

Truth was not one of them. She had chosen the middle ground between science and sorcery—a path neither black nor white, but gray as mist: Thorne Blackburn's path, and now hers. She had sworn to walk it all the days of her life, striving to strike a balance between Light and Darkness—and in doing so she had forfeited her chance to remain ignorant, just as Michael Archangel had warned her would happen.

Truth parked and got out of her car, following the track that led toward the abandoned building. She wondered what had been here back in the long-ago seventies, before this land had become part of Haelvemaen Park. But the history of Nuclear Lake didn't matter as much now as what the basement of the building contained.

Truth pushed the back door open, balancing her bag in one hand and her flashlight in the other. Once she'd cleaned up inside she really ought to see if the Sheriff's Department would put a padlock on the door to keep trespassers out of the place. Abandoned buildings were perfect places for fires to start, and if the spring weather turned dry as it did so often in the Hudson Valley lately, a fire could rip devastatingly through hundreds of acres of woodland and perhaps endanger Glastonbury itself.

Her footsteps echoed down the iron staircase as Truth descended into the basement, her bag of tools bumping at her hip. The beam of the flashlight cast a narrow pillar of light over the walls and ceiling, and the dampness here, away from the cleansing sun, made her shiver.

When she reached the bottom of the stairs, Truth set down the flashlight on one of the lab benches that still remained around the edge of the room and set her bag beside it. She unbuckled the top—it was a canvas plumber's bag, chosen both for strength and capacity—and took out a pillar candle of beeswax, a shallow silver dish and the charcoal to fill it, and a small glass flask filled with a gleaming liquid. Truth had made the Universal Condenser herself, gathering the herbs and the morning dew herself over a period of several weeks and following the laborious and faintly silly recipe set forth in Thorne's writings. As with so many appendices of the Blackburn Work, Thorne was merely passing down the soi-disant wisdom of other occultists, and Truth had already discovered that much occult "learning" consisted of fossilized coincidence—all outward symbols of greater truths, as her teacher, Irene Avalon, had assured her with the serene all-encompassing acceptance that Truth found so hard to emulate. What Truth herself thought was that while magick worked, it didn't always work for the reasons magicians thought it did.

Someone needs to field-test all of this "occult wisdom" to separate the sheep from the goats, Truth thought idly as she lit first the candle and then the charcoal. Once the candle was burning steadily she turned off her flashlight, and when the charcoal was glowing redly, she reached into her bag again and pulled out a fistful of incense. The lumps of resin glowed like cloudy amber in the candlelight. She sifted them over the coals; they sizzled and bubbled and began to distill into a column of pungent white smoke. She took a second bowl from her bag—this one of rock crystal, the faint clouds and bubbles beneath its surface proclaiming its origin far beneath the surface of the earth—and set it beside the first, filling it with the Universal Condenser. The liquid glowed with a faint violet fire to Truth's otherworldly sight, but logically she could not tell whether this was an artifact of its intrinsic power, or of the effort she had put into making it. This was the reality of magick—everything had at least two explanations and often more.

Fire and air; living and unliving earth; water and will—the symbols of the three dualities that the *sidhe* must call upon to work their will. All the Blackburn Work was built upon this central mystery: that of the Bright Lords whose realm this once had been. Truth felt her own *sidhe* blood—her father's gift to her, as the control of the Gates had been her mother's—waken in answer to this summoning.

Easily Truth shifted her consciousness into this larger reality, and now all darkness was gone from the basement. In its place were the colors and shifting auras of the real world—the world of rock and wind and sky.

Truth looked around, sorting through the shifting presences and traces of use until she found the red-and-silver image of the magick worked here so long ago. The images of the hours Hunter Greyson's Circle had spent here fluttered past her senses like the shuffling of a deck of cards.

Yes, there had been power raised here once. Dormant now, its echo could be activated by the presence of any uncontrolled psychic—or by deliberate triggering. Easily Truth isolated the trace of Grey's male energy—youthful and untrained, but holding the promise of mature strength. She looked further, and found to her surprise that there were *two* complimentary female resonances—one powerful but undisciplined, one showing the first signs of an Adept's training. She wondered which of the two had been Winter. This many years distant, there was no way to tell.

Once Truth had located the psychic remnants she sought, she reached one last time into her bag and pulled out a slender rod about eighteen inches long.

One half of it was iron, its surface dark and sheened with the oil that kept it from rusting. The other half was glass, clear as water and gathering light like a lens. A thick ring of pure gold bound the two halves together.

Truth handled it warily, careful not to touch the iron and disrupt the symbolic language she was building. There were times when she thought that her mother's earth witchery and her father's *sidhe* blood were an even worse mix than logic and magick.

In quick succession Truth passed the rod through the candle flame and the incense smoke and over the surface of the liquid in the crystal bowl, reminding herself of the things they symbolized and gathering their attributes into the wand via the Law of Contagion. When she was ready, Truth touched the iron end of the rod to the nearest tinge of red in the room's mingling auras.

She was the iron, and the iron was her will. The rod shuddered in her fingers, pulling to be free.

A member of the Astral Lodges would have called upon the White Light and the Word; a Black Magician upon the powers of Death and Hell. Truth was neither.

"In the name of Time and the Seasons, by the power of the Wheel and the Way," she said in a low voice, "remake this place in the image of this place: All that has been since Time began, Begone!"

She unbound the last echoes of energy, sweeping the rod before her, and, turning, began to walk in a spiral, pushing cleanliness and emptiness before her, as though the slender wand in her hand was a broom.

When she reached the walls, she ran the rod along them as well, draining away the power they had absorbed until they were as neutral and empty as the day they had been first erected.

It was very quiet when she was done.

To a natural psychic or other trained sensitive, the present condition of the room would be more unusual than its previous one, for no place on earth is innocent of contagion by the life that inhabits it. This place, too, would begin to collect impressions again almost immediately—Truth's power was not harsh enough to seal it off completely, nor did she wish to—but the traces the Blackburn Work had left were gone: swept away.

"My work here is finished," Truth said aloud, smiling to herself. Unlike her encounter with the *magickal child* that had attached itself to Winter Musgrave, this exercise of her ability left her vibrant, filled with energy.

Truth wondered—not for the first time—who had sent the artificial Elemental, and why. It seemed murderously furious, out of control—but nevertheless the work of a powerful Adept, and it was hard, looking at Winter, to think of her as anyone who might be familiar with the hidden world of magicians and magickal lodges. Carefully Truth slid the wand back into its protective case and then slipped it into her bag.

With a pang of regret for the work that replacing the liquid would entail, Truth took the bowl of Condenser and sprinkled it all around the room before wiping the bowl dry and putting it, too, back into her bag. She snuffed out the beeswax candle and filled the silver bowl with sand to smother the burning charcoal, then emptied the bowl, ground the last smoldering embers into dust against the floor, and put both objects away. Soon the only evidence that anything uncanny had ever happened here would be a smudge of dirt and a painted figure—now meaningless—on the floor.

Truth went back up the stairs.

The sky was overcast when she got back outside, and the damp wind off the river promised rain in the not-too-distant future. Truth sighed. It was an unfortunate fact of life that her father's magick tended to bring bad weather with it, as well as deriving its greatest power from violent storms. As she made her way toward her waiting Saturn, Truth's mind continued to mull over the odd puzzle of Winter Musgrave and the *magickal child.*

While it was true that Winter was a psychic, and a powerful one—as an adult poltergeist she would have to be, whether her power extended to setting fires or not—it was hardly the same thing as being a trained occultist, and if Truth knew anything for certain, it was that Winter was not trained. Yet someone, somewhere, in her life must be—trained and Adept both.

Was it Hunter Greyson, Colin MacLaren's golden boy? Truth had already spoken to Lion Welland and some of the other faculty who had been at Taghkanic when both Grey and Professor MacLaren had been. Those who remembered them had all said the same thing: that Grey had been planning to do postgraduate work at the Institute directly under Professor MacLaren. And, though it was not widely known at Taghkanic, Irene Avalon, Truth's teacher, had told Truth that MacLaren had made no secret of being an Initiate of the Right Hand Path. Had Hunter Greyson been intending to follow MacLaren in more things than one?

But then Winter left, then Grey left, then Professor MacLaren left, and nobody knows why. Truth frowned. Winter was looking for Grey now, that much Truth knew, but could *she* find Hunter Greyson first?

The wind riffled the reeds along the edge of the lake, and the dimpled surface of the water turned to hammered silver. Truth sighed, shifting her grip on the bag in her hand. The supercharged atmosphere of the ritual in the basement seemed light-years away now in both time and tone.

Find Hunter Greyson? Maybe. If he were still alive, or tied somehow to this world. If he had continued his forays into the Otherworld. If he were willing to be found.

If.

But once she had thought of the possibility, Truth could not simply dismiss it, and so midnight found Thorne Blackburn's daughter once more engaged in her own peculiar blend of magick and science.

The candle she lit this time had a purely pragmatic use—its reflection in the *shewstone* she intended to use would give her a point to focus on visually.

Truth sat cross-legged on the floor in front of her living room coffee table, an oval of polished jet resting on her palms. The candle burned brightly, and she could see the gold sheen of its flame reflected in the mirror's polished black surface.

The theory and technique of *scrying* was extensively documented; whether the focus was a crystal ball, an ordinary mirror, a bowl of water, or a speculum of polished jet such as Truth now held, the object of the exercise was to see pictures of distant people and unknown events; a form of external-projection clairvoyance. As with most divinatory systems, the tool—whether a mirror, a candle, a pendulum, or cards—was only a focus, and had no intrinsic power. The Institute frequently used an entire range of them in their tests, trying to fit the potential psychic expression to its most comfortable tool. Dylan's favorite trance psychic used gaming dice to overcome her occasional clairvoyant blocks.

The living room was dim and quiet, and the only other illumination came from a light in the kitchen. Truth had deliberately chosen the witching hour to work because the psychic background noise that people usually took for granted was much diminished at a time when most of the people in the immediate surrounding area were asleep—one of the many reasons that most hauntings and similar psychic manifestations took place at night.

Truth settled herself more comfortably as the jet—an organic material, just as amber was—warmed in her hands. She wasn't really sure how well this would work; clairvoyance wasn't her strength, even though her mother and her aunt had both been psychics. Her father had once told Truth that her magickal technique consisted mainly of dragging the Powers into compliance by yelling at them until they cooperated in self-defense.

Truth smiled at the memory, trying to relax enough to let her mind float free. She hoped Thorne was right; if yelling was what it took to find Hunter Greyson, that's what she'd do. Winter was outclassed and Truth was all but helpless—*somewhere* there had to be an ally against the pursuing Elemental and its monstrous, destructive hunger, and Truth didn't think she could afford to be too scrupulous about recruiting him.

At last the material world fell away; the constant insistence of Reality that it was the only truth dimmed, and Truth was able to rebuild the world out of the fires of her own conviction and belief. With practiced ease she set the four Otherworld Guardians about herself, so that her spirit had reference points to return to. Once that was done, out of her father's magick, Truth called up her servants and Guardians on this plane: the Red Stag and the White Mare, the Black Dog and the Grey Wolf.

These creatures were the shapes of her power, the astral servants who would do her bidding in this realm; creations of earth magic and *sidhe* magic both.

She mounted the mare and began to ride, with the wolf and the dog loping at her heels and the stag bounding along before, its red coat shadowy in the mist.

Here were the landmarks of the astral temples the other Blackburn Circles had erected; there, less visible to Truth's psychic senses, were the marks of other travelers through this realm; Adepts and *wicce* and others. Beyond that, all was mutable: the Otherworld—called the Inner Planes or the Astral Realms in the books Irene had forced upon Truth—was very much a creation of the observer, taking on the shape its visitors expected.

Which may explain why it looks so much like a foggy, featureless plain to me. I have no expectations of what I "ought" to see.

But even when she had gained access to the Otherworld at last, it did not bring with it success in her quest. Truth wandered for subjective hours in featureless Otherworld grayness, but she found no hint of Hunter Greyson's presence.

The pull to return to her body grew stronger as she searched, until resisting it became an effort and she knew that—this night at least—she had failed to find Hunter Greyson. It occurred belatedly to Truth that perhaps she had been too hasty in banishing all trace of Grey's Circle from Nuclear Lake; she could have used its presence as a starting place for her search, at least. Now, though she had spent hours calling upon the powers beholden to her as far as she dared, Truth could gain no hint of the Master of Nuclear Circle's location.

At last she allowed her body's animal need to tug her back from the Otherworld, and opened her eyes on her own familiar living room.

It was nearly dawn. She was chilled and stiff from immobility, and the candle had long since drowned in its own wax. But Truth was far from defeated.

"Are you sure you're going to be all right?" Dylan said, standing by the door of the car.

"For heaven's sake, Dyl, I'm driving to Massachusetts, not off the edge of the earth," Truth said good-naturedly.

Though many of the staff at the Bidney Institute were also members of the Taghkanic faculty—such as Dylan—Truth was not one of them. Without classes to cover, it was comparatively easy for her to gain a few days' leave.

"It's only a couple of days since you were laid out cold in the lab," Dylan pointed out ruthlessly. "*Where* in Massachusetts?" he added suspiciously.

Truth sighed, capitulating. "Fall River. I was just going to—"

"Meddle," Dylan finished flatly. Truth rewarded him with a dazzling smile that deceived neither of them.

"Right," she said. "But, for heaven's sake, Dylan, it's only a *little* meddling."

"And I can't stop you anyway," Dylan finished for her.

Truth tried to look repentant and failed. "I'll be back in a day or so."

Dylan stood back from the car as Truth started the engine. She waved as she drove off, glancing back at him occasionally through the rearview mirror until she'd passed out of sight.

The closer Truth got to Fall River Sanatorium, the more forbidding it seemed. She drove along a tree-lined road, edged with discreet accesses to private drives, and tried not to think about what lay ahead. Money was power, and Fall River seemed to be the site of a great deal of money—at least if the neighboring estates were any guideline.

Fall River Sanatorium was built on a hill, a gleaming white edifice that did not so much sprawl as recline amid lawns as green and unreal as the turf of a golf course. As Truth drove toward it, she could catch glimpses of artfully landscaped brick paths laid among the ornamental plantings, and once, in the far distance, a solitary gleaming figure in nursing whites.

She had not called beforehand, preferring not to give the sanatorium's staff an additional opportunity to turn her away. The rich were notoriously efficient at protecting their privacy; now that Truth had more of an idea of what sort of hospital Fall River was, she realized that it was more than likely that the doctor who had treated Winter Musgrave would refuse to speak to her at all.

But if Winter had been a patient at Fall River for any length of time the staff must have been aware of the poltergeist phenomenon that dogged her, and the Margaret Beresford Bidney Institute's reputation was almost as well known in psychiatric as in parapsychological circles. Maybe she'd get lucky.

The sign at the front gate said PRIVATE DRIVE, and Truth passed two more signs saying much the same thing before she reached the building. She parked beneath yet another one, located this time in the visitors' parking lot. Her little Saturn looked positively frumpy next to the Mercedes and Lincolns that made up the majority of the occupants of the lot, and Truth tried not to be covetous of the gleaming expensive vehicles. The white BMW that Winter had told Truth she drove must have fit right in here.

And so had Winter. Or had she?

Truth locked her car and walked briskly toward the main entrance, blessing the impulse that had caused her to dress as if she were going to a particularly conservative professional conference. Her dark wool/silk suit and severe cream linen blouse would add an additional air of respectability to what Truth now saw more than ever as a harebrained escapade.

No one in his right mind would have come so far on such a slender hope of information, but now that she was here and the compulsion to come was gone, she recognized it for what it was: some message from the more-than-rational world; beyond instinct, beyond intuition . . .

Yet, having brought her so far, it had deserted her.

Now what?

Truth looked toward the entrance. The doorway was an imposing affair of double doors and leaded glass panels, sheltered beneath a deep portico. As good a destination as any. Truth put her hand to the gleaming brass latch and walked into Fall River Sanatorium.

She glanced around the foyer quickly, taking in the Oriental rugs, the chandelier, the furnishings that looked like costly antiques and probably were, and her hopes for the success of her mission slipped another notch. Everything she saw was designed to give the illusion that the viewer had been invited into a gracious private home—an illusion that was necessarily spoiled by the desk with its sign-in register that stood just to the right and inside the entrance.

"May I help you?"

The woman standing behind the desk was in her midtwenties; immaculately groomed, professionally pretty, and as formidable a guardian as had ever guarded the gates of Hell—one more layer of defense for the protection—or detention—of those treated here. Truth put on her most formal and professional expression and smiled coolly.

"I'd like to see your director of admissions, please," she said. "Or your supervising clinician."

"Do you have an appointment?" the woman responded promptly.

"I'm with the Bidney Institute in Glastonbury," Truth said, letting her voice supply the suggestion that it was a place similar to this one. She held out her card and watched as the woman read it. Margaret Beresford Bidney Memorial Psychic Science Research Institute had a distinguished ring to it, and most people confused "psychic" with "psychological," at least at first glance.

"I'd hoped to be able to consult with . . . ?" Truth prompted.

"That would be Dr. Mahar, the director," the woman supplied. Truth felt a small flare of victory. "Come with me, please, Dr. Jourdemayne."

Truth did not feel it necessary to correct her. She did, after all, have a doctorate—in mathematics.

Her guide conducted Truth down a short corridor to a reception area so luxurious and tranquilizing that Truth was sure this must be where anxious would-be patients awaited their initial interviews with Dr. Mahar. Everything Truth had seen in her few brief minutes inside the sanatorium proclaimed to her the sort of place this was: a sort of psychological factory where human problems were as likely to be tidied away as treated. Another professional sentry, this one an older woman in a starched white suit and slightly archaic gull-wing cap, rose from behind her desk as Truth and her escort entered the room.

"Dr. Jourdemayne to see Dr. Mahar," the first woman said. She offered up Truth's business card to the second receptionist and retreated in the direction of her outside post.

Truth advanced on her new obstacle. "I'm Truth Jourdemayne," she said. "I'd like to consult with Dr. Mahar about Winter Musgrave?"

"Winter Musgrave!" The nurse's mask of professional detachment slipped; as clearly as if she'd spoken aloud, Truth could hear the rest of the sentence: *"She isn't coming back here, is she?"*

Truth smiled a little, saying nothing, as if she hadn't heard anything out of the ordinary. *Winter must have made quite an impression while she was here.* The nurse stood watching her uncertainly for what seemed a long time, but after what could not have been more than a moment's hesitation turned and went through the door behind her desk.

While she was gone, Truth glanced around the room. The more she saw of this place, the less she felt it was the kind of place where unpleasant truths would be welcomed when they were brought to light. As in the foyer outside, the desk was the only hint that this was not a private home. Truth sat down on the couch opposite the fireplace, and picked up the impressive leather-bound book lying on the coffee table.

The Fall River Experience, said the title page. Truth quickly paged through photos of lushly landscaped grounds and ethereal-yet-brave residents—professional models, she supposed, as none of the pampered guests of such a discreet facility would appreciate documentary evidence of their stay. The text accompanying the pictures gave no indication that Fall River was anything more than a particularly well-appointed vacation retreat accidentally equipped to dispense soothing assurances of normalcy. The entire place was engineered to help its inhabitants forget— like the inhabitants of the Isle of the Lotos-Eaters, people who came here forgot their unpleasant past. Only Winter hadn't forgotten. Winter had remembered. And only now did Truth appreciate what bravery that had taken.

Learning this much was worth the trip, Truth told herself encouragingly. Even if she got no farther, Truth felt she knew more about Winter just by having seen Fall River. For a woman grappling with interior demons, desperate to separate reality from delusion, it would have been a particularly harrowing prison.

Truth knew that she really had no authority to slink around asking people questions about Winter Musgrave's past like a character in a bad detective novel. She'd gotten this far under what amounted to false pretenses, and she couldn't expect Dr. Mahar to take a sympathetic view of her actions if he discovered the deception. Once her cover was blown she'd be lucky if she were allowed to beat a graceful retreat instead of being tossed out on her ear; this was self-interested snooping, plain and simple, and as Winter was not even currently working with the Institute at all, Truth didn't have even that much justification.

But something more than mere curiosity had brought her here. . . .

The sound of the inner door opening brought Truth to her feet. The white-suited nurse was standing in the doorway, and slightly behind her was an irritable-looking balding man who could be no one other than Dr. Mahar. Seizing the initiative, Truth briskly crossed the room, holding out her hand.

"Dr. Mahar, how splendid to meet you. I'm Truth Jourdemayne. Might I have a moment of your time?"

Everything about Truth's voice and body language proclaimed her perfect right to be here—the ability to project a self other than the real was the gift that linked the actor with the magician, and even in the modern day caused actors to be distrusted as somehow fey and uncanny.

The nurse moved back toward her desk uncertainly. Dr. Mahar stepped back to let Truth walk past him into his office.

As she entered, Truth glanced around and promptly identified Dr. Mahar as an acolyte of the cult of "Doctor Knows Best": Everything in the dark-paneled office was as hushed and solemn as a church, and Dr. Mahar's professional trophies were prominently and elaborately displayed.

Truth frowned in disapproval. Even when she had been a committed rationalist, the blind belief in the infallibility of the medical profession had been one altar of Science at which she had never worshiped.

"Always a pleasure," Dr. Mahar said meaninglessly. "Now. How may I help you?" He seated himself once more behind the meant-to-be-intimidating desk. If the outer room was designed to soothe and reassure, then this one was meant to inspire unquestioning faith.

"I understand that Winter Musgrave was a patient here until recently. I realize that her records will have been sealed, but I wonder if I might speak to the doctor who supervised her care." *And find out what* HE *thought was wrong with her.*

Dr. Mahar's face settled into an expression of grim dislike at the mention of "patients." "We do not discuss our *guests,*" he said brusquely.

Although it was only what she had expected once she had seen the place, the man's arrogance was such that Truth could not resist needling him a little.

"Ms. Musgrave came to the Institute for help. I know she would appreciate your cooperation."

"'The Institute,'" Dr. Mahar said suspiciously. He looked down at the card on his desk blotter—the same one she had handed to the receptionist at the front desk, Truth realized.

As the woman at the front desk had, Dr. Mahar, studied her card carefully. "'Psychic Science Research Institute,'" he read slowly.

Nailed, Truth thought with resignation.

As the meaning of his own words penetrated, Dr. Mahar raised his eyes and glared steadily at her, his face darkening with unreasonable anger. "Well! I don't know what your game is, young woman, but I must say you show a certain amount of barefaced nerve coming here—" He got to his feet.

Truth stood also, determined to outface him—for the honor of her calling, if nothing else.

"Were there any unexplained fires while Ms. Musgrave was here? More false alarms—shorts in the electrical system—than normal? Did staff and other residents complain of missing small objects—many of which later turned up in places inaccessible to both them and her? You had trouble keeping the french doors in her room closed, I understand. The locks didn't seem to help. You finally nailed the doors shut. Did that work? Or did something pull out the nails every night and open them anyway?"

"That is *enough!*" Dr. Mahar blustered, his face an alarming scarlet.

"No, it is not." Truth's icy tone matched his. "The Margaret Beresford Bidney Memorial Psychic Science Research Institute is a reputable organization with international standing, affiliated with a nationally ranked college. The staff of the Institute is composed neither of frauds nor quacks—as you seem to be implying. It is your decision not to cooperate with my investigation if you choose, *but I will not submit to being treated like a simple-minded con artist.*"

There was a momentary silence as Dr. Mahar all but gaped at her in shock. Truth wondered if he'd ever been spoken to that way by any woman in his entire life—or by any person since he'd received his sacred MD. But despite her expectations, Dr. Mahar was honest enough to try to listen, and Truth watched with surprised pity as the man opposite her struggled against a lifetime of assumption, of tacit promise never to question the bounds of reality as marked for him by equally unquestioning peers, of willful blindness.

And fell, powerlessly, back into that blindness which was far more comfortable than knowledge.

"I have nothing more to say to you," he said heavily. "I'll ask you to leave now. As a professional courtesy I will not have you escorted from the grounds."

Truth turned and walked out—before *she* broke something, and by far more mundane means than that of a poltergeist.

Well, that was a waste of time, Truth thought to herself, stepping out into the hot spring sunlight once more. If she turned back to the building she had just left, undoubtedly she would be able to see white-garbed Cerberuses peering out the windows, waiting to see if Security needed to be called to deal with her after all. Truth felt cross and guilty. Why in God's name had she come here?

"Ms. Jourdemayne? Truth Jourdemayne?" A voice came from behind her.

Truth turned and peered in the direction of the voice, blinking against the glare of the sun. All she could make out was the silhouette of a tall figure. *I guess they called Security after all.*

"You don't have to get nasty, I was just leaving," she said peevishly.

"No. You don't understand. Winter Musgrave—is she all right?"

The speaker stepped forward, blocking the glare of the sun with his body. Truth saw a spare man, closer to fifty than forty, with a tracery of silver in his dark hair and an almost stereotypical mustache and goatee edging his ascetic face. His eyes were a startling pale brown, nearly amber, and he was wearing a white lab coat and dark trousers. The only thing out of the ordinary about his appearance at all was the scarab pendant in bright blue *faience* that hung from a silver chain about his neck and rested against his sober institutional necktie.

The gossip mill in this place makes the one at Taghkanic look slow. "She's . . . all right," Truth said. *At least she was the last time I saw her, but maybe not for long, if that creature catches up with her.* "Who are you?"

"My name is Dr. Atheling; I'm a consultant here at Fall River. Winter Musgrave wasn't my patient, but—may I have a few moments of your time?"

Truth looked past him to the house. "I don't know," she said dryly.

"I've just seen Dr. Mahar, and I think I'm supposed to be getting the bum's rush."

"Ah." Dr. Atheling smiled. "But I have some small sway with Dr. Mahar, owing to my occasional fortunate intervention in some cases of exceptional difficulty. Allow me to take personal responsibility for your continued presence on the grounds."

"Sure. And maybe *you* can answer some of *my* questions." Truth found herself smiling in return. She no longer wondered what purpose had drawn her to Fall River; she knew.

"I first met Winter Musgrave a few weeks after she first came here. She was a patient of Dr. Luty's; he's a colleague of Dr. Mahar's, a very well respected name in his field," Dr. Atheling said.

"And that is . . . ?" Truth asked.

Truth and her new companion were walking along one of the many footpaths that led through the Fall River grounds. Everything around her looked too perfect to be real: Even the weather cooperated in the illusion, bright and warm with only enough cloud in the sky to add the final decorative touch. Though Truth's own sister had been much more harshly treated in a much less luxurious environment, Truth could not banish from her mind the thought of how this artificial perfection would have grated on Winter's shattered nerves, and found sympathetic anger in Winter's defense rising in her.

There must be a better way—a way to help those who are not sick, but different. . . .

"Dr. Luty's specialty is psychopharmacology, as related to post-traumatic-stress-related disorders," Dr. Atheling said. "He's designed a number of quite successful drug therapies. His patients have . . . minimal dysfunction."

Post-traumatic stress. The aftermath of kidnapping, rape, or other violence. "But that wasn't Winter's problem," Truth said. "How could he be treating her?"

"I believe the family arranged it," Dr. Atheling said blandly. He slanted a glance sideways at Truth and his amber eyes glowed in the sunlight. "And certainly Dr. Luty's treatment can have a . . . calming effect on certain forms of stress."

What you mean is, Dr. Luty drugged her nearly insensible! Truth mused furiously.

"Now, let me ask you a question," Dr. Atheling continued. "Why did Winter seek out the Bidney Institute after she left Fall River?"

Truth hesitated, wondering how much she should tell this man who seemed to fit in so oddly with everything else she'd seen of Fall River. "Poltergeists," she finally said. She might as well tell him the truth, after all; she could hardly damage her reputation—or Winter's—further, at least in the eyes of Fall River.

"A classic presentation, wouldn't you say?" Dr. Atheling said.

Truth looked at him sharply. Her eye was drawn once more to the bright azure spark of the scarab Dr. Atheling wore about his neck. Almost instinctively she shifted her sight to see him, not as this world saw him, but as he appeared in the Otherworld.

Blinding white light; a rigorous discipline refined down through centuries; of life after life dedicated to the Great Work . . .

Truth recoiled, involuntarily flinging up a hand to shield herself. Dr. Atheling was an Adept; a follower of the Right Hand Path, but unlike any such Adept she had met before. At the same moment, she saw him quickly sketch a symbol in the air; meant for defense against the Darkness and the Great Unmaking, it barely touched her.

"So," Dr. Atheling said. "It's true. There are . . . others."

He studied her intently, as if trying to solve a riddle that Truth knew to be unsolvable. Not Black, not White, but . . . Gray. "What is *your* interest in this matter?" he added pointedly. His manner was no more hostile than it had been a moment before, but there was a stern watchfulness present now, as of a warrior awaiting the summons to battle once more.

"Winter Musgrave came to the Bidney Institute for help," Truth said honestly, dismissing her personal curiosity for the moment. "If you've heard of us, you'll know that we receive many requests for help each year from people who are certain they are haunted . . . or possessed."

Dr. Atheling gazed at her intently for another frozen moment, then seemed to come to a decision. He relaxed, and smiled at her again with genuine warmth.

"And which did you find Winter to be?" he asked.

"Neither," Truth said, accepting the tacit apology for what it was. "As you say, what our initial interview revealed was *almost* a classic presentation of adult-onset poltergeist phenomena."

"Something that Dr. Luty, alas, could not bring himself to accept," Dr. Atheling admitted. "He felt that drug therapy and the talking cure would answer—but alas, they did not."

"The talking cure"—that quaintly old-fashioned phrase coined by the father of psychiatry to describe the science he had invented. But it had long since fallen into disuse, and no one now living could have studied with Sigmund Freud in the Vienna of the 1880s.

Could they?

"Was Winter comfortable here?" Truth asked, shifting her ground and probing for more information.

"For a while—at least, as much so as was possible to one so harshly medicated; I am afraid my colleagues consider me a bit of a naturopath, but I do not hold with the use of drugs save in *extremis.* But you have not come all this way to hear my views upon the proper treatment of the afflicted, but to hear about Winter." He seemed to gather his thoughts, and when he spoke again his voice had taken on a certain formal timbre, as if he were providing Truth a carefully edited report of events.

"Taken in all, Winter spent nearly sixteen months here. I was—away—on a case of my own when she arrived, but I inquired into the matter once I returned and saw that . . . a case falling within the bounds of my particular interests had been admitted while I was away. Unfortunately, there were reasons I was unable to obtain direct supervision of her care; however, Dr. Luty was reasonably forthcoming. He gave me to understand that Winter was very agitated when she came in—delusional, in fact. He told me that at first she'd even insisted that she'd been in a motorcycle accident. But of course Winter has never even owned a motorcycle, and there had been no accident."

"Are you sure?" Truth could not help but ask.

Dr. Atheling smiled, and this time there was a certain bitterness in it. "You will understand that Dr. Luty was careful to check for himself. It is not always advisable to entirely endorse the family's interpretation of the events in a guest's life."

Truth's opinion of Fall River rose slightly. Not the sort of rubber-stamp place where the inconvenient children of the rich were cached—at least not entirely.

"Her family admitted her?" Truth tried to remember if Winter had said anything about a family—but no, Winter had spoken only of her *recent* past.

"She admitted herself upon the advice of her family. If she had not, it would have been impossible for her to leave in the manner that she did." Dr. Atheling's neutral tones conveyed nothing of the struggle that must have underlain Winter's unorthodox departure from Fall River.

Sixteen months . . . "So Winter was admitted because of . . . stress. And then she left again," Truth said, half questioning.

"Yes—as soon as she realized that her afflictions had their origins in external objective reality, and as soon as she was able. Even so, she was far from well, and in other circumstances I would not have been in favor of it. But as I've said, Winter was not my patient, and though I could advise, I could not interfere in Dr. Luty's handling of the case," Dr. Atheling said somberly.

They reached a gently weathered wooden bench placed at the side of one of the brick paths, and Dr. Atheling indicated that she should sit. Intrigued, Truth did as he wished, smoothing her narrow skirt over her knees. The wood of the bench was warm against her back, and some of Truth's misgiving faded, lulled by the beauty of the place.

"But you must tell me what you have discovered as well," Dr. Atheling said, seating himself at the opposite end of the bench.

Even with this opportunity to study him closely and in bright sunlight, Truth found it hard to gauge either his age or his ethnicity. It was impossible, however, to mistake him for anything but a trained Adept now that her senses had been awakened to the power he wielded, and Truth hoped their paths would not lead to confrontation. Dr. Atheling would be a formidable opponent.

"About a month ago, Winter Musgrave came to the Institute seeking . . . assistance," Truth said, choosing her words carefully. "Dr. Palmer and I were available, so we were the ones who interviewed her. You will understand that the Institute receives a number of requests each year for . . . a type of help it is not equipped to provide."

"Admirably and tactfully put," Dr. Atheling said with a faint ghost of mockery in his voice. "And what did the Institute discover?"

"Although Ms. Musgrave never submitted herself for a formal evaluation, Dr. Palmer and I concluded that the likely explanation for the majority of the presenting phenomena—including an event which we both witnessed—was adult-onset poltergeist phenomena, triggering event unknown."

"For *most* of the phenomena," Dr. Atheling paraphrased. "But not all?"

Although the day was warm, involuntarily Truth hunched her shoulders against the remembered cold of the magickal attack launched against her when she and Winter had summoned the Elemental. "But not all," she agreed.

"Let us not fence any longer," Dr. Atheling said abruptly. "You are aware of who I am, and I am quite aware of what you are. What do you know of the Elemental sending that has attached itself to Winter?"

Truth carefully kept her face from showing her surprise, though such an Adept as Dr. Atheling could certainly read it in her aura even more easily than upon her face.

"That it exists," she said, and half shrugged, embarrassed by her ignorance. "That it wants . . . something, though we haven't yet been able to find out what. That it draws its strength from the blood of the animals it kills—larger ones as its power grows. And that it was sent by someone to whom Winter has an emotional connection." Truth watched Dr. Atheling closely.

"Do you know who sent it?" he asked, his tone mild once more.

"Do you?"

"No," he said, "and if *you* did, you would not be here."

It was no more than the truth, Truth admitted to herself. "I *need* to know," she said slowly, choosing her words with care. "Because it's dangerous. And because it seems to become more powerful with each death—able to command larger blood sacrifices. And because I don't think that Winter has any control over it."

An hour later, Truth drove homeward, her mind busy. Though she had learned a great deal, perilously little of it seemed to have any immediate bearing on Winter's problem. Dr. Atheling, too, had marked the *magickal child* for what it was while Winter was still at Fall River, though he was as ignorant as Truth of its ultimate origin. Bound by a combination of his oaths as an Adept and his oaths as a physician, he had not opposed the creature directly, though he had done what he could to help Winter cope with its effects, and Truth was convinced that the Elemental's power and hunger had increased sharply once Winter had left his sphere of influence.

Back where I started, Truth thought to herself. No answer to *what* was chasing Winter—and *why.*

Only she was not quite as ignorant as before. There was now the puzzle of Dr. Atheling himself to consider. Truth's path and those of the others who studied the Unseen World must inevitably cross if her life continued in the direction it was going. And even after more than a year, Truth wasn't sure how she felt about that.

Though Truth Jourdemayne was only a beginner in the study of the Occult—her gifts having been more a matter of inheritance than training—the months she had spent researching her father's life and his magickal discipline had given her some understanding of the many different coteries who studied that group of arts and philosophy invariably lumped together under the catch-all label "The Occult." Meeting Dr. Atheling made Truth more aware than ever of the fact that, though she thought she moved alone through a labyrinth of scholarship and phenomena, she was in fact only one Seeker among many. Far older than the Blackburn Work, and the source for much of it, was Dr. Atheling's Right Hand Path, the Western Mystery Tradition epitomized by the White Lodges. Though the trappings of each Lodge were different, each traced its ultimate origin back to the learning of Ancient Egypt, and beyond that, to storied Atlantis herself.

Instructed as she was in the Blackburn Work, Truth had made little contact with other traditions. Thorne Blackburn had been a rogue and a rebel against that wellspring of tradition, believing that humankind should seek perfection in the world they had been given rather than seeking an alien perfection in realms that only a chosen few could aspire to—and then only if transformed by a lifetime's rigorous training. The White Lodge in which he had received his earliest instruction had cast him out for such ideas, but though they had pronounced anathema on him, Thorne had not, as many believed, turned to the Dark. The Left Hand Path in all of its guises had, in fact, as little use for Blackburn's philosophy as did the Right.

In the Unseen World, as elsewhere, Truth Jourdemayne walked alone.

As if entirely of its own volition, the Saturn moved left off the high-way, toward an exit that led to a different destination than Glastonbury, New York.

There was one place she could still go to for answers.

The padlocks and chains were back on the iron gates and the gravel drive showed the marks of several seasons' neglect when Truth drove up to Shadow's Gate and parked in front of the gatehouse. Thorne Blackburn's estate was once more in legal limbo; for his children to inherit was now a matter of tedious legal formalities that would take years. For now, the 100-acre parcel remained untouched, a memorial and a monument to the Blackburn legend.

Truth got out of her car, admitting ruefully to herself that her dressy suit would probably not survive this expedition. There was a certain freedom, however, in doing what you wanted no matter how you were dressed. The question was, who was to be the master, as Humpty Dumpty had once said to Alice, and Truth felt that her desires—even her whims—should be more important than a suit of clothes.

It was easy enough to circumvent the gatehouse with its forbidding iron bars, and walk along the fence until the formidable iron spikes became a low fieldstone wall—easy enough to climb over, even in a narrow skirt. A caretaker lived on the property and saw to keeping the grass cut back, so getting across the lawn wasn't a problem. Truth walked up the hill toward the house.

The contrast between Fall River and Shadow's Gate was enormous. Fall River was mannered and manicured, groomed and tamed until it lost all individuality. Shadow's Gate belonged to itself far more than it did to any human force: Since the first Europeans had come to the Hudson Valley and fallen beneath the spell of this land just as their native-born brothers had, Shadow's Gate had ruled the lives and the destinies of all within its reach.

Truth cut back to the drive once she was well past the gatehouse, and walked on a gently upward slope through woods in full spring leaf. Half an hour brought her to the crest of the small rise from which she'd gained her first sight of Shadow's Gate less than three years ago.

The old house still stood in a hollow of ground surrounded by low hills and rambling woodland. To the right Truth could see the boxwood maze whose contours concealed secret passages that would let her into the house itself. The maze was noticeably overgrown now, though some attempt had been made to keep it clipped back. Truth shook her head sadly. Someone would have to do something about Shadow's Gate, and soon. But her destination today was not the house, nor anything that lay close beside it. It took her almost another hour to reach her real destination.

Here in the woods behind the house lay the *henge* Thorne Blackburn and his acolytes had made: a horseshoe shape of man-sized granite pillars in a forest clearing. At the head of the circle, in the place the thirteenth pillar should have been, stood a massive oak tree, its bark thick and twisted with age. Carved into the wood, at the level of her heart, Truth could see the symbol of the Circle of Truth, like and yet unlike the symbols that had been painted at Nuclear Lake. With some difficulty, Truth clambered into the circle and placed her hand over the sign. The wood was warm and alive beneath her hand. She stroked it meditatively.

What should she do? Should she summon the *magickal child* here? This was the place of her greatest power, where her mother's and father's heritage combined—if she had any hope of containing or commanding the creature her hope was here, not at the Institute.

But there was only a slight chance she could prevail, even here. The Elemental had been sent against Winter; it drew its power from the very fact of her existence to such an extent that Truth wondered if anyone but Winter could possibly destroy it. If only Winter were willing to accept her link with that nightmare sending, and use it. . . .

Truth remembered the steely ice-maiden who had come to the Institute for help. Even at her most vulnerable, Winter Musgrave did not seem to be the sort of woman who could yield, gracefully or otherwise. The Elemental would surely destroy her before she would ever accept it into herself. Truth leaned against the tree and closed her eyes.

. . . *Wait* . . .

It might almost have been the wind in the leaves that carried with it that sense of hushed expectation. Truth cocked her head, listening, but heard nothing further. Still, she had the answer she'd instinctively sought. This fight was not hers. Not yet. Perhaps never.

Truth circled the trunk with her arms, and rested her cheek against the bark of the tree. For a long time she stood like that, unmoving, the sun that shone down falling equally on her and the great oak. The sense of peace that she felt welled up from the roots of the earth, carrying with it the promise that there was time for all things. Time, even, to discover her own purpose in the world.

At last Truth roused herself from her trance and stood away from the tree. She felt rested, refreshed—and certain, at last, of her proper course. She turned to go, but before she left the enchanted circle Truth spoke aloud for the first time.

"Thank you, Father."

CHAPTER FOURTEEN

ALL THE WORLD IS WINTER

He disappeared in the dead of winter.
—W. H. AUDEN

DRIVING ONCE MORE THROUGH GLASTONBURY IN THE direction of the college, Winter wondered if coming back here had been a mistake. It felt too much like saying good-bye.

She had never said good-bye to Grey.

Winter set her jaw and concentrated on moving her car through the light traffic on the road approaching Glastonbury. Her bandaged hands were slippery on the wheel, and she grasped it carefully. It had been weeks since she'd left; it was late spring now, less than two months to the end of the school year. There was a certain grisly justice to coming back here now: It was almost as if she were returning to college after spring break, fourteen years too late. She had never finished the part of her life that Taghkanic represented.

And now, when desperation compelled her to go back to what should have been over long ago and stir up old ghosts, she found that the shades of those innocent college days had become something . . . darker. If coming here felt as if she were saying good-bye, it was because she was. All that was left after she'd seen Truth was to go back to San Francisco, find Rhiannon somehow and receive Cassie's message, and then—

Grey. The Elemental. Images tangled in Winter's mind, a web of choking guilt and responsibility that seemed as if it would grow tighter forever. What could she have changed in the past to make the present other than it was?

There was no answer to that; there never had been an answer for as long as people have been asking that question. But if Winter could not find some way to change the present, there would be no future at all.

For anyone.

She pulled her latest rental car into the guest parking lot facing the Institute and parked, an action which brought back the memory of her previous visits here. Despite her constant overwhelming impression of inadequacy, Winter knew rationally that she had come a very long way in a few short weeks—from dependent ex–mental patient to a woman who could reclaim—and take responsibility for—the demons of her own past.

Now all that was left was to say good-bye.

Winter gathered all her poise and self-possession and walked up the steps and into the building.

School was in session; the Institute's outer office was filled with milling students, all of whom seemed to have some urgent business with the Bidney Institute staff. As she came in, Winter glanced at one girl with flaming red hair who wore a brilliant blue stone at her throat. *CZ*, Winter thought automatically—the pendant was far too brilliant to be blue topaz. With some difficulty, she pushed herself to the front of the crowd and got the receptionist's attention.

"Is Truth Jourdemayne in?"

Meg Winslow's startled glance was one more confirmation to Winter of how much she had changed—or perhaps only a tribute to her new wardrobe; Ralph Lauren instead of Calvin Klein; soft, romantic pieces in hopeful pale colors, like the flowers that bloomed in the spring. Winter smiled tightly to herself. Even if the rest of her life was to be a losing fight, she intended to make a good showing. Jack had always said that showing up for the fight won half the battle.

She wondered where he was now. Jack Thoroughgood, her earliest mentor, had retired from The Street after a career of many years a few months before she'd left for Fall River. He'd lasted at Arkham Miskatonic King long enough to become a legend; job burnout on The Street was nearly as high as it was for cops and air-traffic controllers, and to survive at all was itself a victory.

With a wrench, Winter brought her mind back to the present. She couldn't afford to go drifting off here.

"Just a minute, please," Meg said. She started to turn away to deal with someone else.

It was irrational, after Winter had come through so much, that a brush-off from a harried receptionist should have the power to upset her, but it did. As Meg turned away, Winter felt the thrill of power spider-walk up her spine. *Ignore me, will you?* She thought longingly of raising Cain—in a psychic storm Meg's phone would shatter, her computer explode, all the electronic marvels of the twentieth century turn against her. . . .

Suddenly Winter realized how easy doing just that would be: Her psychokinesis was truly an extension of her thoughts now. Hers was the power, under the control of her conscious mind at last: to punish, to avenge. . . .

Very slowly, Winter set her bandaged hand on the counter that separated them and pressed, welcoming the pain of her wounds. Yes, she could hurt Meg and everyone else in this room. With a snap of her fingers she could summon the lightning and turn this room to a storm of poltergeist rage worse than the one that had destroyed her apartment. But if she did, for the first time in her life it would be she, Winter Musgrave, who was *consciously* responsible—not the hate-serpent, whose spasmodic bursts of psychokinetic rage had randomly tyrannized her through childhood and beyond. *Her.*

Winter drew a shaky breath. She had the sense of stepping back at the last instant from the brink of some unimaginable abyss that had opened just beneath her feet. She had claimed her power and acknowledged her anger. Now Winter had to admit that her anger could kill, and vow to chain it forever. Any other choice would make her no better than the monster who had sent the artificial Elemental to stalk her. With an effort, she stepped away from Meg and took a deep breath.

"Winter! I'm so glad you came back!" Truth cried warmly. She stepped through the press of students, holding out her hand in greeting. "Isn't it a zoo today? Dr. Roantree's running an opening screening, and everybody wants to be psychic," Truth finished with a sigh.

"Why do it?" Winter wondered.

"It's the closest thing to a cross-section we're going to get in this field, and if you don't have a statistical baseline, how can you tell when you've deviated from it?" Truth said wryly. "But come on back to my office; I'll get us both coffee."

Leaving Winter in her office, Truth headed back to the coffee machine. She'd actually been watching for long enough to see Winter win the struggle with her own anger. If it had been necessary, Truth would have intervened—in the last several months, she had set enough wards around the Institute to enable her to pull the plug on most consciously directed psychic assaults—but she was glad she had not had to. Self-control was the first step on the Path; to see that Winter had come so far on her own was a greater relief to Truth than she would have realized.

"I'm so glad you came back," Truth said, coming back into her office a few moments later with precariously balanced cups and a plate of cookies. "I like your new look," she added.

"I'm afraid my old look—what's left of it—is locked in a car trunk somewhere in San Francisco," Winter said.

"San Francisco? Was that where you went? I didn't know what to think when you went off that way. . . ."

Winter made an abortive gesture, rising to unburden Truth. "I had to find the others," she said, setting the cups carefully on Truth's desk. The bandages made them slippery to handle, but she knew she was lucky to have escaped as lightly as she had. The glass on her apartment floor could have sliced through tendons as easily as through flesh. "Find them. Talk to them. Find myself—and doesn't *that* sound like something our mothers would say? Not that my mother ever would have," Winter finished with a trace of bitterness.

"It sounds as if you've been busy," Truth said neutrally.

Winter looked away, her manner suddenly stiff. "Not busy enough," she said roughly. "Cassie—I knew her in college—is dead."

Truth was nearly as familiar with Winter's Taghkanic days by now as Winter was. "Cassilda Chandler?" she asked carefully. Winter nodded. But Cassie, like Winter, was in her thirties.

"It killed her," Winter said, and there was no need to explain what "it" was. "It burned her to death in her bookstore in San Francisco. They said she knew it was coming. . . ." Abruptly Winter covered her face with her hands and wept; the fierce angry pain of one who took every loss as a personal failure. After a few moments she sat up and took a deep breath, wiping at her eyes. Truth pushed the box of Kleenex across her desk, and Winter pulled out a fistful and dabbed at her face.

"I'm sorry. But it's my fault she's dead."

"I don't know whether it is or not." Truth selected her words with careful honesty. "But I do know that you didn't deliberately choose her death. I know it sounds inadequate, but would you like to talk about it?"

"I don't know." Winter drew another deep breath. "I don't know if I can. Cassie was a—" She waved her hand helplessly. "I don't know what to call it without being rude. Her friend Rhiannon said she was a witch."

Truth smiled faintly. "They do call themselves that," she admitted. "But wasn't Cassie involved in the Blackburn Work when she was here?"

"With Grey," Winter agreed, pronouncing the name with only the slightest of hesitations. "Rhiannon said that Cassie—I'm not sure I'm remembering this right—had decided that it was more important to depend on yourself than on any gods at all, so she'd sort of *adapted* the Blackburn Work? I hope that doesn't offend you," Winter added dutifully.

Truth smiled to herself. "It's more or less what Thorne did with the magickal tradition *he* was trained in," she said. "Change is usually a good thing, when it helps people and organizations adapt to new truths. But tell me more about Cassie, if you can. You said she was still involved with the Work. Do you know if she tried to summon or stop the Elemental?"

Winter frowned, trying to remember what Rhiannon had said. At the time she'd been to caught up in her own emotions to listen. "I think it sought her out. I think it sought them all out." Winter drew another long shuddering breath. "Oh, Truth, everything's gone so *wrong!*"

It took nearly an hour for Winter to summarize the events of the last month—of her visits to Janelle, who had trapped herself in an abusive marriage out of fear of success, and Ramsey, whose life was another sort of failure. As Winter spoke, the Elemental's attacks and the daily lives of her college friends seemed to meld into one vast tapestry, events super-natural and natural blending together into one long tragedy.

"After I found that Cassie was dead I just lost my head—her friend Rhiannon said she left a letter for me, but I didn't even stop to see if she was telling the truth. I came back East, visited my family, and then went to my apartment." Winter laughed shakily. "It looked like a bomb had gone off in there, and while I was looking around, that *thing* came back and paid me another visit, just like at Nuclear Lake."

"You don't seem too upset, all things considered," Truth said, darting a glance at Winter's bandaged hands.

"You can't be terrified all the time," Winter said, a faint note of gal-lows humor in her voice. "And . . . it wasn't the first time it had come back. I made it leave. But, Truth, I don't think I can do that again—and if I could, it would only mean I was giving it a chance to attack someone else."

Truth sighed. What Winter said was true. "I think you are the only one who has any chance of stopping it," Truth said slowly.

"But you don't think it's a very good chance." Winter stood, more to release tension than from a real desire to end the interview. "That's okay. Nobody lives forever. Ugh. I'm stiff from all that driving. Want to go for a walk?"

"I think this is where I was happiest," Winter said. At Winter's urging, she and Truth had walked across the campus, past the buildings, to where the tended manicured lawns of Taghkanic College gave way to the or-derly ranks of gnarled old apple trees that marched down nearly to the river's edge. "Not any particular place. Just at college."

The water lapped at the shore of broken shale with a sharp choppy motion. It was May; the trees were in full leaf now, their branches spot-ted with hard green spheres that would become apples in the months ahead. The river was wide here, and on the far side the bank rose sharply, its canopy of trees a green vista matching the one on this side, except for a clearing or two that signaled the rolling lawns of a Hudson Valley stately home.

"Many people say that about their college years." Truth had gone to Harvard, spending six years as a hard-science workaholic. She did not remember her college years as being particularly happy. The best years of her life were now.

"It's just that everything after that went wrong somehow. You make choices in college that you aren't ready to make, that nobody tells you how to make. Every choice is built on those, and slowly everything just sort of goes out of control. . . ." Winter fell silent, inspecting some interior landscape.

Truth waited patiently to hear the real reason for Winter's return. Everything else, frightening as it was, could have been handled with a phone call.

Finally it came.

"Tell me what you think I ought to do about the Elemental. I have the feeling I'm only going to get one chance."

Winter's abrupt change of subject did not confuse Truth; it was only an attempt to deal with a subject that, by its very nature, was nearly impossible to deal with. Sacrifice. *Self*-sacrifice.

"You told me you'd gone looking for the other members of your Circle," Truth said. "You mentioned the others. Did you find Grey?"

Winter stooped and came up with a small handful of rocks, heedless of the bandages on her hands. Focusing intently on the task, she began to fling them out into the water one by one.

"I never saw him again after I went home from college that spring." Winter's voice was strained. "I don't think I treated him very well after that. I think he thinks so, too. Or else he's already dead."

No! her mind screamed silently, and a sick heaviness of grief throbbed in her chest. Never to see him again—never to talk, to touch, to kiss . . .

"Do you think—?" Truth began.

"No!" Winter's denial was hot and quick. "He . . . I don't know," she faltered miserably at last. She closed her hands tightly over the last of the stones, and after a moment Truth saw red begin to seep through the layers of gauze.

"Winter!" The exclamation seemed to rouse the other woman; she dropped the stone with a hiss of pain and held out her hands. Rusty flowers of blood bloomed through the tape.

"That was stupid," she said with only a faint quaver in her voice. Truth saw her bite her lip, but her hands remained steady. "As I was saying," Winter continued in a tightly controlled voice, "I don't know where Hunter Greyson is or what he's been doing. I hope Cassie's friend Rhiannon can tell me; that's where I'm going next. After that, I imagine I have to let this occult *thing* of yours catch up with me." Her voice went flat on the last sentence. "You've said you could offer me some advice."

"Yes." Truth did not add to the statement with false words of reassurance. She had too little information—even the warning she had received that this battle was not hers to fight did not mean that Winter would survive it. "But first, let's go get that hand seen to—it looks as if you've reopened a very deep cut."

"Probably." Winter's voice was uninterested. "But the deepest cuts don't bleed, Truth. They don't bleed at all."

A quick stop at the campus infirmary got Winter's hands rebandaged and gained her a stern admonition from the campus nurse. Afterward, Truth steered them toward the faculty dining hall.

"You look like you could use some lunch, and I want to tell you what I've learned while you were gone."

Like most of the college buildings, the interior of the dining hall was done in the Gothic style of the great European universities, imparting something of an ecclesiastical tone to the long high-ceilinged room. The area reserved for the faculty's use was on the second floor of Taghkanic's cafeteria building, and doubled as the faculty lounge. Orders were sent down and meals sent up from the kitchen below by means of the dumbwaiter system that had been new when the college was built.

With the familiarity of long practice, Truth took Winter's order, and added a bottle of wine—a privilege granted only to senior faculty and those nonfaculty, like Truth, who used the dining room. Once the order had gone down she conducted her guest to a table.

"You'll feel better once you've had something to eat," Truth said.

"I can't stay," Winter burst out "—very long," she amended under Truth's level gaze. "Every minute I delay, something could happen. . . ."

"I'll drive you to the airport myself—tomorrow," Truth said firmly. "For now—do you remember Dr. Atheling from Fall River?"

Winter frowned. "He was one of the other doctors, not mine. He was . . . very kind." She shook her head. "It's all jumbled; I'm not sure how much of what I remember really happened. I was on so many different drugs; you know, you never realize how far from normal you've gotten until you try to go back." Winter sighed and looked at Truth, willing her to go on.

"I went to Fall River and spoke with him." As she knew Winter had, Truth left some things unsaid. Winter could not yet have Truth's own hard-won acceptance of the realities of the Unseen World, and to confront her with things she would have to dispute would be needless cruelty. "He asked how you were; apparently he knew even while you were there that an Elemental had been constructed to stalk you."

"But he doesn't know who sent it, or how to stop it, any more than you do," Winter said with brutal insight. Just then, a chime from the dumbwaiter announced the arrival of the food, and conversation ceased while the plates were brought to the table and the wine was poured.

Winter drank thirstily, as if it were water—or as if she were trying to get drunk. "So now what?" she said, with a faint aggressive note in her voice.

"Now you confront it anyway, with Hunter Greyson's help or without," Truth said. "It's the only thing I can think of that might work. You have some sort of connection with it; you're the one it's trying to reach. Magicians don't exactly list in the telephone book, you know—and while I'm not a very good one, I have the feeling that Dr. Atheling is, and he said *he* couldn't control it."

But had he? Truth wondered. Or had he said he *wouldn't?*

"You said you've controlled it before; that's a start," she finished.

Winter looked down at her newly rebandaged hand with a rueful expression. "In a roomful of broken glass I had a lot of incentive. But all I could do was push it away—and that was the hardest thing I've ever done." She drank again, emptying the glass, and held it out for a refill. "It isn't gone for good. And it's going to come back."

In her situation, I'd drink, too. Truth refilled the glass without comment. Alcohol was well known for its depressive effects on the psychic centers; Winter's perceptions of the Unseen World must be spilling over into every facet of her daily life by now, and this was a last-ditch attempt to curb them.

"I just don't see that you have a lot of choice," Truth told her after a moment's silence. "You've said yourself that running away doesn't seem to work; it only finds other targets for a while and then comes back to you. You may have more of a chance against the creature than you realize, though: Elementals are surprisingly vulnerable under certain conditions. What you're going to have to do is choose your ground carefully."

"No moveable objects," Winter interjected mockingly.

"No moveable objects," Truth agreed. "And I'd stay away from power lines or other electrical sources, if I were you. But the Elemental should come fairly readily if you try to bring it—it wants something from you, remember."

"What if all it wants is to kill me?" Winter asked.

Truth met her gaze unflinchingly. There was a long moment's silence.

"Then killing you should make it leave," she said at last.

"Fair enough," Winter said, and drank again.

"When you call it, I don't know how fast it will come, but when it does you can expect the same sort of disturbance that followed you before. You'll probably feel cold and weak—it's linked to you; it draws its energy from you, at least in part."

"What does that *mean,* exactly?" Winter asked. She shifted irritably in her seat as the Taconic Parkway scenery scrolled by. The day was cloudy and overcast, sullen and uninviting despite the thick spring foliage landscaping one of the most scenic roadways in the United States.

True to her word, after a long night spent giving advice and discussion, Truth was driving Winter down to JFK to catch her flight to San Francisco.

"Okay. I'll try to make this as simple as possible. Occultists believe in the existence of what is called the *subtle body;* what it means, in essence, is that every person has what amounts to two bodies; one here on the Plane of Manifestation, and one on the Astral Plane."

"It sounds like science fiction," Winter said tightly. Truth sighed.

"I assure you, it's entirely real. I'm not even saying you have to believe in it, but you asked me a question, and this is the only answer I have. And what it amounts to, in your case, is that a magician has somehow linked this Elemental—which has much of its existence on the Astral— with your *subtle body.* It's as attached to you as if you were at two ends of an extension cord."

"What about my soul?" Winter said, almost at random. "Isn't that really what you're talking about here?"

Truth grimaced. She knew Winter was only trying to change the subject. She'd spent hours last night explaining to Winter how best to confront the artificial Elemental's threat, but one night's lecture could not take the place of years of study.

"No; the soul is—occultists believe that the soul is something different entirely. Look. We don't have enough time for this explanation as it is," Truth said, striving for a light tone, "and if we start talking about the soul we'll never get through it all. Let's get back to the construct. Do you have any questions about what to do once you've summoned it?"

Winter shrugged. "It seems fairly basic; say 'Here monster-monster-monster,' and see what happens. And then—" She fell silent, grimacing. "It all seems so ridiculous, except when that thing's actually in front of me."

"I know," Truth said gently. "But Winter, you have to try to concentrate."

"On communicating with it," Winter said bleakly. "On asking it what it wants. On sucking it in through this astral garden hose that connects us. Frankly, I'd rather drink industrial waste."

"Your choice," Truth reminded her, and Winter snorted. "I wish you weren't making this trip back to California. It makes you so vulnerable. There's a place near here where you could try to call it; I'd be right there," Truth added.

"No. I'll do this alone. It isn't fair to make you face it again," Winter said.

Truth didn't remind Winter that, if Winter died and the creature were still at large, Truth would be doing exactly that. She suspected that Winter already knew.

"Well, after all, I can hardly sit in your office calling everyone in San Francisco and asking them if their name's Rhiannon, and if they used to know a friend of mine, and if the letter they say they have is real, a forgery, or even exists at all," Winter drawled defensively. "If I go back to where I saw her before, she may still be haunting Cassie's bookstore."

With a belated pang of guilt, Winter remembered that her car was still sitting in Long-Term Parking at SFO . . . at least she hoped it was. Her current rental car was sitting parked safely in Truth's driveway; returning it was Truth's problem now.

"And if you do find her, but the message is lost—or has nothing to do with Grey?" Truth asked gently.

"Then I'll come back here," Winter said with bright falseness.

And though Truth knew she lied, there was nothing she could do to stop her. Because finding Grey was still their last, best—only—hope.

She'd relied on the comfort of Truth's mere presence more than she'd known, Winter realized. From the moment she stepped away from the car at the drop-off zone at JFK, Winter had felt lost and alone. It was easier to pretend bravery when there was someone else there to be fooled by the act. Now there was only Winter, all alone, who had even less faith than Truth seemed to in her ability to do anything but die at the bidding of some Otherworld creature. A creature whose nature and desires she didn't understand, sent for a purpose she had never known.

Winter picked up her boarding pass and proceeded to the First Class lounge. She wouldn't reach San Francisco until this evening, though because of the three-hour time difference she would arrive only three hours after she'd left instead of six. Rummaging through her purse, she pulled out the card that Paul Frederick had given her on her last ill-starred visit. *Handmade Music.* That was the place to start.

It began to rain. Small showers of droplets clung to the boarding-lounge window, obscuring the view of tarmac and the waiting planes. The inhospitable vista was the perfect counterpoint to her mood.

The rain seemed to be lying in wait for her; Winter stepped out of the terminal into the dusk to be greeted by a blowy drizzle that was either a very light rain or a very heavy fog. In either event, the weather was cold, damp, and unwelcoming. She shivered inside her cashmere barn coat. The weather wouldn't make driving any easier, either.

She'd tried Handmade Music's number from the airport and gotten no answer. She tried not to let that discourage her; it was a setback, not a defeat. She could always drive to the neighborhood and see what she could find on her own. Without too much difficulty she located her car and paid the exorbitant fee for losing her ticket without a murmur, as if money no longer had any meaning. In a perverse way, Winter found the probability of her death wonderfully liberating. There were no more appearances to keep up.

As if what was left of her life was truly charmed, she reached the corner of Haight and Ashbury streets as quickly and easily as if she were a long-time resident of the city. There was even a parking space, and Winter slid her car into it, shutting down the lights and engine before it occurred to her that perhaps she ought not to be here at all. The streetlight reflected a thousand points of light off the raindrops that starred her windshield now that the wipers were stilled, and all the light was gone from the sky.

Winter looked around. The street that had looked merely shabby and down-at-heels by daylight looked positively sinister now. Though she would have walked unhesitatingly through rougher-looking neighborhoods back home, Winter was off her own turf here and she knew it. Hundreds of tourists were killed every year simply through not being able to read the warning signs of urban violence in an unfamiliar city. The sensible thing to do would be to drive away, find a hotel, and wait for morning and the chance to try Paul Frederick's number again.

Yet, even while Winter was trying to convince herself to follow this sensible course, a gleam of light in her rearview mirror caught her attention. Turning around in her seat, she saw the warm yellow glow of a lighted storefront. Before she had time for second thoughts, Winter was out of her car. Locking it swiftly, she turned up the sidewalk in the direction of the light, half-running through the spring rain.

The Green Man was still a welcoming oasis; Winter did not even stop to remember that this was where she'd had her disastrous interview with Rhiannon as she lunged up the steps and pushed open the door.

It was warm and dry inside the café, in sharp contrast to the rainy darkness outside, and the air was filled with the smell of baking bread. The stained-glass panels hanging in the windows were dark and glittering now, but the polished wood of the spool tables and oak counters glowed brightly, and the plants hanging everywhere filled the place with life. Winter stopped, blinking a little at the brightness. She brushed her hair back from her face, feeling raindrops spatter beneath her hand.

Do something. Don't just stand here like a mooncalf.

Despite the location, the café had a good following; most of the tables were full, and the murmur of conversation and the clink of tableware formed a lulling cushion of sound. Winter looked around. Rhiannon had seemed to know this place when they had been here before; perhaps *they* knew *her?*

There was a booth free; Winter moved toward it and sat down, grateful to be shielded from the illusion of prying eyes. Nobody had noticed her and nobody cared.

But in that much, she was wrong.

The waitress—a young woman with straight blond hair, dressed in tie-dye and a rainbow-colored crochet vest—had barely brought her coffee when a stranger approached the booth.

"Hello," he said. "Do you remember me? I'm Paul Frederick; we met the last time you were here."

The coincidence did not surprise her; it was as if on some level Winter had been expecting him to be here. She smiled invitingly and gestured.

"Yes, I remember you. I don't know if we were ever properly introduced. I'm Winter Musgrave. Won't you sit down?"

Frederick smiled. "Actually, I'm here with my wife. Won't you join us?"

When Winter collected her coffee and moved to the Fredericks' table she received another surprise. The petite brunette seated with him was someone she knew.

"You're Emily Barnes, aren't you? The pianist?"

Husband and wife looked at each other, and Emily laughed. "I suppose you're right, Frodo, and I should stop pretending that nobody knows." She rose gracefully to her feet and held out her hand to Winter. "Yes, I am. If you've heard of me, I hope you've enjoyed my work."

Winter took the hand and clasped it gently, out of respect for the talent in those strong fingers. "Very much. I saw you a few years ago in Japan, when you were on tour with the symphony. You opened with Anstey's *Variations on a Theme for Harpsichord.*"

Emily's smile broadened. "Dear Simon! I always love his work—even though I think he writes some of those transitions just to torment me. He was my teacher, you know."

Winter smiled, and the three of them sat down. There was no one who loved music, either classical or modern, who didn't know the modern-day fable of Simon Anstey and Emily Barnes. At first his protegée, Emily was now coming to be considered the foremost interpreter of his work.

The fairy-tale symmetry of the story was marred only by the fact that the legendary musician-turned-composer had married not Emily, but her older sister Leslie, several years before Emily herself had married. But when Winter had imagined the poised, professional Emily's husband, someone like the elfish Paul Frederick had been the farthest thing from her mind.

"And this is Winter Musgrave, Em. She was a friend of Cassie's," Paul Frederick—Frodo?—said.

"Oh, I'm so sorry." Emily Barnes's eyes filled with genuine sympathy. "I know that saying it was a dreadful tragedy seems so inadequate, but Cassie's death is such a great loss to so many people. Everyone loved her."

And it's my fault. Mine! Winter felt her own grief as if it were still raw and fresh. "Yes," she said briefly, lowering her head.

"It may be more of a tragedy than you realize," Paul Frederick said soberly. Winter's head snapped up, and she locked eyes with him challengingly.

"No," she said evenly, "I don't think so." The warning in her voice was plain.

"Paul!" Emily's voice broke into the clash of wills. "If this is business of yours, can't it at least wait until after dinner?"

Paul Frederick looked sheepish, and smiled apologetically at Winter. "I'm sorry; I was rude. Have you eaten? The Green Man is table d'hôte in the evening unless you just want a snack, but the food here is very good."

"Thanks," Winter said. "I just flew in, and the food on the plane was pretty ghastly."

Paul gestured, and the waitress who'd brought Winter's coffee came over to the table.

As they waited for the food, Emily determinedly kept the talk general. Winter learned that Emily considered herself too impatient to teach, though Simon said she would come to it someday.

"He said if *he* could become a teacher, then there was hope for anyone!" Emily said, with such an infectious merriment at her private joke that Winter could not help but smile, too. For a moment her own problems seemed very far away.

Emily seemed profoundly incurious about Winter's business in San Francisco, but it seemed to Winter that Emily did not share all her husband's interests, and wisely kept herself separate from them. The food, when it came, was a poached whitefish with exotic mushrooms in wine sauce—as unexpected in this atmosphere as was the marriage of neat, disciplined Emily Barnes to the exotic, anachronistic Frodo.

When they had finished dinner and the coffee had been brought, Emily rose to her feet.

"I am going to go powder my nose for about ten minutes," she said determinedly. She strode toward the back of the café with the same queenlike carriage with which Winter had seen her cross the concert stage.

"What's that all about?" Winter said.

"Oh, Em isn't really interested in what she calls 'my other life.' She comes to the big Festivals, but music is the most important thing in her life, and we both respect that," Frodo said.

Winter felt a pang of wistfulness, wondering if Grey would be— would have been—as intelligent and caring a husband as Frodo obviously was. She had made no time in her life for anyone with whom she could form that level of closeness, and knowing her reasons didn't make the loneliness any less.

"And what is 'your other life'?" she asked deliberately.

Frodo met her eyes. "I was a member of Cassie's working group. Her coven," he said quietly.

It took a moment for all the ramifications of that simple statement to sink in, and when they did, Winter found herself blushing with shame. If Frodo talked about the circumstances surrounding Cassie's death Winter did not know if she could bear it. She'd lived her life as if everyone had been put into the world to play a part subordinate to hers, and was only now coming to realize how selfish that had been.

"So you probably know Rhiannon," she said evenly.

"Yeah." Frodo grimaced. "I guess I really got on her case about the way she treated you—just jumping in with what must have sounded like a bunch of messages from the spirit world delivered by a gypsy con artist, when you'd barely found out Cassie was dead."

"Oh, no!" Winter protested automatically. "I suppose I could at least have listened to her," she added after a moment.

She regarded Frodo warily. The aloofness she had always cultivated as a defense against the world made her rebel against the very idea of this stranger knowing anything about her personal life—let alone about the monster that had stalked and killed Cassie.

"It's hard to know what to do sometimes," Frodo said diplomatically.

Winter set her jaw, choking back the words of self-justification before they were uttered. To have to live with what Truth Jourdemayne called the Unseen World was bad enough, but to talk with someone she hardly knew about things that her mind still rejected even as her mouth formed the words . . .

But to her relief, Frodo seemed to be willing to let her lead the conversation, and there was only one thing Winter really wanted to talk about.

"I need the letter Cassie left for me," she said. "Unless you know what it said?"

Frodo shook his head. "No. But Rhiannon can meet us here in about fifteen minutes and bring it with her. If that's okay with you?"

"Yes," Winter said, not trusting herself to say more. *It's going to have to be, isn't it?*

Frodo got up to make the phone call.

Emily had returned to the table, and the three of them had finished with dessert, by the time Rhiannon actually arrived. Winter had no idea what Frodo had said to her in the phone call, but Rhiannon looked almost painfully subdued. She wore a light raincoat beaded with moisture over a pink cotton Shaker sweater, tan corduroy slacks, and oxblood loafers. Her frizzy riot of copper-red hair was stifled in a severe braid that could not quite control the rain-sequined halo of frizz. She carried a manila envelope under one arm inside her coat.

"Hello," she said unsmilingly, looking at Winter.

Oh, just give me the damned letter! Winter felt like shouting. Instead, she rose to her feet and held out her hand. "Hello, Rhiannon. I'm pleased to see you again."

The other woman's mouth twisted, preparing a sarcastic retort, then she caught Frodo's eye and stopped. She took Winter's hand and shook it briefly, and Winter was sharply glad that her particular psychic kink was psychokinesis, not clairvoyance. It was bad enough suspecting the truth about people's inner feelings without knowing them for sure.

With the determination gained through years of practice at keeping emotion at bay, Winter smiled and took charge of the conversation.

"Thank you for coming. I didn't have the opportunity before to tell you how sorry I am for your loss; I know Cassie must have meant a great deal to you." The words were artificial and contrived, but on some level they were true: If Winter had been a better person, she knew, she *would* have sympathized with Rhiannon's loss instead of being obsessed solely with her own.

Surprisingly, Rhiannon accepted the inner truth of Winter's words, not their calculated motivation.

"She was your friend first," Rhiannon said gruffly. "I'm sorry I startled you before. I'm glad you came back."

"We so rarely get a second chance in life," Winter said. "Would you care to sit down?"

"No," Rhiannon said. "I mean, I'm on my way to work. I'm working at Capwell's now, Frodo—it's just temporary, but it's better than nothing," she said in an aside. "Anyway, Cassie's letter is in the envelope. So's my address. If you need any help from us—anything—we owe it to Cassie."

Honest if not gracious, Winter thought.

Rhiannon held out the envelope and Winter took it. She stood as Rhiannon crossed the dining room and went out the door into the rain.

Winter sat down again. The waiter had cleared the table while Rhiannon had been there, and Winter set the envelope on the cleared space in front of her. When it became obvious that Winter was not going to open it, Frodo cleared his throat.

"I hope you'll give me a call when you've had a chance to read that," he said. "I'd like to know what I can do to help. Do you have a place to stay?"

In what she now thought of as her other life, Winter had always stayed at the St. Mark Hotel. She wondered if they'd let her in without a reservation. "I'll find something."

"Will you call me?" Frodo said.

Probably worried that I'm just going to burn Cassie's letter. "Don't worry," she said obliquely. "I've gone through too much to get this." She forced herself to go on. "I'll call you." The waiter came back with the check;

Winter grabbed it automatically. "And, please. I hope you'll be my guests for dinner. I owe you a great deal," she added reluctantly. It was time to get used to being beholden to people, no matter how much her pride rebelled against it.

"Well . . . okay," Frodo said with a warm smile. He stood up. "C'mon, Em. And, Winter, come and see us when you can, okay?"

"Sure." *If I can.* "Good night, Frodo, Emily. It was a pleasure."

When they were gone, Winter put down her American Express card, then signed the slip and left a generous tip. But it was a long time before she could bring herself to slip the envelope into her purse and leave.

The St. Mark Hotel, that gracious relict of what *San Francisco Chronicle* columnist Herb Caen called San Francisco's Silver Age, still stood, in the words of the famous song, "high on a windswept hill." Despite the lateness of the hour when Winter finally reached it and the lack of advance warning, the staff was able to accommodate her. It was true that all that had been free on such short notice was one of the Mark's luxurious suites, but it hardly seemed to matter, and soon she was looking out from the parlor window of her suite over the fog-shrouded Bay. A bottle of wine from Room Service stood on a tray before her, with her briefbag beside it. A corner of the letter poked out from inside the bag, still unopened.

You have to do it sometime, Winter told herself, trying to ignore the clutching ice in her stomach. She reached forward, but instead of the letter, she drew the cork out of the wine bottle and let the scarlet liquid splash into the glass beside it. *You're drinking too much,* she admonished herself, then gulped at the wine angrily. What could it possibly matter now? What could anything matter? She wasn't going to live long enough to become an alcoholic!

She sat back and stared morosely out the window as the alcohol worked its way into her bloodstream. Her conscience nagged at her. Whatever pain Cassie's letter might give her, it was a pain that she deserved.

Winter poured another glass of wine and reached for the envelope. Her hands shook slightly as she tore off the end, and two things fell out. One was a smaller envelope, business-sized, with her name written on it in Cassie's scrawling script; the other, the information Rhiannon had said she'd given her. Meticulously, Winter read over the name and address and tucked the slip of paper into the appropriate pocket in her Filofax before putting its binder back into her bag.

That left only Cassie's letter. Winter pressed the envelope between her fingers, feeling its thinness. Whatever information the letter contained, it was very brief.

Gritting her teeth and closing her eyes, Winter ripped the envelope open.

The fog slid in off the water, blurring the boundaries between the ocean and the land. The rain had stopped, but the air was still filled with moisture as the mist claimed the city for its own, sliding over the walls of stark new office buildings, gracious old hotels, and even the sloping sides of the Transamerica Pyramid. In the City by the Bay, the night slid on toward morning.

In the parlor of the suite in the St. Mark Hotel, time had lost all meaning. Winter stared at the brief paragraph written on the sheet of white paper. She sat cold and silent, unmoving, while inside her mind the screaming had only begun.

CHAPTER FIFTEEN

THE WINTER HEART

Rise up, my love, my fair one, and come away.
For, lo, the winter is past, the rain is over and gone;
The flowers appear on the earth; the time of the
singing of birds is come, and the voice of the
turtle is heard in our land.

—KING JAMES BIBLE

NORTH OF SAN FRANCISCO, THE COASTLINE RUNS TO small coves floored in silvery gravel, and the remains of the mighty sequoia forests stand along the coast like silent sentinels. Along this wild Pacific headland there are a number of small towns that go on untouched from the days when gold, or timber, or even wine—and not computers— were the principal livelihood of the locals. There are frame houses in the exuberant fashion of the previous century, and gracious buildings in the Mission style, and the inhabitants hope that the freeway sprawl that seems determined to make Sacramento merely a suburb of San Francisco will miss them entirely.

She had not slept.

As soon as it was light, Winter had checked out of the hotel. The Mark's concierge had been helpful, providing driving directions and even a road map. She reached San Gabriel a little before noon.

San Gabriel was a sizable town, larger than Glastonbury, though dwarfed by the metropolises surrounding it. By the time she arrived, the early morning haze had burnt off to leave the coast basking in a brilliant, cloudless day.

Winter did not care.

When she pulled into a gas station to ask directions, her voice was harsh as a crow's, her face a stark mask of sleeplessness and psychic pain. She thanked the attendant as carefully as if such worldly courtesies could still matter to her, and drove slowly toward her final destination.

In some cruel incongruity, the place she sought was almost on the water itself, just as if beauty still had the power to affect those within. The Pacific reflected the sun and the sky as if it were poured of blue enamel, and gulls wheeled and cried above the cove. Winter slewed her car into the parking lot and stopped.

"I have to see Hunter Greyson," Winter said to the woman behind the desk. Inside the building it was as if the postcard-perfect day outside did not exist. Tired fluorescents illuminated walls that had been painted a grubby gas-chamber green thirty years before, and the shabby linoleum looked as though it could never really be clean.

"Is he a patient here?" the nurse said. Winter could see her nameplate: CAROL TAYLOR.

Do you think I'd be here if he wasn't? "Yes," Winter said. The contrast between this place and Fall River gave her a sudden unwelcome pang. If Fall River had been horrible, how much more horrible could this place be?

"Are you a relative?" the nurse asked.

Winter's head drooped. *Yes. I'm the woman who should have married him.* "I'm Winter Musgrave."

A simple trick that Winter had learned years before was that any answer, no matter how meaningless, would be taken for the proper answer if only it was uttered in a confident tone of voice. Though she had provided no explanation and no proof, the nurse pressed a button, and an aide in a bright-flowered smock popped out of one of the rooms down the hall.

"Ashley will show you to Mr. Greyson's room," the nurse said.

*   *   *

"And how are we today, Hunter?" Ashley chirped brightly. She walked past the bed by the door, opened the curtain, checked the air conditioner to see that it was running, and then turned back.

Winter stood looking down at the bed by the window. "Hello, Grey," she said. Her lips moved, but no sound came.

The man on the bed was thin and frail. His long blond hair was pulled back in a limp braid. His eyes were closed as if he were asleep.

But he wasn't.

In the space between the two beds a respiratory ventilator worked, its sound an awful parody of human breathing. A blue-tinted hose led from the machine to a bubbling humidifier to a hole in the throat of Hunter Greyson. Through the tube's translucent plastic Winter could see the pale flash of the tracheostomy fittings, and a nauseated wave of denial rose up behind her clenched teeth.

"Is this your first visit?" Ashley asked, her voice low with professional compassion. She moved closer to the bedside, lifting Grey's slack hand and taking his pulse with automatic efficiency. "Come on, Hunter, wake up, guy. You've got visitors."

"Don't," Winter begged. *Grey. His name is Grey.*

Ashley looked at her pityingly. "You've got to talk to them," she said, still holding Grey's hand. "Maybe they know you're here. And sometimes they wake up, even from the machine."

Winter stared at her. She could not have spoken if her life depended on it. After a moment Ashley shrugged almost imperceptibly and moved toward the other bed.

"Hiya, Bobby. How're we doing today? Ready for a little softball on the beach?" she said with bright enthusiasm.

"What happened to him?" Winter asked. Ashley pulled the covers up around "Bobby's" neck and turned to face her.

"Hunter? It was a motorcycle accident, the admitting report said. We got him—I mean, he was transferred here after about six weeks at Sacto; we had the only available bed in the area. He was riding in the rain . . . they found his bike at the bottom of the cliff near Antonia Beach and they're lucky they found him at all. Hit and run, maybe. If he wakes up, maybe he can tell us. Right, Hunter?"

The dark, the rain—hadn't looked like rain when I left; got to get the bike un-

der cover—Headlights in the wrong lane, sliding around the curve—drunk driver; which way's he going to swerve?—No! Oh, God, it's so cold—

Winter jerked back to reality with Ashley's hands clamped around her arms.

"Come on over here; we're going to sit down now."

Winter felt the edge of a chair at the back of her legs and lowered herself gratefully into it, sweating and sick with the sudden flashback to the recurring nightmare that had haunted her for weeks before her admission to Fall River. Only it wasn't a nightmare. She knew that now. It was the truth.

Savagely Winter forced the tears back, wishing she could disown as well the memories of the pain and broken bones, of lying in the rain not knowing how bad the injuries were but knowing they were bad, of feeling life and consciousness ebb like the ocean on the rocks below and praying that someone, *anyone,* would come.

Winter drew a deep breath.

"Are you all right? Shall I get the nurse?" Ashley said.

"No. Yes. I mean— It was just a shock, seeing him. I'm all right now," Winter lied glibly.

"When did you find out?" Ashley said. "About him?"

Winter glanced up at her in surprise.

"You aren't really family, are you?" Ashley said. "A friend?"

There was no point in denying it now. What could they do, other than throw her out? "Yes," Winter said.

Ashley sighed, and for a moment all the vitality seemed to drain out of her. "Oh. I'm sorry to hear it. I was kind of hoping you could sign the papers," she said softly. "We haven't been able to find any family. Do you know where they are?"

Grey had never spoken of his family, not that Winter ever remembered. "No. What papers?"

"To pull the— To turn off his respirator. He came in on one from Sacramento, and by state law we can't disconnect it without the family's consent. But he's been here more than a year, and I don't really think he's going to wake up," Ashley said sadly. "He's only thirty-five. He could be like this for the next thirty years. And sometimes, when I work midnights I come in here and sit with him. I think he wants us to let him go . . . but we can't." Ashley hesitated. "Do you want me to leave you alone with him for a while?"

"Thank you," Winter said.

"I'll be down at the other end of the hall," Ashley said. "It's just me and Mrs. Taylor on today—that's the nurse down at the station. Marcie called in sick. Just press the button if you need anything." Her white orthopedic shoes whispered over the battered linoleum as Ashley whisked out, closing the door behind her.

Winter walked back over to the body in the bed. The thump and sigh of the ventilator was loud inside the room, and the sunny day outside seemed only a mockery painted on the glass.

"Hello, Grey," she said again. She reached out and took his hand.

And vanished.

Or, rather, the world around her vanished, as suddenly as if someone had put a bag over her head. There was a confusing maelstrom of images: the gulls crying, and rain; a roaring sound like a powerful engine running flat-out; and the taste of copper. It was as if some playful god were pawing through some toybox of the senses.

And then, so fast that Winter, scrabbling for her sanity, was sure this was only one more layer of hallucination, she found herself standing in the spring orchard below Greyangels Farm. She had barely grasped where she was—against all possibility—when the apple-blossom petals began to spill from the trees, and the grass to turn to dust. For an instant the branches of the orchard were silvery bare, before the trees themselves withered away to ash, and a cold, cold wind swirled the remains of the orchard away. *I'm going to scream now,* Winter thought, though she knew that once she began to scream she would never stop.

"Hello, Winter."

Dr. Luty was right. Everybody was right. I've been crazy all along.

Winter Musgrave turned around and looked into Hunter Greyson's eyes.

He was dressed as she'd seen him in her dreams, in the white buckskin jacket and jeans he'd worn in that springtime orchard so many years ago.

As she watched, the jacket darkened, became rain-spotted motorcycle leathers, and the lines of age flickered across his face like summer lightning.

She was not seeing Grey, Winter realized with a horrified pang. She was seeing the *idea* of Grey—and she had not seen him in so many years that her mental picture of his appearance was only confusing things.

She was terrified, exhausted, and sick with grief. But more than that, Winter was a woman who refused ever to fail. Deliberately she forced herself to relax, to let go.

Grey's blurred image steadied; a vigorous man of her own age, in his thirties, and not the wasted ghost in the hospital bed. His pale blond hair, still long, was pulled back into a silky ponytail. Instead of anything resembling street clothes, he wore a long white robe with an open-fronted red robe over it. The inner robe was belted in with what looked like a jeweled serpent, and resting on his hair was a laurel-leaf crown made of gold. On his right wrist he wore an iron bracelet set with red stones, and there was a signet ring on his finger. He looked . . .

He looked like the picture of Thorne Blackburn from the front of Truth's book.

"Grey," Winter said wonderingly, and then, with the inanity that was sanity's only possible defense: "What do you *do* for a living?"

Grey—or his image—laughed. "I'm an unemployed actor, what did you think?" He came forward and took her hands in his, and possibly the greatest shock since her arrival was that his skin seemed warm and living against her own.

"You came. I thought you'd forgotten me," Hunter Greyson said.

I did for a while. But not any more. "Grey, what is this place? Where am I? How did I get here?" Winter babbled.

"You aren't here; not really. Your body is right where you left it. This is only a dream. Do you remember, Winter? We built our stronghold here, a long time ago."

Winter looked over his shoulder. The flat featureless light that allowed her to see came from nowhere and everywhere, illuminating a universe as unnatural as a movie sound-stage. In the middle distance she could see twelve cairns of stone, half crumbling and seemingly very old, set in a circle.

"Yes, Grey. I remember." And as she said it, the words were true.

"Help me, Winter. You're my last hope," Grey said. "No one else came."

Once more there came that sick flutter of uncertainty: the night, the road, the glare of the oncoming headlights, and then the cold. . . . She shuddered, pulling closer to him, and Grey embraced her as if her presence could warm him.

"It took me a long time to realize I wasn't dead," Grey said against her cheek. "If I'd been dead, I would have known what to do; after all, I'd been preparing for it all my life. Death isn't the end. It's only a way-station on the journey."

"You're in a coma," Winter said pulling back to look into his face. "Hooked up to a respirator." She felt like Alice having a conversation with the Red Queen—no matter what she said, it would sound totally surreal. As long as she didn't think about where she was or who she was talking to, she was okay, but nothing in the bizarre manifestations of the last several months had come even close to preparing her for this.

"A coma." Grey nodded. "I thought it might be something like that. I can't go on, I can't go back. I'm just . . . here. Not even as real as a ghost. I tried to reach some of the people I knew, but the way I am now, things don't work the way they should. The only way I could reach the physical world at all was to call back the *magickal child* that Nuclear Circle created, and—"

"*You* sent it? It was you all along? *You* killed Cassie?" Winter interrupted. She jerked away from him and stepped back, putting as much space between them as she could. Anger called to her; a fury that here, in this world, would be as tangible as their two bodies. Cassie was dead and Grey had killed her. He'd sent the *magickal child* that had started the fire. He'd said so.

Betrayal fed her anger—only now did Winter realize how much she had been counting on Grey to live up to her dreams of him.

"*Killed—?*" Grey's face went pale with shock. He threw up his hands, sketching a figure in the aethyr—

—and Winter was back in the hospital room, staring down at Grey's body across their clasped hands, her heart hammering with fury and shock.

"Grey!" she cried. The body in the bed did not stir. "Grey, answer me!" She took him by the shoulders, shaking him. His head lolled limply on the pillow.

"Is everything all right in here?" Ms. Taylor came into the room, starched and efficient in her nursing whites, and looked down at Grey. "Is there anything I can do for you?"

Leave my patient alone. Winter heard that unspoken rebuke as clearly as if it had been uttered aloud.

"No," she said, summoning a smile with an effort. "Everything's fine. Could I be alone with my—with Grey, please?"

She didn't dare claim a relationship she couldn't prove, dearly as she wished to. The moment she did there'd be papers to sign and questions she didn't dare face—not someone whose recent treatment in a "sanatorium" could too easily come to light. She had to stay calm, or she could help no one.

"We've always called him Hunter," Ms. Taylor said, seeming to accept the explanation that was no explanation. She smoothed the hair back from Grey's brow. Winter felt a flare of jealousy before realizing that this woman had as much right as she did to touch him—and maybe more.

"The family always called him Grey," Winter said, skating perilously close to a lie. "He hated—*hates*—to be called Hunter." With reflexive pragmatism, she wondered who was paying the bills to keep Grey here, if he really had no family.

"I'll tell the girls, then. We try to call them by name as much as possible. People have come out of comas much longer than this one, Ms. Greyson, you mustn't give up hope. Please stay as long as you want. Oh, and could you stop by the administration office on your way out? Mr. Peters needs to talk to a member of the family about what to do with the billing once the Medicaid runs out." Ms. Taylor smoothed Grey's hair back one last time before she left.

Alone once more, Winter stared down at Grey. If she touched him again, would she find herself back in the Twilight Zone talking to a ghost?

Just how much credence could she give to everything she thought she had heard Grey saying, anyway? Wasn't it so much more likely that the whole thing had been some kind of delusional flashback? No matter how much reason she'd had for it, she'd still had a nervous breakdown—or the next best thing to one.

"Well," Winter said aloud, "you can't have it both ways." Either what had just happened was a hallucination—in which case she had no more reason to believe that Grey had killed Cassie than she'd had before—or it wasn't.

And Grey had killed her friend.

No, Winter told herself. *Think about it. He said he'd sent the* magickal child. *He didn't seem to know about Cassie's death at all—in fact, he seemed pretty shaken up by it when I told him.*

What was she supposed to believe? *Who* was she supposed to believe?

"Why trust anybody, Winter?" Grey spoke to her out of her memory. *"It's a free country. Doubt everything. Question authority."*

"Okay," Winter said. "You're the authority, and I'm going to question you."

She dragged the chair she'd been sitting in before over beside Grey's bed and reached through the guardrails to clasp his hand once more. *I need to know. If you hate me enough to kill me I need to know.*

It was like choosing to step off a high-diving board. She let go and fell through that strange kaleidoscopic disorientation once again; scenes and sensations bizarrely disconnected from all familiar context.

And then, faster than before, the flicker through the orchard—*there's something here I need to understand*—and Grey, the plain, the ruined citadel in the distance.

He was dressed as before, only now the bright scarlet of the outer robe had cooled to a dark wine color, and everything about him seemed less bright. For a moment her senses rebelled against the compelling *reality* of all of this—this—this Stephen King fantasy world that was as concretely *here* as a New York City street.

As she fought it, the world around her flickered and vanished, and the sounds and smells of the hospital room welled up around her once more. She heard Grey cry out—from that world or this?—and belatedly understood that the Otherworld was not something forced on her, but a thing that she was somehow helping to create.

How can this be? a part of her mind cried out, terrified. But this was a part of reality that Truth and others Winter had met on her travels accepted as simply as they accepted the physical world around them, and Winter was out of options. Accept and use it unquestioningly, or more people would die.

She relaxed, and the only world Grey had left came real once more.

She could feel the cold sinking into her bones, and wished, for a ridiculous moment, that she'd brought a heavier coat. But no earthly garments could warm her here.

"Take my hand." Grey's fingers closed over hers, and the world steadied around her. Winter looked up into his face.

He was not the way she had remembered him. Too many years had passed for that. But traces of the boy she'd known remained in the man, and for a moment the memory of how much she'd loved him threatened to overwhelm everything.

For a moment.

"You killed Cassie," Winter said, tightening her grasp on his hand. Determination made a cold weapon of her heart. The answer was here after all.

"No." Grey's denial was slow, uncertain. "I . . . But . . . *you're* here, Winter. Why you? You didn't have any more interest in the Work—" his tone was bitter "—and Cassie did, at least a little; enough that I thought a message from the astral had a chance of reaching her. How did she die?"

"Burned," Winter said brutally. "Burned to death in her bookstore—trying to communicate with what you sent after her."

"But that isn't the way it should have happened," Grey protested. His unhappiness and puzzlement communicated themselves to Winter, tingeing her feelings with his own. "I'm caught between life and death—I don't have either the animal energy of a physical body or the spiritual power of the disembodied to draw on."

"'Your powers are weak, old man,'" Winter quoted, and Grey smiled painfully.

"Something like that. So what I sent was the Elemental that Nuclear Circle had played around with back in college—we pretty much didn't know what we were doing back then, but on the astral every action leaves a trace. The *idea* of it still existed, and I was able to lend it enough will to give it coherence again—but it should never have been able to affect the physical plane at all."

Winter gazed at him steadily. "That isn't what happened."

Grey ran his free hand through his hair, holding tight to Winter's hand with the other. She would have pulled loose from his grip, but she suspected that Grey was the one keeping her anchored here.

"I didn't intend—I've been on the Path too long to say something like that, even if it's true, but I don't understand. Where did it get the power to become real? Even if it were to visit any of the rest of you—we all created it together, so there'd be a link—all that should have happened was a few bad dreams."

"It killed her," Winter said fiercely. "It drove me— It stalked all of us, Grey: me, Janelle, Ramsey, Cassie. Why did you *do* it, Grey?" she demanded.

"Because I didn't want to stay like this until my body finally wore out! The silver cord is broken—I can't find my way back to it, but my body's still alive out there! This should have worked—"

"Well, it didn't! Your singing telegram is very comfortable back in the real world—it started out killing squirrels, but it's working its way up the food chain nicely. Every time it kills it gets stronger, and it doesn't want to tell anybody anything. Don't you think Cassie tried to find out why it was after her? Or Truth? I was there when it came after Truth—it nearly killed her—and she says it's after me."

"Truth . . . Jourdemayne?" Grey said in renewed horror. "It attacked Thorne Blackburn's daughter?"

Winter didn't know why the fact that Grey knew about Truth seemed to make him more real to her, but now Winter believed, both in Grey's reality and in his innocence. His bewilderment was genuine enough to make Winter's heart ache.

"I never meant . . . And I didn't think you'd help me anyway, even if you knew," he finished quietly.

"I—" Winter began, but everything she could think of to say sounded like self-justification, and there was no time left for that. Only one thing mattered.

"You created it. Can you stop it?" Winter said.

Watching Grey's face, she saw him hesitate; his robes—the robes of an Adept in the Blackburn Work—darkened further, from ivory and burgundy to gray and umber. Far away, upon the horizon, flashes like heat lightning played across the sky.

"Maybe," Grey said at last. "There's one thing I can think of to try. If you trust me."

"Trust you?" Winter said suspiciously. "Why do I have to trust you?"

"Because for this to work," Grey said, "you've got to kill me."

* * *

It would be nice to pack it all in and decide that she was actually crazy, Winter thought to herself several hours later. Then all of this could be just some elaborate mental spasm, a sequel to her problematic nervous breakdown. But the hard truth was that she simply didn't care about other people's definition of sanity any more.

She'd signed the papers that afternoon taking legal responsibility for Grey's care. Meaningless signatures, falsely given, but they bought her the few hours that was all the time she would need. By tomorrow—next week—whenever they discovered her deception—it wouldn't matter any more.

Under other circumstances, this would have been a beautiful spring night. It was after midnight; a waning moon rode high in the sky, and the loudest sound was the rhythmic rush of the surf against the beach ahead. She'd left her car parked on a quiet street several blocks away, a few miles into town from the motel where she'd spent the day and evening. No one would be expecting a car to drive up to the facility at this time of night; even a lone pedestrian would rouse suspicion, but that much couldn't be helped. This was something that had to be done at night.

The afternoon's events seemed wavery and unreal, but Winter clung to what he had told her. Stopping the Elemental was what mattered and, tied as he was to a body he could not awaken, the magickal power Grey could wield was almost nil. Once dead—or, as Grey had kept referring to it, *discarnate*—he would be free to move beyond the Astral Plane with much greater power.

But once dead, he would no longer be tied to what he called the Plane of Manifestation, the real world—unless there were someone holding him here. Someone who could be his anchor, lending him the animal power of the physical body and the Plane of Manifestation to blend with the power of the Mental and Spiritual Planes that Grey would have.

Winter.

I'd rather be crazy. It's much more restful.

She didn't know if Grey's plan would sound sensible to another magician; to her it was voodoo, plain and simple. Leaving aside what was going to happen if Grey had been telling her the literal truth, the least of what Winter was going to do here tonight was, by any legal definition, murder—and a hospital full of life-support equipment wasn't the place Winter would have chosen to summon the Elemental's psychokinetic storm to if she'd had a choice. But her choices had been stripped away from her one by one, until she had only one choice left:

Win or die.

Winter walked around to the back of the building and chuckled softly as she reached the back door. She'd expected it to be locked, and it was, but she'd come a long way in the past few months, and it was a small step from moving keys across a table to moving pins in a locking cylinder. This much, at least, she was confident of her ability to do.

The heavy door shuddered under her fingers for a few moments, and when Winter turned the knob again, the door swung open. She stepped into a sort of vestibule, and walked past the cartons of liquid nutrient and the time clock with its row of punch cards. She glanced at the rack. According to the cards, there were only two people here on this shift. She hoped she didn't run into either of them, because even in a Donna Karan white linen duster over gray flannel man-tailored slacks and a beige wild silk shirt, Winter didn't think she had much hope of convincing anyone that she was a doctor making a late-night visit to a patient.

She walked to the inner door and pushed it open.

The lights were lowered for night, and in the darkness and quiet the institution had a bleak, untended air. Wheelchairs and other pieces of equipment lined the halls. Winter looked around dubiously. Where was Grey's room? She'd memorized the room number when she'd been here before, but in the dark, coming at it from this unfamiliar direction, everything looked different and whatever else she did, she didn't dare find herself going past the nurse's station.

She reached Grey's room at last, slipping inside and pulling the door halfway shut with a pang of relief. She couldn't risk a light that might be seen from the hall, but fortunately someone had forgotten to close the window curtains, and the pale moonlight streaming in through the window was enough to see by. Winter crossed the room, pulling the privacy curtains around the bed by the window to shield her further.

"Grey—?" she whispered.

The body on the bed did not respond, and, looking down at Grey lying there, Winter experienced a wrenching sense of disorientation. This wasted body in a hospital bed was not the Hunter Greyson she knew and had spoken to just this afternoon.

But the Grey she had spoken to was a ghost, a sort of psychic echo of the man on the bed, with no more tangible reality than a picture on a television screen. She stood gazing down at him, hesitating. When she turned off the respirator, he'd be gone, just like blowing out a candle.

But that wasn't really true. He was gone already. He'd been gone ever since that rainy night on the coast road when a hit-and-run driver had taken away all of his choices. All that remained was to allow his body to accept that fact.

Winter closed her eyes against the sudden burning of tears, but she knew she was luckier than she really deserved. At least she got the chance to say good-bye.

And, with luck, she might even survive to grieve for him.

She reached for the tube that covered his throat. Removing it should be enough—the respirator was breathing for him; without it, he would suffocate quickly. She closed her fingers around the plastic to pull it free and stopped.

Alarms. There must be alarms of some kind that would go off the moment this thing stopped working, and discovery would be a disaster she could not imagine explaining away. Could she turn the machine off first? Winter walked around the bed and stood in front of the ventilator that breathed for Hunter Greyson. It was as tall as she was, boxy, dark, and threatening. Lights flickered on and off in time to the sounds it made; a bellows worked; there was some sort of dial with the words NEGATIVE PRESSURE on it, and a needle fluttered in the middle of the white zone. She looked further. The respirator had a box plugged into the side that had a red light and a green one on the side and a round speaker grille on the front. The green light burned steadily. That must be the alarm, but she couldn't see any way to turn it off.

Winter continued studying the machine, wishing she'd thought to look at it more carefully in daylight. A thick gray cord ran into the power socket on the wall, elaborately locked into place so that nothing could accidentally dislodge it and interrupt the power supply. Another, thinner, cord, plugged into the wall higher up; the word AIR was printed above it in blue. The unoccupied sockets said OXYGEN and SUCTION. Winter recoiled slightly. This room and what it represented were frightening as no supernatural horror could be.

But she was wasting time, and every moment of delay meant that Grey's *magickal child* might be killing somewhere else. Inspecting the respirator carefully, Winter saw that nothing connected it to the man—Bobby?—in the other bed. What she did here would affect only Grey.

But how? She couldn't unplug it, she didn't think she could just switch it off. . . .

But she could short it out. Somewhere inside this machine was an electrical motor, and electric motors were something Winter knew how to break. She pointed a finger at the machine.

"Bang. You're dead."

The fat blue spark that exploded out of the respirator's casing made her jump back and yelp in startlement, and then hiss in disgust at her own fright. But, to Winter's relief, no one came to investigate, and that was all that happened. The respirator was unmoving, dark, and silent, and so was the alarm box.

She went back to the bedside and looked down at Grey. It was over.

"Good-bye, Grey," Winter said. She swallowed hard. "I could have loved you—if I hadn't been such a damned coward." She reached out and pulled the hose away. Then she took his hand. The room was utterly silent.

"Okay. What are you waiting for?" she said aloud. *Come on, nightmare—here I am.*

When the vertigo struck she realized that she still expected with some part of her mind to hear the bell that signaled the opening of trading on the floor of the Stock Exchange.

She was on the Astral Plane, and it was dark. But the Otherworld, Truth Jourdemayne had said, was created as much from their expectations as by any external force.

Let there be light. Winter willed light and her surroundings brightened, sharp with an eerie blue-gray illumination that made the place look like the Twilight Zone.

—*Winter!*— It was a summons her mind did not recognize as sound; sharp and urgent as the sudden remembrance of a thing forgotten. She turned toward it and saw Grey, farther away from her than he'd ever appeared before, wavering like an image seen through water. She ran toward him, reaching out as he drifted farther away, concentrating on feeling his hands grasping her own.

She touched him; her fingers grazed his as she yanked at him, clutching him tightly. With a sob of relief, Winter dragged him back into reality once more.

"Grey!" she said inadequately. He'd seemed almost insubstantial when she'd touched him, but moment by moment he was becoming more solid beneath her touch.

He freed one hand, brushing the hair back from her face. He smiled, and Winter felt her heart clench in a promise of grief to come.

"Don't let go, whatever you do," Grey said. "Without you, I'll just fade away." His supercilious expression mocked the literal truth of his words.

"All right." Winter held his hand as if they were orphans in a fairy tale about to walk into the dark forest. *How does being dead feel, Grey?* "What else do you want me to do?"

"This is going to sound really simple. We need to walk over there—see the stones?—to where Nuclear Circle's astral temple used to be. Getting there's going to be harder than you think, but then comes the easy part. We rebuild Nuclear Circle's astral temple, and then—"

Winter almost pulled free. "In God's name, Grey—you brought me here for *that?* I make light-bulbs explode—I can't do anything like, like—"

Grey shook his head in frustration—at least, so Winter saw him. "You have to. Just imagine it the way it was; this is the Astral Plane: Wishes *are* horses here, and thoughts are real. You remember the image we all worked on? Just hold that in your mind."

Yes, thoughts were real, Winter thought, at the edge of panic. And how could she tell Grey that out of a past edited by trauma and drugs, the memory of imagining Nuclear Circle's astral temple was one she didn't have?

"Come on!" Grey pulled at her, impatient. Helplessly she let him lead her toward the circle of cairns.

It was like moving through water. Each step was an effort, and Winter quickly understood why Grey had said it would be hard to reach the temple: If she did not concentrate with all her will on the tumbled stones, Winter found herself forgetting where she was going; veering off in another direction, or stopping altogether.

It was her anger that saved her. Not the killing rage that, uncontrolled, brought on the psychokinetic storms that for so long she had ascribed to an outside agency, but a cold quiet determination to do what she had said she would do, no matter how great the odds were against her.

At last Winter was able to lay her free hand atop the nearest cairn of stones. At once the pressure and disorientation ceased, and she and Grey, still holding hands, were able to walk quickly and easily into the center of the circle.

Grey looked around. From the expression on his face he was seeing something different than she was—or perhaps remembering.

"Well, here we are, at the death of hope," Grey said. His voice was cutting, and Winter flinched away inwardly from the anger in it. "You know, for years I hoped you'd come back."

"I forgot," Winter said, and the bare truth sounded far uglier than she'd intended.

"I know," Grey said, and now he only sounded tired. "I looked for you in dreams, on the astral—hell, even on the Internet."

"Did you try New York?" Winter shot back. Why were they arguing now? Wasn't it years and lifetimes too late to matter?

"I got tired of getting thrown off the family estate and then picked up for vagrancy," Grey said. He shrugged and tried to smile, but couldn't quite manage it. "I've got to admit that an arrest record makes a dandy souvenir when you try to get a job, though."

Her parents had done that. Casually. Efficiently. *Damn them.* In this bodiless realm, her spiraling outrage had the seductive force of a jolt of speed. "I didn't do that," she said quietly. "I didn't even know."

"I know." Grey's smile was gentle now. "But it took me too many years to figure that out. I'm sorry. But hurry now. We've got to rebuild the temple—it's coming, and if we can't restrain it when it gets here . . ."

It's going to kill us. Winter's mind supplied the words Grey didn't say.

And it *was* coming. A darkness on the horizon, the heaviness of a mindless hostility that Winter had glimpsed twice before. Grey cried out in a language that, for a confused moment, Winter felt she knew, and where the circle of tumbled stones had stood in the sourceless silver light, the walls of the temple began to rise, shadowy in the wavering air. Winter felt Grey draw power from her living body, but he needed more: her mind, her will, and her heart.

She tried to give him what he needed—and realized, with sinking despair, that she couldn't. There was some fundamental quality that she lacked—if she'd ever had it at all.

"Winter," Grey pleaded. She clutched his hand tighter, wordlessly shaking her head. He wanted her to fly, but her wings had melted long ago.

It was nearly here, and they had no defenses. Grey had said the Elemental had more *reality* here; in this world Winter could feel the ground shake as it approached, and the storm that heralded its coming gained force. Beside her, Grey fought to raise the walls of the temple by himself, and Winter knew he wasn't going to make it.

How could she expect—how could Grey expect—to create alone what it had taken five people once to make?

And then it reached them. The storm broke over Winter like a towering wave: an icy vortex that chilled and deafened her, leaching the strength from her body until she could no longer feel Grey's hand. *This isn't so bad,* was Winter's first, false, reaction. She'd been expecting a monster, some kind of movie alien, not just darkness and crushing pressure.

But her sense of relief was gone before it had truly been, gone in the realization of the true nature of the creature that Hunter Greyson had made.

First came the pain. It was worse than the migraine headaches that had left her sick and dazed for days, worse than she could imagine pain could be. But even that was endurable, was welcome in comparison to the icy needles that slid into her eyes, her brain, carrying with them the knowledge of inhuman hunger and loss. *Pain*—and the soul Winter was not sure she possessed howled its despair. The Elemental had reached her, and here was its message: grief and pain, anger and betrayal, ripping away her sanity and self as easily as she might disjoint a chicken, destroying all that Winter was but leaving behind some screaming spark to know and suffer and sorrow.

Forever.

She didn't know when it stopped, only that she was running. Grey pulled her along, away from the temple, his hand in hers so hot and solid that Winter knew with a distant pang of wonder that even in this unreal place she was nearly on the edge of death.

"Grey— Stop— Grey—" Winter panted. She wanted to scream—she wanted to die—she would do anything to keep that creature from touching her again, anything—

Grey stopped and took her in his arms, holding her body tightly against him. Winter imagined she could feel the fluttering beat of his heart. She would have wept, but terror had burned away all her tears.

"We're toast," Grey said, with a ghost of his old mocking lightness.

"Grey!" Winter protested, as if his disrespect could gain them greater punishment.

"No." She felt him shake his head, denying her false hope. "It's too strong. I broke free this time; I can probably even do it again. But it'll get us in the end."

"No," Winter moaned. And there was no place to run—here or in the real world it would come for her.

Was this what Cassie had felt before she died?

Was it?

Deep within Winter, faint fires of anger and guilt trembled. She coaxed them to life. Anything was better than the terror: anger, guilt, pride—anything she could use to shield herself she would gladly use.

"You told me we could kill it," Winter said, in a voice she hardly recognized. "You lied." Cold. Cold as the hate-serpent; cold as ice; a shield that had been forged only for this ultimate extremity. Useless—dangerous—in the real world, here it was her only hope.

Grey looked behind them. On the horizon, the storm was gathering once more.

"Not kill," Grey corrected her, his voice steady. "Unmake it—understand it, unbind it from the task it was set. Name it, command it, set it free. How could I— I even think it would listen if we could just hold it long enough—shield ourselves from it somehow—but we can't. Lord of the Wheel—" and now Winter heard real agony in his voice "—I would give up all I am, all that I might hope to be, all my advancement on the Path, if I only could stop what I have set in motion here!"

"We need the others."

Where had this sudden certainty come from, the sense that she was somehow something more than herself?

"Cassie's dead," Grey said, but there was a note of uncertainty in his voice now.

"I can get her." Whatever the certainty's source, she had to believe in her own rightness. *Help me, help me—help us!* Winter prayed. A scrap of memory came back to her. *Lords of the Wheel—Lords of the New Aeon—your children call upon you. . . .*

"If you can get them, and bring them here, do it now," Grey's voice was flat. "Because here it comes again."

It was as if sheer desperation had transformed her at last from a creature of careful logic to one of unthinking instinct. The power within Winter beckoned—she seized it, and felt as if she'd plunged her hands into the white-hot heart of the sun.

Cassilda, Ramsey, Janelle . . .

Cassilda stood at the gates of Death, lingering in the borderland, holding on valiantly as she waited for the summons she knew would come. Winter reached for her and took her hand, and it was cold, so cold. . . .

In the courts of Sleep, Ramsey Miller and Janelle Baker lingered.

She found them.

A dream, Winter—something we can all share! Grey's swift demand. *Hurry!*

And remade the world in her own image.

The stadium was packed, a million roaring faceless bodies in the darkness, projecting their passion and energy onto the stage. Winter stood alone upon the empty platform, handmaid of forces greater than herself, and summoned Nuclear Circle into being.

A dream we can all share. To mold them, to bind them, to make them one once more.

The music called, and Winter let it in.

Grey came first, laying down the melody in a dance of electrified strings, smoothing the way for the others, living and dead, to join them—

Ramsey, a little behind, but with a rhythm strong and sure, able to follow where any of them led—

Cassilda, her work in the world cut short, pushed them forward on the insistent beat of the drums, urging them onward—

And, last of all, Janelle danced in and out, the sound of her fiddle mocking the two guitars. Winter drew a deep breath and flung herself into the web of sound, the bright silver skirl of her flute finishing all, sealing the circle and shaping the power. Grey led them on, but it was Winter who blessed and blazed the trail.

Music, Winter. Sound and rhythm, the first awareness; the place it starts—

She looked without sight, seeing them all—and saw, too, that none of them was whole. Each of them had failed, somewhere in the world, once they had left the golden time.

Janelle's failure had been of nerve, Ramsey's of heart, and Cassie's of will, but her own had been the worst, her cowardice a failure of faith, of trust not only in the future but in some essential constant of good.

The music wavered.

But that didn't matter, Winter told herself fiercely. Together they supplied one anothers' lack, strengthening each other against the world, against the past.

The Elemental reached them, and Winter felt it: need and despair, sorrow and rage—but now, against that, she set the best of them: Janelle's bravery and Ramsey's love, Grey's yearning, and Cassilda confident and steady beneath it all. Living and dead together, linked in a covenant that transcended birth, that kept their music strong and sure against it. Here, in this time outside of time, was the golden time when they had all been gods, and nothing was beyond their power.

She concentrated on the Elemental—

And the metaphor shifted again, and now Winter was dancing barefoot and short-skirted on a high hill. The melody they wove was older, richer, deeper: drums and pipes, and she whirled in Grey's arms as the music led in and out, the hounds and the hare, but this time it was the hounds who led the hare on, weaving a web of sound and magick to hold it in.

"Caught!" she heard Grey cry exultantly, but to catch it wasn't enough; Grey had to unweave it, spinning this child of his intention safely back into the starstuff from which the universe was made.

There was something not right in that, something she had overlooked, but there was no time for thought or doubt, and now Winter led the circle again, as the definition of the world slid from Grey's mind to hers and shifted one last time.

And she was reaching out into the electronic architecture, linking the file-servers, pulling up application after application, the definition of the world for a child of the Computer Age—

As the opening bell rang the floor of the Exchange came to its feet in one many-throated roar; here was Chicago, one hour behind New York; it was already afternoon in London and the gold-fix was hours old; Japan was in bed and it was already tomorrow in the Far East and the data poured in across a dozen computer screens and there was only one thing faster, one thing surer, one thing that could integrate that flood of data and build a world from it; a world where time was money, and money was the phantom dance of the EFTs across a thousand world markets. . . .

And this realm of intention and command came alive for her, an extension of her will, her *mind.* Armored in her applications, her programs, her subroutines, Winter reached out, to deal with:

　—*demon*—

　　—*virus*—

　　　—*bad art*—

She felt Grey reach through her. . . .

"That which I commanded is fulfilled, and the term of your years is run. By fire and water, the word and the will, by living and unliving earth I remind you of your making and unmake you now—"

. . . laying gentle merciless hands on the thing that did not belong in this perfect pattern that was the blueprint of all creation . . .

And the Hunt closed in—
And the music swirled to a crescendo—
And the system loaded and began to run—
And all the metaphor was gone.

She felt Cassie slip away first, with a gentle laugh and a last caress, down the Spiral Path to the beginning of creation.

Born again to the Goddess. Good-bye, Cassie.

Then Ramsey and Janelle, tumbling back down into sleep, perhaps to take the courage for change with them into the waking world.

Sleep well, my loves. Dream true.

Gone, all of them, and she and Grey stood alone, hand in hand, in the desolation where only one other thing remained.

She was thirteen, the age she would have been if she'd lived. In her face, Grey's features and Winter's melded.

"Mommy—" The child-wraith wavered; hungry, needing. . . . Winter started forward.

"Don't go to her," Grey said harshly. His grip on Winter's hand stopped her. "She isn't alive. Step outside the circle and you'll wander forever. You won't be able to find your way back to your body any more than I could to mine once the silver cord was snapped."

Surprised, Winter looked down. Just in front of where she was standing was a line of pale quartz river stones, forming a line that curved around to become the circle Grey spoke of.

"I don't care! She's—"

My daughter.

Winter pulled, but now it was Grey who would not release her. He gripped her hand so tightly it hurt; tightly enough that she stared at him in puzzled anger.

"Mommy," the wraith keened again, and the sound came near to breaking Winter's heart.

"I unbound it," Grey said hoarsely. "All that Nuclear Circle once created is gone. But *she* remains." His face twisted with revulsion—and fear. "I created what I could not control, but I'm no black magician—I would *not* bind a human soul into anything I made. She was my— She was our— *I did not bind her here!*"

He tugged against her grip, but this time Winter held fast. After what had gone before, there should be nothing left that could kindle her bruised emotions, but there was one thing left.

"No," Winter said. "I did." Hating, needing, never letting go— *Hate dragged her back. The power of hate.*

Grey said all five of them together had created the Elemental in its original form. If that was true, then there'd been something left of Winter in it even after all those years, enough to let Grey's *magickal child* break free of Grey's fragile control and go searching for—

Their daughter. "This is my fault. I'm why she's here. Grey, let me go. I have to go to her."

"No." Grey's voice was tired. "We have to call her in." His eyes met hers. "Can you do it?"

"Of course I—" Winter began, and stopped. Could she really? Could she accept that she'd brushed this life aside out of her own selfish fear and confusion? Could she accept that its presence here now was a testimony, not to any noble emotion, but to the strength of her self-obsessed hate? Could she bear to see herself that clearly? Was she even willing to try?

And what was the price of failure?

"Yes," Winter said in a strangled voice.

Still clasping her hand—gently now—Grey stooped and lifted one of the stones free of the circle. "Call her."

What name, what name to give to the daughter who had never been? Wordlessly, Winter held out her hand. The child—a girl on the edge of womanhood, really, and everything about her an illusion—drifted forward, through the gap in the circle, and then Winter pulled free of Grey to hold her tightly in her arms.

Cold, so cold . . . I made a mistake. It isn't always, not for every woman. If I'd really thought it through I might have done it anyway. But I should at least have thought hard before I did it!

Grey's arms circled them both, and for a moment Winter could feel his thoughts as well: grief, and self-contempt; an angry guilt that he had not tried harder to soothe her fears all those years ago, to try to be the man she thought she wanted.

But you can't live just for someone else, Grey, Winter thought sadly. *You have to live for yourself, too. There has to be a balance.*

The cold seemed to sink into her very bones as the child-spirit slipped free, unbound at last.

Soon, Mommy. Someday . . .

A line from the half-forgotten Blackburn Work came back to her and Winter spoke aloud: "Here is the Third Gate, the Gate of Making and Unmaking, where Life becomes Death, and Death, Life."

And Winter's arms were empty.

"Now it's my turn."

Winter looked at Grey. He stepped away from her, dressed now as she remembered him best, in beads and buckskin and acid-washed jeans. Behind him a road she had not seen before stretched arrow-straight into the distance; a long straight track, paved, not with yellow brick, but with shining silver.

"Thanks for coming," Grey said, gesturing as if he knew the words were inadequate. "Thanks for setting me free—for setting us both free. I hope— I hope you can be happy." He turned to go, toward the waiting road.

Once he reaches it, it will be too late.

"No—wait!" Winter said, grabbing for him. The fringe of his jacket slithered through her fingers, and she clutched only air.

"Are you just going to give up?" she cried.

Grey looked back at her, faintly puzzled. "Give up? I'm dead, Winter."

"No you aren't—not yet. You said there isn't any time here. You aren't dead yet." There was nothing she could reach him with except her words. "Come back with me—come back *to* me. We can— There has to be some way we can try again," she pleaded.

"I can't do it." There was fear in Grey's voice. "I can't make it back. It's too far—you don't understand. The cord is broken. I can't find my way. You've got to let me go."

"No I don't!" Winter said, willing him to look at her, to *see.* "You said you love me—prove it! Or else it was all for nothing—there's no point in trying because the mistakes we make last forever. Prove that they don't— that no matter what we've done wrong we can take it back, start again, so that it doesn't have to be forever—" Her voice broke.

Grey took a step toward her, away from the beckoning road. There was a sound in the air, a faint and distant wind.

"All right," he said, so low she could hardly hear him. "I'll try."

"Try!" Winter lashed out at him. "'Try' isn't good enough! I didn't 'try' just now—I *did* it! Now it's your turn."

Grey hesitated, and Winter lunged forward and yanked him away from the shining path. His body was cool and unreal in her grasp. He fell against her, gasping a little and laughing at the same time.

"All right," he said. "I owe it. Lords of the Wheel," Grey intoned, and Winter knew he did not speak to her, "I take back the chains of matter willingly, to atone for my pride, according to your good pleasure." His face changed; he looked older, grimmer, as if he faced an ordeal now that she could not comprehend. "Help me, Winter. I can't find the way by myself. Take me with you."

The distant sound had grown louder, and now it was the rhythm of the surf on the rocks below. As she stared up into Grey's face the astral light faded and it began to rain.

There was cold, and wind; the scent of the salt sea and the living earth. Grey's face contorted with pain and he sank to his knees, tearing one hand from her grip and pressing it to his ribs. As Winter watched in fear his clothing shimmered and flowed again, turning to black motorcycle leathers and torn, blood-soaked jeans. She knelt and flung her arms around him, trying to shield him.

The headlights. Oh, God, the cold. Won't somebody come? The echoes of Grey's fear and horror filled her mind. But that was more than a year ago—this was now. In a place where time had no meaning, Hunter Greyson was making the hardest journey of all—into life.

"Don't leave me," Grey gasped. "Stay with me." Winter held him against her, pressing her cheek to his. His skin was cold as rain, and each breath seemed to cost him more effort.

"Never," she said, as her tears began to mingle with the rain and the salt spray from the rocks below. "I'll never leave you, Grey."

HOME IS THE HUNTER

For winter's rains and ruins are over,
And all the season of snows and sins;
The days dividing lover and lover,
The light that loses, the night that wins.
— ALGERNON CHARLES SWINBURNE

DECEMBER IN SAN FRANCISCO WAS A SEASON OF BLUSTERY winds and soaking rain—and a pervasive dampness that struck through even heavy winter coats with a numbing persistence. Christmas lights and holiday garlands looked oddly out of place in a city where the temperature hovered in the high forties and there wasn't even the possibility of snow.

Winter maneuvered the heavy silver Mercedes expertly over the familiar route, grateful for the weight that lent it stability in the rain and wind. Frodo and Emily had teased her when she'd bought the big luxury car, but Winter had pointed out reasonably that she was going to need the space for the therapy equipment and the twice-weekly trips to PT that were a feature of all the foreseeable future.

Fortunately she'd found someone good close to home, so this was the last time for a while that she was going to have to make the pilgrimage across the bridge from Berkeley to the San Francisco Orthopedic Hospital—or, as its patients called it, Resurrection City.

"I'm so excited. I really don't know how I can ever thank you," Janelle said from the passenger seat.

"Jannie, you've been saying that ever since you got here, and that was six weeks ago!" Winter said indulgently. "What are friends for, if not for this?" The heavy slap-slap of the windshield wipers formed a backbeat to her words.

"But you've done so much. . . ." Janelle said.

"I didn't get you that job with— What is the name of that place up in Seattle?"

"Wizards of the Coast," Janelle said, blushing proudly.

Janelle Baker had walked out on Denny Raymond four months before and into the Bergen County Women's Services shelter. She'd gotten in touch with Winter almost immediately, and the two women had kept in close contact, each rebuilding her life as she did so.

"And Ramsey's flying out for Christmas," Janelle added. "Just think—we'll all be together."

"All of us who are left," Winter said, suddenly somber. Cassie would not be here. She wheeled the Mercedes into the hospital parking lot and found a space near the door. "I won't be long," she said. "Why don't you wait here, Jannie?"

The familiar smells of mingled disinfectants greeted her as the elevator opened onto her floor. After so many visits, Winter could just have walked right past the desk, but today was a special day.

"He'll be right out, Winter," the nurse on duty said. "Happy Holiday."

"Thanks, Rachel. Merry Solstice to you." Winter smiled, breathing deeply to cover her nervousness. She'd waited so long for this moment—she wanted everything to be perfect.

Hunter Greyson walked slowly down the hall toward her, a muscular attendant hovering slightly behind. The clothes she had bought him for this occasion still looked painfully new.

"Hi, sweetheart," he said, smiling his crooked grin. "Want to go dancing?"

Winter came toward him and hugged him gently. Automatically, she glanced at Grey's throat. A small white scar was all now that remained of the tracheostomy that had once let a machine breathe for him.

The effects of a year-long coma could not be instantly shrugged off, but Grey's progress toward health and mobility had been rapid, from the moment at San Gabriel when Winter had seen Grey open his eyes in the hospital bed. She'd had a lot of explaining to do about her presence in the building at that hour—not to mention the fact that Grey's respirator was shut down—but the fact that Grey was alive and conscious counted for a lot. Once he'd been able to make his own health-care decisions, Winter had been able to get Grey moved to Resurrection City and started on the long road to rehabilitation.

"Ready to go? Jannie's waiting in the car outside, and Ramsey's getting in tomorrow," Winter said.

"Hail, hail, the gang's all here." Grey put his arm around her waist.

"The chair will be around in just a minute," Rachel said.

"The hell with that," Grey shot back, grinning. "I'm walking out of here under my own power."

The aides and nurses applauded as he walked to the elevator and stepped inside. He bowed carefully as the doors closed, and Winter steadied him as he straightened.

"Dancing, eh? Not for a few weeks, I'd say."

"Maybe for New Year's," Grey suggested irrepressibly. He smiled fondly at Winter. "Now that my time is my own again—or almost— what shall we do with the rest of our lives?"

"I know what I'd like to do," Winter said. She'd meant to say this later, but somehow she felt the time was right. "I'd like to get married. You did ask me, you know—fourteen years ago."

The joy that filled Grey's face told her the timing had been right. "It's about time," he said, taking her hand. "It took you long enough to say yes."

"But it's never too late," Winter answered, her eyes misty. "Not for a beginning."

> *And time remembered is grief forgotten,*
> *And frosts are slain and flowers begotten,*
> *And in green underwood and cover*
> *Blossom by blossom the spring begins.*
> —ALGERNON CHARLES SWINBURNE